Career Girls

Louise Bagshawe

headline
review

'Enter Sandman' written by James Hetfield, Lars Ulrich and
Kirk Hammett © 1991 Creeping Death Music/PolyGram Music
Publishing Ltd. Lyrics reproduced by kind permission of the publishers.

The Publishers gratefully acknowledge lyric reproduction of
'It's A Long Way To The Top' by kind permission of J. Albert & Son
(UK) Ltd., UK administrator.

'It's A Long Way To The Top' (Young/Young/Scott) © 1976 Lyrics
reprinted with permission of J. Albert & Son Pty Ltd (Australia).

First published in Great Britain in 1995 by Orion Books Ltd

This paperback edition published in 2007 by HEADLINE REVIEW
An imprint of HEADLINE PUBLISHING GROUP

2

Cataloguing in Publication Data is available from the British Library

978 0 7553 4049 1 (B format)
978 0 7553 4050 7 (A format)

Typeset in Meridien Roman by Avon DataSet Ltd,
Bidford-on-Avon, Warwickshire

Printed and bound in Great Britain by Clays Ltd, St Ives plc

Headline's policy is to use papers that are natural, renewable and
recyclable products and made from wood grown in sustainable forests.
The logging and manufacturing processes are expected to conform to
the environmental regulations of the country of origin.

HEADLINE PUBLISHING GROUP
A division of Hachette Livre UK Ltd
338 Euston Road
London NW1 3BH

www.reviewbooks.co.uk
www.hodderheadline.com

This book is dedicated to
Barbara Kennedy-Brown,
my partner in crime

Thanks to

Jacob Rees-Mogg, Nicky Griffiths, Ed, Damian, Tiz, Margaret, Rod, James Robertson, James Ross, Nick Edgar, Alexia, Jeremy, Arabella, Stephanie, Melanie, Katherine, Harvey, Nick Little, Edna, Brenda, Marion, Tristam, Pete, Adrian, Alex, Jeremy Green, Sebastien and all my friends at Christ Church and the Union – you know who you are; Gary Williams, Andy Stevens, Luc Vergier, Rachel Robinson and everybody at Sony International; Brian McWheat and Frank Hannon; the infinitely cool Brian Celler; Tom and Claire Zutaut; John and Gina Florescu, Tom Silverman of Tommy Boy; Suicidal Tendencies, Tom Abraham and the crew (ahem); Nigel Kennedy; John Watson and Colin Bell of London Records, James Harman, Rod MacSween, Dave Bates, the C.R.A.B.S., Sean McAuley, Lizzie Radford, Roger Holdom, Vanessa Warwick, Brent Hansen, Brian Diamond, Max Loubière, Lucy, Kate, Sandy, Paul, Paula and Barry at EMI and especially Keith Staton; Pippa, Belinda, Isabella and everyone at Biss Lancaster; Dawn Harris, Angelica Passantino and family, and Claire Bryant.

Special thanks to: Mum, Dad, Tilly, James, Alice, Seffi and all the family; my genius of an agent, Michael Sissons, and the wonderful, brilliant and very kind Fiona

Batty; my awesome editor, Rosie Cheetham, for her guidance, patience and encouragement, and the whole team at Orion, especially Katie Pope for everything and Caroleen Conquest, my copy-editor; Lisa Anderson, the first woman in Britain to run a major label, and Sharon Osbourne, one of the best managers in the world, my all-time heroines – words cannot express my gratitude; Conrad Miles; Jane 'Heaven is . . .' Edwards; Fred 'Court Jester' Metcalf; Nigel Huddlestone and Chris Hall; Richard Hamer; Ged (pronounced 'God') Doherty, Lynn Seager; Andrew Snelling, the world's only rock 'n' roll bank manager; Cliff Burnstein, for three hours of life philosophy at the Don Valley stadium; and to Def Leppard, Joe Elliott, Phil Collen, Vivian Campbell, Rick Savage, Rick Allen and the late, great Steve Clark for the music and the inspiration.

And finally, my thanks to the most appropriately named man in the music industry, Peter Mensch, for taking me along for the ride.

PART ONE
OXFORD

Chapter One

Topaz burst through the door of the President's Office.

'Oh – my – God!' she yelled. '*Oh my God*! I got it! I got it! I can't believe it! Rowena, you're a genius. How can I ever repay you? I don't know what to say!'

She flung herself on one of the faded velvet armchairs, pushing a handful of red curls back from her face.

Rowena turned away from the computer with a sigh. Her delicately pitched letter of invitation to Gary Lineker to come down to Oxford and speak had reached a crucial paragraph. She smiled at her friend. 'What are you talking about?'

'*The Times, The Times*! They read the draft, they like it, they want eight hundred words on student benefits! I'm going to be published in a national! Oh babe, I can't thank you enough,' said Topaz.

'Topaz, that's great. That's really great. I'm so pleased,' said Rowena. 'You're the best, and they're lucky to have you.'

'It's all down to you. I wouldn't have got it without you.'

'That's rubbish and you know it. All Dad did was make sure the right person got to read it. Stevens wouldn't have commissioned it if it wasn't any good,' said Rowena firmly.

The two girls glowed at each other.

'Talent is the only thing that counts,' said Rowena.

'In which case, you'll never have any problems,' said Topaz.

They made a great team. Everyone said so. They were so unlikely to get along, it was almost inevitable that they should become best friends: Topaz Rossi, the brashest, loudest, and by far the most attractive American in Oxford, and Rowena Gordon, willowy, blonde, coldly determined, every inch a gentleman's daughter.

Topaz had interviewed Rowena for *Cherwell*, the university newspaper, in their second term at college, when her sophistication and poise had taken the Union by storm, winning an election to the Secretary's committee by a record margin. The American girl had turned up with a paper and pen cordially prepared to hate her guts: Rowena Gordon, another stuck-up British aristo dabbling in student politics before settling down to a suitable marriage. She despised girls like that. They were the enemy, a living reproach to every woman who'd struggled for the right to work for a living.

When she actually saw Rowena, her second impression was worse than the first; she was dressed in an Armani suit that would have cost Topaz her year's budget, with long, blonde, precision-cut hair, expensive scent, immaculate make-up and delicate gold jewellery.

'Why do you think you won this election?' Topaz asked in a bored monotone.

Rowena had looked at her equally coolly. *Bloody Americans!* Look at this girl, those thrusting breasts in a low-cut top, those long legs stretching up for miles into a suede mini at least three inches too short, and a riot of ruby curls tumbling halfway down her back. Swaggering in here like she owns the place. It was obvious how she managed to be a staffer on the student paper in less than a term.

'Because I worked hard all term, made speeches I believed about, and raised more sponsorship money than anybody else,' she answered shortly. 'Why do you think you're doing this feature?'

'Because I'm the best writer on the paper,' Topaz shot back.

For a second they glared at each other. Then, slowly, Topaz smiled and held out her hand.

By the end of the day, both women had made their first ally.

Over the next two weeks, they became firm friends. At first, this amazed other students who knew them; after all, Rowena was cold, reserved and richer than hell, whereas Topaz was a red-blooded Italian-American, sensual, pushy and scraping by on a scholarship.

But their backgrounds were more similar than most people realized. Both of them had already made one major mistake in the eyes of their parents: they'd been born female.

The Gordons of Ayrshire had been an unbroken line of Scottish farmers for more than a thousand years. Give or take a few acres, the Gordon estate and coat of arms had passed smoothly from father to son down the generations, until Rowena's father, Charles Gordon, had failed to provide a son of his own. There had been three miscarriages, and Rowena was conceived despite doctor's orders. When Mary Gordon, after all the heartache, was finally delivered in Guy's Hospital in London, her proud husband waited all night in the room closest to the ward, turning over names in his mind – Richard, Henry, Douglas, William, Jacob. At 3 a.m. the nurse came in beaming.

'Is he all right?' Charles asked anxiously.

'She's fine, sir,' the nurse smiled. 'You have a beautiful baby daughter.'

Gino Rossi would have sympathized with Charles Gordon. He might also have felt a touch of condescension: after all, he already had three fine sons. He was the envy of his neighbours. But he wanted another, and his wife was getting tired. Gino had already decided this would be the last time for her. When the baby turned out to be a girl, he felt cheated. What should Gino Rossi do with a daughter? He hadn't even had any sisters. No, he patted the little infant on the head and left her to her mother to raise. Anna Rossi called her daughter Topaz, after her favourite gemstone, and because she had a little tuft of red-gold baby hair.

Rowena Gordon wanted for nothing. From the moment she was wrapped in her heirloom christening gown of antique lace, everything was provided for her. When she was six, a pony. When she was seventeen, a car. In between, the finest clothes, the smartest skiing holidays, ballet lessons, a Harley Street orthodontist and anything else her father could think of. Anything that would allow him to ignore his real feelings for her, the acute disappointment, the sense of betrayal. Until Rowena was six, he merely avoided her. After that, he would either lose his temper over the smallest childish offence, or treat her with cold courtesy. Mary Gordon was no better. She resented her daughter as the reason for her husband's coldness towards her. When Rowena was sent away at seven to boarding school, she felt only relief.

When Rowena was ten, a minor miracle occurred. Mary Gordon, at the age of forty-one, got pregnant again and carried the baby to term. This time Charles's prayers were answered: at forty-seven he had fathered a son,

James Gordon, sole heir to the estate and the family name. Both parents were overjoyed; the new baby was the apple of their eye, and Charles Gordon never snapped at his daughter again. From that day forth, he simply ignored her.

Rowena accepted her parents' attitude. Things were the way they were, and no amount of wishing would change it. Her reaction was simple: from now on, she would be in control. She would shape her own world. She would rely on herself.

The grades she was earning at school ceased to be an effort to win their love. Now they became a passport to college. University meant independence, and independence meant freedom. And Rowena discovered something else: she was good at work. She was, in fact, the brightest girl of her year. It was a new revelation. Rowena worked coldly and with complete dedication until she topped the class in everything except art. She had her rivals, Mary-Jane and Rebecca, happy, pretty girls who were much more outgoing and popular than her. They provided a benchmark. They were the ones to beat. If Rowena got only 74 per cent in an exam, she didn't mind, providing Becky and Mary-Jane got only 73 per cent. She discovered she would rather come top than get an A. In most cases she did both.

Across the Atlantic, little Topaz Rossi was also disappointing her family. Where Rowena became arrogant, cold and withdrawn, Topaz threw tantrums, burst into tears and demanded attention. Like the unruly mop of red curls she was sprouting – nobody knew where *that* came from, as Gino remarked – the girl was proving rebellious. She flirted with boys, her poppa hit her. She started to wear make-up, her mom made her go to Mass every day for a month. Her mom tried to love her, but she was worn out. And Topaz was so different! She refused to learn to cook! She wanted a career, like she couldn't find a nice boy, looking like she did! What was wrong with the child, didn't she know she was a *girl*?

Topaz burnt with the injustice of it. In truth, she was more like her father than any of his sons; smart, feisty, passionate when angry. She was so desperate for them to love her. Or at least understand! She was making the best grades in grade school! She was making the best grades in high school!

When Topaz was sixteen, her parents ordered her to quit school and come help in the shop. She refused. She wanted more. Her teachers thought she could get a scholarship to Oxford University, no less. She wanted to make something of herself.

Sullenly, Gino refused his permission. All Topaz's tears were to no avail. Deep down inside, he knew he was wrong, that if Emiliano had been offered such a chance he would have burst with pride, but he was angry. Why did the Lord give him three ordinary sons, no better than the next man's, and suddenly this wild little daughter, who made straight As in courses her brothers couldn't even *spell*? What business did she have, being brighter than her family?

Gino was jealous for his sons. He was jealous for himself. No, he refused permission. She should not take this exam. At eighteen, she would help her mother.

Topaz felt her tears and rage crystallize into a hard diamond of fury. So be it, she thought. If her father turned his back on her, she would turn from him. She took the exam in secret and, as she had known they would, they awarded her the bursary.

Two days later she packed up her few decent clothes, kissed her brothers and mother goodbye and got in a cab for JFK. Her father refused her his blessing.

Though her heart was breaking, Topaz hardened her face. Very well. From now on, she was on her own.

For both girls, Oxford was the way out. In that glorious summer, the beautiful old city nestling in the heart of the soft Cotswold hills represented an opportunity to make a name for yourself. If you were doing it properly, Oxford was a dress rehearsal for real life.

Topaz and Rowena were doing it properly.

Topaz wanted to be a journalist more than anything else in the world. She wanted to talk to everyone and see everything and serve it back up to the public in graceful phrases and snappy paragraphs, underneath a photo of herself and a byline. She would make them laugh, and shock them, and make and break people, and change perceptions. She wanted to give people spectacles, so that when they looked through them they would see life the way she did. She would expose, observe, amuse and enlighten. And make a ton of money doing it.

When Topaz arrived in Oxford, she staggered up the staircase to her room, unpacked her clothes and made a cup of coffee. Then she went down to the porters' lodge at the college entrance, signed her name in the register of new undergraduates, and examined the sixty-odd leaflets stuffed into her pigeonhole from university societies desperate to get freshers – as the new batch of students were traditionally termed – to sign up. One of them was from *Cherwell*, the student newspaper, advertising for volunteers. Topaz folded the little sheet of paper and tucked it neatly in her purse. She threw everything else away without looking at it.

Rowena Gordon was just as sure about what she wanted to do, but she knew Oxford wouldn't give her much help with it. She wanted to go into the record business. Over her last two years at school, Rowena, the icy blonde who was famous for never even *looking* at a boy, discovered rock and roll. It was the first thing she'd felt moved by. The wild, dark rhythms of the music, the blatantly sexual lyrics, the dangerous looks of the musicians – it scandalized all her friends, but it excited Rowena. Hard rock was a world of its own, a totally different world to the one she was used to. It made her feel strange.

Her parents heard about her passion from the housemistress, but could hardly believe it. How could their trouble-free girl possibly be involved in that kind of trash? So the teacher kept her counsel, disapprovingly. It didn't do to upset Mr Gordon. But having known Rowena for some years, she sensed in the girl what her parents did not; a disturbing sexuality buried in that virgin flesh, in the new sashay of her long, slim legs, and the promise of her soft, plump lips.

Rowena was intelligent, and she kept her ambitions to herself. Music would have to wait until she'd graduated, and meanwhile, there was Oxford to attend to.

Her first term, Rowena, newly up at Christ Church, joined the Oxford Union. It was the most important society in Oxford, and so Rowena Gordon intended to be President.

Three quarters of all undergraduates were members of the Union. It owned its own buildings in the centre of the city, and possessed a cheap bar and cocktail cellar that were always packed out. It was regarded as a nursery for Britain's political elite – prime ministers and cabinet members from Gladstone to Michael Heseltine had been officers and presidents. The programme of speakers and events for Topaz and Rowena's first terms had included Henry Kissinger, Jerry Hall, Warren Beatty and the Princess Royal within the space of eight weeks.

Rowena fell in love. She couldn't write, like Topaz, but she could certainly talk. She learnt how to debate and found she adored the almost sexual charge of passionately exhorting a crowd, joking, rebuffing, challenging, holding them locked into her eyes and voice. She started running in the Union elections and found she loved that too; the bitter feuds, the pacts made and broken, the secret meetings in the officers' offices. She loved the rhetoric and the protocol – 'Madam Librarian', 'Mr Chairman', 'the honourable lady from St Hilda's'.

'What's the motion next week again?' Topaz asked, trying not to seem too absorbed in her own triumph. *Published in a national! Published in a national! Editor of* Cherwell *was one thing, but* this! . . .

'This House Believes that Women Are Getting Their Just Deserts,' recited Rowena.

Topaz laughed. 'I can't believe they're letting you off the leash on that one in a Presidential, Madam Librarian.'

Rowena allowed herself a quick smile. 'Nor can I, to be honest,' she admitted. 'Gilbert is such a prat about feminism.'

The Presidential Debate took place once a term and was the final showdown between officers and other candidates for the top job. Rowena's only real competition was the Secretary, Gilbert Docker; one hundred per cent public schoolboy, blood so blue it was obscene. Gilbert found it appalling that women should even be allowed to join the Union, let alone run for office. In the good old days, they had had to watch silently from the visitors' gallery, with all the other peasants.

'You'll have *Cherwell* right behind you,' Topaz assured her.

Rowena smiled. 'Yeah, well. At least you and I can count on each other. Let's go and have a beer.'

They wandered down Broad Street towards the King's Arms, a perennial favourite for students from the university and polytechnic. Most of the tourists that crowded Oxford's lovely streets had climbed back on their buses by six o'clock, and the early evening air was warm and soft. The scent of mown grass drifted towards them from the gardens of Trinity College.

'Have you seen Peter this week?' Rowena asked.

Peter Kennedy was one of the better-known students at Oxford, and Topaz Rossi's boyfriend. They'd been seeing each other for a couple of months, and Rowena was intrigued by the romance. She gathered that Peter was – well – more from her own kind of background, to be honest. He wasn't the type she'd expect to be interested in Topaz Rossi, nor he in her. Still, by all accounts he was drop-dead gorgeous.

'Yes,' said Topaz. She blushed. 'I really like the guy. He's pretty . . . pretty interesting.'

'Pretty spectacular, you mean,' said Rowena. 'Let's not kid ourselves.'

They turned into the pub, grinning at each other with perfect understanding.

'Nice job, Topaz!' called Rupert Walton from the bar. 'I heard about *The Times*.'

'Cheers, Rupert.' Topaz waved to her deputy editor.

'Hey, Rupe,' Rowena called.

'Madam President,' he said.

'Bloody hell, don't say that,' Rowena protested, fighting her way through the crowd. 'Gin and tonic, Labatt's, and whatever Rupert's drinking, please. You'll jinx it.'

'Nothing can jinx it after the piece on him I'm running next week,' he said smugly. 'It's not even editorial condemnation. It's just a long list of his own quotes, starting with "Working mothers are responsible for the crime rate," and ending with "Oxford was designed for the sons of gentlemen, and it ought to be kept that way." I'll have a Guinness, please. Thanks.'

They threaded their way back to the table, nodding at friends. Chris Johnson and Nick Flower, two of Rowena's candidates, were sitting next to Topaz.

'Look out, Rupe, hacks in the area,' she teased. 'You go out for an innocent drink with Miss Gordon, you end up in the middle of a slate meeting.'

'Right,' said Rupert. 'You'll wind up civil servants, the lot of you, and serve you right. No fate is too bad.'

'How's it looking, guys?' asked Rowena. 'Ignore the budding Fleet Street scum over here.'

'Christ Church is solid,' said Nick, 'as ever. Oriel's not.'

'Surprise.'

'Hertford'll give you a hundred and fifty line votes.'

'God bless Hertford,' said Topaz.

'Amen,' Rowena concurred.

'We've got Queen's, Lincoln, Jesus and St Peter's wrapped up. Balliol's a problem. So is John's.'

'Why?' asked Chris.

Nick shrugged. 'Because Peter Kennedy's decided he wants to support Gilbert, and he's mobilizing the old school ties.'

A slight chill fell over the table and Rowena felt her heart sink. Gilbert, really, had never been that much of a threat. Peter was another matter.

Topaz touched her sleeve. 'Don't worry. I'll go see him, talk some sense into him. He'll be cool.'

'Thanks, sweetheart,' Rowena said, wondering what she'd do without her. She didn't want Topaz dragged into a political row between her best friend and her boyfriend. 'But I'll do it. This one's really my problem. I'll sort it out.'

Peter Kennedy versus Rowena Gordon, Rupert thought, looking at the two beautiful girls. Now, that *will* be interesting.

Chapter Two

'Can you tell me where Mr Kennedy lives, please?' asked Rowena politely.

The porter touched his bowler hat gravely, whether in deference to herself or Peter Kennedy she wasn't sure.

'Certainly, madam. Mr Kennedy has rooms in Old Library, number five on the first floor.'

'Thank you,' said Rowena.

She took a quick glance at the spacious lodge, littered like most of Oxford's college entrances with leaflets advertising lectures, plays, jobs and pizza discounts. It was Friday, which meant that a large pile of that week's *Cherwell* had just been delivered, dumped underneath the window next to the noticeboard. She grabbed a copy before they all disappeared.

He *would* be at Christ Church, she thought.

It was the largest, most prestigious and most arrogant college in the university. Only St John's was richer, and only Oriel more despised by everyone else. Not that either of these things bothered the House, as it was traditionally nicknamed; John's was full of 'grey men', hard-working, brilliant undergraduates destined for fellowships and research posts – boring idiots in other words – and Oriel was a poor relation. Christ Church had produced something like twelve prime ministers and nineteen viceroys of India. Its hall was one of the architectural wonders of England. It had a private picture gallery, boasting drawings by Michelangelo and Van Dyck.

Peter Kennedy could not possibly have gone anywhere else, Rowena thought. She smiled. *And neither could I.*

She walked through magnificent Tom Quad, admiring the grey Elizabethan stone, lit gently by the setting sun. Tom Tower, rearing up behind her, began to strike the hour five minutes early, because the college was exactly one degree west of Greenwich. She felt very nervous, as if even the ancient walkways and carved gargoyles were ranking up behind Gilbert, now that Kennedy was on his side. She'd have to talk him out of it. That was all there was to it.

Under the soaring archways of the walk into hall, someone had pinned up the standard-issue poster announcing the Union elections, listing the candidates and somewhat improbably requesting that any breach of the rules be reported to J. Sanders, Exeter, Returning Officer. Since the rules stated that no candidate should solicit votes, much less form an electoral pact – a slate, in other words – they were universally ignored, except on polling day, when the deputy returning officers had fun making life even more miserable for the hacks than it was already. Every hack, once they stopped running, had a go at being a DRO and enjoyed it immensely.

Rowena examined the poster for graffiti and was pleased to find that someone had scrawled 'Prat' after Gilbert's name. She also noticed, laughing, that someone had carefully written 'TOPAZ ROSSI, ST HILDA'S' at the top of the list of standing-committee nominees. My friend the sex symbol. She'd tried to get Topaz to run a million times, but unless she could interview it, report on it or give it an impossible deadline, Topaz wasn't interested. 'Tina Brown didn't have time for the Union,' she'd said dismissively.

Rowena strolled through the glorious cathedral cloisters to Old Library. The door to the staircase was heavy, solid wood, studded with metal bolts like a dungeon entrance. Maybe, thought Rowena fancifully, they locked Protestants in here when Bloody Mary was queen.

She bounded up the narrow stairs to Kennedy's room, her heart hammering, and knocked loudly. I *am* Librarian of the Union, she told herself firmly, and he's a threat, that's all, to be dealt with like any other threat.

Peter, tall and tanned from rowing, opened the door. 'Miss Gordon, delighted to meet you,' he said. 'I've been expecting you. Won't you come in?'

Rowena stepped into the most luxurious under-graduate rooms she'd seen anywhere. 'Thank you,' she said. 'Please call me Rowena, Mr Kennedy.'

'Only if you'll agree to call me Peter,' he said, smiling, waving her to an armchair. 'I am seeing your best friend, after all. I'm amazed that we haven't managed to meet up before now.'

'Then that's settled,' said Rowena, ashamed to find herself momentarily jealous.

Christ, the guy was attractive. He was wearing a dark blue Boat Club tracksuit, with HOUSE emblazoned on the back in large white letters, the colour emphasizing his blue eyes and luxuriant blond hair. To Rowena, his size and strength made him seem even older than twenty-three, perhaps nearer to twenty-five. There was discreet evidence of immense wealth displayed all over the room; an antique gold carriage clock, a couple of leather-bound first editions on his table without library stickers on them. The bed was made up with a feather duvet and crisp Irish linen, and she doubted even Christ Church would run to that. Peter Kennedy was studying Anglo-Saxon under the legendary tutelage of Richard Hamer, one of the most learned and pleasant dons at Oxford, but there were textbooks on advanced economics stacked in rows on his bookshelves. Two pairs of oars were mounted across the bed; blades, traditionally awarded to the finest rowers. And God only knew he was that, Rowena thought.

'Coffee?' he enquired.

'Yes, please,' said Rowena. It might be a little easier when those handsome eyes weren't staring her down.

'You presumably know why I'm here,' she said. 'Word has it that you'll be supporting Gilbert Docker this term. You must realize that without your intervention I'm cruising home.'

'So how can one outsider's influence make any difference to you, more or less?' asked Peter calmly, stirring the coffee.

'I'm not sure,' said Rowena, deciding that honesty might charm him, 'but I'd prefer not to chance it. Believe me, I know how popular you are, how widely you can pull out the Old Etonian vote, the sports vote' – she hesitated, but added, 'the female vote . . .'

Peter handed her her coffee.

'I don't feel that anything could make Gilbert look good,' she said, 'but if there were something, it would be your support.'

He sat opposite her, sizing her up. Nice. Long blonde hair, green eyes, slim body, long legs, a lady evidently. A virgin for sure.

'Why should I support you?' he asked. 'Gilbert's the son of a friend of my father's. You'll have to give me some very good reasons to withdraw my backing from him.'

My God, Rowena thought. He's considering it. Is he seriously interested in my qualifications for the job? Most people couldn't give a monkey's about that.

'I'm the best candidate by miles,' she said, 'and you're rumoured to be a meritocrat, Peter.'

He smiled, amused. That was a clever slant.

'As Secretary, I doubled the number of social events and made a profit on entertainments for the first time in four years. As Librarian, I managed to get speakers from David Puttnam to Mick Jagger. I've served time on every Union committee. I've debated for Oxford in the world championships.'

'Did we win?' asked Kennedy, interested.

'We came second to Edinburgh,' Rowena grinned. 'The Cambridge judges were copping an attitude.'

'Classic inferiority complex,' agreed Kennedy.

'Gilbert ran straight for Secretary, just scraped in on the O E vote because there was no serious opposition, can't be bothered to turn up for standing-committee meetings, and has put on exactly two parties, using hangover sponsors from my term. He only wants to put "President of the Union" on his application to the merchant banks. He probably wouldn't bother with his own debates, if he got it.'

Kennedy nodded, accepting this. 'I need some more time to think about it,' he said. 'I won't give you a glib answer.'

Rowena got up and offered him her hand to shake, pleasantly surprised.

He turned it over, raised it slowly to his lips and kissed it. A shiver ran with little electric feet all over her body.

'Really, Topaz is terrible,' he said. 'Keeping you away from me like this. If I'd had the pleasure of knowing you beforehand, I wouldn't have committed myself to Gilbert in the first place.'

For a second Rowena wondered how on earth Topaz had managed to hook up with this devastating guy. She was amazed that he would choose an American. Still . . .

'Well, thank you for seeing me,' she said. 'I'll be in touch.'

Topaz and Rowena sat in Topaz's cramped room in Hall Building in St Hilda's, companionably drinking huge mugs of tea and stuffing their faces with chocolate biscuits, leafing through back copies of *Cherwell* to select the best pieces for Topaz's portfolio. What there was of Topaz's room was very nice, as it had once belonged to a don, but in order to create two separate rooms for lowly undergraduates someone had partitioned it straight down the middle. Topaz thus had half a window, which looked out on to the river, past the gorgeous Hilda's gardens which were ablaze with roses and thick honeysuckle. Both girls loved it here.

'God, I'm so tired,' Topaz complained. 'The fucking computers crashed at three o'clock this morning and we all had to stay up and retype everything. Ever tried drinking out of a Coke can someone just used as an ashtray? No? Well, don't bother.'

Rowena smothered a laugh, her mouth full of Hob-nob.

'I've got a tutorial first thing tomorrow on Molière, and I can't skip it because I went sick on the last one, so that means essay crisis tonight . . . and I gotta pick something out here to show the big boys when I'm job-hunting, and I'll just screw it up because I'm pissed-off.'

'You're always pissed-off, Topaz,' said Rowena.

'I brought you a present,' Topaz said, throwing her the latest issue of *Vanity Fair*. 'It's got a massive piece on David Geffen in it.'

'Oh, great!' said Rowena, grabbing it. 'David Geffen –'

'– is God, I know, I know,' said Topaz.

Rowena worshipped David Geffen, the legendary American music mogul who had started two record companies from scratch and made a huge success out of both of them. He was a self-made billionaire who had started out without a cent to his name. She kept a *New York Times* profile on him tacked above her bed.

'So?' said Rowena defensively. 'You'd walk a mile over broken glass for five minutes with Tina Brown.'

'I'd walk ten miles,' sighed Topaz, imagining it. Tina Brown was young, beautiful, happily married and the greatest magazine powerhouse the world had ever seen, or at least that's what Topaz Rossi thought. She had left Oxford, gone into editing and seemed to double the circulation of any magazine in whose direction she glanced. Now she ran *Vanity Fair*, and had produced a cocktail of glitz and gravitas that made it the hottest title on the shelves, hotter even than *Cosmopolitan*, if that were possible.

'I want what she's got, damn it!' Topaz said.

'You've got *Cherwell*.'

'It's hardly *Vanity Fair*, now is it?' asked Topaz sarcastically.

'It's a start,' Rowena insisted. 'It got you *The Times*.'

'That's true,' admitted Topaz, her bad mood evaporating. 'How's the debate coming along?'

'I've got no problems,' said Rowena, supremely confident. 'Gilbert Docker? I'll slaughter him.'

'What did Peter say?' Topaz asked, with an uncharacteristic blush. Somehow, talking about Peter in front of Rowena always made her feel a bit dirty. Rowena was still a virgin, amazingly enough.

'He said he'd think about it,' Rowena told her. 'Are you seeing him tonight?'

'Yeah,' Topaz said. She was glad Rowena had dealt

with it herself. She'd hate to have to discuss slate politics with Peter.

There was a slight pause.

'Let's get on with it, then,' Rowena said, picking up a feature on the Magdalen May Ball.

Topaz arched her back from the pleasure of it, feeling the night dew of the meadow wet beneath her. Over her head she could see the spires of the ancient city, black against the night. They were a few feet away from the riverbank and somewhere under the urgent heat of her pleasure she could hear the gentle murmuring of the water. God, it was so beautiful. In New York the neon lights of the city obliterated all the stars; here, under Peter's exquisite touch, she could see them scattered across the whole sky, like sherbet.

Peter's tongue was flicking up and down her spine, his fingertips lightly tracing her ribcage, half tickling, half caressing. Her whole body felt sensitized, alive. Topaz parted her legs, ready for him, enjoying the weight of him, the feeling of his large, thick erection pushing into her. She liked his strength. Sometimes she might even have liked it a little rougher, but that wasn't Peter's style; sex was an art for him.

She felt his fingers slide around and underneath her, reaching for her belly, for the delicate little skin patches just under her hips, wanting to stroke them, to feel them flutter under his touch. It sent a new spasm of wetness through her, and she moaned. He had taken his time discovering her body. He knew where he could turn her on. Topaz pressed against him, squirming into his hands. He liked that. His cock leapt against her.

Topaz moved with him, getting hotter. She was close, she could feel it. She wriggled about, so she could push up against his cock with the cheeks of her ass. Peter gasped when she did that, surprised by a new surge of desire. He pulled back, positioned himself to enter her. Topaz opened herself wider, waves of heat spreading through her.

'Now, baby,' she urged, and Peter began to thrust, in and out, pulling so far back he was almost withdrawn, and then plunging back inside her, slick with her juice. He was getting harder inside her, he was nearly there. He put his hands on her shoulders, gripping her hard, pushing into her faster, pleasuring her. Topaz sobbed. Maybe someone would walk across the meadows. Maybe someone would see them. She moaned, she was going to come. The block of pressure in her stomach dissolved and shattered, rippling through her, a long shiver of orgasm. Peter went rigid with pleasure, came, and relaxed on top of her.

Topaz kissed his shoulder. 'You were amazing,' she said.

'Me? Oh, baby,' he said. 'You're fantastic.'

He rolled off her, and they lay on the riverbank together, exhausted.

'This is so romantic,' Topaz said. 'I just can't believe it.'

She was incredibly happy. Peter was so gentle, so imaginative, so tender with her. The fumbling boys back in Brooklyn had never been like this. And her father had wanted one of them for her husband! If Gino could see this stunning, rich English gentleman, he'd throw a fit. Topaz had a brief, vengeful fantasy about taking Peter back for dinner and watching her poppa fall over himself to kiss his ass. Not that she'd ever darken *that* asshole's door again.

'I'm glad you think so,' Peter said. He grabbed his jacket, took out a packet of cigarettes and lit up. The smoke curled up in the darkness, white and fragrant.

'Your friend Rowena came to see me today,' he added. 'About the Union. She wants me to drop out of supporting Gilbert.'

'She mentioned it,' Topaz said, warily. One thing she had learnt was that Union politics got deadly serious. She suppressed the memory of her friend's mute appeal for help this afternoon; she didn't want Peter to think she was interfering.

'Trouble is, I'm committed to him,' Peter said easily. 'Are you cold, darling? No? I might get out of it, but it'd be tricky.'

Topaz curled against the warmth of his side. She still tingled from his caress. 'You guys can sort it out,' she said.

Peter allowed his arm to drop round her, enjoying the feeling of her firm, full breasts. It was pleasant, being with Topaz Rossi. She was eager, enthusiastic and fun. He was slightly surprised that Rowena Gordon was her friend. They were so different.

Idly he pictured Rowena as she had come to deal with him that morning. The shimmering blonde hair. The graceful poise. The confident manner. If being with Topaz was exploring the exotic, talking to slim, elegant Rowena Gordon was like looking in a mirror. And that was something else Peter Kennedy enjoyed.

'Leave it to us, sweetheart,' he said. 'We'll find some solution. Tell your friend to come and see me again.'

Chapter Three

'Topaz, please,' Rowena said, twisting her fingers around under her cuffs.

The two girls were walking down the wide gravel path that bisected Christ Church meadows, strolling down to the river. It was the middle of Eights Week, the traditional summer rowing contest. Every college fielded male and female teams – except St Hilda's, which didn't admit men – and the students took it very seriously indeed. Topaz had two whole teams of *Cherwell* reporters asigned to it, and every hack in the Union took up position outside their college boathouse first thing in the morning. Ambition aside, where else could you be? The sun was beating down, the water was glittering and the alcohol was flowing. Thousands of kids were packing the riverbank, this year like every year. Rowena and Topaz were threading through a crowd on their way down there, and it was only ten in the morning. The crack of dawn. Normally they wouldn't even be awake.

'No. Jesus, how many times? I said no, and I meant it,' Topaz answered, with something of an edge to her tone. 'I'm not gonna discuss it with Peter for you. I don't want to get involved. *Capisci*?'

'I get that, but I need your help,' Rowena said,

hammering away. 'I *have* to get Peter, if not to go with me, at least to hold back from supporting Gilbert.'

'What part of "no" don't you understand?' Topaz asked, sarcastically. 'The guy's my boyfriend. This stuff is as important to him as it is to you. If I start interfering, he's gonna be turned off like a light switch. I'm devoting every damn issue of the paper to what an asshole Gilbert Docker is. Isn't that enough?'

'Yeah, and you know I'm really grateful, but –'

'No. No buts,' Topaz interrupted her impatiently, pushing a handful of scarlet curls away from her forehead, and yet again Rowena was struck by how terrific, how brazen, her friend looked. Today she was wearing cut-off denim shorts that fitted snugly round her taut, curvy ass, the tiny threads on the fringes just kissing the tops of firm, tanned thighs, and a yellow-checked shirt tied above her flat midriff, the fabric pulled hard against those overripe breasts. She felt another quick burst of frustrated envy, immediately followed by a stab of guilt.

'You'll have to talk him into it yourself, Rowena. That's your specialty, anyway.'

'I'm seeing more of him than you are, these days,' Rowena said softly.

For a second Topaz glanced across at her. 'You can't hate his company as much as you're making out,' she said. 'Peter's not so bad. Hey, you're gonna have to get to like him. You'll have to dance with him at our wedding. That's in the chief bridesmaid's job description, says so in all the books.' She grinned.

'Wedding! Don't you think you might be rushing this just a little bit?' Rowena exploded.

'Maybe. Let's not talk about it any more,' Topaz begged. 'I don't want to have a row with you. But I'm not getting involved. OK?'

'OK,' Rowena said, looking away. She swallowed her fury. 'I'll see you later, Tope, all right? I want to see how we're getting on.'

'Sure,' her friend said, giving her a cheerful wink as she headed towards a hot-dog stand.

Rowena fought her anger all the way down the riverfront as she strolled towards the Christ Church boathouse. Not that anyone watching her would have known it; she walked slowly, waving at anyone who looked even vaguely familiar and flashing a dazzling smile at everyone else.

She looked good, she knew that. Beautiful and happy, confident and stylish. The brilliant sunshine made her blonde hair look almost platinum, and the long cotton dress she'd picked out that morning flowed closely round her slim body. She'd picked out just a kiss of make-up – clover lips, beige eyeshadow – and in her own way she looked just as sexy as Topaz Rossi.

But it was Topaz Rossi who was dating Peter Kennedy, not her.

Yes, and he'd really dump her for bringing up politics, Rowena thought, blowing a playful kiss to Emily Chan, a friend of hers from Lady Margaret Hall. Why can't she just do this for me? Why do I have to be closeted with her fucking boyfriend? If I was dating some guy at a national paper I'd talk to him about *her* . . .

The path exploded with cheers as Merton's women's crew tore past, oars slicing up the water with powerful strokes, and Oriel only seconds behind.

'Go *on*, Merton!' she shouted, jumping up and down. Ancient college rivalry between Christ Church and Oriel. Anybody was preferable to those guys winning . . .

'Yeah, move it!' a voice agreed behind her. The sun was blacked out by a Christ Church scarf being looped around her head from behind, knotted and pulled tightly together. 'Guess who?' the voice whispered in her ear. A low male voice, laughing at her.

'Cut it out, Kennedy,' Rowena snapped.

He loosened the scarf, letting her see again. 'You're too easy, Rowena. Don't look where you're going. You could get into all kinds of trouble that way.'

She reached up to her neck and ripped it off. 'What are you doing here?'

He raised an eyebrow. 'Same thing you are. Supporting Sam and the guys.' He nodded towards the Christ Church boat, moored just ahead of them, where Sam Wilson, Captain of Boats, and the main men's crew were waiting to race. 'That *is* what you're doing, right?'

'Of course,' Rowena replied icily.

Damn, why did he have to look at her like that? Look her up and down like that? What was she supposed to do about it? Say, 'Hey, you belong to Topaz'?

'Sure you're not here to hack?' he teased her. 'All these votes, within such easy reach . . .'

'Sure you're not here to relive past glories?' she countered.

Last year Peter Kennedy had been Captain of Boats and had led Christ Church to a record victory. There had been talk of Olympic trials, but Kennedy had chosen to give up sport to concentrate on his finals. Now Sam Wilson looked as though he might be leading them to Head of the River again, and the Olympic coaches were sniffing round new stars, like Johnny Searle.

'You know how to hit where it hurts,' Peter said, not taking his eyes off her. He made it sound vaguely obscene. 'Rowing meant a lot to me. Still does.'

'I can see that,' Rowena answered, struck by the closeness of his body, the broad, tanned chest in a white

T-shirt inches from her face. Peter Kennedy would have graced any beach in California.

'Are you flirting with me?' Peter asked, catching her green eyes on his body.

Ridiculously, Rowena felt her breath catch in her throat. Where the fuck's Topaz? she thought.

'Don't be absurd,' she said coldly.

'Maybe you *should* flirt with me. Kiss up to me a little,' Peter suggested, smiling at her with a lazy grin. 'You do want my help, right?'

'Not that badly.'

'Don't be so uptight. I'm just kidding,' he said, putting one hand on her waist and steering her towards their boathouse. 'Topaz wouldn't want us to quarrel.'

Despite herself, Rowena stiffened beneath his touch.

Peter Kennedy smiled.

'Rowena! Peter! Hurry up!' said James Gunn, a friend of theirs, pulling the two of them into the Christ Church crowd. 'You nearly missed it, we're about to start.'

Rowena felt herself surrounded by bodies in college colours, hundreds of them, all seething forward towards the bank, shouting and clapping. Somebody flung an arm round her. She flung an arm round somebody. The college was going berserk.

'*House! House!*'

They were about to cut the boat loose. Rowena was lost in a press of navy blue, thrown forward towards the mooring boards. 'I can't see anything!' she complained to no one in particular.

Suddenly she felt herself being lifted up from behind, as lightly as a doll, and hoisted backwards over the heads of the crowd. Amazed, she looked down, to see Peter ducking between her legs, supporting her on his shoulders. She had a perfect view of the boat, the river, everything.

The back of Peter Kennedy's strong neck pressed against her white cotton panties.

It felt good.

'Put me down!' she insisted, weakly.

He grinned up at her. 'Later.'

With a roar from the crowd, the Christ Church boat sprang away from its moorings, finding the stroke at once. The eight rowers moved in perfect harmony into the water, their oars churning it up at terrific speed, chasing the Oriel first boat. The supporters on the bank immediately broke up and started to run alongside it, screaming encouragement at the tops of their voices and cursing the rival crew amicably. Peter ran with them, carrying Rowena above him, his hands holding her thighs in an iron grip, ignoring her protests. Her weight was evidently nothing to him.

Rowena, startled, cheered and shouted with the rest. It was too much fun. Besides which, she couldn't help but think, every single person here could see her getting into it, supporting her college – she'd be kind of hard to miss, with her fair hair streaming out behind her like a banner, piggybacking on top of Peter Kennedy.

There was a cry of triumph as Christ Church inexorably rammed into the tail of the Oriel boat.

'Bumped!' Peter yelled. He reached up and swung Rowena gracefully down from his back with one hand.

She touched her feet to the ground, smoothing down her dress, suddenly embarrassed, wondering what to say.

'We win again,' he said.

'Thanks, Peter,' she muttered.

He raised her hand to his lips and kissed it, casually. 'That was fun. Let's do it again some time,' he suggested.

Rowena Gordon blushed bright red, nodded as coldly as she could, and walked off down the path.

*

Cherwell was buzzing.

It was two weeks to the Union elections, and it looked as though they were going to be close. Every college was being hacked full-throttle by eager candidates from the opposing slates. Each new day brought a fresh crop of rumour, treachery and malicious gossip; Tori had defected, Joss wasn't pulling his weight, rival candidates were still sleeping with each other . . . Topaz loved it. It was an editor's dream.

Of course, the biggest rumour of all was that Peter Kennedy and Rowena Gordon were on the verge of doing a deal. If *that* happened, all bets were off. Rowena would be home free, the first woman President of the Union for five years. Gilbert Docker needed Peter to survive.

Whenever Rowena or Gilbert went round to Peter, the news trickled back to *Cherwell*. Mostly Topaz didn't report it. She wanted to throw as much weight as she could behind her best friend, and she concentrated on articles about Gilbert's sexism or the bully-boy tactics of his followers. God only knew they made the best reading; one of her writers at St Anne's had come in just that morning with a story of how Gilbert's Secretary candidate, a popular Scottish guy reading law, had stuck a ten-inch carving knife into the door of his female opponent on Rowena's slate. Topaz had been ecstatic; the story was dynamite. She'd lead this Friday's edition on it.

The only thing she would *not* do was interfere personally. Rowena had asked her to take over with Peter three times this week, but Topaz always turned her down flat. She knew what the Presidency meant to Rowena, but even so, she couldn't risk her boyfriend over it.

'Have you seen my layout for the jobs pages?' Rupert

asked, weaving in between their rickety photocopiers with a full cup of coffee. 'I'm sure I left it on top of my desk . . .'

Topaz shook her head, preoccupied with the carving knife. College authorities had pulled it out of Lisa's door, and she was wondering if she could get away with sticking a similar knife in the door and taking a photo of that.

'You're bloody useless, Rupe,' Gareth Kelly said. 'We had two thousand quids' worth of advertising from McKinsey in that.'

'I'll find it, OK?' promised her deputy editor, sounding harassed. Rupert was scatty and untidy, but a great journalist. Topaz could see that clearly. Even on a college paper he had a knack for ferreting out the real stories: single-parent students, harassing tutors. Rupe had been the first to congratulate her on her *Times* commission. He was the only person on the staff who realized it meant more than a £150 cheque.

'Here it is,' shouted Jane Edwards, the features editor. Rupert leaned gratefully across and grabbed it, answering the phone at the same time and slopping coffee all over his desk.

'*Cherwell*. Yeah. Who should I say is calling?'

He handed the receiver to Topaz with a wink. 'It's for you. Geoffrey Stevens at *The Times*.'

Topaz grabbed the phone, swinging her long legs over the desk to reach it. Every guy in the place sighed mentally.

'Miss Rossi?' asked a cool voice.

'That's me,' Topaz replied, trying to sound flip and unconcerned. She'd posted off her article two days ago. What if the guy hated it?

'This is Geoffrey Stevens,' he said. 'We received your article on student benefits yesterday. We were wondering if you might like to consider a new use for it?'

Topaz's heart sank. It wasn't good enough for the *Educational Supplement*. 'What did you have in mind?' she asked.

'I think this is a bit too good to tuck away in a supplement,' Stevens said. 'I've shown it to the features editor and he agrees with me – we want to use it in the main paper.'

Topaz put out a hand to steady herself against the desk. She was too stunned to speak.

'I know what you're thinking,' Stevens went on, 'you're wondering where we're going to put it. And you're right, of course, that's a problem just at the minute. We're full up, but if you can bear to wait a fortnight we'll run it two weeks on Monday. Would that be OK?'

'That'd be fine,' Topaz said, trying not to sound too overjoyed.

'Terrific! I hoped I could count on you. And send me some more, if you've got it. We're always looking for new talent.'

'Thanks, I will,' said Topaz. She hung up, and looked at the six faces gazing at her expectantly.

'Oh my God!' she exclaimed. 'I'm *in*!'

Rowena planned her campaign with military care. Every speech was dramatic. Every outfit was sexy. Every hack on her slate had his or her orders, and everyone followed them. Rowena had found out who the weak links were early on, kept them out of slate meetings and assigned them to the smallest colleges. She just wasn't taking risks.

She wanted to be President of the Union.

She wanted it *badly*.

She would do almost anything to win.

And that was the problem. Because in this case, 'anything' involved Peter Edward Kennedy, her best friend's boyfriend, the power behind Gilbert's throne. The one man who could hand her what she wanted on a golden plate.

Since that first meeting, Kennedy had swung back and forth like a pendulum. Yes, he would support her. No, he'd given his word. OK, Gilbert was a sexist and an elitist. He would back her slate. Well, maybe he wasn't sure . . .

Rowena knew she could not let this go. However annoyed, however exasperated she got, she never let it show. If Peter Kennedy could be won over, it was worth any effort. It was worth going to see him four times a week.

And that was the *real* problem.

Rowena Gordon, the proverbial ice maiden, was having to deal with something more than annoyance. Something so new she didn't even recognize it at first, but which slowly took a hold of her, until it was all she could do to control herself. She was falling for Peter.

Every day she had to deal with it. He forced her to sit in his rooms and discuss politics with him, a subject which normally fascinated her. But with Peter Kennedy she found she was tuning out. She wasn't listening to him, she was watching his lips move. The square, bold set of his jaw. The thick flaxen hair. The well-developed muscles sliding under the brown, healthy skin.

Peter entranced her. He was so intelligent, so masculine, so assured. Normally Rowena despised men of her own class: wimpy chinless wonders, the lot of them. Gilbert Docker was a typical specimen. But Peter Kennedy wasn't like that. He was a thorough gentleman, but he was sexual too. He was graceful, but he obviously knew how to fight. He was accomplished, but he was also a fiercely competitive athlete. He interested her. He *excited* her.

'What do you *want* out of life?' he asked her. 'When is it enough?'

'I want everything!' Rowena replied. 'It's never enough!'

'When you die, they'll put "Dreamer" on your gravestone,' Peter said, looking at her admiringly. 'You remind me of something Henry Ford once said – "Whether you think you can, or whether you think you can't, you are right." '

She'd glowed with pleasure at his approval.

She knew it was dangerous. She knew it was wrong. Topaz was in love with him, for God's sake! But what could she do? Without Peter's backing she might fail. And failure was something Rowena Gordon wouldn't stand for.

She began to get angry with Topaz. Why couldn't *she* do this? Peter was her boyfriend. He'd listen to her. If Topaz would talk to him, she wouldn't have to torment herself, but no, her friend just refused to help. It was the first breach that had come between them. Topaz wouldn't even discuss it. She's too absorbed with her goddamn paper, Rowena thought angrily. Student Journalist of the Year. Young Editor of the Year. Future *Times* columnist.

So Rowena walked in and out of Christ Church's magnificent Tudor stone four times a week, because Kennedy refused to let her off the hook. He wanted to be persuaded, talked into it. He told Rowena he enjoyed her company, that she was beautiful, brilliant and enthralling, and that since he had all the cards, she'd have to humour him.

Rowena tried to convince herself that this annoyed her.

Silk. Satin. Swirling chiffon. The lawns of St Hilda's were covered in ballgowns. Thin, sparkling sheaths clung tightly to their owners' bodies, short, bias-cut numbers displayed miles of pretty calves, and old-fashioned crinoline gowns swept regally to the ground, their delicate hems brushing the close-mown grass. The only women's college left at Oxford was preparing for the Union Ball.

'What do you think?' Topaz demanded. She struck a pose against an oak tree wreathed in white dog-roses.

'Very sexy,' Rowena said. Topaz was wearing a tiny, barely-there outfit of navy velvet which contrasted beautifully with her auburn hair, bright blue eyes and healthy tanned skin. The dress was boned at the ribs to emphasize her magnificent breasts, and cut off six inches above the knee, displaying acres of firm, rounded thighs. It was a knockout; even the old porters couldn't stop staring at her.

Rowena tried to hide her disapproval. What *did* Topaz think she was wearing? She looked like a tramp. That little scrap of fabric hardly hid her underwear. How could – she tried to smother her snobbery, but failed – a gentleman like Peter Kennedy want to date her? She was so brazen!

'Do you think it's possibly a little short?' she added coldly.

'What's the matter, am I embarrassing you? Huh?' Topaz grinned. 'Wondering what Peter's going to do with me when he checks this out?'

Rowena blushed scarlet.

'Hey, hey, I'm only teasing,' Topaz said hastily. 'You're getting a little uptight these days, that's all.'

'Election pressure,' offered Rowena, ashamed of herself. She was letting jealousy sour her friendship.

'You look wonderful,' Topaz said warmly. 'Fantastic. It's a little conservative for me, but I'm sure it'll win you hundreds of votes. Who could see you tonight and *not* vote for you?'

Rowena had chosen a family heirloom, an antique Regency gown in light pink silk. It was embroidered with a subtle design of heather sprigs, picked out on the bodice in cloth-of-gold. She was wearing her long hair straight, letting it tumble in a blonde curtain over her shoulders. Her shoes were satin heels from Chanel, and she was carrying a small fan and an elegant clutch bag. Long washed-silk gloves reached up to her elbows. Cinderella would have been proud.

'Thanks,' Rowena smiled. 'That's the idea.'

Topaz glanced at her again, more slowly. 'You devious bitch,' she said affectionately. 'They could stick a picture of you in the dictionary next to "ladylike". It's all part of the masterplan, am I right? Look feminine, talk feminist? You'll hook the women with their ears and the men with their eyes.'

Rowena laughed. 'For a foreigner, you're a quick learner.'

A porter shuffled across the manicured lawns towards them. 'Taxi, Miss Rossi,' he said.

'So when are they printing it?'

'Two weeks from yesterday,' Topaz said. The taxi crawled across Magdalen Bridge, the Gothic splendour of the college rearing up to her right. Undergraduates in full evening dress were picking their way along the High Street, but Rowena didn't want to walk. Not that the locals paid any attention. Every year, ball dresses, dinner jackets and drunken students were a standard fixture in the summer term. 'And he asked me to give him some more stuff, said they were always looking for talent . . .'

Excitement and happiness bubbled in her voice.

'They'll print it right after the election,' remarked Rowena. It was so close now. Anxiety balled in her stomach like a fist. She *must* win, she must! The Presidency of the Union would be her crowning achievement so far. After she graduated, she was going to give everything up, sink herself into rock music, carve out a new life. Mavericks like David Geffen were her heroes. But all that had to wait. Rowena Gordon was totally single-minded, it was part of her control. If she was going to drop out later, fine. But she had to drop out as a winner, and the Presidency was the ultimate prize.

'Yeah,' Topaz agreed. 'And it means I'm on my way. I can't get over what you did for me, getting your dad to make Geoffrey Stevens look at my work. I could wind up working for *The Times* now.'

'For *The Times*?' asked Rowena, confused. 'Won't you go back to New York?'

'I was planning to, but not any more,' Topaz said. She stretched luxuriously. 'Not now I've met Peter.'

The car took a right down Cornmarket towards the Union. The early evening air was mild and warm, perfect weather for a ball. The event was sold out, and student politicians from both slates would be there, hacking the crowd for all they were worth. Rowena dragged her mind away from Peter Kennedy. There were more important things at stake.

'James!' Rowena said. She fought her way through the glittering crowd of bright young things crowding the lobby, dragging Topaz with her. 'Topaz, you must meet my escort, James Williams. He's running for Treasurer with us.'

'As if I didn't know,' Topaz smiled, shaking hands with a gorgeous young second year in army dress uniform. James Williams was a rising star, honest, popular and very good-looking. He was also up at Oxford on a military bursary, and even in the left-wing student atmosphere that commanded grudging respect.

'Delighted,' James said, gripping her hand firmly. '*Cherwell* gets better every week. I see you've won a fistful of awards.'

'You certainly know how to charm a reporter,' Topaz said. 'And everybody else, I hear.'

'What's this, Williams?' demanded Peter Kennedy, coming up behind them. 'Chatting up my girlfriend? We can't allow that, can we?'

James grinned. Peter had been in the year above him at Eton. 'When are you going to do the decent thing and back us, Kennedy?' he demanded.

'Subtle as an H-bomb,' Rowena apologized.

Peter just smiled at her, and turned to kiss Topaz's hand. 'What a sensational dress.'

You're nearly wearing, finished Rowena silently. Watching Peter Kennedy eat Topaz alive with his eyes was just too much. She burned with envy and total inadequacy. God, Topaz had curves on her curves, while she was a mere stick insect. And Topaz was probably his fantasy in bed, as well. She was just a frustrated, ignorant little virgin. How could she ever have imagined she could compete with a sassy, gorgeous American? It was politics that interested Peter. Not her.

'And Rowena,' he said. 'Stand back and let me look at you.'

Rowena took a pace back, aware of a crowd of onlookers watching her, including some of Gilbert's supporters, dismayed to see Peter Kennedy getting so friendly with her. She managed a radiant smile.

'Breathtaking,' Peter said, after what seemed like an eternity. 'James, you are a lucky bastard.'

A shiver of delight rippled through her. He almost sounded like he meant it.

'Come on, babe, they've got business to attend to,' Topaz grinned. *And so have we*, she thought. *Somewhere dark and private.*

'Absolutely,' said Peter, gently squeezing her hand. He nodded at Rowena. 'You and I will have to hook up again later, Miss Gordon. I've come to a decision.'

'Come on, Rowena. Let's get some champagne,' James said, not wanting to push him.

Topaz was having a good time. The crowd was partying hard, the music was great, the food was plentiful and Peter was with her. How could she not enjoy herself? They'd been to the masseur, the video room, the manicurist, the fortuneteller and the handwriting expert, who proclaimed that Peter was trustworthy and confident and that Topaz had a good sense of humour.

'I wonder why they never see anything bad in there,' Topaz commented afterwards.

'With you, there's nothing bad to see,' Peter said.

They'd found a wildly drunk bunch of her compatriots who tried and failed to teach Peter 'The Star-Spangled Banner', danced cheek-to-cheek to a chamber music quartet, and roasted marshmallows together in a bonfire lit in the gardens.

'At least I found one American custom you like,' Topaz teased him.

'Oh, I like a lot of American things,' Kennedy replied, letting his right hand slip to the back of her dress.

When he took her in his arms and kissed her by the firelight, she felt pure happiness flood through her. All the time she'd struggled in New Jersey, for attention from her family, for popularity at school, to make *something* of the only life she had, she'd never dreamed college could be like this. More friends than she could count, English and American. A student paper she ran by herself. A best friend whom she relied on completely. And a boyfriend whom she could easily fall in love with.

'You mean the world to me,' she said breathlessly when they stopped kissing.

Peter smoothed her hair, gently. 'You're incredible,' he said.

She's far more innocent than she makes out, he thought. He lifted her to her feet. 'We ought to get back inside,' he suggested. 'I have to abandon you for a few minutes. I need to find Rowena. Anyway, I don't want you catching cold.'

'All right,' Topaz agreed, looking lovingly at him.

Peter didn't like it. Why did she have to get that devoted shine in her eyes? He wasn't her father, for Christ's sake.

Laughing. Smiling. Applauding loudly. Flirting. Joking. Rowena was on automatic pilot. Three hours of this rubbish and she could hardly bear to tell one more overweight postgraduate how stunning she looked in cherry velveteen, but she did it anyway. You had to lead from the front, right? All her female politicos were going through the same thing. Rowena didn't worry about the men. *They* didn't have to cope with heels.

'Brought you a margarita,' Chris Johnson said, shoving through a crowd of freshers to get to her. Chris was her Librarian candidate, a clever, nice, scatty guy with a shock of brown hair that made him look like a young Albert Einstein.

'You lifesaver,' she said gratefully, taking a refreshing sip. 'How's it going downstairs?'

'Oh, pretty well,' he nodded. 'All our lot are pouring double measures into every drink they serve.'

Rowena grinned. Handing out ridiculously generous measures of drink was a time-honoured way of making yourself popular with the voters.

'Not my money,' she and Chris said in unison, and laughed.

'You should go up to the masseur,' she suggested. 'A bunch of helpless voters trapped in a queue.'

'You got it,' he said.

Rowena finished her drink slowly, glad of the break, and smoothed down the fragile silk of her dress. Amazingly enough she'd managed to prevent it from getting torn in the crush, God knew how. She was fond of this gown, it had been in the family for generations and she'd like to see her daughter wear it to a ball some day. Better than turning up semi-naked like Topaz.

'Rowena,' Peter Kennedy said.

She spun round to find him standing at the foot of a pillar draped in gold streamers and ivy leaves, watching her. He was leaning against the wall, casually, his black dinner jacket slightly crumpled from holding Topaz outside.

'Hello, Peter,' she said, flushing red. 'Are you enjoying yourself?'

He nodded absently. 'I wonder if you could spare me five minutes?' he asked.

God, how beautiful she is, he thought. Attractive in exactly the opposite way to Topaz. Rowena was so obviously embarrassed, blushing whenever he turned up, trying to get out of coming to see him. He felt the familiar twitch in his thighs. Rowena Gordon was a challenge, much more of a challenge than her best friend. A virgin. And very loyal to Topaz, or so people said.

She was struggling with herself.

She *wanted* him.

'Of course,' Rowena said. She glanced around her at the ballgoers cramming every available inch of space in the main building. Only one thing for it.

'We can go into the Officers' Offices,' she suggested, beckoning him to follow her. She turned into what looked like an under-stair cupboard and punched a code into a security lock. The Officers' Offices, for the Librarian, Treasurer and Secretary, were a little back annexe closed off to the public. It was about the only place that would be private.

Peter shut the door behind him and whistled softly. 'Ali Baba's cave,' he said.

Rowena shook her head. 'Hardly. They don't even heat it. A few computers, some files and leftover cans of low-alcohol beer don't add up to limitless riches.'

She couldn't look him in the face. Suddenly, they were out of all the noise and the crush and she was alone with him. Her best friend's man.

IIow *can* you be with Topaz! Rowena thought angrily. You're so different from her!

'You said you'd come to a decision,' she said, as coolly as she could.

'That's right,' Peter agreed. He moved closer to her, and she could smell the faint scent of his cologne. 'You've talked me into it. I can't actively campaign for you, but I'll withdraw my support from Gilbert. I'm going to break it to him tomorrow.'

Rowena felt overwhelmed with relief. He'd just handed her the election. Gilbert Docker had a snowball's chance in hell without Peter Kennedy's help. He was talentless, elitist and completely disorganized. At the debate on feminism next week she intended to prove that.

'I don't know how to thank you,' she said, beaming with delight.

Peter took a step towards her. 'I do,' he said. He bent forward and kissed her lightly on the lips.

A second later, Rowena pulled back. But it was a second too long. Kennedy had already felt her soft mouth welcoming his embrace, her nipples stiffen against his shirt – he could feel them through her dress – the telltale brightness in the eyes and the shortness of breath. Desire surged through him. Topaz Rossi was a skilled, passionate lover, but Rowena's timidness and uncertainty was something else. He wanted to have her. To teach her about sex. He'd never taken a girl's virginity. The thought of it aroused him almost unbearably.

'What are you *doing*?' Rowena hissed. 'What about Topaz?'

He nearly said, 'What about her?' but stopped himself in time.

'I know, I feel so guilty,' Peter admitted, undressing her with his eyes. Oh, look. She was blushing from head to toe. How sweet. 'Topaz is a great girl, and I'm fond of her too, but . . . I can't help the way I feel about you.'

'Topaz is my friend,' Rowena insisted. 'That's all there is to it.'

God, she wanted him.

'We'd never have lasted together,' Kennedy said smoothly. 'You know that. She's American, she wants different things out of life to me. I only realized it once I started seeing you and talking to you. We're the same, Rowena. We might have a chance together. Let me talk to Topaz and explain things to her.'

'No, no,' said Rowena. She felt as though she could hardly breathe. To hear Peter say what she'd been thinking for so long . . . it was killing her. 'Just leave me alone. I can't talk to you again,' and she wrenched open the door and ran out, her eyes brimming with tears.

Peter Kennedy watched her go.

Not long now, he thought.

Chapter Four

The air in the chamber was thick with tension.

Rowena sat on the opposition benches, her beautiful face frozen in stone. She appeared to be listening gravely to Gilbert Docker's bumbling, inept attempt at proposing the motion.

At the moment, he was making jokes about male executives having their innocent, appreciative comments towards female juniors totally misconstrued by dykey feminists. It wasn't going down too badly, on the face of it; a crowd of drunk, upper-class rugby players and Oriel boaties had turned up and were cheering every sexist innuendo to the rafters. Gilbert's normally squeaky voice was climbing higher and higher with pleasure, and his face had gone red and sweaty from the heat; he was annoying everyone else, Rowena noticed.

She put a delicate hand to her temple, trying to make the sick, dizzy feeling go away. Why me? she thought. Why now?

Chris Johnson, who as top of standing committee was sitting in the Secretary's chair while Gilbert spoke, glanced across at his slate boss. He was very worried. The chamber was packed solid with students, cramming the benches, squeezed up on the floor, thronging the gallery upstairs. It was Wednesday; the election would be on

Friday week. Presidential Debates and officer hustings were usually held on the night before the election, but Crown Princess Victoria of Sweden was due to speak that day, so tonight's showdown had been brought forward. The unusual timing made the debate even more crucial for their slate; Oxford would have more than a week to reflect on this evening's performances.

And Rowena Gordon was a star. A brilliant speaker. She could wipe the floor with Gilbert Docker, ninety-nine times out of a hundred. Indeed, a large chunk of the crowd had turned up specifically to see a bloodbath.

Oh, there'll be a bloodbath, OK, Chris thought grimly. But it might not be Gilbert's blood.

Rowena *looked* stunning. No problems there. She was wearing a strapless ballgown of crushed red velvet, a Balenciaga original of her mother's which emphasized her perfect small breasts and tiny waist, and then cascaded to the floor in sumptuous raspberry folds. The richness of the colour picked out her shimmering hair, and her ice-mint eyes were sharp and glittering.

Glittering far too brightly, Chris thought. The girls who were looking at her enviously and the guys who were sizing her up hadn't seen her like he had this morning, her hair slick with perspiration, her skin pale and shining with sweat. They'd called the doctor: Rowena Gordon, on the morning of her Presidential Debate, had a temperature of 103 and was immediately confined to bed. Chris, as her friend, had tried to talk her out of it, but as soon as the doctor had left, she got up, staggered over to her sink and swallowed ten Nurofen.

'It's not worth it, for Christ's sake,' Chris had said, aghast. 'You'll kill yourself.'

Rowena, shivering with fever, looked at him.

'No I won't,' she said levelly. 'I'll kill Gilbert.'

*

In the gallery, Peter Kennedy was watching Rowena intently.

Something's wrong, he mused. I know it is.

He thought about how amusing it would be to console her for the loss of the Presidency. Ladies simply had to learn not to bite off more than they could chew. He looked at her again, unsure exactly what it was, but confident that Gilbert would be fine now.

He had a killer's instinct for weakness.

Topaz Rossi was really trying hard to concentrate on the debate, but couldn't. Rowena looked great and she'd cruise it. And if, by some disaster, she did say anything stupid now, or miss some chance to shred Gilbert, Friday's *Cherwell* would wrap it up for her.

Rowena tried to think her way through the lightness and fuzz in her brain. She tugged at the red silk wrap around her shoulders. *Get it together, girl, get it together.* She knew the drugs had sent her ten miles high.

She smiled at her friend, Richard Black, the Treasurer-elect, who was sitting directly opposite her. He grinned tentatively back, but was making frantic gestures at his chest.

Rowena raised an eyebrow. What are you trying to say?

Richard just kept on gesticulating. In the end, unable to work out his signals, she shrugged amiably and turned a contemptuous gaze on Docker.

Gilbert sat down to polite applause, punctuated by whoops from the Oriel contingent.

Jack Harcourt, the President, got up to introduce Rowena. 'And I'd like to thank the Secretary very much indeed for that speech, and it now gives me great pleasure –'

'Oh, Jesus, no,' Chris said.

'– to call upon Rowena Gordon, Christ Church –'

Other people were noticing it now. Murmurs and laughter started to bubble through the chamber.

'– Librarian, to come and oppose the motion.'

Rowena mustered a brilliant smile and got to her feet, making her way to the dispatch box.

For a moment there was a stunned silence. Then the chamber erupted into the loudest roar of cheers and applause Rowena had ever heard. She smiled, bewildered. Not even Gary Lineker had had this enthusiastic a reaction. People were yelling, smiling, drumming their feet on the floor. She smiled again. They were going insane.

Then she saw Gilbert's smug grin and Chris's stricken expression. *Oh my God*, she thought.

She glanced down at herself, and time seemed to freeze, and then pool like treacle.

Her strapless dress had slipped; the bodice was hanging down, useless, at the waist. She was standing semi-naked at the podium, displaying her breasts to the entire chamber.

Afraid she might faint, Rowena grabbed at her wrap and pulled it across her chest, clutching on to it for dear life. The cheers had by now turned into roars of laughter; a thousand students all clapping and whistling. Everybody on the Gordon slate just wanted to die. Of all the ways to lose an election . . .

In the gallery, Topaz, jolted out of her daydreams, had started to cry from shock and compassion.

Peter Kennedy was quietly beside himself. Those perfect little exposed breasts had given him a rock-solid erection.

Rowena stood frozen at the centre of the storm, paralysed like a rabbit in the glare of headlights. She felt hot tears prickling at the back of her eyes, nausea welling in her throat. She would never live this down as long as she stayed at Oxford.

The cheering went on and on.

Why don't they shut up? Rowena screamed silently. *What are they waiting for?* Then she realized. They were waiting for her to burst into the inevitable tears and run from the chamber. She looked at Gilbert Docker, who shot her a triumphant smile of pure malice. Something inside her snapped back into place. Still clutching at her wrap with her left hand, she raised her right hand for quiet, and, surprised, the audience shut up.

Rowena waited until she had total silence, and then she smiled. 'Well, Mr President,' she said in a loud, clear voice, 'there's only one lesson to be learnt from what just happened – and that is that the Proposition should watch themselves.'

She took a step forward. All eyes were now fixed on her. 'Be warned,' she went on, turning dramatically to Gilbert, still grinning. 'Because for those of us on this side of the House, no sacrifice is too dramatic, no humiliation is too great, *to win this bloody motion*!' and she laughed.

The chamber erupted again, but there was a different quality to this applause. As the bravery of what she had just done sank in, people started to rise from their seats, and all of a sudden she had a standing ovation. Rowena wasn't finished yet, though. Still covered by her wrap, she pulled up her bodice with her free hand and held it against her. Then she let the wrap fall.

'Mr President,' she said loudly, 'if – given the appalling speech the honourable Secretary just made – it isn't against his principles to assist a woman, I wonder if Mr Docker would give me some help with my zip? I seem to be having a little trouble with it.'

And she immediately turned round, presenting her

back to a helpless Gilbert, who got up and fastened his rival's dress, boot-faced with anger.

Chris, Topaz and Nick led a fresh round of cheering.

By the time the debate was over it was the middle of the night and rain was thundering down in the Union gardens. Students spilled out into the street, rushing back to their colleges or sordid digs, or attempting to shove themselves into the sardine-like Union bar for last orders. Baby hacks from the Secretary's committee stood outside in the downpour, arguing furiously over whether Rowena had done it on purpose. She had gone on to deliver a moving, passionate speech, and had won the motion by a huge margin.

'We'll still win the fucking election,' Gilbert Docker snapped at Chris Johnson on the way out.

Chris just laughed in his face. He'd already had the pleasure of turning down Gilbert's Treasurer candidate, who'd rather pathetically tried to switch sides.

Topaz cannoned out of the chamber, whooping, kissed Rowena, and ran in the other direction.

'Hey, where are you going?' she yelled.

'*Cherwell*,' Topaz shouted back at her. 'I've been dying to get on that computer since the second you sat down! What a story, girl! I'll have you on the front page!'

'OK, if you say so,' Rowena shouted at her friend's departing back.

It was true, it *was* a great story, and Topaz had been so wrapped up in it she didn't notice the way Peter had stiffened beside her when she hugged him in elation.

Rowena, utterly euphoric, accepted congratulations and pumped hands like a dutiful hack for an hour and a half before slipping back to her tiny digs in Merton Sreet, hardly noticing the soaking rain.

*

In the *Cherwell* offices, Topaz flicked on the lights and turned on her Apple, trying out a few headlines. Everything came up *Sun*-speak: 'MAY THE BREAST WOMAN WIN.' 'GORDON BENNETT!' 'TREASURE CHEST!' Topaz laughed out loud. Maybe it *was* time for a break from the quality tradition, after all! She tapped in a huge headline: BREAST FOOT FORWARD, and lit a cigarette.

'You thought you'd seen it all before,' Topaz typed away, 'until last Thursday's sensational speech by Rowena Gordon, 34–22–32 (obviously).'

Around her, the empty *Cherwell* offices were quiet and deserted, the silence broken only by the soft hum of the computer and her own breathing. She enjoyed a brief fantasy about how different it would be in a year's time, working on a real paper in London.

Topaz felt contentment seep through her. Rowena would be President of the Union. She would get to be a journalist – *The Times*, no less, and maybe, just maybe, Mrs Peter Kennedy, too.

Peter bawled Gilbert out.

'It's not my fault,' he whimpered for the hundredth time.

'Look,' Kennedy snapped, losing his temper, 'just go home, OK, Docker. I'm going to sort it out now.'

'There's nothing you can do,' Gilbert whined, and then, seeing Peter's face, thought better of it.

Peter started to walk towards Merton Street. Christ Almighty, why did he always have to do everything himself?

Rowena sat in her study sipping a cup of weak tea and watching the fire crackle in the grate. She was comfortable and warm in her thick soft towelling bathrobe, her half-dry blonde hair hanging fresh and glowing around her shoulders. The summer rain drummed against the dark skylight; through the streaming glass she could see the slippery, melting lights of the stars.

She was far too excited to sleep.

She glanced at the faded article on David Geffen, pinned over the bed. When she was President, she'd be able to invite him over to speak . . . She was still fantasizing about what she'd say when they were introduced when the doorbell rang.

'Let yourself in, sweetheart,' she called to Topaz.

'That was a warmer welcome than I expected,' Peter Kennedy said, ducking his head as he stepped into the room.

Rowena shot out of her chair, belting her robe even tighter around her. 'What are you doing here?'

'You asked me in, I believe,' said Peter calmly, shutting the door behind him and offering her a cigarette. She declined; he shrugged and lit up. 'It was a good speech, if I may say so. Very gutsy of you to carry on.'

'Thank you,' said Rowena, relaxing slightly. She couldn't help it, she was glad to see him. Peter hadn't come round since that kiss at the Union Ball a week ago. Who don't I trust? Rowena asked herself. Him, or me?

'It was that or give up on the whole thing, and nothing would persuade me to do that. I've got a duty to the other guys on the slate, anyway.'

He took a long drag on his cigarette. 'Nothing could persuade you to drop out?'

'Nothing,' said Rowena, wary again. There were only two reasons, in this university, for someone like Kennedy to be in her rooms at this hour: sex or politics. And he was still dating her best friend, so it couldn't be the former. 'Tell me what I can do for you, Peter.'

'I want you to withdraw from the election.'

Rowena leant back, and took another sip of her tea. She was surprised, but not shocked; she'd seen too much of this stuff, treachery, indecision, switching sides, on her way up the ladder, to be taken aback now. Plenty of it had been last-minute, too. She wondered for a second if Topaz had known, and then dismissed that idea: Topaz was her closest friend. This was a blow, when it looked as if she had everything wrapped up, but it wasn't all that serious. She doubted even Peter Kennedy could save Gilbert now, not after this evening's triumph.

'I have no intention of doing any such thing, I'm afraid,' she said coolly. 'I rather thought you were supporting me, Peter.'

'Then you thought wrong,' Kennedy said with equal coldness.

'Does Topaz know you're here?' Rowena asked. Her heart was hammering now. Why had Peter come? Why had he switched sides again? Because she'd turned him down?

She looked at the handsome face, the muscular body, the golden hair soaked from the rain. She didn't want him to be angry with her. She wanted him to like her.

'I can't go back on my word to Gilbert,' Peter said, furiously. 'Why can't you see that? Why are you making me feel like this?'

'You gave your word to me, too,' Rowena answered. He looked so angry and guilty and mixed-up. She knew he was battling with himself to sort out his motives, do the right thing. She was stupidly pleased by it, that the way he felt about her had confused him. A small ache of lust began to gather inside her.

'I know,' Kennedy said. The sapphire eyes stared directly at her. 'I should never have said it. I couldn't help myself.'

For the second time that evening Rowena felt time slow down around her. For a few seconds she didn't reply, and they listened to the fire crackling in the grate and the gathering storm outside, the wind moaning across the Elizabethan gables of the house.

Finally she asked, 'What do you mean?'

Her heart was hammering in her chest, her mouth was dry, waiting for his answer.

Peter reached out tenderly and stroked her cheek. 'You know exactly what I mean,' he said. 'Tell me I was wrong. Tell me you have no feelings for me. That you don't think about me. That I can never be more to you than your friend's boyfriend.'

Overcome with desire, Rowena was silent. His touch on her skin sent a small, burning ribbon of heat down between her legs.

'Tell me any of those things,' he said, 'and I'll leave.'

For a split second Rowena remembered Topaz telling her how much Peter meant to her. How she'd stay in England because of him.

Then she looked again at the handsome, aristocratic face, the hard, masculine body, and the way he was watching her, and put the thought out of her mind.

'No,' she said. 'You weren't wrong.'

Chapter Five

Life seemed to carry on as normal.

In the run-up to the election, Rowena was as ordered and focused as she'd always been: drawing up college lists, organizing secret car runs to carry friendly voters in from around the city, planning speeches and working parties and making sure everybody on the slate did the same. Peter was definitely sticking with Gilbert and they had to work twice as hard. This would be close.

The tourists who crowded into Oxford this summer like every other would have been amazed if they could have seen what was going on behind the bicycles, the billowing academic gowns, and the spires and turrets and champagne picnics – a dirty, bitter struggle for power that would have done credit to a Congressional race. The public schoolboys were going to fight for their turf, and Rowena's assortment of non-privileged candidates couldn't afford to underestimate them.

They had allies, of course. *Cherwell* for one, which had supported them all term. Colleges of their own. Kids that turned up to debates regularly. Anyone who had heard about Rowena's performance in the debate.

But to the other side, merit didn't matter. A socialist idea. Gilbert *wanted* to be President, so he should be. Support the old school. His father's regiment. His mother's receptions. All the old, solid things that had been certain fifty years ago and in the late eighties meant absolutely nothing – except to the disinherited youth which liked to pretend that they did.

Words were had in the appropriate places. The Gridiron Club. Vincent's, where Oxford sporting Blues with matching blue blood liked to get very drunk on fine port. The Disraeli Society. And all the older, established colleges, which despite their PR to the outside world liked things exactly the way they had always been – Oriel, Lincoln, Jesus, Balliol, Queen's, and especially Trinity. Only Christ Church held back. Rowena was one of their own.

And that was what really got the boys going. Because Rowena was being defiant. Charles Gordon's daughter, educated at St Mary's, Ascot, she should have known better. Gilbert and Peter could have arranged the Presidency for her next term. But she still insisted on fighting them. And on picking her own team.

It was obvious that Gordon was walking away from the whole deal. She had hung around with that brash American practically since she came up. She talked loudly about going into the music industry, of all things.

She was a feminist.

She was a traitor.

They would teach her a lesson.

If Gilbert Docker could have seen underneath the cool mask Rowena was presenting to Oxford, he might have relaxed a little. At the moment, with all the organizing and whispering and trading of favours he could pull off, the relentless work of the other slate still put them ahead, and most people saw Rowena herself as their greatest strength.

They didn't know what Peter Kennedy did.

Rowena Gordon was out of control.

*

She gasped. Peter's hands had moved from her thighs to her nipples, brushing her skin with the featherlight touch he knew fired her up most. She was slippery wet between the legs, loving how he felt inside her, his cock pushing deeper and deeper into the quick heart of her pleasure, his gentle rhythm never faltering, never letting up, sending a light, sweet orgasm rippling across her stomach, and then another a few minutes later, just enough pressure for one or two contractions, keeping her hot, never letting her reach the final climax.

'It's not so bad, is it?' Peter teased. 'Sleeping with the enemy?'

'I'm Mata Hari,' Rowena managed. 'Using you.'

He gave a low, confident chuckle and answered her with an exquisite little twist of the hips, stroking her inside her body, letting her response speak for itself.

Rowena moaned with pleasure. This close to orgasm, she forgot all the other emotions that crowded into her mind whenever Peter came round. The guilt. The jealousy, because he was still seeing Topaz. The shame, at not being able to dismiss him. And the bittersweet joy at seeing him again.

Every time, Rowena said it was the last.

It never was.

She was simply no match for him. Closed away in a convent school, a virgin, faintly contemptuous of boys, Rowena had never come across anyone who called to her body like Peter did. She had been a cold girl, determined, closed-off, proud; Topaz Rossi had been the first really close friend she'd had. For the sake of that friendship, she'd tried to hide her feelings. She'd even turned Peter down at the ball.

It wasn't enough. Her desire was too strong.

She drew back from Topaz, refusing to admit to

herself what she was doing. After all, there were a thousand excuses. Topaz was all wrong for Peter. Too brazen. Too foreign. Too poor. And she was perfect: from the same country, the same background, the same class. Kennedy was a gentleman, she was a lady. Prejudices which Rowena had fought against all her life, which she'd always despised, she started using to convince herself of what she needed to believe. She became cold and distant when Topaz tried to talk to her. Told herself the friendship was a mismatch from the start.

'Do it again,' Rowena said, intently. Her nipples were throbbing with pleasure. 'Again. Now.'

'You're good,' Peter whispered, excited. It was true. She was a natural at sex. She loved it. The way she leapt under his touch aroused him. She responded to every tiny caress, every hot glance, every touch of his fingers.

Even that first time, she had come.

Cold, haughty Rowena Gordon.

Kennedy grinned to himself, thrusting deeper into her. Life was full of surprises.

Topaz Rossi walked along Broad Street, heading towards Christ Church. She was in a good mood. Unlike all the English kids who took it for granted, the beauty of Oxford always enchanted her. Compared with small-town New Jersey, this is another planet, she thought, looking across at the wrought-iron gates protecting Trinity's immaculate gardens, the spectacular busts of the Roman emperors ringed round the entrance to the Sheldonian Theatre.

Some scholars cycled past her, long black robes billowing out behind them, on their way to Blackwell's, the university's bookstore of choice. She smiled, wondering whether they were picking up obscure textbooks or a sex-packed trashy novel. One of the things Topaz liked best about studying here was that it could just as easily be either.

She turned down towards the main Hertford entrance, glancing into the courtyard of the Bodleian, Oxford's main library and one of the finest in the world. Topaz walked around there sometimes just for the sheer beauty of it, but you couldn't take out books there, so she didn't use it often. She was a modern girl. She preferred to study in her rooms, where she could make a cup of coffee and listen to Aretha Franklin.

A couple of young *Cherwell* wannabes waved hi to her. They were assigned to the arts pages, covering some new student production at the Playhouse.

'How's the report going?' she asked.

'Well,' the younger girl replied. 'Looks like a couple of West End scouts were in the audience last night. I want to interview Mary Jackson, since she's directing.'

'What she means is, she wants a part in the next one,' her friend said, grinning. The other girl hit her.

'As long as we get our story,' Topaz told them, feeling extremely grown-up. She wasn't in the mood to rain on anybody's parade just now. She was on her way to surprise Peter, she couldn't wait to see him. Life was good.

The two girls waved and walked away.

Topaz pushed back her mass of red curls from her face, enjoying the easy camaraderie of the moment. Some American kids had a tough time here; not understanding the dry English teasing, they left Oxford convinced that the natives hated all foreigners with a passion and Americans in particular. Topaz knew better.

Or maybe Rowena's just blinded me to their faults, she thought.

Or maybe Peter has.

Her skin still felt warm where he'd caressed it that morning. Where he'd licked off the champagne. 'A congratulations present,' he'd said, 'for finishing your second article for a national paper.'

It was a good article, too. She'd submit it as soon as the first one had been published, after the elections. Rowena would be thrilled, once she was a bit less nervous and stressed-out. She'd been acting weird lately.

Topaz paused for a second at the top of Oriel Square, the back entrance into Peter's college, thinking about her article, her lover and her friend, letting it all shimmer round her head. The soft warmth of the sunshine beat down on the nape of her neck. She felt like she was taking a bath in pure happiness.

Rowena felt the fist in her chest again. As though she couldn't breathe, certainly couldn't cry. A gut reaction, probably, to help her keep control.

'We have to stop,' she said bleakly. 'I shouldn't have done this.'

Peter offered her a cigarette, but she shook her head.

'But you did do it,' he said.

A sense of power came to him. That every time he could overcome her scruples, her conscience, whatever. It appealed strongly to his vanity to know that he could fuck both Topaz Rossi and Rowena Gordon in the same day.

Not that Rowena knew that, of course. But she knew he was still seeing her best friend. And that counted.

'I've told you before, I have to let Topaz down gently,' he continued. 'I thought we'd agreed on that.'

Rowena was silent, staring at the wall. Shame and heartache and restless desire were all mixed up inside her.

'What is it? The election?' Peter demanded. 'You know how I feel. I have to keep my word. What we have together is nothing to do with politics.'

She shook her head, no. They both knew that the sex was better because they were opponents. It added another edge.

'What about your word to Topaz?'

'You said it was the last time yesterday,' he reminded her cruelly.

Rowena flushed. It was true. Yet again she'd given in; partly as a result of her deep craving for him, partly because he'd refused to let up. He'd climbed up the drainpipe outside her window, sent her two dozen red roses and a bottle of vintage champagne. He'd sat next to her at every meal in Hall. Waited for her in the porters' lodge when she came to get her morning post. He had been as insistent as a Sherman tank and as romantic as Lord Byron. It was almost a relief to give in to him, to let him do what she longed for him to do.

We're at the same college, Rowena thought. I can't get away from him.

Out loud, she said, 'I mean it. This isn't about not hurting Topaz. It's about you refusing to give either of us up.' She wanted to cry.

'You're the one I want,' Peter said carefully, hearing a new note in her voice. He took her in his arms.

Despite herself, Rowena felt too weak to resist. She wanted him to comfort her. To tell her he loved her, that it would all be OK.

'Topaz is my best friend,' she said. A fresh wave of shame beat up in her. How could she say that? She'd sneered at her, despised her, pulled rank on her, the works. All because Topaz had done the unforgivable thing. She'd been betrayed. And Rowena had let a guilty person's dislike for their victim take over.

Peter looked down at the sexy, lithe body, stiff in his arms. At those full lips set dead against him, strong with rejection.

Neither of them noticed the door swing open. Neither of them saw they were being watched.

'What are you talking about?' he said. 'You were the person who told me the whole thing was crazy. A hick from New Jersey and a girl like you. She wouldn't even help you with *me*, remember? I seem to recall you told me last night you'd break if off after the election. She does edit *Cherwell*, after all.'

He touched her cheek, softly. 'Don't blame Topaz Rossi for what you feel about me. She doesn't matter to you. Don't try and hide behind that. You owe me better.'

'Hide what?' Rowena murmured. The smell of him, the nearness of him. She wanted to cling to him. She didn't want to let him go.

'The fact that you don't love me,' Peter said.

'That's not true.'

There was a pause, while he sensed her sexual heat blossom again.

'Show me,' he said, and Rowena, with a little sob of capitulation, lifted her lips to his.

At the door, Topaz found her eyes had brimmed over with tears, so she could hardly see. She blinked, and felt the salt water roll away down her cheeks. In total silence, she backed into the corridor.

Neither of them noticed her go.

The *Cherwell* offices were crammed. It was Wednesday, the final review meeting day for copy. Everything had to be filed by Thursday afternoon and they went to print that night. The atmosphere was fun, a cocktail of apprehension, excitement, moaning about the work. Seventh week of Trinity Term was going to be a thick edition, too. There was sports news from the rowing, gossip from the various college balls, a bundle of recruitment ads, advice on the final examinations for unfortunate third and fourth years, and, of course, the Union elections. And that didn't even touch on the features: benefits, computing and the city homeless. Students were jamming the place. It was a good paper to write for, a good thing to put on the résumé. And, since Topaz Rossi had taken over, everybody read it. Shock and amaze your friends! They were future media barons. They were ready to go.

People stopped chattering when Topaz and Sebastien walked in together. The editors had that kind of presence: good for a laugh, motivational, fun to work with, but you shut up when they told you to. Topaz never settled for second-rate writing, photography or design.

You got it right, or you were out.

'OK', Topaz said. She was wearing a sexy outfit, a cut-off black tank top that emphasized her magnificent breasts and bared her flat midriff, teamed with low-slung black 50I's which hugged her ass. Her red hair was wound into a coil and piled loosely on the top of her head, letting a few rebellious strands swing round her temples. Uncharacteristically, she was also wearing make-up: a dash of colour on her high cheekbones, soft brown eyeshadow, an inviting pink lipstick. Long chain earrings swung from her lobes, following every movement of her head. Her eggshell-blue eyes were sparkling with fierce determination.

Half the male journos in the room found they didn't know where to look.

'We've got one major change this week,' Topaz said. Her Italian-American accent seemed more pronounced than usual. 'Roger Walpole, I'm afraid it affects you.'

Roger, sitting in one of the comfortable black chairs, looked across at her. 'What's up?' he asked. 'You didn't like the piece?'

He'd been writing the lead story on a Student Union plot to increase the price of alcohol, a matter of concern to every undergraduate in the city, if not a personal tragedy. It would have been a terrific headline.

'No, it's superb, as usual,' Topaz smiled. 'It's going on the front page. But we're running a new lead. I've written it.'

A murmur of surprise ran round the room. 'About what?' somebody asked.

Topaz paused for effect, feeling the white-hot rage, the burning satisfaction of a tiny measure of revenge.

'About Rowena Gordon's candidacy for President of the Union.'

The place erupted, with everybody shouting questions at once.

'I thought you were friends,' Phil Green said.

Topaz shrugged. 'A story's a story.'

'What are you going to say?'

'That I've discovered that Rowena plans to cheat on her own slate; she's not going to pull any votes for anyone but herself. That the whole thing with her dress in the debate was a deliberate publicity stunt. That she made up the story about the knife in Joanne's door just to slander Gilbert.'

'Is it *true*?' Roger asked, shocked.

Topaz looked him straight in the eye. 'Every word.'

'What a bitch,' said Jane. 'But we come out on Friday morning. The morning of the election.'

There was another burst of noise as the room realized what that meant. 'She'll be destroyed!' someone yelled.

Topaz waited for them to quieten down, then looked at them calmly. Every eye was fixed on her.

'That's the idea,' she said.

*

Rowena Gordon felt good about herself for the first time in weeks. She'd actually done it, she'd told Peter Kennedy to go screw himself and she'd meant every word. He'd sent flowers at lunch, she refused delivery. She put the phone down on him three times. When he turned up at her door, she threatened to call the porters if he didn't leave.

It was madness, she told herself, but it passed.

Of course, it nearly hadn't done. After that kiss this morning, she must have been seconds away from falling back into bed with him. She had no idea what gave her the strength to pull back. To push him away. To insist that he leave, and actually make him do it.

Rowena brushed her long fair hair, standing in front of the wall mirror in her chilly bedroom. The silky fall of the fine strands against her back was a sensual feeling. She moved and pirouetted, admiring her own slender, leggy reflection, the pale pink nipples on her small, tight breasts. She'd always envied Topaz her magnificent figure, but tonight she decided she was happy with her body. It would look graceful, sitting in the President's chair.

There was a hard knock on the door.

'Who is it?' Rowena demanded, reaching for a silk bathrobe. If her rooms weren't quite the picture of luxury that Peter's were, Charles Gordon, with his customary disregard for money, had seen to it that they were handsomely equipped.

'It's Topaz,' came the reply.

Rowena felt little spiders of fear crawl up and down her spine. She'd nearly said, 'Get lost, Peter.'

'Just coming,' she shouted, tying back her hair. She found herself blushing. Should she confess to Topaz? she wondered, and in a split second decided against it. That would only salve her own conscience at the expense of her friend's happiness.

She took a deep breath, and opened the door.

Topaz walked into the familiar room quite calmly. She'd rehearsed this meeting over and over in her mind, so she'd get to take it slow, say everything she needed to. She didn't want to lose anything in the heat of passion.

Rowena, that cold, betraying English bitch, was looking her normal immaculate self. Topaz checked out the robe, noticing the expensive designer-green silk. A lot of things in this room were expensive, she guessed. The feather duvet. The bottle of port on the sideboard. Rowena's brushed-leather overcoat, hanging on the back of the door.

Things that were way too good for a hick from New Jersey, right?

Topaz sauntered past Rowena, looking at her with the deepest contempt.

Rowena felt her heart leap into the roof of her mouth. She had seen Topaz act like this only a couple of times before. When one of the *Cherwell* old guard had called her a Yank wop and tried to kill some of her early stories. It had been one of the reasons she'd liked Topaz so much in the first place.

'You should know something about Italian-Americans,' Topaz had told him, right in front of Rowena. 'We always avenge an insult.'

Two months later, the guy had resigned from the paper. Topaz never offered to tell her what had happened and Rowena never asked. It was just there for all to see.

I am who I am. Don't fuck with me.

She had that same look on her face now.

'You know,' Rowena said.

'Yeah, I know,' Topaz said. 'And please don't insult me with an excuse.'

Rowena couldn't look at her. Shame overcame her. 'I left him, today,' she said, eventually.

'Did you?' Topaz asked. She suddenly wanted to cry. The double rejection came back at her again, with the force of a kick in the stomach. Her friend. Her lover. Had they laughed about her together? she wondered. 'It didn't look like that when I saw you in his arms this morning.'

Rowena sat down heavily on the bed. 'I can explain –' she said.

Topaz shook her head. 'It's over, Rowena,' she said. Her eyes were hard. 'I brought you a copy of *Cherwell*'s front cover story for tomorrow. I thought you might like a preview.'

Her hands trembling, Charles Gordon's daughter picked up the story that would wipe out three years of dedicated work. That would deny her the last prize she wanted before she dropped out of society. That would brand her as a traitor and a liar in front of her whole university.

She finished the story in silence. When she turned to Topaz, her face was drained of blood.

'If you print this,' she said, 'I'll call my father and I'll have him speak to Geoffrey Stevens. Your article will never see the light of day.' She drew herself up, rigid and haughty. 'I promise you.'

'I thought of that,' replied Gino Rossi's daughter. Her face was murderously angry. 'It's worth it, to see you crash and burn.'

She paused, looking for the right words. 'You see, Peter doesn't matter,' she said. 'He was nothing. He was good in bed, he was charming, I'd have found out what he really was soon enough. It's *you* that matters, Rowena. Because I was your friend. Because we trusted each other.'

Topaz leant closer. 'I promise *you* something,' she said. 'I promise you this is just the beginning. When you find what you really want to do – records or whatever – I'll be waiting for you. Wherever you go. And I'll have my revenge. I swear it.'

'A nice speech,' Rowena answered coldly.

Topaz turned at the door, the two beautiful girls staring at each other with candid hatred.

'You never had to fight for a thing, did you? Life's just a fucking tennis match for you, right?'

Topaz nodded at the *Cherwell* article spread out over the bed. The headline, in black type three inches high, read FOR SHAME, ROWENA.

'Fifteen-all,' she said, and slammed the door.

PART TWO
RIVALS

Chapter Six

Sophistication was the first thing to go.

'*You* wanna rent this place? You must be joking,' the third landlord said when Rowena turned up to view his bedsit. He examined her camel-coloured wool coat, her Armani pantsuit, her delicate shoes. His eyes narrowed. 'You're mucking me about. What do *you* wanna live in Soho for?'

'It's the only thing I can afford,' Rowena answered. She wished the guy would step back; his breath recked of garlic and curry. She tried to smile, to make him want to rent to her. The first two places she'd seen, the landlords had taken one look at her and slammed the door in her face.

Rowena was getting desperate. The money she had from her own account was running very low, she couldn't find a job in the record business anywhere, and her parents had cut her off without a penny until she agreed to come home and give up any idea about working in music. Rowena had refused point-blank. When she graduated, she'd decided to conquer the world. There was no way she was crawling back to Scotland to apologize and behave, like a beaten puppy.

'Sure,' the landlord said. He leered at her. 'On the game, are we, darlin'?'

'I beg your pardon?' asked Rowena, stunned.

He winked. 'Oh, don't look like that. I won't tell if you won't. It's fifty-five down and cash at the start of each month, in advance.'

For a second she didn't understand. 'You're renting it to me?'

'I ain't giving it to you,' he said, extending a sweaty hand.

Rowena hurriedly opened her purse and gave him the notes. She'd already learnt not to offer a cheque.

'Any problems, please don't bother me with them,' the guy said, leering at her again and waddling out of the room.

Rowena took a long, hard look at herself in the grimy mirror. A high-class prostitute? *Her?*

Then she took another look. The figure-hugging clothes. The impeccable make-up. The precision-cut hair shimmering down her back.

He was right. It wasn't Soho.

The next day, Rowena took all her designer clothes down to an exchange store and sold every one of them. She hawked her brooches, her Patek Phillipe steel watch and her gold pendant, and forced herself to haggle over the price. The woman upped her offer by 30 per cent. Rowena knew she was probably still being ripped off, but it felt like a victory. She was learning.

She invested in a good pair of Levi's, some ankle-boots, sneakers and a black leather jacket. T-shirts were cheap and she picked up Indian-print scarves at the markets. By day she traipsed round London, looking for a job. By night, she practised her cooking – not being able to afford Marks & Spencers was a revelation – and went to every cheap rock gig she could scam her way into.

Looking back on that first month, Rowena wondered how she'd ever got through it. All her romantic notions about rebelling against her parents and living in poverty until she found the job of her dreams! How come she'd never stopped to wonder what 'poverty' actually meant? To be cold, hungry, watching every penny all the time – Rowena Gordon, who'd never so much as compared the price of two lipsticks the whole time she was at college! How come the image of bravely tramping the pavement, banging on every door in sight, had never included the sick feeling of failure that consumed her whenever she lost out on another entry-level position?

Two or three times she nearly gave up. She didn't have to do this, after all. She had a good degree and a useful set of A-levels. She could have become a lawyer, joined a management consultancy – all sorts of high-pay, high-respect jobs where doing well at Oxford would count for something. She was only getting rejection after rejection because she wanted to go into the record business, where a degree was a negative, not a positive, and nobody gave a monkey's if your hobbies were riding and skiing.

But in the sweaty little clubs, packed out with bikers and rock fans, filled with acrid smoke from the dry ice and Guns n' Roses pumping loudly on the stereo, Rowena Gordon had her first taste of freedom. She became accepted on the scene. She got to know the bartenders, some of the regular kids, and they accepted her for what she was. Without questions. Without judgments. Another 21-year-old kid that liked music.

And there *was* the music.

Rowena got to know all the coming bands. Most of them were tired, derivative rubbish – pale imitations of the LA glitter boys, or the New York metalheads. But sometimes, just *sometimes*, she'd hear a band that excited her. And that made it all worth it.

Arrogant, cool Rowena Gordon was surprising herself.

She couldn't bear to give up on the dream.

One night she walked into the Arcadia, in Camden Town, to find the place almost deserted.

'What's up?' Rowena asked, walking up to Richard, the barman and a friend of hers, who was chatting to an old man in a trenchcoat. 'Did Blue Planet cancel?'

He nodded.

'That's OK, they're overrated anyway,' she shrugged, perching on a barstool. 'Can I get a Jack Daniels and Diet Pepsi, please?'

Richard pushed across her drink, glancing slyly at the guy he'd been talking to. 'I hear Musica Records just signed them for two hundred grand.'

Rowena chuckled. 'They would. Musica can't tell a rock band from a rubber band.'

The old man coughed. 'Why do you say that, missy?' he demanded, in a brittle American accent.

Rowena blushed. 'Are you their manager? I'm sorry.'

'No, I'm not their manager,' he said. 'But I'll buy you that drink if you tell me what you think's wrong with them.'

'You should listen to Rowena,' Richard told him. 'She goes to every gig in town. Every club, too.'

'Rich girl?' the old man asked.

Rowena laughed. 'Hardly. I don't *pay* for any of it. Friends let me in. You know how it is.'

'Yeah, I know how it is,' he said wryly, trying to remember what it was like hanging out at New York Jazz dives in the thirties.

Rowena took a swallow of her drink. Her friends from

Oxford wouldn't have recognized her; sitting without make-up, comfortable and relaxed in a scruffy pair of jeans, she looked even younger than she actually was. She'd lost weight, developed muscle tone, and pulled her long hair back in a casual pigtail. She looked terrific.

'You want to know why it was a bad deal for Musica Records?' she asked cockily. 'Fine. I'll tell you.'

Ten minutes later, her eyes sparkling with enthusiasm, she was still talking about dime-a-dozen unsigned bands.

'Enough, enough,' Richard laughed, putting a hand on her arm. 'He gets the message.'

'No, that's OK,' the old guy said. 'What do you do when you're not fighting for a place in the front row, missy?'

She shrugged. 'Nothing. I want to work in a record company, but I can't get a job. I'm still trying, though. Who's asking?'

As Richard grinned, the American pulled out a gold-edged business card from his battered wallet. 'My name's Joshua Oberman,' he said shortly. 'You know who I am?'

Rowena felt herself spread crimson from head to toe. Josh Oberman was an industry legend. He was also President of Musica Records UK.

'Yes, sir,' she said.

'I said my name was *Joshua*. Don't act cute. Just report in to my Personnel division at ten tomorrow morning. You're hired,' he added as an afterthought, and got up to leave.

'What as?' asked Rowena, stupefied.

'A talent scout, of course,' Oberman snapped. 'What do you think?'

The first day Rowena walked through the doors of Musica Records as an employee was one of the happiest of her life. She took one look at the futuristic lobby, its black leather and polished chrome, the young, hip secretaries strolling in and out of reception with their T-shirts and attitude, and the wall-mounted TVs pumping out music videos, and knew she'd found her vocation.

Nothing could dent her mood. Not the surly, prim woman in Personnel who filled out her details and insisted on calling the president's office to get confirmation that Rowena wasn't making it up; not the way the other A&R scouts refused even a pretence of friendliness to the new competition when she was being shown round; not even her tiny cubbyhole of an office, or the minute amount of money she'd be getting paid, which meant she'd still have to keep her seedy apartment.

Rowena was prepared to sweat blood for Musica Records. They had given her a chance.

'Hi, welcome to the team,' said Matthew Stevenson, with a total lack of enthusiasm. 'Have a seat.'

He waved Rowena to a cavernous armchair in soft buttery leather at one corner of his huge office. Sun came streaming through the windows overlooking the Thames, illuminating the state-of-the-art stereo system and the framed gold and platinum discs that covered the walls.

'I'm the head of A&R, or Artists and Repertoire,' Stevenson said, sighing. He was a fat, bald, hook-nosed industry veteran and he liked to pick his own scouts. But Oberman got what Oberman wanted, and he'd taken a shine to this girl.

Stevenson had seen it happen before: some kid would impress Josh at a concert or write him a good pitch letter and Oberman, always hungry to discover a new David Geffen, would stick them in Marketing or International and there was nothing anyone could do about it. They usually lasted a few months, maybe even a year, and then lost interest and quit or got fired after a decent interval. He was sure this girl would go the same way. But what could he do about it? The old man was capricious.

'That means we try and sign talented bands to the label, and then we help them develop repertoire, i.e. songs. That used to mean we'd choose songs for them to cover, but these days it mostly involves helping a band choose the right producer. Is that clear?'

Rowena nodded eagerly. She knew all this stuff backwards, of course, but she didn't want to look cocky.

'Your job,' her boss continued, 'is to listen to tapes the hopefuls send in, mail them back with a rejection letter, and go out at night looking for bands.'

'But what if someone sends in a good tape?'

'If they're good, they play live. Someone has heard of them. They have a manager. Understand?'

Rowena crossed her legs. She didn't want to annoy her new boss, but she couldn't help herself. 'Then why do we bother listening to them at all?'

'Just in case I'm wrong,' Stevenson answered with an unpleasant grin, and held out a clammy hand. 'Welcome to the music business.'

He wasn't wrong. After three days, Rowena was quite clear on that point. Every morning, the secretary she shared with four other scouts dragged a huge sackful of tapes into her cubbyhole and left Rowena staring at them in dismay. At first, wanting to be fair on everybody, she listened to half of each tape. When she discovered that one sack was replaced by two, and two by three, as she made no inroads at all on the mountain of work, she cut it back to one song. Eventually, Jack Reich, the scout who worked next to her, took pity on her hopeless amateurism.

'Look, Rowena,' he said, yanking her headphones off her ears. 'Thirty seconds, OK? *Thirty seconds*. You've got hundreds of these suckers to go through, *and* all the paperwork, *and* all the bands that are serious enough to actually play gigs. Ninety per cent of these acts you're making notes about have split up by now.'

He grabbed the tape she was listening to and held it up. 'See the date of that? September. Five months ago. That's how long it takes to get round to unsolicited tapes.'

'Thirty seconds?' Rowena repeated.

'Thirty seconds,' Jack insisted 'is *generous*.'

He wasn't kidding. Rowena was getting disillusioned about musicians. She'd had no idea how much bad music it was possible to make until she started looking for a band good enough to invest in. Her days were filled with tape after tape of utter rubbish – people would submit tapes of themselves singing along to Karaoke machines. Her nights were filled with long, backbreaking drives around the country, watching a succession of lacklustre singers and laughably dreadful rock bands. She got to know every mildewed, dank little club from Oxford to Truro, and as the lowest scout on the totem pole she was never allowed within ten feet of more juicy chances.

It was difficult to make friends at work. Jack Reich treated her kindly, but he was an A&R manager with three signed acts, and always busy. The other scouts, all male and all younger than herself, refused to give her the time of day. The secretaries made it clear that they preferred flirting with the boys to typing up her paperwork, and Matthew Stevenson called by her office every week like a circling vulture, Rowena thought, itching to sack her.

'Found anything yet?' he'd smirk, and she'd have to say, 'No, not yet.'

God, she really wanted to! It was heartbreaking! Here she was, a rock fan, a music junkie, and now a talent scout for a major label, pleading, begging to be impressed. And she saw or heard hundreds of bands a month, all of whom were begging her to be impressed by them.

But she couldn't. She couldn't do it. There was no answer to Matthew, because everything she checked out was so awful, every song was so dire.

She ploughed on, feeling more and more isolated and depressed. Maybe she should forget the whole thing, become a lawyer. Maybe there was a talent drought in Britain. Maybe there was nothing *to* find.

And then she stumbled across Atomic Mass.

Chapter Seven

Topaz was miserable. It was not supposed to turn out like this, she told herself for the millionth time as she huddled over the street brazier, frozen to the marrow of her bones. There is nothing on God's earth so cold as a New York winter, and Topaz Rossi was catching the full brunt of it.

She stared across the river of grimy traffic, crawling though the slush, at the marbled Fifth Avenue skyscraper from which David Levine obstinately refused to appear. Persistence, Topaz told herself, persistence is 99 per cent of what makes a good reporter. True, she could duck into Rockefeller Plaza and grab a cup of hot chocolate – with whisky – and a slice of warm sachertorte. But if she did, and God knows she was longing to, it was a hundred to one on that Levine would choose that exact moment to appear and she'd lose her shot at an interview with the hottest film star on the planet. Not to mention her job.

Topaz stuck her hands into the pockets of her snug black jeans, cut to show off every curve of her magnificently pert ass. She may have felt like shit, but she looked like a million dollars, even if the tips of her ears were so cold they matched her lipstick. The guy selling chestnuts on the brazier raked over the coals some more, in the hope that it'd be warm enough to keep this incredible babe standing there for just a bit longer. Maybe if he got *really* lucky, she'd stamp her feet again to warm up, because when she did that she jiggled slightly under the clinging cashmere jacket, showing him a little bit of paradise right here on earth. He wondered, not for the first time, who she was waiting for. If it was a guy, he was one hell of a lucky sonofabitch.

Topaz let her mind drift back as to why she was there, answering her own questions as usual. This might be a cold fucking assignment but it was a lot better than none at all. She had a vision of herself just three months ago, clutching a smart little leather folder full of neatly mounted examples of her work on *Cherwell* and letters of recommendation from her tutors, hawking herself around the New York magazine houses until her feet bled. It was the same story everywhere.

'I'm sorry, we have nothing for you.'

'You do need *some* experience to write for the *New Yorker*, kid. Sorry to have to break it to ya.'

'We have no vacancies at this time.'

'He's in a meeting.'

'She's in a meeting.'

'He's still in a meeting.'

'What is this stuff? You're bringing me stuff from *school*? We're a national publications group, Ms Rossi. If you don't realize that this isn't good enough without me telling you, you aren't cut out to be a journalist,' said Nathan Rosen, not unkindly.

Topaz felt as though two or three big rocks were sitting leaden in her stomach. It was her sixth interview of the day.

'I was commissioned to write a piece on student benefits for the London *Times* once,' she murmured miserably.

Rosen brightened. 'Well, that's different. I'd like to see the piece, you got it with you?'

She shook her head. 'It didn't come off.'

Rosen looked at her sceptically.

Rowena Gordon, I hope you rot in the hottest corner of hell, Topaz thought, suddenly pierced with a white-hot anger. She pushed back her chair.

'Mr Rosen, I'm obviously not suited for *Westside*. Thank you for seeing me. I won't waste any more of your time.'

'Hey, hey, wait up,' Rosen said softly. 'I didn't say you could go. One of the juniors in entertainment is off sick this month. You'd be pasting, setting, making coffee, typing . . . it's pretty menial stuff, but it's a way in. You want the job?'

No I don't want the job, Topaz screamed silently. *I'm the most intelligent goddamned woman that ever set foot in your stinking rathole office, and I'm nobody's fucking gofer!*

It was the only thing she'd been offered in more than a hundred interviews.

'What's the pay like?'

'It's shit,' said Nathan Rosen.

'I'll take it,' said Topaz.

For the next two weeks she seemed to run on adrenaline, substituting the electric atmosphere of the office for more normal human fuels like food and sleep. She lost weight and learnt how to gulp down a cup of coffee whilst running from the art department to the newsdesk with six different layouts in her hand. She typed up articles, corrected spellings, pasted photographs on to mockups, checked up on facts for investigative pieces. She made coffee, typed letters, photocopied headlines and hated herself. She suggested captions and ideas to the journalists and felt she was making a mark. She pushed herself in everyone's face.

The first Saturday Topaz had off, she slept all day.

She learnt quickly because she had a fast eye and instincts about people. Jason Richman was writing a piece on the weirdest food in New York? Topaz had seen a guy selling chocolate pizza off West 4th Street. Josie Simons complained at the top of her voice that there was no one in the whole world with a fresh take on rock 'n' roll, and Topaz suggested she interview the doorman at CBGB's. Josh Stein, the art director, couldn't fit a long headline on to a page? Splice it across the diagonal, maybe, said Topaz. Write the article around it.

'I need a title for this piece!' bellowed Nathan Rosen across the features desk, drowning out the incessant whirr of telephones, voices and computer typewriters.

'What's it on?' asked Elise DeLuca, the deputy features editor.

'Modern art at the Met . . . Henry Kravis is thinking of endowing a national collection of American avant-garde stuff – its the lead story next week,' Rosen yelled. 'Biggest thing since J. P. Getty got the painting bug.'

'Modern Masters,' said Elise.

'The Tate comes to NYC.'

'New York, New Pictures.'

'Cutting-Edge Kravis.'

'All of those suck. *They suck*!' bellowed Rosen. 'All I'm asking for is one good goddamned line!'

'How about "State of the Art, Art of the State"?' murmured Topaz, passing his desk with two armfuls of photocopies.

Rosen looked at her. 'That's good. I'll use that,' he said quietly.

Later in the afternoon Rosen stopped by her desk, where she was typing up some hack's drastically edited play review for setting. 'See if you can do something with this one, Rossi,' he said, trying not to stare at the beautiful firm young cleavage positioned directly under his nose. 'I got two pages in the business section on Häagen-Dazs ice cream and how good it's doing in Europe – four hundred per cent growth a year, stuff like that.'

'I'm not surprised,' said Topaz, remembering the Häagen-Dazs café in Cornmarket and how it was full of undergraduates even in December.

'Yeah, well. This is a real smart piece of business reporting but it's just that – business. I'd like to get some feel of ice cream in there, remind people what Häagen-Dazs tastes like. Association makes the figures a lot more interesting. So.'

He held up a sheet with the article, entitled 'Häagen-Dazs Spearheads Growth of Upmarket Snacks'. It was one and three quarter pages of close text, with a tub of rum-raisin filling the upper left-hand corner of the second sheet.

'I need a killer caption for the packshot,' said Rosen.

'OK. Gimme just a second,' said Topaz. She had the line already, she'd thought of it the moment he explained the article, but she wanted to bask in Nathan Rosen's presence for a few more seconds. Hey, any junior would be flattered to have the editor by their desk. The fact that he was so good-looking had nothing to do with it.

'No hurry,' said Rosen impatiently.

'Well,' said Topaz slowly, 'how about if you put "Häagen-Dazs: not so much of an ice cream, more of a religious experience." '

'Could you say that again?' asked Nathan Rosen, wondering if he could have heard her right.

'Not so much of an ice cream, more of a religious experience,' Topaz repeated.

Nathan pulled himself together. The sentence was

perfect. 'OK. Let me get a few other suggestions. You make sure you stop by my office when you get off work today.'

'Whatever you say, boss,' Topaz smiled. *I'm getting there*, she thought. 'You won't get a better caption than that one!' she shouted after his retreating back.

The editorial rooms of *Westside* were quieter by 8 p.m.; there were still a few journalists hunched over their consoles, faces lit by the flickering screens, who might well be slaving over their pieces till one or two in the morning. Topaz heard a telephone ring in the art department, a fax machine whirr on the newsdesk. But basically the place was emptying out. She felt slightly sick with excitement as she looked at the editor's office, still flooded with golden light. She was exhausted after another gruelling day; the job left her feeling like a human punchbag.

Better check myself out first, Topaz told herself, slipping into the ladies. Hardly the most luxurious restrooms in the universe, at least they had adequate supplies of what she needed most right now: lights and mirrors.

She glanced at her reflection, dabbing a little cover-up over the shadows under her eyes. Pretty good. Her black Donna Karan tunic emphasized her large bust and tiny waist, the latest stack mules made her calves look thinner, there were a few long curly red strands which had escaped from her swept-back look, but that was cool; they looked sexy, and they looked like she'd been working.

'Yes. I am a working girl. I am going to get a promotion,' Topaz told herself, then she took a deep breath, left the ladies, and strode across the floor to Nathan Rosen's office.

Rosen watched her coming. She excited him every way he looked at it. Day-to-day, she was a free-range magazine-improver and staff-energizer. Mentally, he felt a rush of joy as one print man discovering another; looking at her, he saw a female version of his younger self: all journalistic brilliance and brass balls wrapped up in an intense love of the story and how to tell it. She would make it in spades, and he would be her guru. But physically – damn it! – he had distinctly unpaternal feelings which refused to go away. He watched the tight muscles of her ass rolling under her clothes as she came across the room, her breasts rising and falling, her legs clicking and pumping . . . he felt that treacherous tickle in his groin . . . God, look at the way she moved when she walked! It was poetry, it was a symphony to the beauty of the human female.

Stop it! Right now! Rosen lectured himself. She's twenty-one years old, I'm thirty-nine. I could be her father.

Topaz knocked and came in, smiling.

My God, she's attractive, thought Rosen. 'Sit down,' he said coldly.

Topaz sat.

'You're coming up with some good stuff, Topaz,' he said, leaning forward. 'Really good. And I know you realize this. I also know you realize that you're outperforming your job description, and that you deserve a pay rise and a promotion.'

Topaz nodded intently. *This is it. I did it. He's gonna make me a reporter*.

'Well, you can have the pay rise,' Rosen said. 'But I'm not gonna make you a reporter. That, you can forget. You've only been here a month. You got five months to go before I'll even consider it. And I don't want you making any waves around the office – all the assistants are jealous enough of you as it is and I can tell you right now, some of the junior reporters feel threatened.'

'What?' said Topaz, bewildered.

'You gotta pay your dues and that's just the way it is. I'm sorry if you don't like it. That's all. Congratulations on your pay rise,' said Nathan bluntly, and turned to a file on his desk in dismissal.

For a second there was silence, as Topaz was suffocated with fury. But only for a second.

'Fuck that! And *fuck you*,' she spat. 'So that's it, huh? Six months of typing from seven a.m. to eight p.m. so the other secretaries can feel comfortable! How can you sit there and tell me talent means nothing, pay your dues? You're scared of your junior reporters? I'll tell you why they're threatened – because I prove every day out there that I can do what they do *better*. You practically said so yourself. Who's the editor here? You or them?'

'*I* am!' roared Rosen, out of his chair now and incensed. '*Me*, not *you*! And don't you *ever* forget it!'

He sat down again heavily, enraged. 'You listen to me, Rossi,' he said. 'You're lucky I don't fire you on the spot' – Topaz went white – 'for the way you just spoke to me. I've been running this ship for ten years and you've been here five minutes. I've seen hotshots like you before, you come in the door, put in long hours, come up with a couple of snappy lines and you think you're Ralph J. Gleason. Well, coming up with a title or a caption does not make a reporter. You know what it makes? An *advertising copywriter*!' he bellowed again. 'You wanna sell ice cream? Take a cab to Madison Avenue!'

Topaz trembled. It was like standing directly in the path of a ballistic missile.

'I'm sorry,' she mumbled, and was appalled to hear her voice quiver. Oh God, she panicked, I think I'm going to cry.

Rosen looked at his protégée, staring at her lap and obviously terrified. He had been violently angry, but that had passed and now he kind of admired her spirit. And she looked so vulnerable. Part of him wanted to soothe her, kiss her, stroke her hair. Part of him wanted to throw her over the desk and fuck her right here in the office. *Don't think about that! Be fair. But be just.*

'OK, look,' he said. 'I can't go on with you like this, it's disruptive. But you think I'm holding you back, you're as good as the junior reporters . . . so. I'm giving you a chance to prove it. David Levine has a meeting at the GE building at three o'clock tomorrow, I got a tip-off, nobody else knows. You know nobody's been able to get a comment from him on this story that he hit a teacher at his kid's school. Get a comment. You know where he'll be, follow him, get a comment. You do, you get a promotion and a secretary. Screw up, and you're out on your ass. Understood?'

'Understood,' said Topaz, and now she was glowing.

David Levine emerged out of the General Electric building, and across the street Topaz felt time, her heartbeat and the revolution of the planets grind to a resounding halt. She sucked in her breath. He was unmistakable even at this distance; the golden hair that had introduced a generation of American pubescent girls to their own sexuality glinted in the thin winter light, and she could see his broad, tall frame and arrogant jawline from here. David Levine combined an intense, Jewish, Richard Gere-type sensuality with the looks and physique of a Viking. Topaz had seen ten of his movies herself. He was one of a handful of stars who could 'open' a movie nationwide; and now ugly rumours were surfacing which could wreck his career if they were true. Certain sussed journalists had heard that America's Mr Romantic was a woman-beater, and had broken the nose of his mistress, a young teacher at his son's primary school. Not a word had appeared in print. The woman was too scared to talk. Levine was too powerful to libel.

Topaz felt for her Dictaphone recorder, securely in her pocket, and dashed through the traffic. 'Mr Levine!' she gasped, running up to him. 'Excuse me, sir?'

Levine turned round, noticed a girl with a great-looking body in shades and a baseball cap, blushing furiously. He gave her a lazy smile. 'Hey, sweetheart,' he said. 'Not too loud. I don't want to get mobbed. Who shall I sign it to?'

He thinks I'm an autograph-hunter!

'Oh no, I'm not a fan,' she blurted. 'Well, I am a fan. It's just – I mean, I'm a reporter . . . you know, there's a story going round that you hit a teacher. I was wondering if you had any comment, you know, to clear your name?'

David Levine's green eyes had crystallized into chips of ice.

'Get lost, you cheap whore,' he slurred. 'And you can tell that tramp from me, if she's been talking . . .'

'What?' demanded Topaz. 'You'll finish the job?'

All of her nervousness had evaporated. She was right in the middle of a breaking story, and this bastard was high.

Levine glared at her. 'Print a word of this, slut, and I'll sue you to kingdom come. I don't see a tape recorder.'

And he stepped into a swooping cab.

Topaz barely had time to register that he was right, she hadn't had the Dictaphone switched on. She hailed the next taxi in line. 'Can you follow that car? And don't let the guy know.'

'No problem, lady,' said the driver, pleased to have his boring day livened up.

The cars tore through glittering Manhattan, weaving through the traffic like it was water. Topaz stared out of ·

the window, at the mirrored skyscrapers jabbing into the sky like accusing fingers, and raced through her information. Number one, he was guilty as hell. Number two, he was on some kind of drugs, and not totally together – maybe she could get something past him. Number three, the way he spoke, she'd bet her last dime the teacher was not the only woman he'd hit . . .

Topaz thought for a second. Then she took off her cap and shades and stuffed them in her bag, unbuttoned her jacket and unpinned her hair so that it fell round her shoulders like a blazing waterfall. She loosened the top three buttons on her shirt, took out her lipstick . . .

David Levine relaxed some more. It was good cognac, good coke and a nice club, the kind where people were too cool to bother him. He'd screwed three more points on the gross from them in the meeting today, and told a dyke reporter where she could get off. And now he was here, talking to Jo-Ann, some Texan chick with wide baby eyes, soft lips and awesome tits. She had a good attitude, too. She appreciated her luck in getting to sit with him. She was the type that liked a strong man. He could hardly wait to stick it to her.

'. . . though you prob'ly don't approve, being a New Yorker,' she murmured, eyes downcast. 'Y'all are prob'ly one of those feminists.'

She pronounced the word with a delicate distaste.

Levine roared with laughter. 'No, ma'am. No way.'

'Well, that's good to hear,' she said. 'I know I'm real old-fashioned, but I swear that's the way the good Lord intended it to be. It tells us so in the Bible. I admire a man who keeps discipline in his own house, although you don't meet too many of those in this day and age.'

Levine wondered if she'd get off on being spanked before he took her. Well, no matter, he was going to do it anyway. The thought of her delicious Southern ass exposed across his knees started to give him a hard-on.

'Well, you got one here, Jo-Ann,' he said. 'Last time my ex-girlfriend decided to get out of line . . . let's just say she never did it again.'

Topaz leant forward, pressing her breasts together, the rolling Dictaphone whirring under her dress.

'My!' she purred. 'Why don't you tell me *all* about it?'

Chapter Eight

The subway car was crammed, absolutely full to the brim. Smart businessmen in crisp linen suits stood shoulder-to-shoulder with maintenance men in their overalls and joggers in tight Lycra on their way home. Topaz didn't mind; not even the fat Italian housewives clutching shopping bags bothered her any more.

For the first couple of weeks, she'd felt uncomfortable, wondering if all these big-city slickers could see through her no-nonsense jeans and trainers, her tight little skirts and black briefcase. She'd felt transparent, like everybody could tell by looking at her she shouldn't be here: Topaz Rossi, a pushy kid from New Jersey, playing at being a journalist on a big magazine. She imagined that everybody could tell she was earning slave wages, living in a scuzzy walk-up on the Lower East Side. Who was she kidding? Nobody'd be fooled because she'd learnt to *dress* right. She was bound to look gauche and awkward. To make a fool of herself.

Three weeks after that, she'd become neutral, tuning out like everybody else.

Today, she was loving every minute of it.

The David Levine article, typed, neatly laid out and over eight thousand words long, was safely folded in her briefcase, together with a copy of the tape of her interview. She felt as though it must be burning a hole right through the leather, this thing was so hot. It had taken her all night to write it up, and it was worth every second. She didn't feel tired. She felt young, and terrific, and bursting with energy. She was on her way.

Topaz smoothed her skirt down on her hips, oblivious to the admiring glances of the men around her. Her mind was racing with plans, with exactly how she should present this to her editor, with what she could get out of him in return.

Because this was it.

This was her big break.

Nathan Rosen had given her Mission Impossible, and against all the odds she'd come through. Yeah, she mused, he won't be expecting *this*. He wanted to punish me, show me I'd been getting too big for my boots, that I couldn't handle the stuff I was asking for. He probably expected me to come see him a couple of days later, in tears, begging him not to sack me. Topaz shook her beautiful head, sending her earrings jangling about her throat. The scene wasn't gonna play that way.

The train pulled up at 53rd Street and 7th, and Topaz pushed out of the doors, looking forward to the walk to the office. Several bored commuters admired her ass as she strode purposefully up the escalator, enjoying the rare sight of a girl with curves. Topaz had an hourglass figure, and she refused to starve it into waiflike submission. If Kate Moss wanted to look like a boy, fine. She doubted men like Nathan Rosen would look twice at Kate Moss.

Broadway glittered in the early morning sun as Topaz stepped out of the station. The air was faintly humid and warm, promising a baking hot day later on. She shivered with pleasure, feeling enthusiasm and energy beat up out of the streets towards her. Her sneakers seemed to bounce off the pavement. Midtown Manhattan! Why *shouldn't* she love it?

All the way to the American Magazines tower, Topaz Rossi was bubbling with excitement. When you were young and on your way, New York was the only place to be, paying no attention to where you were from, just where you were going.

And I, Topaz thought, pushing through the revolving doors into the marble lobby, am going straight to the top. No more Gino putting me down. No more Rowena Gordon, stamping on me with her blue-blooded feet. No more sons-of-bitches like Peter Kennedy tricking their way into my pants. And no more assholes like Geoffrey Stevens refusing to take my calls—

'Topaz? Anybody home?' Jason Richman asked. 'God, where are you *at* this morning? I called out to you three times on the street, but you just walked right past with your head in the clouds.'

She smiled at him apologetically as they both walked into the elevator. 'Jase, I'm sorry. I had my mind on a story.'

'Yeah? Whose? Did Rosen ask you to copy-edit that Josie Simons thing on ticket scalpers?'

Topaz shook her head, grinning. 'Not exactly. This is one of my own.'

'Of yours?' asked Jason, surprised. Topaz was obviously very good, but Nate Rosen would surely never promote her so quickly. She'd only been at *Westside* a month. Even Elise had had to wait six months before she got a reporting gig.

She nodded. 'It's kind of a . . . a test. He wanted to see what I could do.'

The heavy metal doors hissed smoothly open, and they stepped out together onto *Westside*'s floor. The offices were deserted at this time in the morning. Only

Jason liked to get into work early; he left early too, to hit the cool, crowded little restaurants he reviewed before the rush started. Today, Topaz wanted time to think, to go over what she could get out of this hot little bombshell. If only she could keep a lid on her excitement long enough to think straight.

'I'm intrigued,' Jason said. 'Spill it, Topaz. What did he say? You want some coffee?'

'Yes please,' she said, already a shameless caffeine addict. 'Black, no sugar. Can you keep a secret?'

'Sure,' said Jason, curiously.

'He asked me to get an interview with David Levine. Said that if I did, he would make me a reporter, and if I screwed it up, I was fired.'

'No!' said Jason, perching on the edge of his desk. He handed her the coffee. 'That's not like Nathan, to be hard on a junior like that. He's normally so laid-back. You must really have pissed him off, Topaz. Would you like me to talk to him? See if I can calm him down?'

Topaz grinned. 'I got the story, Jason.'

'Get out of here.'

'I did, I did!' she burst out, unable to control the huge grin spreading across her face. 'I trailed him! In disguise! And I taped him! And it's dynamite!'

Jason laughed at her affectionately. 'Come on, babe, you're not Lois Lane, and this isn't the *Daily Planet*. What did you do, make something up? I'm not gonna report you. Nathan'll probably let you off for being inventive.'

Without another word, Topaz bent down and unclipped her briefcase. Gingerly she extracted the double-spaced typescript of her story and handed it to her friend.

Jason read it in silence, occasionally raising an eyebrow or letting his lips move in surprise. It was extremely well written. And it was indeed dynamite.

At the end, he said simply, 'Topaz, can you prove this?'

She nodded, eyes sparkling, and threw him the tape of their conversation. Richman slotted it into the cassette player by Elise DeLuca's desk.

'. . . tell me *all* about it,' said Topaz in a soft Southern drawl.

'Well, Susie should have known better,' David Levine's unmistakable voice asserted loudly.

Jason sat bolt upright, staring down at the pages in his hand. He realized what he was hearing, but he still couldn't quite believe it.

'She was a teacher. Seemed like *I* had to teach *her* a lesson,' Levine went on, his voice clipped and tight.

'Coke?' Jason asked, reaching for the off-switch. He didn't want to hear any more. The stuff Levine admitted in this article made his stomach turn.

'Yeah. And he was on something different when I first stopped him in the street,' Topaz answered. She was swelling with pride. Jason's reaction was exactly what she'd hoped for. 'He told me he'd sue if I printed anything, because he didn't see a tape recorder. So I switched my Dictaphone on and . . . and I hid it inside my bra,' she explained.

Jason glanced involuntarily at her firm, full bust. Damn, the girl had no business looking like that. It was distracting when he was trying to concentrate on the scoop of the goddamn year.

He sighed. 'Topaz, do you know what you've got here?'

'A story that'll make me a reporter,' she said confidently.

Richman marvelled. For a smart, independent kid, Rossi could sometimes be incredibly dumb.

'What you've got here,' he explained patiently, 'is a

front-page lead item on the six-o' clock-news-type story. An exclusive that could sell millions of papers. That will ruin a major film star's career, embarrass his studio, and make you personally into a celebrity, at least for a few days. Now you *could* hand in a story like that to your boss and get made into a reporter, on twenty-five thousand dollars a year. That's a big step up from where you are now, of course.'

He gathered up his stuff, wanting to get over to the Gotham Café in SoHo for breakfast. 'Or you could figure out what a story like that is worth. To Nathan Rosen or anyone else. Don't be a *putz*, Topaz. You're not in Kansas any more.'

And with that he winked at her and strolled out the door.

Nathan Rosen stepped into his kitchen, wondering what to fix for breakfast. French vanilla coffee and a toasted bagel with lox, perhaps. Nothing too heavy. It was too warm a morning to want to eat heavy food.

A few years ago he'd have just grabbed some ice cream from the fridge, or made himself a chicken sandwich. Or more likely skipped breakfast altogether and picked up a doughnut at the office. Things were simpler then. After the divorce, eating what he liked where he liked had taken on a delicious sense of luxury.

But Rosen was a born New Yorker, and a high achiever at that. He liked to be the best at everything, and he liked the attentions of women. And somewhere in the mid-eighties, how you looked became as important as what you were.

As usual, Nathan refused to be left behind. He joined a gym and worked off his soft belly and spreading thighs, and cut excess fat from his diet. He still ate like a horse, but he ate high-protein, high-carbohydrate foods. The one thing he couldn't give up was ice cream, but then again, he was only human.

It had been a struggle. But it was worth it, Rosen thought with a touch of vanity, checking himself out in the wall mirror. His large frame was now solid muscle. He had a clean, strong jawline with no hint of fat around the chin. There was nothing he could do about his thinning hair and the flecks of grey at the side of his skull, but basically Rosen looked good. And he knew it. Hell, how could he fail to notice? He was getting laid so much more. Women came on to him at the gym. After the workout class. While he was out jogging. At parties. At baseball games. Yeah, Nate Rosen was a big fan of the exercise revolution.

He'd dated a few of the women he met socially, but not for long; no relationship since his marriage had lasted more than five months. But that didn't bother him. He was in no rush to get another thin gold band. After years of fidelity to a sexually selfish woman, Rosen was enjoying his freedom too much to give it up. If the right person came along, fair enough. But it was a case of proceed with caution. He'd been wrong the first time.

Rosen switched on the percolator, waiting for the pleasantly bitter coffee smell to fill the airy kitchen. He loved this time in the morning that he had for himself, swinging into his stride, psyching himself up for another day in the office. *Westside* was a fun magazine to edit; not only cutting-edge, but, since he'd taken over the editor's job, highly profitable.

In fact, the rumour was that he was about to be promoted. Henry Birnbaum, the director of American's East Coast operations, was due to step down in the fall. Nathan had been told by the President, Matthew Gowers, that he was first in line for the job.

Director. It would be a good way to turn forty, Nathan

thought, grinning. He looked out of his window towards Central Park, enjoying the clear blue skies, the sunlight, his own feelings of success.

Maybe he'd been a little hard on Topaz Rossi.

Now where the hell did that come from? Rosen wondered, angry with himself. What *was* this thing he had about some new kid? Some talented, pushy new kid who'd only been in the office a month? He could not stop thinking about her. Getting enchanted by her enthusiasm, fascinated by her intelligence, enraged by her arrogance. He'd never had so much chutzpah at her age. At least, he thought not. And she had been way out of line the other night, no question. But would he have reacted in that way if she'd been a guy? Wouldn't he just have laughed at her, told her to calm down? What was with this stupid do-or-die mission he'd sent her on? David Levine? Right. Like some kid could manage to swing an interview with *him*. She was probably over there this morning, cleaning out her desk. And she had talent, Topaz Rossi; Nathan reckoned she'd make a good writer some day. It wasn't his job as her boss to be taking out his feelings on her.

Because, Rosen admitted to himself, spreading lox on his bagel, I *do* have feelings for that girl. I like her. And I want her.

But that was natural. She was beautiful, with those delicate blue eyes and that mass of curly red hair. It was impossible not to think about the hair elsewhere on her smooth, young body. And she was stacked, with a waist he could encircle with his two hands swelling out to an invitingly curvy ass. Rossi would grace the cover of *Sports Illustrated*'s swimsuit issue, so it was only to be expected that he imagined her the way he did. On a beach, in a tiny bikini. Naked on top of him. Being made love to, slowly, in his jacuzzi upstairs.

Rosen, feeling the first stirrings in his groin, dragged his thoughts away from those images. Topaz was way too young. He despised middle-aged men who chased students. And he had enough girls without screwing around on his doorstep. In the nineties, the office romance was totally taboo. It had always been bad news, but these days you didn't even think about things like that. The office *compliment* was taboo, for Christ's sake. If Topaz was a little older, she'd understand these things. She wouldn't come on to him so damn obviously, with those smiles and little breathless glances and tight T-shirts. She was a nice kid. He had to be a responsible adult.

This morning, Rosen decided, I'll call the kid in and let her off with a warning. A *stern* warning.

David Levine and Topaz Rossi? he thought, grinning. It would be Christians and Lions all over again.

'What's up with Topaz?' Elise asked Josie. 'She's been locked on the phone all day.'

'And circling property ads in the *Village Voice*,' the music writer agreed. 'I don't know. I guess she's moving house.'

'On what we're paying?' Elise shrugged.

Topaz felt her heartbeat speeding up. Adrenaline coursed through her. Thank God for Jason Richman! Thank God she'd even got to talk to him! How *could* she have been so blind?

She was holding for Geoffrey Stevens. Amazing how good this felt. It had come to her like a blinding flash of inspiration, after Jason left this morning. So the article was worth $50,000 and she hadn't spotted it? Fine. Well, now she was going to make it $100,000. And get herself a little revenge into the bargain.

She had to move secretly. And she had to move fast.

'Miss Rossi.'

There it was, at last. That clipped English accent she thought she'd never hear again, not once Charles Gordon had killed her student articles with one phone call. Oh, she remembered all that. 'Mr Stevens is unavailable.' 'Mr Stevens is not in the office.' 'Mr Stevens has asked me to tell you we can't use your material, Miss Rossi. Sorry if there was any misunderstanding.'

Topaz felt her Italian blood pump through her, thrilled at the prospect of revenge.

'I got your fax,' Stevens said. 'A very interesting snippet.'

Yeah, you're interested in this *material, right, you limey prick?*

'There's more where that came from, Mr Stevens. A lot more. And a tape to go with it.'

There was a pause. Topaz could almost see the greedy asshole licking his lips.

'We would be very interested in publishing this story, Miss Rossi. You would have a byline, of course. And a picture.'

She almost laughed out loud. He must think she was still at college. 'Of course,' she agreed. 'That's standard. Now we must discuss the small matter of my fee.'

'My budget is limited, Miss Rossi,' Stevens said coldly, as if to imply his contempt for such a mercenary attitude.

Topaz grinned. 'My options aren't,' she observed.

Silence. He could feel it slipping away. 'What do you want?'

'Seventy thousand pounds,' said Topaz coolly. The office fax wasn't numbered, and she wanted him to think she was still in England. That was an important part of the plan. 'Today. Paid directly into my bank account. You get a European exclusive, and it has to run in the *Sunday Times* next week. I'll fax you the first half of the story today, with a tape to match, Fed ex'd to the office. If I get my money, you'll get the second half of the story tomorrow.'

'How do I know it isn't a complete fabrication?'

Topaz held her Dictaphone up to the receiver and pressed play, letting the tape run for twenty seconds.

'That should be enough, Mr Stevens. If you can't trust me, just say so, I'll sell it to the *Mail on Sunday*. Do we have a deal?'

'Yes, damn it!' the man spat.

Topaz heard the line click dead.

Smiling, she called her bank.

Nathan arrived at *Westside* about eleven fifteen and went straight into his office, refusing all calls and his mail, and worked solidly through the proposed budget for a new colour supplement the board wanted to see installed. Nobody disturbed him; it had been Rosen's habit for years to concentrate completely on the most immediate problem they had, and sort other things out later. If Elise wanted a new features layout or Josie wanted to run a rock concert promotion, they got to see Nathan Rosen – but only after lunch. If you got summoned to the office before 2 p.m., everybody knew something was up.

At noon the internal phone buzzed on Topaz Rossi's desk.

'Yeah,' she said absently, hunched over mortgage calculations.

'Topaz? This is Oriole,' said Nathan's assistant, sympathetically. 'Could you come over to the editor's office right away, please? He wants to talk to you.'

'Sure,' Topaz said, feeling her palms begin to sweat. God, she hoped she'd done the right thing. Not that she should worry. She'd made herself rich. Or at least richer.

Seventy thousand pounds is $100,000, Topaz told herself firmly, trying to calm her nerves, to control the ball of anxiety in her stomach. She got up, tugging her skirt round her hips, futilely trying to make it a little longer, pulling back her snaking red curls into a neat ponytail. It was no use. Her reflection stared back at her from Elise's glass door, the long, well-turned legs stretching up for miles, the smart black leather hugging her ass provocatively, the tiny waist emphasized by a leather belt, and the full breasts, tilting youthfully upwards from her ribcage, blossoming under the tight pull of her crisp white shirt. In fact, the ponytail somehow *added* sex appeal – it made her look like an overripe schoolgirl.

Blushing, she unfastened the blue velvet scrunch that held it in place, grabbed her story and her tape and marched across the corridor to Nathan Rosen's office.

Why should I care if he fires me? Topaz thought rebelliously. I can get another job in a second. I don't need *Westside*.

But she knew that she did care. Very much. Because Nate Rosen worked at *Westside*.

'Hi, Topaz,' Oriole said. 'You can just go right in.'

She sauntered into Rosen's office, looking over the spectacular city view. Nathan, jabbering furiously into the phone in Yiddish, motioned to her to take a seat. Topaz sat gratefully down in a black leather chair opposite his desk, trying to look like someone who knew how to bargain. Someone who sold a major story to two papers every day of the week. And not someone who was terrified she'd just blown her career.

Nathan growled into the phone and hung up, then sat down heavily, glaring at her. 'So you remember our last conversation,' he said.

Topaz summoned up her courage. 'Yes I do,' she said. 'And I got you the interview.'

Her editor raised an eyebrow.

'I taped it,' Topaz blurted. 'I mean, I disguised myself and I taped it secretly. I hid the Dictaphone . . . on me, and he admitted everything, so I transcribed it in a story and I have copies of the tape and . . . and it's all there,' she finished breathlessly, shoving her typescript and the tape towards him.

Nathan looked at his protégée for a long moment, then glanced at the top page of the interview, not bothering to flick through it. Then he looked slowly at Topaz again.

'OK, kid,' he said coldly. 'What have you done?'

'Wh – what do you mean?' she stammered.

Rosen sighed. 'Ms Rossi,' he said, 'I've been editing this magazine for two years. I've been a journalist for eighteen years. I think I can read a case of guilty nerves pretty well. I'm sure you *did* get this story, like you say. Now that ought to be a coup, am I right? But you walk in here like you've been summoned to the principal's office, not like you wanna tell me you're up for the Pulitzer. So please don't insult my intelligence. Just save us both some time and tell me what you've done.'

Topaz swallowed, hard. 'OK,' she said. 'I–I've sold the European rights on the story to the *Sunday Times* and they're running it next week. But they think I'm still in England. They don't know I'm here, so they didn't ask for world rights. Which means that we can lead Wednesday's edition with it and still be first with the story.'

'Let me get this straight,' Nathan said slowly. 'You have sold this story to another publication, a major international paper, and you are proposing to double-cross them by having us print the story in America first. Where it will, of course, make the news around the world, thus making it almost useless to them.'

'Yes,' Topaz admitted weakly.

Rosen's voice was calm. 'How much did you get for it?'

'A hundred thousand dollars,' she mumbled.

'One hundred thousand dollars,' he repeated. 'I see. And what did you want from me? A chunk of the stock, perhaps?'

'No, no,' Topaz protested. 'I swear. I just wanted you to make me a reporter . . .' Her voice trailed off miserably and she stared at her skirt.

'Sit there,' Nathan ordered. 'While I read this *lucrative* piece of investigative journalism.'

Topaz waited for five minutes that seemed like five hours, squirming on her seat in embarrassment as Rosen worked through the article, his face impassive. She was obviously about to get fired. Nathan seemed to think she'd torn up the rule book of news ethics. *Santa Maria*, and she only wanted to please the guy! He was so gorgeous! And yet he never seemed to notice she was alive, unless it was to yell at her or reprimand her for some little thing. The shorter her skirts, the more figure-hugging her blouse, the less interest Nathan showed. She couldn't understand it. She'd never come across a man that didn't at least *look* at her appreciatively. And Nathan Rosen was definitely not gay – according to the other girls in the office, outside of *Westside* he was a goddamn womanizer. So what the hell, Topaz thought angrily, is *wrong* with me?

Finally, Rosen looked up, and to her astonishment she saw he was smiling.

'What kind of a reporter did you want to be?'

'Excuse me?' she said, bewildered.

'Come on, Rossi,' Nathan said. 'Pitch me. Tell me what you want to do. Tell me how you can sell more magazines for me.'

'I could write a column,' Topaz said. It was the first thing that came into her head. 'About New York. As an out-of-towner who's new here. Things most people wouldn't notice – it'd make them look at Manhattan with a fresh eye. I'd call it "NY Scene".'

'What about your salary?' asked Rosen, still smiling.

'Thirty-five thousand dollars,' Topaz said boldly.

Nathan shrugged. 'That's ten thousand more than new reporters get.'

'But I'd be a *columnist*. And like I told you before, I'm better than they are.'

'Don't push it,' Nathan said. He extended one hand across his desk and Topaz grabbed it eagerly, feeling a little electric shock of sexuality as his flesh touched hers.

'Congratulations, kid,' he said. 'You scored.'

'You're not mad at me for selling it to an English paper?'

Nathan chuckled. 'Rossi, that was the first piece of real initiative you've shown since you got here.'

'And thirty-five thousand a year!' she breathed.

Nathan smiled at her again. 'With a story like this, you could have asked for fifty thousand. But you wouldn't welsh on a handshake, right?'

'You sonofabitch,' Topaz said, angrily.

Nathan laughed. 'Relax. Consider it valuable vocational training. You're not the only one who can pull a fast trick, kid. Just remember – I'm still better at this than you are.'

For a second she glared at him, and then broke down under the warmth of his teasing and smiled. Damn, damn, *damn*, he was attractive.

'Want to grab a beer with me to celebrate?' she asked, tentatively.

Nathan Rosen looked her over, the thrusting breasts, the handspan waist, the round ass and long, beautiful legs, and felt himself sorely tempted. Her desire was written in a bright glow on her face, on those delicious half-stiffened nipples.

'No, I have to work,' he said. 'Unlike some people I could mention.'

She turned away, trying not to show her disappointment.

'Topaz,' Nathan said. 'You can take the day off. Go find a new apartment. You did good.'

'Thanks, boss,' she said lightly, and walked out of his office, closing the door behind her.

After she'd gone, Nathan Rosen stared at the typescript on his desk for a long moment. He'd have to watch this girl carefully. Because unless all his instincts were mistaken, the pushy little Italian was a force to be reckoned with.

Chapter Nine

It wasn't a promising start. Of all the places Rowena least liked having to trek to see bands, working men's clubs in the north of England rated amongst the worst. Usually she had to argue for forty minutes with some surly bloke who blew smoke in her face before he'd even let her in, and then stand at the back and do her best to blend into the chipped paint or peeling wallpaper. Not easy, when drunk fifty-year-olds were wandering up to you and making breathtakingly obscene comments every five minutes. The only women welcome in those dives were strippers, and the punters made sure Rowena knew it.

So some bunch of talentless Northerners called Atomic Mass are playing Crookes Working Men's Club in Sheffield, Rowena thought as she parked her battered mini down the road. Terrific. Great. And Musica Records, right on the cutting edge as usual, is here to check them out.

Once she got inside, she bought two triple Jack Daniels and Dict Cokes, and finished one off before the band even hit the stage. She was obviously going to need them. The place was mercifully half-empty, but the barman had taken great pleasure in informing her that Atomic Mass were a bunch of young kids who'd got together at college, with an American from the university on lead guitar. Bound to be strictly amateur-hour stuff. By the time they wandered onstage, Rowena was seething with resentment at Matthew Stevenson for making her waste an evening like this.

And then they started to play.

Barbara Lincoln, elegantly dressed in an Armani pantsuit in cream linen that set off her slim figure and soft chocolate skin, was trying to figure something out. Her secretary had brought in her mail that morning – the usual stuff every Business Affairs executive had to deal with in a record company – and one memo. Not that she didn't normally get memos. But this one was different: hand-delivered early in the morning, and from a talent scout in A&R, Rowena Gordon, some new girl whom Barbara had never met.

It was so weird.

She glanced at it again. *Dear Ms Lincoln, I would be grateful if you could allow me ten minutes for a meeting with you today. My extension is 435. Regards, Rowena Gordon, Artists and Repertoire.*

Why on earth did one of Stevenson's *scouts* want to meet with her? Why not Matthew himself? He was the one who handled contract negotiations. Barbara was twenty-five and the number two in Musica's Legal and Business Affairs Department, and she'd never met a scout in her career. There was just no reason for it.

Intrigued, she dialled Rowena's extension.

'I wanted some advice,' Rowena said nervously, shutting the door behind her. Maybe this hadn't been such a good idea. Barbara Lincoln's secretary had shot her a strange look when she'd turned up for her appointment, dressed in her normal office clothes of jeans and trainers. Over in Business Affairs, the look was obviously more formal.

Christ, Lincoln dressed the way she had at Oxford, in the old days when money was no object. That seemed several lifetimes ago now.

Barbara eyed her up. She looked intelligent, a well-spoken young girl for a talent scout. There was something about this one she couldn't pin down.

'I don't mind at all,' she said. 'I'm just curious as to why you wouldn't tell me what this was about.'

Rowena nodded. 'I understand,' she said, 'but I couldn't say in front of Matthew Stevenson. You see, I've found a band I think the company should sign, and I don't think Matthew will listen to them with an open mind if I play them for him.'

'Why not?' Barbara enquired calmly.

'Because Josh Oberman hired me himself,' Rowena said.

Barbara smiled. 'Did you know that's how I got hired?' she asked.

'That's why I'm here,' Rowena said simply. 'You've obviously survived. I hoped you might be able to help me to.'

Barbara laughed. 'Very inventive. Did you bring a tape with you? I'll put the headphones on.'

The older girl listened in silence for several minutes, then slid the headpiece off and looked at Rowena with something approaching respect. 'Well, I'm into business, not music,' she said, 'but it seems to me like you have something here. If I were you I'd go to see Oberman direct.'

'How would I get an appointment?'

Barbara picked up her phone and tapped in some numbers. 'Josh?' she asked. 'Hi, it's Barbara Lincoln. Fine, thanks. Look, Josh, I was just wondering if you could see Rowena Gordon some time today.'

Rowena, her face flaming red, made a lunge for the

phone, but Barbara stood up, grinning, and held it out of reach. 'She's found a good act and she wants you to hear it. Doesn't think Matthew will give a rock band a chance, and she's too shy to tell you herself. Yeah, OK. OK. I understand. Thanks, boss.'

She hung up and turned to a mortified Rowena. 'He wants to see you in his office in five minutes,' Barbara told her. 'And don't look like that. He's not gonna fire you. I've been working with Josh for a couple of years, and I tell you, that guy knows the score. He's been doing this since before either of us were born. He'll understand Matthew's problem. He'll only think well of you for coming to me.'

'Are you sure?' Rowena asked, anxiously.

Barbara gave a self-assured nod. 'I am. And come and see me when you're through. We should go out for a drink.'

Rowena smiled. 'I'd like that,' she said.

Joshua Oberman sat hunched in his chair, listening to the tape. The sound quality was dreadful, the production non-existent, and Gordon didn't have so much as a picture to show him.

They were *awesome*.

Excitement rippled through his withered veins. Seventy years old, and good music could still turn him on. He couldn't get an erection any more but he still felt like a teenager when he heard stuff like this. It was the old Guns n' Roses syndrome. The thrill of hearing an act nobody else had heard of, and knowing, just *knowing* that in a couple of years they'd be packing stadiums and making thousands of teenage chicks cream their pants. Fat bass. Fresh guitar. Great vocals. Cool songs.

The kind of stuff that got arena seats ripped up.

Music that caused riots.

'So where did you see this act?' he asked impassively, staring sternly at little Rowena Gordon, sitting fidgeting in her chair like she was up before God at the Day of Judgment.

'At a working men's club in Sheffield,' Rowena admitted. 'They're really young, Josh. And they look really good.'

'Music sells music, kid,' Oberman growled. 'Remember that.'

She nodded hastily, but couldn't help adding. 'And they moved really well live . . . hardly anyone was there but they still played their guts out . . .'

'Where are they playing next?' Oberman asked casually.

'At the Retford Porterhouse,' Rowena told him. She leant forward on her seat. 'Josh, you've got to come and see them. Please.'

She groped for something he would understand. 'Look, they'll sell records in America,' she tried. 'I'm just sure of it.'

Josh Oberman raised an eyebrow. He'd grown up on the Brooklyn Heights, his career had spanned three continents, and for the past fifteen years he'd ruled the British record industry with a rod of beat-up platinum discs. In all that time he'd found exactly three European bands who'd had substantial success in America. Now there was a pretty little English rosebud sitting in his office, telling him she was *sure* this unknown act of hers would break in America.

The trouble was, he agreed with her.

'Listen to me, kid,' he growled. 'It's seven years since I've been to a fleapit rock concert. So you'd better be right about this, because I've got six companies to run here.'

Rowena took a deep breath. So she was gambling her

career. So what? If she couldn't get *these* boys signed, she was in the wrong industry.

'I'm right, Josh,' she insisted. 'If you don't agree, I'll quit.'

Oberman pretended to think about it. 'OK, Gordon. You have yourself a deal. I will neglect all the needs of the Musica group of companies in the UK and go see –'

'Atomic Mass.'

'Atomic Mass, right. And you should pray that they're good. Come pick me up tomorrow night, and don't bother to bring your car. We'll take a limo.'

What an incredible-looking girl, Oberman thought as he watched Rowena leave his office. All legs and hair and pouty lips.

He wished he was young enough to wish he could fuck her.

Rowena could hardly make it through Wednesday, she was so excited. And nervous. And hopeful. And scared.

If Josh didn't like them, that was the end of it. Forget about music. Forget about dropping out. It would be back to the drawing board, and a nice safe life as a lawyer or something.

But if he *did* like them—

She hardly dared think about it.

As soon as the time on her computer flashed 6.30, Rowena logged out, stood up and almost ran out of A&R to the president's office. She'd taken great care with her appearance this morning; black jeans, a tight black body to emphasize her minute waist, fashionable workmen's boots and a black leather jacket. A sexy look. A tough-girl look. She hoped she seemed like someone who knew a talented rock band when she heard one.

'Goddamn, what the hell are you wearing?' Oberman

demanded, thinking how hot she looked. The long blonde hair shimmering down her back was almost obscenely golden against the black leather.

'What's wrong with it?' Rowena asked, practically dragging her boss out to the lifts.

'You look like you're gonna mug me,' the old man grumbled, leading her towards his car.

Rowena took a step back. Of course, she was hardly unused to luxury. And she realized that the presidents of record companies don't drive Renault 5s. But this was something else. A liveried chauffeur holding open the back-seat door on a long, gleaming black monster that looked as if it had driven straight out of a Jackie Collins novel.

'Well, what are you gaping at?' Oberman demanded, secretly amused. The kid was half brilliant and half totally naive. 'Get in and quit wasting time. They're only the support act. You want me to miss them, or what?'

'No, no, sir,' Rowena said hastily, slipping into the back seat with a refined movement. Josh noticed that, too. So she was used to chauffeurs. Although she'd been dirt poor when he found her, and she was earning a pittance right now. Curiouser and curiouser, as Alice said in Wonderland.

He clambered in next to her and told his driver where to go, and the limo pulled smoothly out of the car park and melted into the early evening traffic.

Rowena glanced at her watch.

'Don't worry, kid, we'll get there,' Oberman said. 'Lewis is a good driver. Knows all the short cuts. Right, Roger?'

'Right, Mr Oberman,' the chauffeur answered briskly in a soft Welsh accent.

Rowena paid no attention. She was trying not to stare at the incredible array of equipment in Oberman's car.

Two phones. A fax machine. A television. A CD-player on a stack system. Discreet Surround Sound speakers built into the camel leather. An IBM computer and a drinks cabinet.

'The swimming pool's out back,' Oberman added dryly, and chuckled when she spun round. 'I do a lot of work in the car,' he explained. 'Works out cheaper than a second office.'

She nodded, trying not to feel that she was way, way out of her depth. What was she thinking of, dragging her boss out to a tiny, sweaty club in the provinces? That was her job, not his!

'OK,' Oberman said briskly. 'Tell me everything you remember about the first time you saw these guys play.'

The limo pulled up in a grimy street a couple of hours later. The summer evening sky was black with rain, and by the time she'd shown him across the road to the club they were both soaked to the skin. She stumbled into the entrance, drenched, and gave their names to the doorman, who insisted on making Oberman wait outside in the downpour while he laboriously searched the guest list. Rowena's heart sank. She could see that this gig was packed out with kids, no place for an old man to have to stand listening to a new act. And he was bound to be in a filthy mood at the weather and the delay.

'Yeah, all right,' the doorman yelled. 'Oberman, Joshua. 'E can go in.'

'Thank you,' Rowena yelled back, pulling her president inside.

'No readmittance,' the doorman added sourly.

Oberman's face was murderous.

Rowena swallowed hard and pushed through the open doors, grabbing her boss's hand and forcing a way through the slamming crowd, so they had somewhere to stand. It was tough going. She was used to metal crowds, but she was still a girl. And acting as a bodyguard for an old man was a tough gig. At least he's tall, Rowena thought gratefully, craning to see Atomic kicking up a storm on the tiny stage.

Josh Oberman watched the band in silence, a huge grin on his weatherbeaten face. He was pleased that Gordon couldn't see him. He didn't want to let her know how delighted he was with her.

In front of him, a bunch of five kids looking as though they were barely out of school were tearing up the little hothouse of a club as though the world would end tomorrow. Jesus, Oberman thought, the drummer looks like he's never fucking *shaved*. The songs were original and new and had an insistent beat, clever harmonies and a crashing bass. The front rows were a mass of flailing bodies, teenage boys slamming into one another, slick with sweat and rebellion.

They had passion.

They had music.

They had youth.

And, Joshua Zachary Oberman told himself when the house lights came up, they had a record deal.

'Come with me,' he said to Rowena. 'We're going backstage.'

Knowing better than to ask him to wait a few minutes, Rowena followed her boss round to the side, picking her way across puddles of beer and crushed styrofoam cups and flyers. The security guards spoke briefly to Josh, then ushered the two of them into a minute dressing room, where Atomic Mass, drenched in sweat and towelling off, looked at them questioningly.

'Hi, I'm Joshua Oberman, president of Musica Records,' Josh said.

Two cans of beer halted simultaneously in mid-air.

Oberman shoved Rowena forward, noting the appreciative glances the lads shot her. 'And this is Rowena Gordon, an A&R girl who works for me. She thinks we should give you a record deal. And so do I.'

Chapter Ten

In the sweltering heat of the *Westside* offices on Seventh Avenue, the phone rang on Topaz's desk.

'Rossi,' she said briskly.

'Topaz?' crackled the voice at the other end.

'*Rupert*?' shrieked Topaz, delighted. 'Rupe! How *are* you? Give me your number, I'll call you right back.'

'It's OK, I'm at the Union,' said Rupert, with the airy disregard of someone not paying the phone bill.

'How's it going down there?' she asked. The comparative peace and quiet of college seemed very attractive right now.

'I made editor,' said Rupert. 'James Robertson's President for Michaelmas Term; and Rod Clayton made another great speech.'

'Rod's great, I wish I'd been there,' sighed Topaz. Rod Clayton's speeches made her laugh till her stomach hurt. She glanced down at her piece on the demise of the Mets; no matter how hard she reworked it, it wouldn't come right. Much like the Mets, in fact. Topaz was a big Mets fan and she wasn't having history's best day.

'Anyway, I didn't call you about that,' Rupert went on. 'I called about Rowena.'

Topaz froze. 'What about Rowena?' she asked casually.

'Didn't you hear? You *must*'ve heard,' said Rupert

incredulously. 'First she just disappeared from sight for months. Then it turns out she's got a job at Musica Records, right, and she barges into the president's office or something and told him he was a prat. Apparently things like that get you big brownie points in the music business. Anyway, he goes to see this brilliant band she'd found and offers them a deal on the spot! So now he thinks Rowena's a genius, and he's making her AR or something – that means she gets to sign acts . . .'

Topaz Rossi had suddenly become oblivious to the flashing phone lights and deadlines and spewing fax machines and all the office chaos. She sat still as a statue. Rowena's success was a white-hot knife in her heart.

'Everyone at Oxford's taking bets on which of you guys is going to make it first,' Rupert went on. 'Someone faxed your *Westside* exposé of that bastard David Levine to *Cherwell* – we led on it! It was *unbelievable*, Topaz, even for you.'

'Thanks, Rupe,' said Topaz mechanically. 'It's going OK here.'

Then it dawned on her that this would get back to Rowena. 'In fact, I'm probably going to get a syndication deal,' she added quickly. 'I got creative control, I report direct to Nathan – he's the editor – and *Westside* just gave me my own column.'

'Bloody *hell*, Topaz!' said Rupert, astonished.

'I've even bought a little apartment,' said Topaz, 'so if you're ever in New York . . . it's on Clarkson Street in the Village . . .'

'In the *Village*?' spluttered Rupert. 'Are you rich, too?'

'I'm getting by,' said Topaz.

Choke on it, Rowena.

Nathan Rosen passed her office, flashing her a 'rescue me' look. A tall, thin, blonde woman in a fur coat was propelling him towards his own, one hand on his shoulder ostentatiously flashing a gold Rolex.

'Who is that?' hissed Elise to Topaz.

'No idea,' she whispered, shaking her head. 'Ask Jason.'

Elise buzzed Jason Richman.

'Don't you guys recognize her?' Jason asked. 'That's Marissa Matthews.'

'The gossip columnist?' demanded Elise in a strangled screech. Marissa Matthews' bitchy chronicles of New York high society made her the highest-read journalist in America.

'His ex-wife,' Jason added.

'His *what*?' gasped both women.

'Nathan was married?' asked Elise, who'd been at *Westside* two years.

'For seven years,' Jason said. 'He doesn't talk about his private life.'

'Jesus! You can say that again!' muttered Elise, twisting her own wedding ring.

Topaz was shocked at the wave of jealousy surging through her. Nathan Rosen was going to be hers. He'd resisted all her advances so far, but he'd see reason. They were having dinner this evening to talk about the column, and she had high hopes even for tonight.

'I'm getting him out of this,' she said to Elise, jumping out of her chair and striding across the floor to the editor's office.

'Topaz Rossi's on the warpath,' said one of the features subs to a secretary, catching sight of her face.

'So what else is new?'

'Baby!' Topaz purred, throwing open the editor's door. 'What time are we meeting up tonight? Oh, hi,' she added warmly to Marissa. 'I'm Topaz Rossi. I see you've met my boyfriend, but I don't think we've been introduced! Nathan, you're such a forgetful boy.'

She gave Marissa a dazzling smile.

Rosen suppressed a wild desire to laugh.

'Sweetheart, I don't think you've met my ex-wife, Marissa Matthews. Marissa, this is my girlfriend Topaz Rossi, a rising star at *Westside*,' he said pleasantly.

Marissa stared at her with a look that would have lowered the temperature at the North Pole as Topaz sauntered over to Nathan and ran her hand affectionately over the seat of his pants.

'Nathan and I were together for a very long time,' she informed Topaz acidly.

'Oh well! Shit happens, huh?' said Topaz, with a cheerful smile. 'Still, every cloud has a silver lining,' she added maliciously, standing on tiptoe to kiss Nathan's cheek, which she did slowly and luxuriantly, touching his rough skin with the hidden tip of her tongue.

Rosen felt flames of lust lick up and down his body.

Marissa's thin lips pursed in disapproval. *What a foulmouthed little Italian tramp!* 'I must be going, Nathan,' she snapped.

'Let's do lunch!' called Topaz after her retreating back, letting go of Nathan's hand reluctantly.

Rosen smiled at her, wondering how long he could hold out. She was just a child, damn it, and she worked for him. He absolutely must *not* take advantage of a young girl's crush.

'Thanks, Rossi,' he said. 'I owe you one. How's "NY Scene" coming along?'

'Great,' shrugged Topaz. 'I just spent a day in Central Park, interviewing everyone who used the carousel.'

'Sounds good,' Rosen nodded curtly, pleased because it did. 'We'll talk more at dinner.'

'Sure,' Topaz said, turning to go.

Work, work, work, she thought sadly. You never look at anything else, do you?

Rosen drove down Baxter Street into Little Italy.

'Where are we going?' demanded Topaz, pissed off because he hadn't noticed her low-cut dress.

'Silver Palace,' said Nathan, keeping his eyes locked on the road, as if that would help him forget about those incredible breasts staring him in the face. *Dear God, please don't let me get hard right in front of her.* 'I hear they have incredible dim sum.'

'I want Italian,' said Topaz mutinously.

'Well, I want Chinese,' replied Nathan amiably, 'and I'm paying.'

'You're the boss,' Topaz snapped.

He turned into Hester Street, heading for the Bowery, and ignored her.

Topaz watched the high tenement houses with their beautiful iron fire escapes slip past her. She felt more relaxed out of the office, in crowded Little Italy with its cafés and Chinese shops and almost European sense of clutter. Anyway, watching the scenery might take her mind off the close-shaven grey and black hair at the side of Nathan's head.

Miraculously, they got to the restaurant without another row.

'What do you want?' Nathan asked, as one of the dim sum carts wheeled its way across the packed floor towards them.

'Spring rolls, prawn dumplings, steamed pork dumplings,' said Topaz, somewhat reconciled to Chinese from the mouthwatering scent of the food all around them.

Nathan heaped his plate. He worked out three times a week, drank no alcohol, and considered good ice cream the ultimate human pleasure this side of sex, so he'd pig out if he damn well felt like it.

Talking of sex, he was getting hard for Rossi. Her skirt had blown up just a little as she'd climbed the stairs in front of him. He couldn't help himself.

'. . . and I think it'd be a great twist, you ask six celebrities what they read at school . . .'

'. . . that would be a winner, Nate, for the men's titles – "My Favourite One-Night Stand" by sportsmen . . .'

Rosen, making notes, choked on a spring roll. 'Rossi!' he protested, shocked.

'Why not? Sex sells, especially men's titles. And I think you should suggest a cover-mount CD for *White Light*. Some books tried it in England last year when I was at school, circulation quadrupled.'

Nathan jotted it down. It was fantastic, a never-ending torrent of ideas. Where did she get it all from? He'd talk to Harry Birnbaum about her, he'd have to. There was a vacancy for a features editor over at *US Woman*, and Topaz Rossi was obviously perfect for it. Whoever heard of a features editor with only one year's experience? Well, they were about to.

He watched her, leaning towards him, blue eyes sparkling with passionate enthusiasm.

'I thought we were gonna talk about "NY Scene", not what you'd do if you ran American Magazines,' he said weakly.

Topaz shrugged. 'You got a problem with "NY Scene"?'

'No.'

'We getting a good reader response?'

'Pretty good,' Nathan conceded. In fact, *Westside* had never seen so many letters.

'So what's to discuss?' demanded Topaz.

He looked at her. 'Young lady, I should take you across my knee and spank you.'

Topaz felt herself getting slick between the legs. 'Promises, promises,' she said, touching him with her shoe.

Nathan battled with himself. He was as hard as a rock. 'Quit that,' he said through gritted teeth.

'Quit what?' asked Topaz innocently.

They stared at each other for a long moment.

'I'll get the check,' murmured Topaz, jumping up and turning to the counter to pay. She almost ran down the stairs and out of the door, waiting for him. She needed to get him out of the crowded restaurant.

Rosen emerged on to the sidewalk two seconds later, grabbed her by the shoulders and backed her up against the wall.

Then he kissed her, his body stretched along hers, the hard weight of him pushing against her right there on the street, so her soft breasts were crushed into his chest and she could feel his erection.

Nathan softly prised her mouth open and ran the tip of his tongue along the underside of her top lip.

Topaz moaned.

He pulled away from her and stared into her eyes, wild and surprised and aroused and scared. 'Topaz Rossi,' he whispered in her ear, 'I'm going to fuck your brains out.'

Topaz sat rigid in the cab in the darkness, trying not to betray herself in front of the driver. Nathan had his left hand, hidden by her coat, in her panties, and was stroking her very gently with two fingers, relentlessly, back and forwards.

'We'll go to the American Magazines tower on Seventh, please,' he said casually. 'I got a little unfinished business at the office.'

The two of them walked into the marble lobby,

Nathan supporting Topaz while he collected his keys. Once the elevator door had shut he ran his hands all over her, barely able to restrain himself. Topaz was faint with desire. She was burning for him over her whole skin, her entire body sensitized to his touch. He put both his palms on the insides of her thighs, caressing her, tantalizingly close to her ass and her pussy but never quite touching them.

'Please, Nathan,' she gasped, '*please . . .'*

For answer he led her out of the elevator and across the deserted *Westside* office. Barely able to walk, Topaz stumbled after him.

Nathan opened his office but didn't bother flicking on the lights; the dull neon glow of New York at night was more than enough to see by. He looked round the room at his Eames chair and his files and his silent computer. Then he looked at Rossi, leaning against the door for support, squirming with longing for him. Rosen stared at her for a second, mesmerized by her; the flawless young skin, her lips wet and parted, the blue eyes liquid with desire.

Jesus Christ, she's every man's fantasy, Nathan thought, overwhelmed with lust. His cock was so hard he was starting to ache. He felt half frightened to touch her, unsure what she could do to him, where this would take him.

He'd sworn he wouldn't do this.

She'd shown him what she wanted.

He wondered who was seducing who.

'That's a nice dress,' he said hoarsely, 'but it'd look a lot better in a crumpled heap on the floor. Take your clothes off.'

Topaz stripped, her fingers fumbling from her heat. She saw Nathan Rosen gazing at her, transfixed. A new flush of sex rippled through her – look what she could do to him, look at the way he was staring. She unhooked her bra deliberately, delicately, letting him see the wisps of chocolate-coloured lace brush against her erect nipples, shrugging the tiny silk panties slowly off her thighs.

'Well?' Topaz asked insolently. She pirouetted for him, displaying herself, taunting him.

Rosen could hardly believe her body. His cock reared in his pants. 'Come here,' he breathed.

Topaz crossed the room and reached for him, sliding her hand across his fly, feeling the hardness of him through the denim. Nathan's rough hands gripped her shoulders, moving over the sleek skin, the pressure betraying his impatience. She reached for the buttons of his Levi's and undid them, slipping her hand over him, hard as flint, hot against her palm, and opened and closed her fingers around him in a smooth, fluttering movement, feeling him pulse under her touch, his breath catching in his throat.

Rosen moaned, harshly, utterly unable to control himself a second longer. He caressed her, squeezing her ass and stroking her firm full breasts with their exquisite swollen nipples, before turning her gently round and pushing her down over the desk.

A second later she felt him slide into her, in and out, in and out, and all her pent-up desire crystallized into a huge block and she looked round and saw Nathan behind her and above her, smiling, fucking her slowly, and she felt the sweet pressure spread out across her body and she started to come, feeling it in her fingers and toes, and her whole skin, convulsing in orgasm . . .

Chapter Eleven

Rowena Gordon leant back against the soft fabric of her seat as the plane dipped sharply in the sky, veering in to the landing approach. She craned her neck, trying to catch a glimpse of the Manhattan skyline spread out below her, full of threats and promises. At this very moment, a cab assigned to her would be pulling up at JFK. Waiting to take her to Mirror, Mirror, the famous, luxurious and totally exclusive New York studios. Nicknamed the 'Dream Factory'. Where good bands went to become great ones. Where stars went to become multi-platinum supernovas. Where a kind of weird magic descended on the recording of just a handful of albums each year, turning them into volcanic eruptions of sound that could blow you away even on a tinny home stereo. Magic that transformed your bedroom into Madison Square Gardens. That gave drums a wild kick, guitars a glittering distortion, vocals a savage precision, and shot your record to the top of the charts and the cover of *Rolling Stone*.

Because Mirror, Mirror was the studio where Michael Krebs recorded.

And Michael Krebs was the best producer in the world.

And Rowena had to have him.

At first she'd just been dreaming out loud. Things were going so well, after all: Josh had signed Atomic Mass, she'd got a big promotion and pay rise – and a nice new flat in Earl's Court, thank God – and the band were media darlings of the week. Their small shows became bigger shows. The bigger shows sold out. No less than five major acts offered them the support slot on their tours. And in the middle of all the excitement, the boys were keeping their heads screwed on and writing some incredible songs . . .

So Rowena had joked to Josh Oberman that they should get Michael Krebs to produce. Yeah, right. The *legendary* Michael Krebs. Who only ever worked with superstar bands, who was probably booked for a decade upfront, and who'd expect a couple of million dollars for his services alone.

Of course, a multi-platinum record can make six or seven million. So for a huge act, it wasn't unreasonable.

But Atomic Mass were a tiny new band, freshly signed, with not even a single to their name. And Rowena's budget was £100,000.

So it *was* a joke.

Christ Almighty, what am I doing here? she thought, smoothing her long blonde hair into a ponytail and trying to look cool, as though she flew Business Class to New York all the time. What am I going to say to him? A hundred and fifty thousand dollars? He'll laugh in my face. I'll probably crack a rib when his security goons throw me out on the pavement.

But that was Joshua Oberman for you! When the old guy liked an idea, he really liked an idea.

'You think Krebs should produce Atomic Mass?' he'd asked his protégée.

'Oh, sure,' Rowena grinned. She patted her demo

tapes like a proud mother. 'They're the best band around, they should have the best producer. And just as soon as I've saved up a spare million, we'll hire him for them.'

Oberman got up and padded around the soft carpet of his office, like a twitchy leopard.

'I know Michael from way back when,' he said suddenly. 'Gave him his first job when I was working for Elektra. In seventy-four. He'll see you if I ask him to.'

'Josh, you can't be serious,' Rowena protested. 'He'd cost more than ten times our budget for the whole thing!'

'We could go to a hundred and fifty thousand dollars,' Oberman replied with an air of reckless generosity.

'You must be –'

'No buts,' Oberman insisted. 'You fly to New York and meet with him. Take a demo. If he likes the stuff, he might do it for that money. Starting a band from scratch could appeal to Michael. He's a risk-taker. I'll have him send a cab to bring you to the studio, and I'll let you take it from there.'

'Boss, you are out of your mind. This will never work in a million years.'

Oberman looked across at her, with a strange expression. 'Atomic Mass are your band, Rowena,' he'd said. 'Make it work.'

'Can I take your champagne glass, ma'am?' asked a handsome steward in a gentle American accent. 'We'll be coming in to land in just a few moments.'

'Thank you,' Rowena said, startled out of her thoughts. God, she was really doing this! Coming to New York for the first time. Trying to pull off a deal with a superproducer. In person. By herself.

There it was, look! The Statue of Liberty!

'Oh God,' said Rowena out loud.

She had never felt so nervous in her life.

'What kind of business?' the customs officer asked pleasantly. Not that he gave a damn. The girl was obviously not a drugs smuggler, criminal or illegal immigrant, but as long as he could ask her questions he could enjoy the sight of her long, slender legs in those tight pants, the gentle swell of her breasts under the clinging Lycra body, her tumbling blonde hair, her almost obscenely sexy lips, soft, plump, with a slight natural pout that belied the businesslike jacket and smart briefcase.

'I have a meeting,' she replied, in crisp English tones. The officer brightened even more. What a babe. She sounded like Princess Diana, all haughty and impatient. Made him want to warm her up.

'With who?'

'With a producer.'

'Oh,' he said, glancing at her slyly. 'An actress, huh?'

Rowena shook her head, smiling. 'Not that kind of producer.'

'Well, welcome to the United States,' the guy said, sighing. Back to the grind. Fat tourists and screaming kids. Terrific . . .

Rowena, glad to have it over with, pushed her trolley through into the arrivals hall, praying that the Mirror cab hadn't given up on her and driven back. This was impossible enough without her annoying Michael Krebs. She peered through the throng of relatives, company reps and minicab drivers, jostling against the barrier with their little cardboard signs. Nothing. She checked again. Definitely no 'Gordon'. Damn! She'd have to call and explain . . .

'Ms Gordon?' asked a respectful voice.

She spun round, and was confronted with a tall chauffeur, decked out in full uniform – peaked cap, grey suit, the works.

'Yes, I am,' she answered, trying not to stare.

'Mr Oberman gave us a description, ma'am,' he explained, taking her trolley. 'If you'd like to follow me, I've got your limousine parked round the front. Mr Krebs wanted to know if you'd like to come and see him straight away, or if you'd prefer to go to the hotel first?'

'We should just go straight to the studios,' said Rowena. *A limo! Jesus Christ!* 'If it's convenient for Mr Krebs to see me now.'

The chauffeur touched his cap respectfully and led her to the exit, Rowena walking three paces behind him in the vague hope that everyone might stop staring at her. She couldn't believe this. It was a message to Musica from Krebs. When Oberman suggests he might send a cab, he responds . . . with . . .

Rowena, emerging into the bright sunlight, felt her mouth open in astonishment.

Parked in front of the regular car queue was the biggest, longest, most ecologically unsound car she'd ever laid eyes on. It stretched out in front of her, gleaming, polished and totally ostentatious. It had *three* back doors. The chauffeur was loading her suitcases into a vast trunk with infinite care, as if they were Louis Vuitton filled with the crown jewels instead of her scruffy T-shirts and Marks & Sparks pyjamas. As he walked round and held open the third of the back doors, she forced herself to stop gawping and try to behave naturally. What would Josh do? Probably wouldn't bat an eyelid.

A small knot of people had gathered outside the airport doors, watching the scene curiously. Rowena felt centuries of gentlemanly Scottish restraint screaming in protest at such vulgarity. She blushed scarlet and hastily clambered into the car, shutting the doors, thankful that this monster came with one-way mirrored glass. At least nobody could see who it was in here. They'd probably assume it was Madonna . . .

Forty minutes later, she'd relaxed a little. The car was so smooth it felt as though they were floating. She'd called London from the in-car phone, switched on the TV and tuned it to MTV – wherever you go in the world, some things stay the same – and pulled out her Walkman. *Remind yourself why you're here.*

Atomic Mass's newest, best demo flooded into her head as they spun through midtown Manhattan. Dazzled by the beauty of the city – soaring skyscrapers, vast neon bill-boards – she settled into her leather seat and just let herself enjoy it. Oh, she could get used to this, Rowena thought, as they turned off Times Square, heading for the studios. So what if Krebs wanted to send a limo? He might still agree to $150,000 for a new band. After all, they *were* very good. And like Josh said, he was a risk-taker.

A little voice inside her head said she had to be kidding.

There was no way this was gonna work.

And Oberman had told her to *make* it work.

Jesus.

The limo purred to a halt. Rowena switched off her music and looked outside; they'd stopped in front of a square, low-slung, black granite building.

'We're here, ma'am,' the chauffeur announced. 'If you care to go inside, I'll take your cases on to the hotel for you.'

'Thank you,' said Rowena, nervously overtipping him $20 and stepping outside.

Her reflection gazed back at her from the car: hair long and tousled, eyes tired from the flight. She should have freshened up at the hotel first. Oh well. Too late now!

Rowena took a deep breath and walked into the reception area, automatic doors hissing open in front of her. The studio lobby was decorated in sumptuous apricot tones, a Persian rug spread on the carpet, dark mahogany furniture everywhere, soft lighting arrangements on the ceiling and walls giving an instantly soothing effect, and a kidney-shaped reception desk bearing a huge crystal vase crammed full of white roses.

'Can I help you?' asked the immaculately dressed receptionist, giving Rowena a disapproving once-over. She felt hopelessly awkward, standing in this bloody palace in her crumpled clothes, with her two-bit little demo tape and pocket-change offer for Michael Krebs. Lord, even his receptionists wore Chanel.

'I'm here to see Mr Krebs,' she said, as confidently as she could. 'He's expecting me. My name is Rowena Gordon, from Musica Records in London.'

The girl tapped the name into her computer and gave Rowena a more friendly look. 'Yes, ma'am. I'll just let him know you're here.'

She spoke quietly into an internal phone, then turned back to her. 'That's fine. If you want to walk right through those doors, someone will meet you and escort you up to his office,' she added, giving Rowena the benefit of several thousand dollars' worth of cosmetic dentistry. Rowena nodded briskly and went though into the main recording complex, feeling her heartbeat speeding up.

Come on. You can do this.

'Ms Gordon?' asked another polite minion. 'If you'll just step this way –' and Rowena followed the guy through three studios to the main office, where he held open the door for her with a beaming smile.

Rowena tucked her hair back behind her ears and stepped into the producer's office. It was a large room all gleaming chrome, black leather and hi-tech luxury. Michael Krebs was working on something at a desk made entirely of cut glass, heaped with phones, faxes, an expensive-looking IBM and a range of sound equipment.

Her heart sank. Offering this guy $150,000 would be an insult. But that was her goddamn budget! As far as her boss would go . . .

'Michael Krebs?' she asked.

He stood up, punched a few keys on his computer and turned round to her, smiling.

'Rowena, good to see you,' Krebs said, walking over to her and shaking her hand warmly. She noticed the way his eyes ran quickly over her body, checking her out. 'Josh Oberman's a big fan of yours. Told me everything about you, except why you're here.'

'I'm grateful you could find time to fit me in,' Rowena replied. 'And thank you for the car.'

She was dismayed to find herself blushing. Oh, God! Why hadn't she gone to the hotel and changed first? He was absolutely, totally drop-dead gorgeous.

Michael Krebs was in his early forties, about twenty years older than her. He was tall, muscular and lean, with intelligent black eyes and grey hair round his temples. He carried himself with a natural air of total confidence and power; Rowena noticed he was wearing a sweatshirt, jeans and sneakers, no Rolex or jewellery or any kind of status symbol. Even these magnificent offices had no gold or platinum discs anywhere in sight, and she knew he could have wallpapered the entire complex with them if he'd wanted to. Everything about him said *I don't need to boast.*

But it was the eyes that she couldn't get over; mesmeric, gripping eyes, fringed with the most incredible thick dark lashes, lush as a woman's. She could not break his gaze. She felt transparent, as if he could see right through her.

A small point of sexual heat started to burn between Rowena's legs.

'The car? That was nothing. We keep some on-site for the acts that record here,' Michael said. He waved to the black leather couch. 'Won't you have a seat? I hate to keep you standing up. You must be exhausted.'

'Thanks,' she said, sitting down and reaching for her demo. She felt sick with nerves. Michael Krebs was a world-class producer, and she'd flown across the Atlantic to ask him to work with a totally unknown act with a Mickey Mouse budget. She didn't know where to start.

Krebs pulled a chair up opposite her and sat down, completely relaxed. What a great-looking girl. Fantastic hair. Very sensual lips. He had a brief vision of her giving head with those lips. And *endless* legs, Jesus, a guy could get lost in there. Almost made him wish he was single. It was too cute, the way she was obviously completely terrified and doing such a lousy job of hiding it. Poor kid, Oberman had probably got some crazy idea into his head and sent a stunning babe over here to do his dirty work for him.

What had the old buzzard said? That this kid was bright, ballsy and a great talent scout? 'A natural feel for rock music,' wasn't that it?

Looking like that? *Sure*.

'To what do I owe the pleasure?' he asked gently.

Rowena started, and fished in her bag for the demo tape. She held it out to him. 'We'd like you to produce this band we've signed,' she said. 'We think you'd be perfect for them. They're called Atomic Mass.'

Michael Krebs shook his head, perplexed. 'Atomic Mass? Doesn't ring any bells,' he said. 'I must've blanked out. Remind me what their last album was called.'

Rowena swallowed hard. 'They've never made a record,' she replied. 'This would be the first.'

He stared at her. 'Oberman wants *me* to work on a *baby act*? Now I've heard everything,' he said. 'He's gonna spend that kind of money on a new band?'

Oh, God, thought Rowena. 'We could offer you' – *Josh will* kill *me* – 'two hundred thousand dollars.'

Krebs, amazed, broke into a huge grin. 'Did I hear you right? Two hundred thousand?'

Rowena nodded. She was still clutching her little demo like an idiot. He hadn't bothered to take it from her.

'Ms Gordon, you've been misinformed,' Krebs told her. 'I do have a space in my schedule for the next two months, but the price is a million. At *least*. And I never work with unestablished bands.'

'But wouldn't you like to break a new act? From scratch? I thought you were a risk-taker, Mr Krebs,' Rowena said, rather coldly. To her surprise she was getting angry. How could he just dismiss Atomic like that when he hadn't even heard them?

Michael heard the challenge in her voice. Interesting. Maybe the girl did have some balls after all.

'I used to do that. But times have changed,' he answered, equally coldly. 'And the price is one million dollars, minimum.'

'We don't *have* a million.'

'I wouldn't get out of bed for two hundred thousand.'

Rowena stood up, furious.

Too bad Oberman hadn't bothered to explain the rules of the game to the girl, Michael thought. She seemed smart and passionate. He'd give a good report of her back to Josh when he rang him up to yell at him for wasting his time. But that was Oberman for you; the guy was completely fucking insane, he played by his own rules.

'I'm sorry you've had a wasted trip,' he said, smiling at her.

Rowena lost her temper. 'Times *have* changed, haven't they? You used to be a hero, Mr Krebs. A real visionary. Christ, I had articles about you on my walls at college. It's incredible what a few platinum records will do, isn't it?'

She threw the demo at him. 'Take it, it's a present. Might remind you what a bunch of teenagers who give a damn are capable of. But I guess you don't care about music any more. Just the chinging of cash tills, right?'

She sprang to her feet. 'Don't bother to get up. I'll show myself out.'

Astonished, Michael Krebs watched her go.

Rowena turned round in the shower, letting the hard jets of water pummel her neck and shoulders, massaging away the strains in her muscles. She pushed her long wet hair down her back, squeezing the conditioner out of it, rinsing it clean.

There's nothing like washing your hair to refresh you, she thought, switching the water off and pulling on one of the hotel's soft white bathrobes. The shower had made her whole body feel alive again, her nipples hard from the cool air of the room, her skin warm and vital. She would definitely go out tonight. She'd slept, and she felt good. Maybe she'd buy a copy of the *Village Voice* in the lobby and check out what bands were playing.

Rowena had one night in New York. She wasn't going to waste it sitting in her room. Outside her window, Manhattan stretched in front of her, sparkling in the night, traffic moving through the gridlike roads in melting rivers of light. It was exciting and alive. She wanted to move into the slipstream, to be part of it.

There was a loud knock on the door.

'Come in,' Rowena yelled, belting her robe. Great. She was starving. She'd ordered a huge pastrami sandwich on rye and a chilled beer – when in Rome, after all . . .

'Hello again,' Michael Krebs said, walking in.

Rowena jumped out of her skin, automatically clutching the bathrobe tighter around her. 'What are you doing here?' she gasped.

'We had the hotel address, remember? We sent your luggage ahead of you,' he reminded her. 'I thought I better come and see you before you flew back.'

She didn't reply.

'You know, it's been a long time since somebody told me to go to hell,' Krebs remarked, glancing at the slim lines of her body under the robe. *Stop that!* he ordered himself. 'Oberman said you were pushy. He wasn't wrong.'

Rowena, embarrassed, started to apologize, but the producer cut her off. 'So I listened to your band. I was curious,' he said. 'They're pretty good.'

'Yes they are,' she agreed, holding her breath. Was he about to say what she hoped he was?

'OK, I'll do it,' Michael Krebs told her, black eyes glittering. 'But not for two hundred thousand. If I'm gonna chance working with these boys, I want a stake in their future. Musica doesn't pay me at all, but I get a five per cent royalty. Of the gross.'

'Five per cent gross? That could be a lot of money,' Rowena countered, trying to contain her excitement.

Krebs looked at her. 'Don't push it, kid. Do we have a deal, or what?'

'Yes, sir,' Rowena said, feeling triumph flood through her. 'Thank you, Mr Krebs. I'm sure you won't regret it.'

Michael Krebs! Michael *Krebs* was going to produce Atomic Mass! It was the coup of the fucking century!

'I'd better not. And you can call me Michael,' Krebs said, enjoying her reaction. He checked her out again. His wife was visiting her parents this week, and he didn't have to get home. And this girl was intriguing him; talented, brave, smart, a little reckless . . . Well, he rationalized, I'm working with her now.

'Why don't you get dressed, Rowena?' he said. 'I'll show you New York.'

Chapter Twelve

'So it's between those two, then,' the chairman concluded, toying with one of the files on his desk.

'I would have said so.'

Nathan Rosen stared out of the glass walls of the
penthouse office, somewhat uneasily. He didn't normally suffer from vertigo, but this was the sixtieth floor,
the summit of the American Magazines tower. It was a
famous quirk of Matt Gowers, the CEO, that the walls of
the top floor should be three feet of clear glass, so he
could survey the whole of New York, right out to the
ocean. 'Because journalism is observation,' Gowers had
reportedly said.

Nathan Rosen was new to the American Magazines
board, and he wasn't used to the effect. Anyway, he
preferred to convince himself it was the view that made
him nervous, not the fact that he was secretly dating one
of the candidates he was recommending to his boss.

'Kind of young, aren't they?' Gowers commented.

Joe Goldstein was thirty; Topaz Rossi, twenty-three.

'Yes, sir. Child prodigies,' Nathan smiled, only forty-
one himself. 'But they've both proved they can run
magazines. Circulation and revenue are up and costs are
down on all the books they cover.'

Gowers nodded, acknowledging this. 'I have a lot of

money riding on this project.'

'Yes, sir, I know.'

'Joe Goldstein's got an MBA, from Wharton,' said the chairman. 'Does Rossi?'

'She's completing her first year. She's taking a course in the evenings and at weekends, doesn't want to take time out from the job.'

'Is the programme Ivy League accredited?'

'Yes it is.'

Gowers considered this. 'That's a good attitude,' he said. 'That's good. Have these two kids met each other yet?'

'No. Goldstein's only just moved to New York. He used to work out of the Los Angeles office.'

'Get them together, Nathan,' the chairman ordered. 'They've got a right to check out the competition.'

Joe Goldstein was in a bad mood.

I just don't want this shit, he thought angrily. I don't need any of this bullshit. It's not like we have time to waste here.

He fiddled aimlessly with an already perfect bow tie. God, he hated wearing a tux. It made him feel stiff and awkward, and he thought he looked like a waiter. But you don't turn down an invitation to dinner with Nathan Rosen, director of American Magazines, East Coast. And if it says 'Black Tie,' you wear black tie.

A handsome and annoyed young man glared back at him from the mirror. Joe regarded his reflection coolly, his impassive gaze sweeping across the jet-black hair trimmed ruthlessly short, the dark, intense eyes flecked with silver, the broad, clean-shaven jaw. Goldstein was darkly attractive, his smooth skin tanned to a deep brown from the California sun, and he had a muscled chest and long sturdy legs, uncomfortably encased in stiff black linen. He frowned.

At thirty Joe Goldstein was resolutely single, and doing a pretty good impression of the Man Who Had Everything. He had been born the eldest of four sons to a moderately wealthy Massachusetts retailer, and the power and responsibility of being a big brother had lent him the air of someone who naturally expects to be put in charge. Joe had been ambitious all his life. He'd excelled in high school, firstly to show his brothers, Cliff, Martin and Sam, how to do it, and later because excelling had become second nature. Joe Goldstein made straight As, was a quarterback in the football team, and was voted 'Most Likely to Succeed' three years running. His parents, who believed in hard work, God and family values, set standards for their eldest son which he followed almost absolutely.

Joe helped old people across the road, gave part of his allowance to charity every week, and stood when a lady entered the room. Only two things prevented Goldstein from being a caricature of the perfect Republican All-American boy: first he was Jewish; second, he was an inveterate womanizer.

The Goldstein boys had been sent to a private school that stretched the limits of what their parents could afford. It was an old, prestigious establishment, and although they were not the only non-Christian pupils attending, they were part of a tiny minority, swamped in a sea of rich Boston kids with trust funds and establishment backgrounds. Joe never felt completely secure there. One day he went to check on his youngest brother, Sam, then aged six, and saw him sobbing in a corner of the playground. Some older boys were kicking and punching him and shouting abuse. The eldest was repeatedly giving the Nazi salute, and appeared to be trying to force little Sam to do the same. Joe tore across the concrete.

He was seventeen, twice as big as any of them, and

when he crashed into the group they instantly laid off his baby brother and looked terrified.

Two of them burst into tears. The ringleader, a fourteen-year-old, spat at him. 'Kike,' he said.

He gave the Nazi salute, right in Goldstein's face. He wasn't about to worry over a punch or two. Everyone knew what the Yid quarterback was like; he wouldn't really hurt a kid half his size.

Joe glanced at his brother. 'You OK?' he asked.

Sam snuffled yes.

Joe grabbed hold of the ringleader's right wrist and held it in a vicelike grip. He turned to the other bullies, who were watching horrified.

'This is what kikes do to fascists,' he said.

Then he broke his arm.

None of them were bothered again, but Joe never forgot that incident. He ceased making any attempt to fit in socially with people he despised. From then on, he became highly selective of his friends, choosing to spend time only with the boys whose morals and dedication matched his own. Academic achievement became a matter of pride, too. Joe worked harder and won bigger, as if proving his worth to himself. His only distractions were sport, and later, women.

Girls came easily to Goldstein from puberty onwards, and he took full advantage of the situation. He used to tell himself it was because he was a football player, but once he reached Harvard and turned to the *Lampoon* instead of the sportsfield, the flow of women did not dry up. Nor did it dry up once he graduated *cum laude* and lunged straight into Wharton Business School.

And Joe indulged. Why not? He was good-looking, muscular and well-endowed. He was also, more importantly, a skilful, sensitive lover who took care that his partners were pleased. He practised safe sex and was upfront about what he wanted. Joe had a strictly defined set of rules: he didn't get involved with girls who got involved. He liked female company, he liked sleeping with women, but that was it, and he made that clear. And even under those conditions they flocked to him, Jewish girls and shiksas, white girls and black girls, Asian girls and Hispanics. Joe didn't discriminate. He just liked women, all kinds of women.

There was only one type of girl Goldstein didn't get on with, and certainly didn't want in his bed, and that was the driven, aggressive career woman. He thought feminism was OK, to a degree – that is, he thought ladies should be *respected*. But he didn't like women who pretended to be men. Joe admired compassion and nurturing in women; protecting and providing he reserved for himself. His old-fashioned values ran all the way down the line. He thought Naomi Wolf's *The Beauty Myth* was a bunch of hysterical nonsense. He knew a lot of men privately agreed with him.

Joe Goldstein had turned out a nice guy, but a sexist.

Joe did *not* like women like Topaz Rossi. He didn't like having to eat dinner with them. And he particularly didn't like having to pretend to compete with them for the managing director's job on a new, upmarket economic title. A man's title. A title clearly earmarked for him, but one he'd have to pretend to compete for, so American Magazines could look politically correct.

He hated to waste time.

Topaz sighed. 'God,' she remarked to a pigeon, 'I envy that guy.'

She'd never met Joe Goldstein and didn't know much about him. One thing she was certain of, however, he was a man. Therefore he was to be envied at times like these. For Nate and Mr Goldstein, 'Black Tie' were two simple words, not a command to strike fear into the soul.

She twisted round in her sixth outfit, wondering if this would do. She was wearing a short skirt of supple brushed leather from Norma Kamali, a chocolate-brown silk shirt from DKNY, and slingback mules from St Laurent. A mixed heap of gold bangles jingled on her right arm, and her slender legs shimmered in light-reflecting hose from Wolford's. It was an aggressive, expensive look, the sexy-but-businesslike style that was the height of fashion at the moment. And after all, fashion was what she did for a living, so looking good and looking professional were synonymous for her these days.

Outside her window, Central Park shone green and gold, bathed in the evening sun. Topaz permitted herself a smile. Even by New York standards, her rise had been meteoric. She'd only been features editor of *US Woman* for a few months before the managing editor's job at *Girlfriend* magazine fell vacant when the boss left to get married. At first, Topaz hadn't even considered applying. She'd only just got a major promotion, and anyway, nobody gets to run a flagship teen title at twenty-three. But then the board had announced internally that they were opening the vacancy to group tender; any executive or senior enough editor could pitch for it, anonymously, by submitting a blind portfolio of ideas, covering everything from layout to advertising strategies to subscriptions. The portfolios would be anonymous, so, like an exam, the judges would not know whom they'd liked or disliked until the results were out.

The initiative had come direct from the chief executive, Mr Gowers. It was an attempt to bolster internal competition, and Topaz realized that as a features editor, she was eligible to apply – and nobody would know if she failed.

She changed her mind. For two months she immersed herself in teen fiction, teen music, teen television and hundreds of teenage magazines. She researched statistics on box-office young audience figures and called account executives at fifteen major advertising agencies. She worked nights and weekends and told nobody she was pitching, not even Nathan.

The dummy issue she came up with was dynamite, a mixture of baby feminism, cheap makeover ideas, New Kids on the Block and Sega games. The accompanying dossier of financial projections and consumer profiles was eighteen pages of taut research.

Topaz's submission was outstanding, so much the best it wasn't even funny. She became the youngest managing editor in the history of the group, and within six months the new-look *Girlfriend* had increased its market share by 16 per cent.

She was beautiful, successful, and just twenty-three years old.

She became a media property herself, although Nathan, on his way to the board and once again her immediate superior, forbade her to agree to a *Vanity Fair* profile. 'Sell magazines for American, not Condé Nast,' he said.

Oh yeah? thought Topaz to herself, adjusting a cuff. Somehow she suspected the new director had a more personal reason for wanting the spotlight away from her vicinity. And that attitude presented her with a big problem, one she would soon have to turn her attention to.

But forget about that, for now. Tonight was not about her personal life. When it was announced that American would be looking for an editor for *Economic Monthly* from inside the company, Topaz had spent two whole weeks on her application. She had no experience of finance, or men's magazines, but she put her ideas across with such passion and clarity that Nathan *had* to put her forward to Gowers. Although he'd made it clear that the other contender was by far the favourite.

So tonight was about this Goldstein guy, and the formidable opposition he represented to her next step up the ladder. Because Topaz was determined to prove that a woman was good for more than one woman's title. She wanted to demonstrate that she was an all-rounder.

She wanted to be a *player*.

She wanted *Economic Monthly*.

Nathan Rosen, the newest director of American Magazines, prayed Topaz would behave herself. She was the only element in his life he couldn't control.

He paced round his apartment, checking for the millionth time the immaculate table setting of Irish linen and Italian glassware. He forced himself to take a deep breath, and looked round the drawing room, finding some comfort in the emblems of his success all around him – the marble fireplace, the small Cézanne hanging above the Chippendale cabinet. The place was a model of discreet bachelor luxury, from the soft, buttery leather armchairs to the wafer thin stereo system, currently playing 'Eine Kleine Nachtmusik'. This was one of the most exclusive co-ops on the Upper East Side.

Not bad for forty-one, Nathan reminded himself. I can handle Rossi.

He stopped pacing and smiled. Maybe that last thought could have been better phrased. It was his inability to *stop* handling Topaz that was causing him problems.

Rosen had been seeing Topaz ever since that wild night when he fucked her over the desk in the *Westside* editor's office. He couldn't help himself. To this day, he could remember her teasing over that meal, taunting him with her body and her beauty, challenging him to come and take her. Well, he had, and it'd been fantastic. It had been the best sex he'd ever known. Nathan had no doubt at all that half the pleasure of that night had derived from the fact that he'd been fighting his desire for Topaz from the moment she'd walked into his office.

The million reasons why he shouldn't have fucked her then remained just as true now – she was so young, he was her boss. And if anything, they seemed to have been amplified by time. There was a larger downside too, given that those two years had seen her make editor of one magazine, and him become a director, with responsibility for New York and the rest of the East Coast.

Which led to situations like this. Where he, Nathan, was going to sit on a panel choosing between two candidates. And he was dating one of them.

Topaz told him the simple answer was to just admit it. To see her publicly. To tell Matt Gowers that they were lovers, and see what the CEO said about it, which she insisted would be nothing at all.

Nathan wasn't so sure.

And the fact was, he was totally embarrassed about becoming a living cliché – 41-year-old man with his 23-year-old girlfriend. What did they call them? Jennifers, yeah, that was it. It was the modern equivalent of wearing a T-shirt saying MIDLIFE CRISIS IN PROGRESS! And he was *not* having a goddamn midlife crisis! He was doing very well and he knew exactly where he was going – two doors down the hall, to Matt Gowers' office. By the time he was fifty-four, he thought his life's ambition would be within his reach.

On the other hand, he couldn't give Topaz up. She was no Jennifer, no dumb ditzy blonde. She was one hell of a strong, confident girl, and a natural print woman.

Her intelligence and enthusiasm charmed the pants off him. So to speak. Oh God, the sex . . . he couldn't help being pleased that she wanted him, when he knew for a fact that half the guys in the company would give a month's wages to touch her breasts *once*. She had evolved sexually too: she would throw him down on a bed, mount him and walk out when she'd finished, just as often as she wanted him to dominate. Topaz needed variety and experimentation. Which was partly why he stayed so hot for her.

He was going to have to make a decision; she'd said to him last week that she either moved in or moved on. God Almighty! Rosen thought. To have Topaz around all the time . . . that red hair, those creamy breasts, everything about her that drove him nuts, wandering around this place all the time. And she'd need satisfying, *all the time* . . .

The idea was breathtaking!

The idea was terrifying!

He'd asked for grace, to be allowed to think about it after this selection process, but she refused flat out. 'What you and I do out of hours has nothing to do with business,' she said. He could see her clearly right now, moving closer to him, her hand on his thigh, pushing that tricky, sexy, maddening tongue into his ear.

'I can't be patient. I want you. I *love* you,' she whispered, and Nathan Rosen had felt the familiar silver tendrils of desire trawl across his body, sending little hooks and claws digging into his groin, and he'd had to get her out of the office.

He passed a hand through his greying hair, unsure whether to be furious or elated. Man, he never thought he'd be going through this again. Checking into hotels at lunchtime because his need for a woman was so urgent he couldn't wait.

The selection procedure, Rosen, Nate reminded himself, dragging his thoughts back to this dinner. Maybe that would enable him to prove to the board that there was no undue favouritism going on here, because, he was certain, he'd be voting for Joe Goldstein. A new title like *Economic Monthly* was *designed* to be run by somebody like Joe. Rosen didn't think that Topaz, smart though she was, talented as she had proved herself to be, was yet ready for a serious, big-budget, male-orientated title like this one, and Nathan planned to vote impartially for the best candidate for the job.

And unless Joe really screwed his application up, that would not be Topaz Rossi.

She wouldn't hold it against him. She was fair where business matters were concerned. His only worry was that she'd tease him in front of Joe, let something slip. If that happened, his relationship with Goldstein, which he valued, would be jeopardized.

The doorbell rang. *Oh God*, Nathan Rosen thought.

He let his guests in, Joe just before Topaz. They had arrived within seconds of each other.

'Nate Rosen,' Joe greeted his old friend.

'Hey, Joe, how are you finding Manhattan?' Nathan welcomed his first discovery, grasping him in a bear hug.

Rosen had first noticed Goldstein at the *Lampoon* and hired him while he was still at Wharton, to work in the finance division of two titles. Goldstein had been another sensational success. Nathan smiled at his friend; what a great talent-spotter I am, he thought complacently. He had no doubt that Joe would be as brilliant a manager of the new title as he already was of *American Scientist, Executive Officer* and *Week in Review*.

'Hi, Topaz,' he added.

He wished she'd gone for something a little more

formal; the best he could hope for was that she'd make a useful friend and ally in Joe. She could learn a good deal from him, he had a grasp of formal business strategies that were outside Topaz's experience. He doubted Goldstein would approve of this look for a businesswoman; it was too feminine, too distracting.

Well, it was distracting *him*, goddamnit.

'Joe Goldstein, meet Topaz Rossi, our managing editor at *Girlfriend*,' Rosen introduced them. 'I know you've seen Joe's résumé, Topaz.'

'Nice to meet you,' said Topaz, offering Joe her hand to shake. Why hadn't he been sent *her* résumé? She sized him up. Handsome, muscular, pleased with himself. She disliked him on sight.

Goldstein shook hands with her briskly, suppressing his annoyance. He was being asked to compete with *this*? The girl was barely out of diapers, and just look at that skirt. No need to ask how she'd got this far this young. He'd never seen so much T&A in all his life.

'How do you do,' he said.

Nathan handed them both a glass of champagne. 'Let's eat,' he suggested.

They sat down to a starter of Jerusalem artichokes with asparagus butter.

'So, Ms Rossi,' Joe said. 'Do you know much about economics?'

Rosen shrank in his chair. *Oh no. Oh no. Please, no . . .*

'Why wouldn't I know about economics, Mr Goldstein?' asked Topaz, angered by his tone. 'Because I'm a woman?'

Not only a bimbo, thought Joe, a militant feminist bimbo. Wonderful! OK, you want the gloves off, cutie? Fine.

'It was an innocent question, Ms Rossi. Perhaps you'd

prefer it if I were more specific. What nation do you see as having the greatest potential for growth in the next five years?' he enquired, waiting indifferently for the inevitable reply: 'Japan'.

Topaz considered for a few seconds. 'Korea,' she replied. 'Although the question's way too general. How can anyone accurately predict where we'll be in two years, let alone five?'

Joe was surprised, but caught himself. So she'd read a few back issues of *The Economist*. So what?

He decided to play hardball. 'Korea is yesterday's news,' he said. 'You should be looking to China. Growth rates indicate –'

'Yesterday's news!' Topaz interrupted. 'I'll tell you what's yesterday's news: looking at the provinces which border Hong Kong and assuming that the rest of China can get just as rich just as quick, without the whole economy totally overheating –'

'There's nothing to stop it from doing so,' Joe snapped. 'But doubtless fashion shoots in Beijing have made you an expert.'

Topaz flushed. She knew all Goldstein's existing titles were aimed at the exact same market as *Economic Monthly*, totally unlike her own. 'I'm an expert at selling magazines,' she retorted.

Unnoticed to either of them, Nathan had sunk his head in his hands.

He'd *known* this damn dinner was a stupid idea.

'Well, Rosen, how did they get along?' Gowers asked.

'I – I think it's safe to say that there will be a healthy spirit of competition for this title, sir,' said his director.

The chairman chuckled. 'Fireworks, were there?'

'It was the Fourth of July, sir,' said Nathan.

*

Over the next two months, the battle for *Economic Monthly* became the American Magazines spectator sport of choice. Joe and Topaz were scrupulously polite to each other at management meetings, but that was the extent of their co-operation. People were fascinated by the open rivalry, and betting on the board's decision became a minor cottage industry, although after the first week nobody would accept a bet on Goldstein, even at 15 to 1 on. Only the staff of *Girlfriend*, *US Woman* and a few *Westside* reporters, who'd watched their former colleague pull off wildly improbable promotions twice already, would risk putting money on Topaz. Joe Goldstein, after all, was five years older, had his MBA, and ran three books to Topaz's one – all of them pitched at the educated, affluent male.

The more Joe saw of Topaz Rossi, the less he liked her. At the second editors' meeting they attended together, she chewed him out for opening the door for her. Goldstein hardened his resolve. So be it. As far as he was concerned, she had now renounced all special considera-tion to which a lady was entitled.

Topaz took her seat, laughing inwardly at Goldstein's face when she'd flown at him. She did it on purpose to annoy him. Goldstein was the worst type of jerk; he put women on pedestals and gave them no real respect at all. And on top of her dislike for his attitude problem, she was well aware that the whole building thought that *Economic Monthly* was as good as assigned to Joe already. They dismissed her chances, and she blamed him for that.

Early in the meeting, Jason Richman, who'd replaced Rosen as *Westside*'s editor, discussed his forthcoming series on leading women clergy.

Joe laughed. 'As Dr Johnson remarked,' he said, ' "a woman's preaching is like a dog's walking on his hinder legs. It is not done well; but you are surprised to find it done at all." '

There was a hush around the table as the execs waited to see if Topaz Rossi would come back. She didn't disappoint them.

'As Topaz Rossi remarked,' she mimicked him. 'Dr Johnson was a stupid asshole who probably couldn't get it up.'

There was laughter.

'Why don't you just back off, and save us both some time?' Joe murmured to Topaz when they left the room.

'Go fuck yourself,' she hissed. 'I could do the job just as well as you.'

'Oh, don't worry, honey,' said Joe. 'There's a place for you at *Economic Monthly* – I've always got room for an assistant with a cute tush.'

He patted her on the backside and walked out, leaving Topaz speechless with fury.

The next morning, *Executive Officer* began running the first in a series of in-depth profiles of leading economic figures; Joe Goldstein, the managing editor, was personally interviewing Alan Greenspan of the Federal Reserve. The article received wide acclaim, and was discussed on WHRT's *Good Morning Manhattan*.

Topaz Rossi and Joe Goldstein would present to the board in six weeks' time.

Chapter Thirteen

'Let's look at the situation,' Joshua Oberman said.

He pointed to the bright graphics on the presentation stand, showing the board of Musica Records what they wanted to see. Profits were up. Costs were down. And for the first time in years, Musica had some promising new acts.

'We can be happy with the results we have now,' he told them. 'Sam Neil and Rowena Gordon have each signed three good acts. Sam prefers to concentrate on mainstream pop, and Rowena has managed to find us talent from various' – he groped for the formal marketing term – 'niche sectors. Her soul singer, Roxana Perdita, had a debut album that went silver, and a rave act, Bitter Spice, has the number eight single this week.'

Blank faces greeted this summary around the table. Oberman sighed inwardly. Why did he bother? The bottom line was the only music to their ears.

'And Sam's bands have done equally well,' he concluded. 'But I feel that we are losing market share by limiting our search for talent to England and Europe.'

'But we have no base in America,' objected Maurice LeBec, President of Musica France.

'Which is what I propose to set up,' Joshua replied. 'It's true that we've always been a European company.

But being the only major label in the world *not* to have a base in the States is becoming a liability.'

Hans Bauer, President of Musica Holland, sniffed sceptically.

Josh took his meaning at once. *You would say that. You're an American.* Bauer was his main rival for the job of chairman of Musica Worldwide, when John Watson retired next year.

'Gentlemen,' the old man went on, 'I need hardly remind you that only the English company has successfully found any new acts that sold albums last year. Now I have an executive with a particular gift for developing offbeat talent. Just the sort of talent that's crowding New York. And for her to operate properly she needs a company base there. I don't want to lease her out to Warners or PolyGram and have them poach her.'

'How much will this cost?' the chairman asked.

Oberman named a figure.

'That's a lot of money,' Hans said disapprovingly.

'We could make it back off three big records.'

'Just how talented is this girl, Joshua?' the chairman asked.

Oberman smiled at his boss. 'John,' he said, 'Michael Krebs is producing her act for *free*.'

'Do it again, Joe,' Krebs insisted.

Rowena sat on a spare chair behind the production console, watching them work. Joe Hunter, the singer, was laying down vocals for 'Karla', the album's big ballad.

'Rowena, make him stop,' Joe said into the mike, so she could hear. 'This has to be against the bloody Geneva Convention!'

'Michael's in charge,' she shrugged helplessly,

grinning at him. 'Far be it from Musica to interfere in the creative process.'

'This is the fourteenth time we've done this take, Michael,' the singer complained. 'And it's one bloody line of the song . . .'

'Come on, Joe, you'll get it,' Krebs ordered him implacably. 'We don't settle for second best, right? Not for Atomic Mass. Go again.'

'Slavedriving bastard,' said the singer, but he did it again.

Rowena hugged herself for pure pleasure. It was so good to be involved like this, exactly what she'd wanted. Joe and the rest of the boys were all friends of hers now, and Barbara Lincoln had quit her job at the record company to manage them. So Rowena had got to be involved at every stage of their career – finding a live agent, getting them a good accountant and planning the tour, as well as the normal A&R stuff like supervising marketing. She cared like hell about all her acts, but Atomic were the only band that kept her up at night.

'That's good,' Krebs agreed. 'You can go from "it's good to see you again" now.'

'Wow, the second line,' Joe growled sarcastically, but he looked pleased.

Michael glanced at Rowena and winked.

He was wearing a black sweater and black jeans and he looked amazing. Rowena thought Michael should live in black. It picked out his eyes. It made him even more attractive than usual.

She loved to be with him.

It had started in New York four months ago, when he'd come to the hotel and said he'd show her the city.

That wasn't fair. He'd had her at a disadvantage – first he blew her out, then he offered her the break of the fucking century, then he put her in another of those monster black limos and showed her some of the sights. A man whom Rowena had hero-worshipped for years, whom she'd literally fantasized about talking to, was driving her to the Russian Tea Rooms for dinner, and ordering her strawberries and champagne. Then he took her to an Aerosmith concert at Madison Square Gardens, where they had access-all-areas passes and got to stand at the side of the stage.

Everyone they met treated Michael like a king. Rowena felt dizzy from the glory of it.

Krebs was intense. That was the main thing about him. She'd met guys as good-looking as he was, or at least she thought so – but never, never, had she found someone so completely in control of every situation. He'd decided that Rowena Gordon was of interest to him, and that was it. At the Aerosmith show, he'd introduced her to so many record moguls they dissolved into a smiling blur. She was 'Musica's great white hope'. 'A rising star'. 'Incredibly talented'. And Krebs had told absolutely everyone that Rowena had personally convinced him to produce her band for nothing.

She'd had record company *presidents* lining up to shake her hand. Several of them offered to double her salary on the spot.

But Rowena shook her head, smiling and overwhelmed.

'Why didn't you take them up on it?' Krebs asked.

'I owe Josh,' Rowena said simply, smiling at him, and Michael Krebs looked at her, her long, freshly washed hair gleaming in the bright lights, and thought how glad he was she'd walked into his offices.

'Yeah, you do,' he said severely. 'And don't forget it.'

In the car on the way home, he'd demanded Rowena tell him her entire life story. 'I want to know *everything*.

And you have to tell me. You owe me, because I took you to Aerosmith.'

'Took me to a show? Michael, you're producing my band.'

Krebs shook his head, giving her a smile that melted her bones. 'You don't owe me for that, honey. I have five per cent of the album. I'll get mine,' and she believed him.

When the limo pulled up outside her hotel, and Michael kissed her hand gallantly as she got out – man, it was weird to have an American heavy-metal producer do that – Rowena suspected she was in big trouble.

And when she got to JFK the next morning and found that Krebs had arranged for her to be upgraded to first class, she *knew*.

Her return home had been fairytale stuff. Although he had wanted this, Oberman could hardly believe Rowena had actually pulled it off. He gave her a senior manager title and another pay rise. Atomic Mass, meanwhile, were dumbfounded by the idea of working with Michael Krebs, and their extreme gratitude turned into friendship, as Rowena found them places to live in London and took charge of their affairs. When Barbara quit to manage them, they got even closer.

The two women had a lot in common. Barbara wasn't the music freak Rowena had turned into, but she was cool, logical and very ambitious. She had no interest at all in the secretaries' gossip, or who was fucking whom, nor did she give a damn if Manchester United won the league. The result was that she was branded a cold bitch, stuck-up and the rest of it. Nobody understood what Joshua Oberman could possibly see in Ms Lincoln. Behind her back, and sometimes even to her face, they called her 'the token black woman', a piece of positive-discrimination window-dressing.

Rowena knew better. In fact, Barbara made her feel small; she'd only had to fight sexism, the disapproval of a privileged circle and prejudice on account of her looks. Barbara had clawed her way up by herself: law at London University, an MBA at nightclasses, and heavy specialization in entertainment law. Her tutors wrote her glittering reports, her papers were published in eminent legal journals. And then she had suffered the utter humiliation of being turned down again and again at record companies, always getting to the final interview, never getting hired.

'Overqualified', 'underexperienced'. What they never said was 'Black'.

At first Barbara had thought she was being paranoid. Maybe she was just presenting herself wrongly. But when she asked for a list of senior black personnel at the seven major labels from industry associations, the reply confirmed all her worst suspicions.

There were none.

Not 'one or two', not 'a bare handful', *none*.

She refused to give up. She went on trying, banging on the Human Resources doors and doing everything else she could think of. Finally, she had written a long letter to Joshua Oberman, President of Musica UK, and marked it 'Private and Personal'.

Oberman had seen her. And he'd hired her on the spot.

Rowena learnt all this from Josh himself on the drive back from the Retford Porterhouse, and she'd bought Barbara lunch the next day – partly as a thank-you for getting Oberman to hear her tape, and partly to satisfy her curiosity.

Now they were best friends – the first woman Rowena had been close to since Topaz Rossi.

Whom she never thought about.

Whom she buried deep in her mind.

She was, she told herself firmly, a different person now. One who'd totally outgrown social snobbery. One who would never betray a friend.

Barbara enjoyed watching Rowena adjust to having money of her own, money she'd *earned*, for the first time in her life, helping her buy a flat in Holland Park, start shopping for her food in Marks & Spencer's and, most importantly, dress designer. Since she'd been disowned by her father, Rowena had almost forgotten how.

'I can't believe how much this *costs*!' she gasped, holding up a sexy little Krizia dress.

'If you want to be a player, you better dress that way,' Barbara laughed, folding the dress over her arm.

Rowena abandoned the elegant, refined clothes she used to wear in favour of younger, brighter, more confident stuff. Where Barbara preferred Armani, she liked to slink around in Donna Karan. When Barbara wore Chanel to industry parties, Rowena turned up in shimmering Valentino. They complemented each other perfectly.

They were inseparable.

And then, on 15 March, Michael Krebs arrived.

'Can you come up to Oberman's office?' Barbara asked, sticking her head round Rowena's door. 'We've got a visitor.'

She'd gone upstairs without thinking, totally preoccupied with how Bitter Spice were playing in the clubs. Too preoccupied to notice the sidelong glances that Barbara was giving her, and the jealous looks from the secretaries on the executive floor. When her friend opened the door of the president's office for her, Rowena jumped out of her skin.

There he was. A week before she'd expected him. Michael Krebs, dressed in beat-up jeans and sneakers and a Mets baseball cap, chatting to Josh Oberman as though he did this every day of the week.

He looked so fucking gorgeous, Rowena's heart stood still.

'Miss Gordon, we meet again,' Krebs said, giving her a beaming smile and standing to greet her. 'Oberman, I tell you, you are so lucky to have this young lady working for you it isn't even funny.'

Josh snorted.

'You're early, Michael,' Rowena managed.

He shrugged. 'I had a free week. I thought we might do a little pre-production. Think you can get the band together for me?'

'Oh, I expect we can manage that,' she replied, glad to be on safe professional grounds.

'Good,' Krebs said, looking her over slowly. Rowena felt a wave of desire flood through her, and she coloured, hoping Barbara wouldn't notice.

'And you'll have to show me London, too. If I'm going to be here for a few months, I'll need some help getting around.'

'I'm not sure how good I'd be as a tour guide,' Rowena said, but Krebs shook his head.

'You'll be fine,' he said implacably.

'You can't steal my A&R manager, Krebs,' Oberman objected. 'She's got three bands to look after.'

'Relax,' Michael said, not taking his eyes off Rowena. 'She'll have plenty of time. I just want to show her how I record an album.'

'You never let a record company within ten miles of your studio,' Oberman scoffed.

Krebs turned back to his friend with a shrug. 'Rowena's different,' he said.

For two weeks, Rowena held out. She never saw him alone. She tried not to think about him. She kept herself busy, going scouting for bands, attending parties, seeing stupid amounts of films. Because Michael Krebs spelt danger. Heady, reckless danger, the kind any intelligent girl should avoid.

He was an extremely powerful man.

He was twenty years older than her.

He was married.

Rowena knew all that. So she did her best to resist her feelings for him. Because whenever she did have to see Michael – with Barbara, or with the band – she only became more fascinated by him. More attracted to him.

Not only was the guy a legendary producer, he was also highly intelligent and well educated, to Rowena's surprise. He had two degrees, from the Universities of Chicago and Boston. He was an exercise fanatic and went to the Harbour gym in Chelsea every morning. He loved dogs. He loved history, and made Rowena take him round the National Gallery and the British Museum.

And he loved the record business. With a passion.

'I'm gonna teach you everything you need to know,' he told her.

'You can spot talent. And that means the sky's the limit,' he said.

'You're going to surpass me by miles,' he said. 'You can conquer the world. Believe it.'

Rowena was half embarrassed, half thrilled by his interest in her. It overjoyed her to see how well Atomic were getting on with him – Zach Freeman, the lead guitarist, and Alex Sexton, the bassist, especially – and what incredible depth he was bringing to the album. Even the quality of the songs the boys were writing had improved dramatically. It was as though everybody was outdoing each other to impress Krebs. He had that effect on people, Rowena thought. Like any born leader, he made you want desperately to please him.

It felt like he was producing her life.

Of course, she couldn't be sure she was right about how he felt. Maybe he *was* just a friend. Maybe he only wanted to mentor her. He did flirt with her outrageously, and she responded in kind, but there was nothing wrong with that. He never made a pass, he never avoided questions about his family, and he bugged Rowena about getting herself a boyfriend. So she was confused. She told herself she was being ridiculous.

But sometimes, when she caught him watching her in the evenings, she thought differently.

As the days went by, Rowena's attitude changed. Without even admitting it to herself, she started to try to make Michael Krebs notice her – as a woman, not a record executive. She began to wash and condition her hair every day. She wore Red by Giorgio Beverly Hills whenever she went down to the studio. She selected her sexiest outfits, the clinging grey cashmere dress by Georges Rech, the black Donna Karan suit, the Ann Klein miniskirt. And she put on make-up.

Michael reacted by ceasing to even flirt with her.

'He doesn't know I'm alive!' Rowena complained to Barbara.

'Don't be pathetic. I feel like holding up a match between you two, to see if it'll catch fire,' her best friend replied. 'The sexual energy you guys are giving off could power the National Grid.'

'He's married,' Rowena said, with an air of finality.

'I *know* he's married. That's what makes me nervous,'

Barbara replied. 'Rich, powerful men like Michael Krebs eat girls like you for breakfast.'

'So you think all the stuff he says about me being talented is rubbish, then?' Rowena asked, winding a strand of blonde hair round her fist.

Barbara shook her head. 'Actually, no,' she said. 'He believes all that. And he really likes you as a friend. The trouble is, he's having trouble suppressing his sexual feelings.'

'No he isn't,' Rowena said. 'He's stopped flirting with me now. He doesn't ask me to dinner. He's even stopped introducing me to people.'

'You want to know why? Because you're a threat now. When it was harmless to flirt with you, he enjoyed it. But now you've turned up the heat, and he wants you.'

'I think you're wrong.'

'You'll see,' said Barbara calmly.

So now, at the end of the session, Rowena watched Michael wrap it up with Joe with her normal mixture of interest, admiration and confused longing.

'OK, my man. You're out,' Krebs told the singer dryly, flicking a couple of switches on the production console.

Joe raised a hand to the two of them and walked straight off the studio floor, without further pleasantries.

'Nice manners. Maybe I'm working them a little too hard,' Krebs remarked unrepentantly.

'The song sounds good, though,' Rowena said. She curled on her chair, a sinewy, catlike movement.

'What would you know?' he asked gruffly. 'You can't tell take one from take fifteen. You've got ears like Beethoven.'

'Oh, I just look for the big picture. I let guys like you sweat the details,' Rowena said, smiling at him.

There was a pause. Both of them were acutely aware that they were now alone together.

'Are you free for dinner tonight?' Rowena asked suddenly.

Krebs spun round slowly on the big leather producer's chair, looking at her. He'd been preparing for a moment like this for weeks. What he would say. How he'd let her down. How he could preserve a great friendship without risking anything further.

Except that if she'd waited a second longer, he'd have asked Rowena the exact same question.

Dinner's just dinner.

'Why do you want to have dinner with me?' he asked, almost savagely. 'On our own?'

'Just for the pleasure of your company,' Rowena answered quickly, blushing bright red.

'For the pleasure of my company? That's sweet, but you've been in my company all day,' Krebs said, hearing his own cruelty but unable to stop himself. He couldn't tear his eyes off Rowena, her long, slender legs tumbling out of a light blue Krizia dress, her firm thighs shimmering in reflective hose, her small breasts clearly visible through the white Bill Blass shirt she'd chosen that morning. Her long hair fell loose and sleek around her shoulders, and her eyes were wide, her lips parted.

For weeks now she'd been like a trembling reed in his presence, so brimming with desire that he could practically smell it.

For weeks now a general appreciation of an attractive, intelligent girl had become a raging lust which he could scarcely control.

And Michael Krebs was always in control.

He ached to fuck this woman. To really have her. To put her through her paces in ways she'd never dreamed of.

'Hey, it's no big deal,' Rowena said, her green eyes flashing.

'You've got a crush on me, Rowena,' Krebs insisted, his expression unreadable. 'And I'm married. I have three sons.'

'Nonsense, Michael,' Rowena said coldly. 'I'm not remotely attracted to you.'

They glared at each other.

The phone rang, shattering the tension.

'Krebs,' Michael said shortly, picking it up. 'Oh, hi, Oberman. No, it went fine. Yes, she is.' He held out the receiver to Rowena.

'Can you come over to the office and see me?' the old man asked. 'I need to talk to you about something urgently. Right now, Rowena.'

'Of course,' Rowena said, dragging her mind back to business with an effort. 'Is something wrong?'

'Nothing's wrong. Just be here,' Oberman said testily, and hung up.

She looked at Michael. 'I have to go.'

'Rowena –' he said suddenly, but she moved away from him, not wanting the quarrel to get any deeper.

'I really have to go. I'll see you tomorrow.'

'Call me tonight,' Krebs said, and although Rowena wanted to tell him to go to hell, she knew he wouldn't take no for an answer.

'I will.'

'You'd better,' Michael said, grinning at her in that way of his that weakened her knees. She felt a great rush of wanting sweep through her, and turned way from him as fast as she could, almost running out of the studio.

'Tell me something, Rowena. What do you think of New York?' Oberman asked her forty minutes later, as she sat across from his desk.

God, she looks stunning, he thought. I don't know what's happened to this girl lately. She was always special-looking, but now she's something else. Check out that pale blue dress with those light green eyes! Goddamn, no wonder Stevenson had resented her! How could a babe this beautiful be so good at her job?

'What do I think of New York?' Rowena repeated, bewildered. 'I've only been there once, Josh. It's a great city. What can I tell you?'

'What do you think of the bands there?' Oberman pressed her.

Rowena shrugged, a cascade of blonde hair falling about her shoulders. 'Right now, it's got the best bands in the world.'

The old man gave a satisfied grunt. 'OK. Now let's play a different game. What if I made you Managing Director – and don't get too excited, the title's only protocol – of a small subsidiary? A *tiny* subsidiary, just a name really, an outpost company. Your only job at first would be to look for talent, but over time I'd expect you to build it up. Do you think you could handle it, working on your own for a couple of years? With just an accountant and a secretary?'

'Of course,' she replied, wondering what the hell he was talking about.

'You mean that? You think you could be totally self-sufficient?'

Rowena shifted in her chair. It dawned on her that Oberman wasn't just playing 'Let's Pretend'. 'What about Atomic Mass? I wouldn't want to be too far from them right now.'

He made an expansive, dismissive gesture. 'Thought of that. We'd transfer them to record at Mirror, Mirror.'

He paced around behind his desk, looking at his protégée as though he was trying to see past her actual flesh and bones to her character, her self-reliance.

'I got the impression that you'd made a conscious decision to change your life when you got into this stuff, Rowena,' he said. 'Well, I hope that *was* what you wanted. Because I've just come back from an extended board meeting and I think I can guarantee that your life is about to change completely. Congratulations, Miss Gordon. You're gonna run a new label for us.'

He leant forward towards her, his craggy old face broken by a mischievous grin.

'In New York.'

Rowena didn't get back to her flat until 11 p.m., she'd spent so long talking about this with Josh, and Barbara, and even a little with Alex and Mark, the bassist and drummer for Atomic, who were in Barbara's management offices when she drove over there. She felt nervous and excited at the same time.

She flicked on the dimmer switch, letting a soft light flood the drawing room of her flat, illuminating the oyster-white carpet, the elegant chintz sofa and Georgian writing desk. As she slipped off her shoes and padded across to the kitchen, wanting to make herself a gin and tonic and a light supper before she crashed out, the phone rang.

With a sigh of annoyance, Rowena picked it up.

'I thought you were gonna call me,' Michael Krebs said.

It was like an electric shock. Small prickles of desire crawled all over her skin at the sound of his voice, teasing, friendly, definitely turned on.

'I meant to. I've been so busy, I only got home a second ago.'

'Rowena, you can always make time for your friends,' Krebs said softly.

Rowena took a deep breath. 'I thought I was making too much time for you,' she answered.

'I didn't mean to bite your head off,' he said. 'But I was right, though, wasn't I?'

She felt her palm holding the receiver go moist with sweat.

'You *have* been thinking about it, haven't you? For a while, now, I guess.'

'And you haven't,' she managed.

'We're not talking about me, we're talking about you,' he said relentlessly.

'Christ! Michael, you're so arrogant,' Rowena replied. 'I haven't got the faintest interest in you.'

There was a pause. She could almost feel his desire reaching down the telephone line. It was late at night, there was no one to see them, no one to stop them. She knew that they were trembling right on the cusp, on the brink of something from which there was no going back.

'Rowena,' Michael said.

It was just one word. A light rebuke. A tease, as if to say *Come on*. But his knowing, mocking tone pushed her over the edge.

To Rowena's astonishment, she heard herself moan with lust. A soft, wild sound she couldn't control.

Michael heard it, and his erection pressed so hard against his zipper it hurt.

'I'm at the Halcyon Hotel, in room 206,' he said. 'Get in a fucking cab. *Now.*'

It took twelve minutes for Rowena to get to the hotel, and during that time Krebs paced the room, thinking about her, imagining her in different positions, lightly touching himself from time to time. His erection remained rock-solid. When he heard her timid knock, he had to restrain himself from running across the room to wrench the door open.

'Hi, Rowena,' he said. 'Come in.'

She stepped into his suite, hearing the heavy door lock itself behind her. She was squirming and wet between the legs. Her heart was crashing and thudding so loudly against her ribcage she was sure he must hear it. She stood awkwardly in the middle of the room, not sure where to put herself.

Krebs regarded her impassively, his arms folded, for a few moments, looking her over at his leisure. She blushed deeper. She wanted him so desperately now she thought she might collapse.

Michael calmly picked up the phone and spoke to the operator, not taking his eyes off Rowena. 'This is Mr Krebs in 206,' he said. 'Hold all my calls, and have room service send up some champagne and leave it outside the door. I'm taking a shower.'

He replaced the receiver and beckoned to her. 'Come here.'

She walked unsteadily towards him.

'Closer,' Michael ordered, and she moved nearer, until her lips, wet and slightly parted, were inches from his face.

Staring deep into Rowena's eyes, Krebs shoved his hand up her dress and roughly yanked down her panties, pressing his hand against the damp hair between her legs, and slid a finger inside her, finding the hot, melting centre of her.

Rowena sobbed with pleasure, her legs shaking.

'What happened to "I'm not remotely attracted to you", "I haven't got the faintest interest in you"?' he enquired, caressing the urgent knot of heat in her belly.

She couldn't speak. She couldn't take her eyes off him. The mesmeric quality Krebs had always had, the dominating influence he'd had over her, in sex became a control so complete it sent spasms of ecstasy convulsing through her. Rowena couldn't believe what she was feeling. Not with Peter, nor with the other men she'd dated since, had she ever experienced anything like this. She was almost hypnotized. The force of his will was like a ten-ton truck.

And she was amazed at the depth of her response. She'd felt desire before. She'd felt pleasure. But never, *never*, had she felt anything like the heat that was flooding her body now.

'Say it,' he insisted. 'I want to hear you say it.'

'Michael, I – I think you're the most attractive man I've ever seen in my life, and I always wanted you,' Rowena said, half choking on the admission. She pressed herself against him, feeling his thick erection, letting him understand how great her need was. She pressed her lips to his throat, covering it with kisses. 'Please,' she said.

Michael took her head in his hands and twisted it about, looking at her like he wanted to drink in her face. Then he kissed her, fiercely, crushing her lips, running his hands over her body, under her dress, unsnapping her bra and playing with her erect nipples, stroking her in between the legs until she was weak with pleasure.

'I have dreamed about this,' he said. 'You're so beautiful. You're so different, you could drive a man mad.'

Then he pulled back, forcibly holding her away from him. 'I fantasized about you that first time,' he said. 'I looked at your mouth. I want to see your lips round my cock. I want to see it disappear into your mouth.'

He pushed her down on her knees before him. 'And tie your hair back,' he added. 'So I can see what you're doing.'

Rowena fumbled with her hair, barely able to get her

fingers to work properly. She was already approaching orgasm, her feelings were so strong. She had trouble unbuttoning his fly because the denim was pushed out tight from his cock hard against it. Krebs did not help her.

When she finally freed him, Rowena drew breath.

He was big. No doubt about it. Long and thick. The thought of that inside her was almost frightening. She longed to taste him.

Rowena had always flatly refused to give head, no matter how much her partners had begged her. The thought of it disgusted her. But there was no question, now, of refusing Michael Krebs anything he wanted. She was being completely controlled and she loved it.

She wanted him inside her mouth. She wanted to please him. To submit to him.

Delicately, gingerly at first, and then bolder, harder, more confidently, she began to suck him.

Krebs felt the sweet relief of her tongue and pleasure surged through him, violent, intense sexual pleasure. He knew it was her first time, and that somehow made it better. He watched her, her eyes shut in rapture, her soft, plump lips caressing him eagerly.

When he finally forced himself to pull out of her mouth, he dropped down beside her without a word, spread her legs and entered her immediately, holding her head steady in his hands so he could watch her come.

Rowena felt the orgasm seconds before it started, the waves of sex running through her gathering and deepening, rushing towards her groin from her fingertips, her toes, her neck. The ecstasy was so intense she felt dizzy, and all she could see was Michael's face, and those brilliant dark eyes watching her, and she was coming, a huge, crashing climax ripping through her, and she thrashed about in Michael's arms, and she felt him erupt inside her with a groan of bliss, and she was still coming, and then finally it subsided, and she was staring into his eyes again, and she knew, with absolute, helpless certainty, that she had just found the one great passion of her life.

Chapter Fourteen

From 7 p.m. onwards, fleets of limos streamed down the Avenue of the Americas, towards the Victrix, the smartest hotel in Manhattan.

It was the party of the year.

It was the party of the decade.

Invitations had been harder to come by than tickets to the best Clinton Inaugural Ball, more sought-after than A-list places at the late Swifty Lazar's annual post-Oscars bash. An invitation to this party marked you out as the cream of the New York crop; fail to get one, and you failed to make the grade. Social death. Effective immediately.

Because there was something different about this party, quite aside from the eleven million dollars it had reputedly cost. This was no ordinary hymn to American excess, with a safe guest list drawn up from the usual social old guard: Mr and Mrs Billionaire Financier, Mr and Mrs Millionaire Publisher, and their summer neighbours from the Hamptons. Elizabeth Martin couldn't care less about those sort of people. She wasn't interested in the richest. She was only interested in the best.

Elizabeth was twenty-eight years old and married to the wealthiest man in the Western world, which meant that money no longer concerned her. Achievement was all she gave a damn about, and she threw parties for the people at the top of each individual tree, their bank balance being incidental. Your ancestors came over on the *Mayflower*? So what? If you couldn't compete on a worldwide scale, Elizabeth didn't have time for you.

Her parties were strictly for the great. The good could take care of themselves.

Young, cool, competitive Manhattan was hosting the Meritocrats' Ball.

Topaz Rossi and Rowena Gordon had both been invited.

Oberman arrived at Rowena's new apartment on West 67th street at 8 p.m. There had never been any question that he wouldn't fly over for this one, and in any case Rowena needed an escort, since she didn't know any of the American players yet, and invites were for one person only; no wives, no husbands, no lovers.

'Just come in, Josh, it's open,' called Rowena from the bathroom. He took a look round, pleased with himself; with no time to hunt for a place, Gordon had taken the first thing he recommended, and he obviously hadn't failed her. The co-op had a façade of elegant white stone, with Gothic carvings of gargoyles entwined around the porch, which led into a lobby of polished black granite with efficient, discreet 24-hour security. Rowena had four huge, high-ceilinged rooms with breathtaking views over Central Park, and she'd decorated them with a few small English watercolours and exquisite Georgian furniture. He nodded to himself, satisfied. No disgrace for Musica's youngest-ever MD to live somewhere like this.

'Holy shit,' he said as Rowena walked into the drawing room.

She was wearing a white chiffon gown by Ungaro,

high-waisted in the Regency style and bias-cut in the skirt, so that it flowed around her, following every slight swing of her hips. The chiffon was studded with tiny fabric roses, complementing her classic peaches-and-cream complexion. Her blonde hair was swept up into a regal pile, secured by tiny ebony combs. Rubies glittered at her ears, throat and wrists, the dangling earrings in particular giving a sexy emphasis to the movement of her head and setting off her sparkling green eyes. Delicate pink satin heels peeped out from under her hem.

'Do you like it?' asked Rowena anxiously.

'You look unbelievable, toots,' said Oberman, with fatherly pride. 'Have a drink. You'll need it.'

'If you say so.' She smiled at him. What a sweetheart he was. She hoped she'd get the same reaction from the two people she was really dressing for: Michael Krebs and Topaz Rossi.

Topaz received her gold-embossed invitation at the office, just as she was winding up a particularly tough advertising deal for *Girlfriend*. She was one of only four people invited from American Magazines.

Mrs Alexander Martin requests the pleasure of Miss Rossi's company on Wednesday, 28 June, for a party in four acts.
The Victrix Hotel, 8.30 p.m.
Dress as you please.

She spent a fortnight agonizing over what to wear, and then decided that less was more and went for a Chanel sheath in light green silk with matching shoes. She wore her hair loose, and no make-up or jewellery of any kind. The dress let her figure speak for itself, hugging her curves like a second skin, and the sea-green colour lit up the deep cobalt of her eyes. It was a look to stop traffic.

Nathan Rosen, Marissa Matthews and Joe Goldstein were coming too, and since they were all ridiculously busy people, they met up in the limo.

Nathan was wearing a tux.

Joe was wearing a tux.

Marissa was wearing a golden creation in six layers of organza, laced with silver thread and covered head to foot in solid gold sequins. She had added a three-row pearl choker and sapphire and diamond bracelets.

'What's the matter, honey? Couldn't you at least have *hired* something to go in?' she asked as Topaz settled into the leather seat, furious because neither Nathan or Joe would stop stripping her with their eyes.

'I didn't realize it was a fancy-dress party, darling!' Topaz countered. 'How original of you to come as a Christmas tree!'

Nathan hastily turned a snort of laughter into a cough, and the limo eased smoothly away.

Rowena clutched on to her boss's arm, trying to catch her breath.

What was normally the ballroom of the Victrix Hotel, occupying the entire twenty-fourth floor, had been turned into a landscaped garden, with mossy turf laid down wall to wall and ancient-looking stone paving. To the right and left were orchards of orange trees in full blossom, delicately scenting the air. Footmen in full court livery paraded around with mahogany trays of caviar and truffles, and maids appeared and disappeared silently, ensuring that no glass was ever less than half full of vintage champagne. Tiny bells had been garlanded into the branches of the trees, filling the room with soft, delicious chimes. White peacocks wandered among the crowd.

And what a crowd! Rowena had passed Madonna on her way in, and then found that she and Josh were sharing an elevator with Arnold Schwarzenegger and Si Newhouse, mogul head of Condé Nast magazines. Oberman had had to edge past Henry Kissinger, deep in conversation with Henry Kravis, just to get Rowena some champagne.

'Come on, kid,' he said, seventy-two and unshake-able. 'I'll introduce you to a few people.'

For the next ten minutes Rowena Gordon, who lived and died for the record business, was catapulted straight to heaven.

'Ahmet Ertegun, Rowena Gordon.'

'Rowena, you haven't met Sylvia Rhone, have you?'

'Tommy Mottola. Clive Davis. Michelle Anthony. Joe Smith. Alain Levy.'

Rowena shook hands, suppressing the urge to curtsy.

'This is Rick Rubin,' said Josh, steering a huge man who looked like a bear towards her.

Dear God, thought Rowena, as she shook hands with the ultimate Heavy Metal prince, you can almost smell the testosterone. The guy's masculinity must walk into a room three paces in front of him.

'I like the rushes of that Atomic Mass record Krebs is working on,' growled Rubin. 'Word of mouth on that band is huge.'

'Yeah, they're great,' agreed Rowena, glowing with pride. 'I thought you did an awesome job on "Licensed to Ill".'

'Thanks,' said Rubin.

'Stop flirting with everybody, Rowena,' said Josh loudly, making her blush even worse.

'Get out of my face, Oberman,' said Rubin amiably.

'Oh my God, Batman and Robin,' said Oberman, grabbing a pair of guys who were walking their way.

'Hello, gentlemen, come say hi to Musica's new woman in New York. Rowena, say hello to Q-Prime, and then go sign me an act they can handle.'

Rowena was afraid she might drop her glass. If it was good and it used a guitar, Q-Prime represented it. *Sweet Jesus! The two most legendary managers in the world* . . .

'Hi, nice to meet you,' said Cliff Burnstein and Peter Mensch.

'How are you finding New York?' asked Burnstein, who basically didn't give a shit about anything and had turned up in a Metallica shirt and jeans.

'Er, it's very big,' muttered Rowena, her powers of conversation deserting her. They kindly agreed that it was indeed very big, and then launched into an animated discussion of the prospects for the Mets that season, finishing off each other's sentences.

'Do me a favour,' Oberman murmured to her after they'd moved away. 'Never, ever fuck with those guys.'

'I wasn't planning to, Josh.'

At the other end of the garden Topaz had also taken up residence on cloud nine, because Nathan had finally introduced her to Tina Brown, and the editor of *Glamour* had complimented her on *Girlfriend*.

'Excuse me, Marcelle,' simpered Marissa, dragging a highly reluctant Topaz away from the exquisitely dressed editor of British *Cosmopolitan*. 'Topaz, didn't you know Rowena Gordon when you were at school?'

'What about it?' snapped Topaz.

'Because she's right over there,' Marissa purred.

At that moment, Rowena happened to glance to her left, and froze, paralysed to the spot.

They had not laid eyes on each other for three years.

'Ladies and gentlemen,' announced a waiter. 'Dinner is served.'

*

Elizabeth Martin had outdone herself this time, everybody agreed. The menus announced 'Act II: A fairytale meal', and she had certainly delivered.

The dining hall looked like a missing chapter of *Charlie and the Chocolate Factory*. It seemed as if Alexander Martin must have bought the entirety of F. A. O. Schwarz to decorate it. The centrepiece of the room was a table for 200 people crafted out of hard-baked, solid gingerbread. Miniature trains ran round the table, laden with quails' eggs and celery salt in one carriage, Godiva chocolates in the next, and still more caviar in the third. Humanoid robots stumbled about, bearing various trays of drinks: champagne cocktails, fine wines, fresh pressed raspberry juice, even ready-mixed Long Island Ice Teas and Cokes in glass bottles. With a fine disregard for the seasons, various trophies of childhood festivals stood around; pumpkins complete with flickering candles and jagged smiles, fireworks for the Fourth of July, Easter eggs and chocolate bunnies, and Christmas trees everywhere, strung with tinsel and baubles and laden with gifts to which guests were expected to help themselves: Rolex watches, silver cufflinks, Hermès scarves, bottles of Joy and Chanel No. 5. You just didn't know where to look first.

'Fucking fantastic!' laughed Joe Goldstein, seated on one side of Topaz.

'Awesome!' agreed Nathan, and indeed all around them the movers and shakers of New York had started to laugh in wonder, smile and relax. Nobody had ever seen anything like it. You almost saw the pressures of the city lifting and the years evaporating. Normality was suspended.

As waiters dressed in penguin suits served them with starters of smoked salmon mousse or honey-glazed roast vegetables, guests started unwrapping the presents laid beside each individual place setting, parcels of various different shapes and sizes. A chorus of gasps arose amongst the delighted hubbub. Someone had spent a long time on the known preferences of each guest; Elizabeth had apparently cast herself as everyone's fairy godmother. Beside each plate was an object of desire longed for by the recipient, but never acquired.

'Oh my God,' said Topaz, delicately lifting the gauze off a letter to an academic written, and signed, by J. R. R. Tolkien.

'I don't believe it,' said Josh Oberman, pulling out a small Fabergé egg. 'It can't be what I think it is.'

'Look at *this*,' said Rowena in astonishment, holding up a first-pressing copy of the Def Leppard EP and a bootleg tape of the MC_5.

'Look, Joe,' said Nathan Rosen, showing him his battered football with the autographs of the entire Giants team.

Silence descended on the room as people started to enjoy the food.

Topaz couldn't eat anything. She toyed with her meal, trying not to stare at Rowena. The force of her loathing gripped her inside her stomach, twisting her guts. God, she was just the same: English, cold, haughty. So stunningly beautiful, so perfectly tasteful. Rowena could wear as many rubies as she liked and carry it off, whereas Marissa just seemed vulgar. Look at her. She didn't give a damn about anybody or anything.

I worshipped you, you hateful bitch, Topaz thought, choked. I shared everything with you. And it obviously meant nothing to you.

She felt weak, she thought she might cry. The bitter pain of Rowena's treachery came flooding back, and the terrible hurt of betrayal by the only friend to whom she'd ever fully revealed herself; the hurt of Rowena, whom she'd totally trusted, teaching her that sisterhood was a sham, and that the only person in this life that Topaz Rossi would ever be able to believe in was herself.

Rowena sliced up her duckling breast, precisely and automatically. She was determined not to show how badly she felt, knowing Topaz Rossi's cruel blue eyes were boring into the back of her neck.

She had betrayed a friend. Cheated on her. Stolen her lover. And used her class and breeding to excuse herself – as her father had done to justify his own rejection of her. It was a system she had previously denounced as an archaic, imperialist British hangover, best forgotten.

But you used it against an Italian Yank when it suited you, accused a nagging little voice in her head.

Rowena shook her head, as though she could dispel the past. She hadn't given Topaz a second thought! Why should she be looking at her like this now? Water under the bridge, right? Christ, they were only kids at college.

Trust Topaz Rossi to get worked up about it.

Anger mingled with her guilt. That terrible *Cherwell* headline flashed in front of her.

Deliberately, Rowena pushed back her chair, and stood up, smoothing down her dress. The room was seriously overstocked with men, and at least thirty pairs of eyes followed the flow of the material over her breasts.

There was a tension in the air. The main course wasn't even finished. What was she doing?

'Sit down,' hissed Josh Oberman.

Rowena, apparently, could not hear her boss. She walked carefully over to where Topaz was sitting, and the other woman shot out of her chair to meet her.

Two places down, Marissa Matthews was ecstatic.

Something was very wrong indeed, and very right for Friday's column. She strained to listen.

'It must be hell for you, Rowena,' said Topaz, in bitter, measured tones, 'having to break bread with all these ghastly colonials.'

'I see that you're doing well in American Magazines, Topaz,' said Rowena evenly, 'although I'm not surprised, since journalism is a profession where the scum usually rises to the top. Do you find a better class of interviewee to sleep with these days?'

'No wonder you're succeeding in the record business, Rowena,' answered Topaz, barely restraining her fury. 'So few women to get in your way, and you can contribute to the feminist agenda by promoting male heavy-metal bands. But then this sister was only ever doing it for herself, wasn't she?'

They stared at each other, constrained by the presence of the glittering crowd.

'This is my patch,' hissed Topaz.

'This *was* your patch,' spat Rowena.

There was a moment's hung silence. Then, slowly, both girls turned aside and returned to their seats.

Michael Krebs moved casually towards Rowena across the dance floor. He didn't enjoy dancing, but he did enjoy watching his beautiful woman whirl gracefully from the arms of one mogul to the next. Her intelligence and her poise were captivating the whole of New York. All of these men thought she was the ice queen. He knew better.

'Do you mind if I cut in?' he said to the deeply famous movie director, who was pissed off because he wanted to get Rowena to consult on his project for the life and times of Led Zeppelin.

Rowena, who'd been searching for him all night, tried

to stop herself melting into his arms with relief. Michael hated emotion. He demanded complete detachment. Maybe it took his mind off the wedding ring glinting on his left hand, she thought with renewed agony.

Krebs took her easily into the sedate rhythm of the waltz, one hand on the curve of her waist. He felt her body respond to his touch as if he'd given her an electric shock, and immediately his cock started to swell for her. The intensity of her lust was almost frightening. He knew he could get her wet just by looking into her eyes. It sent a flood of powerful joy through him, to do this to her. Her own sexuality had her in chains.

'You look lovely,' he told her quietly.

'Thank you, Michael,' said Rowena, determined to keep her cool. 'It's quite a party.'

'Yeah,' said Krebs, adding matter-of-factly, 'you'll meet me in the lobby downstairs in ten minutes. Don't excuse yourself to Joshua, just come downstairs.' Rowena felt the familiar convulsions of longing.

'I can't,' she murmured.

'You can and you will,' said Michael Krebs, and she looked at his determined black eyes, and his wiry salt-and-pepper hair, and his beautiful, callous face, and knew she would do whatever he wanted.

'But the party –' she protested weakly.

'I know what happens now,' said Michael in her ear, 'so you won't have to stay to see. For Act Three, everyone goes downstairs to the fourteenth floor, which they've turned into a giant ice rink. Then for Act Four, everyone goes up to the roof garden and gets into a fleet of helicopters which ferry them to Alex Martin's private airstrip, and then two Gulfstream 4 jets take everybody out and back for six hours' dancing in the Florida Keys.'

'You're kidding,' breathed Rowena.

Krebs made an impatient movement with his hand.

'No, I'm not kidding. But I want to fuck you, so you're not going.'

He took another look at her in that cream-and-roses dress, the rubies sparkling round her long neck as she moved. She reverted to type, they all did, these aristocratic little rich girls playing around in business. She was a class piece, a European lady, the kind that he dreamt about in college but would have stammered in front of if he'd actually had to speak to her. Now he was everything she hoped to be; now, in this new universe where class counted for nothing, he was a lord and she was still a peasant.

Michael Krebs, twice Rowena Gordon's age, her mentor in business, her tutor in sex.

He splayed his fingers over her ribcage, feeling her slight involuntary squirm. He would have her like this, exactly like this. He wouldn't let her change a thing. He wanted to see this English lady in her fine clothes down on her knees with her mouth round his cock, with her warm soft lips and eager tongue working him so he could come in her mouth. That would be first. Then a little later, before he was even hard again, he'd make her take his limp prick in between her lips and hands and work him back up to erection, so he could put her on her hands and knees on a hotel bed, shove up that elegant chiffon and screw her from behind, just fuck all that British reserve right out of her. She'd have to please him like that. She'd have to earn her sex.

Topaz fastened her seatbelt as the Gulfstream soared into the skies above New Jersey. She'd got a second burst of energy now, even without the aid of the poppers and speed pills which most of the guests were on. Stewardesses in the navy uniform of Martin Oil moved up and down the spacious aisles of the private jet,

presenting passengers with orchids, cigars and minia-
tures of cognac.

Marissa, orgasmic at the confrontation she was
announcing to the world, had already phoned in her
copy to 'Friday's People'.

Topaz knew it and she welcomed it. There would only
be one winner in this war. New York was her turf, born
and bred, and the stuck-up bitch would never survive.
Everybody knew she hadn't even lasted this party,
whereas, she, Topaz, had tied up two joint ventures and
optioned a bestseller.

She tapped Joe Goldstein on the shoulder. He was an
arrogant, sexist bastard, but she had a use for him.

'Yeah, Rossi,' he said, engrossed in his *Wall Street
Journal*.

'Joe,' she asked, 'what do you hear about a rock band
called Atomic Mass?'

Rowena gripped on to the edge of the mixing desk with
one hand, her feet splayed against a Marshall stack, her
other hand in her mouth, muffling herself.

Michael stood in between her legs, rocking his cock
into her with perfect control, in and out, making her
look at it as he fucked her. He felt her pussy rippling
round him, young and tight and hot with pleasure. She
was trembling on the brink of orgasm, mutely imploring
him to push her over it.

'Absolutely,' he said into the phone. 'No, the second
Atomic album, Josh, I'll make the time. Yeah, well, what
can I tell you. Two per cent of nothing is nothing! Sure!
You know I love doing business with you, Oberman, and
with Rowena Gordon as well. She's a very good friend of
mine. Yes, very talented.'

He could feel the insistent clutching of her belly,
unable to resist him much longer.

'Well, I'll catch you later,' he said casually, and put the phone down.

He moved deeper into her. 'You like that, don't you?' he asked her conversationally. 'You like having me fuck you while I'm doing business.'

Rowena had her head back, and her eyes were wild. She couldn't speak. She made little choking noises, which he loved, as she gasped in ecstasy.

'God these rivers of passion,' he said. 'You're a slave to it, aren't you? Is this everything you dreamed it would be? Is it as good as you remember it?'

'Michael! Michael!' Rowena sobbed, abandoned utterly to pure desire. Krebs grinned to himself, as the pleasure in his own loins began to build. She was in New York for good. Now she belonged to him.

Chapter Fifteen

Topaz stood in front of her new bedroom window, looking across the Village.

The blue expanse above the warm red brick of the elegant townhouses shimmered, holding out the promise of another scorching day. She stared at the view below her, drawing strength from it. After all, she was a New Yorker now.

Like the city itself could help her stay on top of things.

She turned away from the window and padded towards her dressing room, across the lush blue carpeting of the bedroom, noting with satisfaction the Art Deco table, the Lalique lamps, the huge Moston bed with its silk sheets still rumpled from the way Nathan and she had christened it last night.

Nathan Rosen. Her lover. Her partner.

He'd been superb last night, probing, stroking, kissing her everywhere. Almost as good as the first few weeks they'd been lovers. And she was glad of that. She couldn't understand why Nathan wanted to take it slow. 'Let's pace ourselves.' 'Later.' 'Sweetheart, I'm beat right now.' He'd been like that for weeks.

Not that they hadn't made love. *Sometimes*.

Topaz adjusted the belt of her Yves St-Laurent silk gown, feeling it flow round her magnificent body like water. Her full breasts still thrust upwards despite their weight, tilting towards the sky with the confidence of youth.

She caught sight of her reflection in their full-length wall mirror, and pirouetted, pleased with that at least. No way she needed an uplift, Topaz thought. Although the second she did she was gonna get one. Why should she have sagging breasts, when she had plenty of money to ensure otherwise? Of course, Rowena Gordon would probably think plastic surgery was low-rent. Well, she could go fuck herself. This was America. Where pasty complexions and sexual repressions weren't something to be proud of.

Topaz shook her head, as if to dispel thoughts of Rowena. Time enough for that when she got into the office. Christ, she'd kept that anger bottled up for years. It could wait a few more hours.

Her Italian blood was raging for revenge. She still couldn't believe Rowena Gordon had had the chutzpah to actually get up in the middle of dinner and confront her. Of course she'd known Rowena would be there. Just like she knew she'd been posted to New York, and that her act Atomic Mass were being talked about all over knowing circles in the city.

British live sensation.

Michael Krebs producing. No fee. Just a piece of the action.

Five young boys with looks MTV would eat alive.

Debut single out this week.

If the rumours were true, Atomic Mass were about to burst on an unsuspecting world as the biggest new band since Nirvana.

Topaz made it her business to know these things. Somebody else might have sneered at the hype, dismissed it as gossip flavour-of-the-month stuff. But she remembered Rowena's passion for music – yeah, she remembered *everything* about Rowena. In those days, in the cloisters of Oxford, it had been the one rebellious trait in her personality. She'd had the elegant clothes, the social grace, the ever-present volume of medieval poetry or some other scrupulously academic book tucked under her arm. Rowena Gordon wouldn't have dreamt of relaxing with a Jackie Collins or a John Grisham. But her rock 'n' roll Rowena loved too much to hide, even for the sake of her precious image.

And Topaz wasn't about to underestimate her opponent. That was a mistake for amateurs. That was what Rowena Gordon did to Topaz Rossi, and was she ever going to pay for it.

I said I wasn't going to think about her now! Topaz lectured herself, and strolled into the kitchen. Light was streaming in from the windows and skylights, flooding the polished wood floor, the expensive oak table and the European Aga cooker, which Topaz had insisted on. In fact she'd insisted on the whole thing. Moving in together. Nathan selling his co-op. Her selling her chic single-girl's apartment. If they were going to be partners, she'd persuaded Nate, they ought to be *partners*. In love. Money. Everything.

And who could deny that it was a good move? she asked herself, setting up the coffee machine so Nate could get his fix when he came back from his early morning jog. Pooling their resources, they'd been able to buy a *house*, an actual house, in the middle of Manhattan! West 10th Street, prime Village property and very suitable for a media couple. And their place even had a garden. OK, so it was a tiny scrap of a garden, but in New York that was saying something.

Specifically, that was saying, *we are very rich*.

So? Topaz thought. They *were* rich. Who could deny

it? Nathan was a director for American Magazines, and she was editor of *Girlfriend* and about to become editor of *Economic Monthly*.

Whatever Joe Goldstein thought.

Joe thrust again, twisting his hips a little, pushing himself deep into the pulsing heart of her, feeling for the hot, wet core that would send her crashing over the edge. The excitement in his cock seemed to feed through into his whole body, making his bloodstream sing as though it were liquid fire. He gently caressed her fine, pointed breasts, taking the swollen nipples into his mouth and circling each of them with his tongue, then sucking them, while she moaned and gasped with delight, making those small guttural sounds in the back of her throat that turned him on even more. They rolled over and she was on top, her dyed blonde hair tumbling round her face, eyes still closed in bliss. He hadn't missed a beat.

Joe pushed up her breasts in his hands, more urgently now, feeling the first tremors of orgasm start to build. The ecstatic expression on Lisa's face had triggered it; he took pleasure in the woman's pleasure, always making sure they came several times, always leaving them hungry for more.

On automatic pilot he gathered himself for the final seconds and plunged deep, deep inside her, hitting the g-spot, the little tender melting spot on the wall of the vagina, the place some sexologists and most women swore didn't exist. But not the ones who'd slept with Joe Goldstein.

Well, it had taken men a while to discover the clitoris, Joe reckoned. They'd get round to the g-spot eventually.

Of course, it helped to be a connoisseur of women.

Of course, it helped to have a twelve-inch cock.

'*Joe!*' Lisa screamed, her entire, perfectly flat belly visibly rippling with the force of her convulsions. 'Joe! Joe! Oh, my God!'

'Lisa,' he breathed, feeling his orgasm tear through him and explode inside her.

They were immobile for a few seconds, gasping for breath, recovering.

'Jesus Christ, you are the best,' she said, rolling off him and pushing the damp hair out of her eyes.

'You're something special yourself,' replied Joe automatically. 'You always were.'

She got up and sauntered towards the shower, displaying a firm, full body, with nice breasts and legs, maybe a little chunky around the hips, and sassy, uneven blonde hair with the roots showing. Joe and Lisa had screwed on and off for years. She was married in name only to a Wall Street financier who could rarely get it up, and she was as careful in choosing her lovers as Joe was in choosing his: no involvement, no commitment, and plenty to offer in the sack. Lisa Foster was a sensualist, but she was also a materialist. She didn't want to take any risks. And neither did Joe.

'Baby, you could fuck for World Champion,' was her parting comment to him as she left, wrapped in a garish pink Ungaro suit.

Joe smiled and kissed her hand. He liked Lisa. Girls like her were worth missing sleep for. They were easy to please and fun to screw, and they didn't insist on beating you up with a big feminist stick. She didn't want to debate the difference between men and women for five hours, she just wanted to enjoy it. He supposed Topaz Rossi would despise a girl like Lisa. Living off her husband's money, or whatever it was she'd say.

Goldstein lit a cigarette, annoyed. Even thinking about that woman ruined his good mood. He wandered into the kitchen, spread a couple of bagels thickly with cream cheese and put on a fresh pot of coffee, switching on his IBM. The notes for his presentation to the board flashed up on the screen, the speech amusing, well paced and lucid.

That made him feel better. The speech was a killer. It should nail *Economic Monthly*, if it hadn't been nailed before. The title had his name on it anyway – a serious new monthly: glossy, upmarket, aimed at men. He ran three magazines just like it for American Magazines already, and he ran them very successfully. And it wasn't just the circulation of his own titles that he had to offer the group. Since the time he'd been at Wharton and discovered by Nate Rosen, he'd been using his *cum laude* MBA to American's advantage, submitting cost-cutting proposals, helping to review supplier contracts, helping out on acquisition titles.

Goldstein was more than a hotshot editor. He was a businessman. And he saw *Economic Monthly* as a direct leap to the board.

Topaz Rossi! What made her a goddamn candidate? OK, so after a couple of weeks at American's New York offices he realized he'd been wrong about her, at least at first. She was a very talented journalist, dynamite columnist, had been a good features editor at *US Woman* and had done wonders for the circulation of *Girlfriend*. Fair enough, she had more going for her than her physical charms. But still, the girl was in charge of only one magazine. Aimed at teenage girls. And she had no corporate or business experience at all – well, a little MBA work at night school, big deal. God, she'd never been within a mile of running a high-profile men's magazine.

So why am I letting her get to me? thought Joe angrily. I'm gonna *cream* her over *Economic Monthly*. And that's all. End of story.

But it wasn't.

Topaz Rossi was under Joe Goldstein's skin, and he didn't like it. She annoyed him and she bothered him and she made him mad. Usually, when he met a woman he couldn't stand, he put her out of his mind. He had better things to do. Annoyance was a futile, pointless emotion, and Joe Goldstein didn't indulge in time-wasting.

But Rossi refused to get out of his mind.

Maybe it was the harsh feminism, but he met a lot of feminists. Maybe it was her personality. That brash, bold, in-your-face way Topaz had about her. She seemed to be everywhere he went, shouting encouragement to the *Girlfriend* staffers, carrying great stacks of layouts past his office to her own, greeting everybody in the goddamn building like they were her bosom buddies. And it seemed most of them were, which made it worse. In meetings, she was polite and courteous to him, but that was as far as it went. She was curt. Blunt. Almost dismissive of him. In the LA bureau where Goldstein had been operating, people compromised from time to time to let something get done. Not Ms Rossi, though. 'Compromise' was not in her dictionary. That girl would argue for two hours rather than concede *anything*.

She was fucking *relentless*.

Maybe it was her dress sense, Joe thought, moving back into the kitchen to finish off his bagel. He glanced at his Rolex. Eight forty. He'd have to get a move on; lucky the Brooks Brothers suit was already pressed and ready to go, the white shirt hanging on the back of his closet. Yeah, her dress sense. Totally inappropriate for the working environment, he thought severely. Always showing off her figure. Bright colours. Designer names. Rich fabrics. By rights, she should come over as vulgar, but her innate self-confidence and sense of style enabled her to carry it off. He'd never met another redhead who could wear a shocking-pink suit by Vivienne Westwood and get away with it. It was just so – so – off-putting, this bold, brassy, ballsy Italian girl storming round the place like an ongoing nuclear explosion.

Joe dressed quickly, without fuss or undue worries about his reflection. He never thought about that stuff.

Of course, he'd fantasized about Topaz. Or tried to. Hell, she was awesomely beautiful and she had the best body he'd seen outside the covers of *Playboy*.

But something was wrong with that picture. Every time he tried to imagine her naked on a rug, he found himself remembering something annoying about her, like the last time she'd shaken his hand at an editors' meeting with all the warmth of your average iceberg.

He ran off a new copy of his speech notes and put them in his custom-made briefcase. No time to think about that now. There was only one day to go before the board got to pick the first editor of *Economic Monthly*.

Joe Goldstein had worked hard on the construction of his speech for this presentation, harder than he'd worked on anything for some time. Possibly he was being underconfident. After all, he was meant to be a dead cert for this job.

But he wanted to polish this speech till it gleamed.

There was no way he was gonna lose out to Topaz Rossi.

'I wanted to break it to you myself,' Josh Oberman said, spearing a stuffed mushroom with vigour.

He was meeting Rowena Gordon for breakfast at the Pierre. When back in New York on business, Oberman always stayed at the Pierre and he always had the same suite. He knew what he liked. Elegant décor, impeccable service and a nice view of Central Park. The Royalton or the Paramount were the music-industry hotels of choice right now, with their futuristically equipped rooms and ultra-hip atmosphere, but Joshua Oberman sneered at that. Hotels were somewhere you slept when you were doing business. Period. He couldn't give a damn about how good-looking the bellboys were.

'Break what to me, boss?' Rowena asked, picking at her fruit salad. The New York body fascism was already starting to get to her, but she didn't mind. How could she? Her slim, naturally blonde figure seemed to be the American ideal. And she wanted to be perfect for Michael, absolutely perfect. Her desire for him was fast becoming obsession.

'The reaction Warners had to the first Atomic Mass single,' Josh said gravely.

Rowena stiffened, little prickles of fear rising on the nape of her neck. Warners were going to distribute the first Atomic record in the States, just like they packaged, shipped and sold all the Musica records out here. Rowena's little talent-scout outpost of a label notwithstanding, the company had no real presence in America. So they did a deal with a major, like every other semi-independent, and took a royalty payment on each of their CDs sold out here.

So if Warners hated the single, forget it. Her band were sunk.

'What reaction?' she demanded. ' "Karla" is brilliant! It's *brilliant*! How could they not love it?'

Josh let her hang for a second, savouring the moment. He admired her outfit again, a shaped black suit by Anna Sui, legs tapering down in sheerest black nylon to stack-heeled mules from Chanel. Her long hair, shaped with a soft new fringe at the front and precision cut at the back, swung behind her like a shining golden curtain.

'Relax,' he said. 'They did love it. More than that, even.'

Rowena leant back in her chair, feeling relief flood through her. She smiled at her boss. Capricious old bastard! She shouldn't have risen to it like that, but any teasing about Atomic Mass hit straight home. The first single was about to be released, the record was nearly done, and everyone connected with the band was wound up as tight as a bedspring.

The boys themselves, naturally, were completely at their ease, just glad to be wrapping up *Heat Street* and going back on the road. And they were still getting to know New York. The bars. The clubs. And the women. *Especially* the women. Christ, they weren't even known here yet, and they were getting snowed under with girls. She'd never seen anything like it. No, the band weren't uptight, the band were in seventh bloody heaven.

'I wish I could draw you a picture of Bob Morgado's face when he heard it,' Oberman said, smiling broadly at the memory. 'Oh, they thought Christmas came early this year. If the rest of the album matches up to "Karla", we're looking at the top of the priority list.'

He attacked his cheese omelette, cackling. 'Know how I really know they loved it?' he asked. 'They wanted to renew the Atomic contract. Separate from the general Musica deal. I guess they must realize we plan to get our own distribution going sooner rather than later, and they still want a piece of Atomic Mass.'

'What did you tell them?' Rowena demanded.

'I said we'd think about it. Depending on how good a job they do with *Heat Street*,' Oberman grinned, thoroughly pleased with himself. 'And how are you settling in, kid?'

'Oh, fine,' said Rowena vaguely. She wasn't about to belabour her boss with her business problems. The office. The overwork. The commercial fucking Siberia she found herself in as a lone gun.

Fix it first, talk about it later.

'Good. Haven't seen you since you ducked out of Elizabeth Martin's party – without saying goodbye,' Oberman added severely. 'No, don't give me whatever excuse you're desperately trying to cook up. You don't want to jet to Florida, it's your problem. Who was that woman you were catting with at the dinner, Rowena? The stunning redhead? Is it something I should be concerned about?'

'She's nobody. A magazine executive I didn't get on too well with at Oxford, that's all,' answered Rowena, her tone going cold. She resented Topaz shoving herself into a conversation she was having with Joshua Oberman. Josh was her mentor. Josh was sacred.

Oberman lifted his fork, warning her. 'Babe,' he said, 'nobody at that party was nobody.'

The sixtieth floor of the American Magazines tower on Seventh Avenue was pleasantly cool, despite the blazing sun that streamed into it through the glass walls in every director's office. Lower floors in the building were at their normal, mind-melting level, but not this one. The board had the benefit of the latest Japanese air-conditioning systems, silent and effective, so that they could run America's second-largest magazine empire with total concentration, the freezing winters and baking summers of New York being totally immaterial.

Indeed, to the unwary visitor used only to the rest of the building – editors barking orders, reporters yelling into phones, computers and printers clattering, photocopiers whirring and the rest – the sixtieth floor could seem like another planet. Chaos and bleeping phones and mundane things like deadlines seemed miles away from the calm, almost churchlike tranquillity of the executive floor.

Nathan Rosen, the company's young director, East Coast – a mere forty-one years old – sometimes missed the constant hustle of actual magazine offices. But not often. He'd been working up to his current position all his life. He was ready for the big picture work now – acquisitions, sales, disposals. It *was* busy up here. It was just that you'd never know it.

At least, Topaz Rossi didn't seem to know it.

'I can't talk,' Nathan protested. 'Not today.' He gave a small shrug, the tightness of his movement betraying his annoyance. 'You and Joe are presenting *tomorrow*, Topaz, for Christ's sake.'

'Why does that matter? I know you'll be objective,' Topaz said, moving towards him.

She knew she shouldn't be here. But she couldn't help it. Some innate desire to tease her lover had proved too strong to resist. She loved seeing his face like that, taut with anger and impatience, as though he despaired of her. Topaz knew it reminded him of the difference in their ages, and she played on that mercilessly. Making him do things he'd sworn not to do. Forcing him to consider all the taboos he was breaking with her. Forcing him to remember *why* he was breaking them.

Anything to provoke.

Anything to arouse.

Anything to help his passion, his vitality, match up to hers.

Nathan leant across his desk and took her head in his hands, gazing at the soft, tanned skin, the sparkling blue eyes, the wild red hair. She'd picked out a short Mark Eisen suit in bright yellow, set with pretty enamel buttons shaped like large daisies. She was wearing some fresh, summery perfume – Chanel No. 19, he thought. She was sensational.

Rosen pressed his lips down on hers, her riot of colour muted by the sober navy of his Savile Row suit. 'Think Jewish, dress British.' One of the only pieces of advice his father had bothered to give him, and pretty good advice too, Rosen had always thought.

He pushed his tongue into her mouth, enjoying her instant response, enjoying her surprise.

The young are so arrogant, Rosen mused.

'Now get out of here,' he said firmly as he pulled off her. 'You've got work to do, Ms Rossi. Didn't you tell me this morning that you were planning a piece on that new girl over at Musica Records? The one who's just set up here? I thought you were hot on doing some kind of exposé for *US Woman*. She's got quite a reputation already, this girl. What's her name again?'

'Rowena Gordon,' said Topaz, drawing back from him. Her face had taken on a new hardness. 'But she's not important. It's the band I'm interested in. There has to be a story there.'

Nathan looked up. Interesting. Now she was fidgeting, couldn't wait to get back downstairs. He sighed. The girl was a mystery to him.

'OK, good,' he said curtly. 'Atomic Mass, isn't that their name? Joe told me you were digging around them, now I come to think of it. Should make a good story. The rumours about them are wild. Apparently they're the next –'

'I know,' she said shortly.

He smiled at her. She was crazy and mixed up, but he adored her.

'I'll see you tonight,' Nathan said, as she turned to go. 'I love you. And by the way, Rowena Gordon *is* important, Topaz. If she makes something of this new company, she'll be in a very powerful position.'

*

Thursday, 6 July dawned muggy and overcast. Grey skies loomed over the city, hardly dissipating the heat that seemed to steam up from the crowded sidewalks and logjammed roads.

The two candidates for editor of American Magazines' new upmarket glossy, *Economic Monthly*, rode the elevator to the boardroom on the fifty-ninth floor, one floor down from Gowers' glass cradle of power. Both were wearing suits and immaculately groomed, but Joe Goldstein looked by far the more confident and relaxed.

He was carrying a large canvas folder containing charts and statistics for his presentation. It was an understandable, witty and highly expert summary of macroeconomic conditions, designed to demonstrate once and for all how suitable he was to edit this title – if his existing magazines hadn't already established that beyond doubt.

He glanced at Topaz, who'd come armed with nothing at all. She was nervously tapping one hand against her thigh.

Joe hardened his heart. Little girls that bite off more than they can chew get hurt; if Topaz Rossi insisted on playing out of her league, she was just going to have to learn her lesson the hard way.

He looked her over again, surreptitiously.

He'd been right about that cute ass, though.

The senior committee watched Joe Goldstein giving the most polished, urbane performance of his life. They were fascinated, laughing and nodding from time to time. Nate Rosen glanced at the papers of the man seated next to him; he'd made a note to call his broker.

Actually, Nate thought Goldstein was being pretty gracious about this. He was paying Topaz the compliment of giving it his best shot, not just showing up to have management rubber-stamp a decision which was basically already made.

He glanced at Topaz, sitting in a chair against the far wall, watching Joe with polite attentiveness. She was dressed soberly – navy Dior, rebellious red curls swept back in a severe bun – and she seemed anxious. Rosen felt a pang. He wanted to comfort her, to tell her it didn't matter, that she was only twenty-three, there'd be plenty more titles for her later. He noticed the way her full breasts rose and fell as she breathed, pushing against the stiff linen of her jacket. He wanted her.

Nathan turned resolutely back to Joe, embarrassed. He was supposed to be concentrating. Damn it, this whole situation was his fault. His judgment wasn't sober or impartial, not these days. He veered too far one way, then too far the other. This so-called contest for *Economic Monthly*, for example. It was one instance where he thought she was totally off-track competing for it and Matt Gowers was just trying to look liberated by fielding a woman candidate. But it was his fault too. He had endorsed her for it, when she'd insisted on trying out. He'd sat there in the chairman's office and told his boss it was between Joe and Topaz.

Who was he trying to kid? Joe was always going to destroy her, and now here he was, destroying her right on cue. He, Rosen, both as Topaz's lover and her boss, should have been cruel to be kind and refused to put her name forward. Now his own judgment would be called into question.

But that was his mistake, his error. And he'd been making Topaz pay for it. Coming down on her like a ton of bricks in the editors' meetings. Cutting her dead in front of their colleagues.

'. . . if it's dinars or dollars,' Goldstein concluded to warm laughter and applause, and walked over to the chair next to Topaz, offering his hand to her as he sat down. She shook it briskly, avoiding eye contact with him, murmuring congratulations. The board at the table in front of them had their heads down scribbling brief comments on their sheets of paper. But it was obvious from the genial smiles on their faces what they thought.

He did look terrific up there, Topaz admitted to herself. Absolutely terrific. It's a shame he's such a jerk, because that is one handsome, self-possessed sonofabitch.

'And now,' said the presiding secretary, 'the board will hear Ms Topaz Rossi, editor of *Girlfriend* magazine and still a journalistic contributor to many of our other titles. Ms Rossi, if you please.'

Topaz got to her feet and regarded the seven pairs of eyes looking at her with little more than polite interest.

'Mr Goldstein's presentation was the best, and the funniest, piece of economic analysis I think I've ever heard,' she began in a clear voice. 'And if he were applying for the job of chief correspondent or senior features writer, I would give it to him without hesitation.'

She paused.

'But it isn't the editor's job to write the magazine. I had dinner with Mr Goldstein last month, and I admitted to him then that I was no expert in economics. I said that I *was* an expert in selling magazines. And that's still true.'

The seven pairs of eyes now looked considerably more interested.

'The job of editor – the *editor*, mind you – at *Economic Monthly* will not be to explain the General Agreement on Tariffs and Trade. It will be to take advertising and circulation away from *The Economist, Forbes, Fortune* and *Business Week*. And this is how I would do that.'

Holy Shit! thought Nathan Rosen.

The board watched her, riveted.

Chapter Sixteen

The public rivalry started with Marissa Matthews' column, 'Friday's People', published two weeks after the party.

Seeing Topaz with Nathan as a couple in public, and hearing what had happened at the *Economic Monthly* pitch, Marissa didn't pull any punches. On either of them.

Catfight at the most important party of the year . . . Musica Records executive embarrassing her boss . . . Fiery redhead Topaz Rossi . . . innuendo about 'sleeping with interviewees' . . . do we remember the mysterious David Levine exclusive? . . . Watch out, Manhattan, here come the Career Girls!

'Ridiculous!' said Topaz, annoyed. She flung the paper on to the kitchen table and dialled Marissa Matthews at home. 'What do you mean by this?' she demanded.

'Who is it, please?' purred Matthews, as if she didn't know.

'It's Topaz Rossi,' replied Topaz, furious.

'Darling!' Marissa crooned. 'Are you a little bit upset about the column?'

'Marissa, I –'

'Journalistic integrity, sweetie. You, of all people, should understand that. I mean, just look what you did to that ravishing film star.'

'He was a woman-beater!' Topaz snapped, incensed at the comparison.

'Well, darling, I haven't ruined your career, now have I? It's simply the truth that you and your friend did make a scene at dear Elizabeth's party, and it was so very dramatic! All that wonderful stuff about territory, and sleeping with people to get interviews! Not that I *personally* believe it, of course, but one always wondered how you got that story . . . it did kick-start your career in the most fabulous way, and I *do* have a duty to my readers.'

She paused, then repeated with relish, 'To my many *millions* of readers, especially in New York – I mean, sweetie, anyone who is anyone in this town reads . . .'

Topaz slammed the phone down on her in disgust.

'I think it's funny,' Michael Krebs told her. 'It's a hell of a way to announce your arrival, though. You have some kind of history with this girl?'

'I don't want to talk about it,' Rowena answered wearily. Her phone had been going all day from reporters wanting to run a 'Rivals' story in various magazines.

Krebs nodded. A story like this was bad news.

'Did Oberman have anything to say?'

'Yes he did,' she said shortly. Her chairman had the 'Friday's People' column faxed to him every week, and was none too pleased to see his newly appointed MD starring in what was described as a bitch-fight during the most important social event of the year. He'd given her a lecture of businesslike conduct, ending up with 'You know what, Rowena? A lot of people in this industry don't like me putting a woman in charge. Don't make it harder for me by giving them ammunition.'

She had burned with shame at the rebuke, more so because he was right.

'Forget about it,' Krebs told her. 'You've got enough to do setting up this label. I know it's been tough.'

'It has. It is,' she said, under pressure and anxious.

'I could help,' Michael offered, brushing her hair out of her eyes. She felt the cool metal of his wedding ring against her temple.

'It's my problem. I'll handle it,' Rowena said, but already part of her was wondering if she could.

BOOM! Atomic Mass were everywhere. And that meant *everywhere*.

Displays in the store windows. Ads in the music magazines. Billboards across the city, cleverly designed to show a picture of the boys, slouching together against a wall and looking meanly at the cameras, like five long-haired versions of James Dean. The one-word strapline at the base of the posters said simply: COMING.

MTV had an exclusive right to show the video, and it was making good use of it. God, sometimes heavy rotation means *heavy rotation*, Rowena thought, delighted, as she switched on yet again and found it pumping away.

Zach Freeman, holding his guitar like an offensive weapon.

Alex Sexton, strumming hard at the bass and checking out the girls in the front, cute pieces of jailbait with the darkly kohled eyes that were in fashion amongst the alternative music crowd right now. Despite the perfect street-cred calling cards, the camera showed all the women in a very old-fashioned state of high sexual excitement.

Mark Thomas attacking his drumkit like it just insulted his mother. Pan to shots of guys in the audience, screaming approval and hurling themselves into a raging mosh-pit.

Jake Williams, rhythm guitarist, grinding out a swing that you wouldn't believe.

And Joe Hunter, lead singer, six foot three of Lancashire muscle, with his tumbling brown hair and handsome, slightly slanted eyes, taking total control of the stage, prowling like a wild panther, all his youth and inexperience counting for nothing. He didn't need experience.

He was a natural.

He was a star.

'But is it on the radio? We need airplay,' Josh fretted, ringing her the first day Warners had released the track to radio.

'Oberman,' his new managing director soothed him, 'it's on the radio. It's on the playlist for every Top Forty station in New York. The song is a fucking phenomenon.'

'Is it getting out to the other markets? Dallas, LA, Chicago, Minnesota?' Josh asked the next day. 'Warners swear it is. But they would. You tell me.'

'It's breaking out like a rash. Like it was contagious,' Rowena assured him.

'You know what? This business is going to rot your brain,' he told her. 'Forget that Oxford education, your vocabulary is about to contract into two sentences – "It's a hit." "It's not a hit." '

'This,' said Rowena firmly, 'is a hit.'

Oberman laughed, his grating roar reaching across the Atlantic, rich with satisfaction. 'I think you might be right,' he said. 'That bastard Krebs! I thought he was doing us a favour, but he was just spotting talent. Now he gets five per cent off the top. Sonofabitch! I've known the guy for long enough, I should have guessed.'

Rowena couldn't resist it. 'If you'd come up with a million five in the first place,' she pointed out, 'we wouldn't be getting royally screwed now. Anyway, why *did* you tell me to go and get Michael Krebs for a hundred and fifty thousand dollars? You must have known that was never gonna happen.'

'I did,' Oberman admitted. 'I dunno, kid, it was an impulse. I wanted to send you in to get him with your back against the wall. See what you'd come up with. I had a sense that you two would be good together, and I wanted him to get interested in you. With the right amount of money, you'd have been just another client to him. And Atomic Mass would have been just another band.'

Rowena put the phone down, feeling yet again that Josh Oberman was one of the most cunning, knowing men alive. How well he'd understood Michael Krebs. How well he'd understood *her*.

And the rise of Atomic Mass continued at full force.

Barbara Lincoln had flown over and checked into the Paramount and Rowena was to meet her there every morning to begin the promotional round. Officially, it was none of her business. Rowena worked for Musica, and until they built up a distribution network Atomic Mass's label in the States was Elektra. But Barbara and the band insisted, so that was that. Rowena, and usually Michael Krebs, too, piled into the limo with the guys as they headed off to the Warners building to start the day's round of interviews, photoshoots and radio phone-ins.

She had no time to attend to the new label. Forget that, Rowena thought. It'll wait.

'Hey, Rowena! How's it going?' Barbara asked her, kissing her on the cheek. She admired the burgundy Donna Karan tunic, the Charles David pumps, the silk hose from Wolford's. 'You look terrific.'

'So do you,' her friend said, returning the kiss and the admiring glance. Barbara was dressed in a silk slip Armani dress, complete with beaded straps, Italian heels and a Hermès scarf. Every day she turned up in something impossibly glamorous and totally impractical. Barbara made no concessions to minor matters like the dirt of Manhattan or the fact that all the Warners people wore jeans.

Let's face it, Rowena thought, smiling. Barbara makes no concessions to anything.

'It's the only reason we're working with you,' Mark teased them. 'Can't be surrounded by anything except beautiful women now. Bad for our image.'

'Our image! You fucking prat,' Joe snarled, pushing his drummer in the shoulder.

'Hangover?' asked Krebs, who was sitting directly across from Rowena in the limo. He'd nodded curtly at her as she got in the car, and that was about it. Michael was supercautious these days. The old gushing about her talents had gone completely, and since she'd arrived in New York he had scarcely complimented her publicly. Rowena had been forced to point out to him that unless he acknowledged that they were at least friends, everyone would assume they were having an affair. You don't go from red-hot to ice-cold without a good reason. God, men were so stupid. Especially the smart ones.

Joe nodded, grimacing. 'Went down to Continental Divide. I was on shorts all night.'

'You'll pay,' said Michael, like a stern father.

The singer shrugged as their limo pulled smoothly away into the traffic.

'What he doesn't say is that he was up all night with these three girls who –'

'Zach!' Krebs warned sharply, glancing at their manager, but the guitarist grinned.

'Barbara don't give a fuck about that,' he said, quite accurately.

She nodded, smiling at the producer with elegant indifference. Rowena marvelled at how changed she was. Just a few months looking after a rock band, and Barbara already understood the first instinctive rules. Like, you don't mess with your act's sex life.

'They can do what they like. They're not old married men like you, Michael,' Barbara said. *And even so I wouldn't give a fuck*, her tone implied.

Krebs grunted.

When the band and Barbara had got deep into a discussion of promotion for the album launch, he finally looked over at Rowena. Cute dress. She looked like a schoolgirl in that dress. Michael felt himself getting aroused. He was disturbed, he'd planned on giving her up by now. Any longer and something must surely slip, she'd tell Barbara, she'd mention something to Josh, the band would pick up on it. There was no way he could risk Debbie finding out.

He loved his wife, and he lived for his sons. The family. It was the most important thing in life, Michael always said. His own parents had provided for him, but little more; to this day he resented them for it. Ten thousand dollars' worth of therapy swore his control-freak tendencies came directly from that. And Michael thought it was true. He could remember deciding that if that was the way it was gonna be, then he was going to be in full control. Permanently.

Maybe that was the lure of Rowena Gordon, Krebs thought, letting his dark gaze travel slowly up those slender calves, to the shadow under the fall of her skirt, and then further up, as if he could see through the darkness through sheer force of will, please himself by gazing at those pale, supple thighs and the delights that lay between them. There had been many women, some more beautiful, more skilled in bed than Rowena. But few so intelligent as she was. Michael Krebs, like many Jewish men, prized intelligence in everyone, including women. It didn't scare him off, it attracted him. Amongst other things it meant that Rowena came to him with her eyes open, having understood the hopelessness of her position, but coming to his bed anyway. And maybe that was the lure. His complete control over her.

I love my wife. I've been a good father to my sons, better than my father was to me, Krebs thought, and then Rowena shifted in her seat and caught him staring at her. He watched her instant reaction, the lips parting, the blood rushing to the face, her green eyes glancing at him, then away again, pretending to watch midtown Manhattan through the limo's tinted windows. His cock hardened in his pants. Bang, just like that. He had her again.

The band and Barbara were still jabbering away at each other.

'Rowena,' Michael said softly. Her name, a command.

She looked at him, her thighs flaming from the feeling that he'd been looking at her, thinking about her, reminding himself of the last things they'd done together. Lust started to lick at her. It had been four days ago, just before the release of the record. Michael had taken her to her apartment on West 67th and made her undress for him in her bedroom, removing her clothes exactly as he instructed. He had been excruciatingly slow, making her wait, turn and move as he directed, so that by the time she was naked Rowena was so aroused she could hardly stand up. Krebs had sat there, fully clothed, his erection clearly visible under his jeans, and made her just stand before him, naked, while he talked to her about what he was going to do with her and how, getting Rowena hotter and hotter, until she was weeping with sheer desire, but he'd still made her stand there. She remembered how the combination of being so exposed in front of a clothed man, and what he was saying, and her submission to him, had brought her so close to the brink that when Krebs stood up and came across to her, still not touching her, and had very deliberately walked round her, staring at the whole of her body, her ass, her breasts, her legs, and finally let his gaze trail obviously and slowly between her legs, Rowena's haunches had shuddered in an uncontrollable movement and she'd climaxed, coming for Michael Krebs when he hadn't even laid a finger on her.

'Yes, Michael?' she replied now, the coolness of her tone belying the wild heat in her belly.

What's wrong with me? Rowena thought. I can't even be near the guy without melting all over the seat.

Krebs smiled, his liquid black eyes refusing to accept her outward calm. 'Wanna have lunch?' he asked casually. 'I can play you the final mixes for the b-sides.'

'Sure,' Rowena said, anticipation oozing from every pore.

Oh, love was a drug. It made you higher than acid or ecstasy or anything. Michael, Michael, the universe itself was less important than his smile, he was the first thing she thought of when she woke in the mornings and the last image in her mind at night. There was the trial of setting up the label. The triumph of watching Atomic Mass break. The danger of Topaz Rossi, something Rowena sensed, feared, and knew she'd have to deal with.

But over that and above it was Michael Krebs, and the heady, maddening passion Rowena felt for him. Love. Like a fine, golden mist, settling over everything. Informing everything she did. The backdrop to life. *What will Krebs think? When can I tell him? What would Michael do? Where is he now?*

Yes, she knew he was married.

Yes, she knew he had children.

Yes, she knew it was wrong.

But Rowena Gordon didn't care. She was in love, in that rare, complete thraldom that true first love demands. Anyone who has ever experienced it knows exactly what it's like. Rowena, as she sat in that car, looking at her married lover, was prepared to sacrifice anything and everything in order to keep him around. Her pride. Her heart. Her principles. Her honour.

'It's your turn, I think,' Michael said, holding her in their private conversation, locking her gaze in his.

'To buy lunch? Yeah, I think so too,' Rowena agreed, inflecting her tone with just that subtle shade of extra meaning Michael had used.

They both knew what he meant. That Michael had pleasured Rowena the last time they met, and it was her turn now. She would do what he loved, sweeping her long, fine hair across his body so it teased him with millions of featherlight strokes, then moving down with her lips and her tongue until she reached his groin, then teasing the wiry grey hairs around the flat of his stomach, circling the base of his cock until he couldn't stand it any more, and grabbed her head by the hair, insistently pushing her down on him. Sometimes Rowena licked him first, the tip of her tongue running round the tip of his cock, flicking at the sensitive little triangle just under the crown, and then when the pleasure got too much for him to bear without coming, moving down to the base again, then holding him hard and wet in her hands, using her fingers and tongue to bring him to a crashing orgasm. Other times, she simply responded by taking him deep, deep into her mouth, carefully angling his thickness so it got to the very back of her throat. Michael could only take a little of that before he came, erupting into her with a groan of satisfaction, staggered at how incredible it felt to see this girl swallow him whole. She was so good at sucking cock, he thought he'd died and gone to heaven. And she loved it. That was what truly aroused Michael so much that sometimes he woke up in the night, next to his wife, with a raging hard-on for Rowena that refused to go away. Other women would either refuse or grudgingly agree to it, as a special favour to their men. You could order a groupie to do what you liked, of course. But that was quid pro quo. Rowena was so into Michael, so wild with lust for him, that she *fantasized* about doing it to him. She begged for it. And he'd never known *anything* – not on tour, not with girlfriends, not with his wife – like the rapture he felt when Rowena Gordon was kneeling in front of him, her long blonde hair halfway down her back, her little bud nipples erect, giving him head, her eyes closed in sexual frenzy, making those tiny choking sounds at the back of her throat that drove him fucking crazy, as he rammed himself into her, roughly, forcing her to take it all in, asking her how he tasted, if she wanted more, if she loved it. Once she'd even reached up blindly, groping for his hands, and he hadn't known what she wanted until with a fresh rush of sex he understood she was putting them on the back of her head, asking for it harder, deeper, more.

Michael felt his hard-on swelling.

Rowena saw it.

A conspiratorial look passed between them, shared desire, shared annoyance at being in company, shared helplessness to do anything about it. And then Rowena grinned, and Krebs winked at her, and they felt a huge surge of affection and friendship, on top of the desire.

Christ, I like *him so much*, Rowena marvelled.

That girl is terrific, Michael thought.

The limo purred to a halt outside the Warners offices, and as it did so, a small crew of photographers ran forward, poised to snap pictures of the band.

'Get used to it, guys,' Barbara said, glancing at her producer and A&R girl with evident satisfaction. 'You'll need to.'

HEAT STREET – OUT NEXT WEEK, screamed the banner ads.

New British Invasion? asked *RIP* magazine, giving a picture of Joe space on the cover.

Oh, You Pretty Things, cooed the *Village Voice*.

'What's heavy metal got that rap and country don't?' asked *Rolling Stone*. 'Precious little, if recent sales are anything to go by. Except, of course, metal can lay claim to Atomic Mass, a new band from England who are causing a sensation on MTV with "Karla", the first single on their Krebs-produced debut *Heat Street*, out on Warners next week. Playing music brutal enough to appeal to fans of early Metallica, and good-looking enough to steal young girls from the teenybop bands, the act are tipped as the next Led Zeppelin. Can you say *crossover*?'

Overhyped. Overrated. Over here ran the headline in *Westside's* influential music section atop a devastating attack, sneering at alternative fans for falling at the feet of a band 'snug in the arms of the machine, protected by Warners' marketing might and Michael Krebs's Midas touch'. The Wednesday that article ran, the band's low-key gig at CBGBs was half empty.

'Fuck 'em, if they want to stay away because some paper tells them to,' Jake snarled, but he wasn't used to playing to an audience with gaps in it and it pissed him off.

'Is Topaz Rossi behind this?' Josh Oberman demanded from London, spitting with rage. 'I've got the fucking *NME* and *Melody Maker* all ready to run articles on Atomic Mass being a heavy metal Suede. And MTV Europe reported the CBGB show on the news.'

'Yes, she is,' Rowena said, her anger returning.

'That bitch!' her boss swore. 'Is this her idea of revenge?'

Rowena smiled grimly. 'Oh, this isn't Topaz's revenge,' she told him. 'This is just a calling card.'

Topaz needn't worry herself, Rowena thought. She was having enough trouble here without needing any help.

Everyone took Atomic Mass seriously.

No one took Musica Records seriously.

As the scout who'd signed the flavour of the month, Rowena Gordon was respected, regularly showered with job offers, and had her ass kissed by promoters and agents and anyone who thought she might have some clout with Barbara Lincoln.

As the 'Managing Director' – *yeah, right!* – of Luther Records, the name she'd given to Musica's new subsidiary in New York, she couldn't persuade an act to sign with her. No big-time managers would commit their new acts to a European company that was just tinkering around in the United States. No, they were all happy to deal with Musica in Europe, but let a US major sign the act first and then rent it out to Musica for Europe.

The trouble with that was that the US label took a royalty. Just like Musica did when Elektra sold an Atomic Mass single.

And they'd go on missing American repertoire.

And she, Rowena, would have failed.

Rowena looked out at the lights of Manhattan from Luther's tiny, cramped offices at the top of a narrow building on Leonard Street, and knew there was no way she was giving up. Michael Krebs lived here, Atomic Mass were tasting their first big success here, and fifty per cent of all the records in the world were sold here. Anyway, she loved New York. She'd made friends in her building, friends in the clubs, friends down at the Marquee, the Bottom Line, and all the other venues where her face was getting known. Josh Oberman had been right about her wanting to change her life.

Here people were interested in what she did, not who her parents were.

Hadn't Rick Rubin managed it? Rowena reminded herself sternly, after another door slammed in her face. Surely she could do it. All she had to do was find a really talented, really good new band who'd be happy to sign with her despite the risks. A band so new they didn't *have* a fucking manager.

She stared out at the city. It was the place to be, she could feel that in her bones. Lady Liberty, wasn't she the patron saint of career girls?

Fuck you, Topaz Rossi, Rowena thought. *I'm here to stay*.

All she had to do was sign a good band. Fast.

Chapter Seventeen

The rivalry escalated with Joe Hunter on *Oprah*.

'But why do you guys get such adulation from some of the press, and yet other magazines are . . .'

She held up a copy of *White Light*, the cover plastered with a shot of Mark Thomas taken during some gig, in motion. His mouth was open and his eyes were shut in a pose that made him look like a moron. The strapline was WORST BAND IN THE WORLD?

The audience laughed. Oprah held the magazine between thumb and forefinger, as if it were a piece of trash, the wry expression on her face making her distaste clear.

'Oh, it don't bother us,' Joe answered firmly, the northern accent making some women on the audience visibly squirm on their seats in delight. 'We don't care about the press, we only care about the fans. We've just hit number one in America with our first single and we're on tour with bloody Guns n' Roses. *White Light* can go . . . stuff themselves,' he finished carefully, remembering just in time that they were on coast-to-coast TV.

The host smiled, charmed by the singer's forthright speaking. In an age where most rock stars' *hairdressers* had publicity agents, and said exactly what they were told, Atomic Mass obviously couldn't care less. They smoked, they drank, they ate red meat, they screwed a lot of girls and they said things like '*White Light* can go stuff themselves' on primetime shows.

They were likeable.

They were dangerous.

They meant *ratings*.

'Fair enough,' she said. 'And you have no idea why opinion on you is so split?'

Joe gestured to the magazine she was holding. 'With that one there I do,' he said. 'That article was written by Josie Simons. She writes in-house on music for American Magazines, and her boss is a girl called Topaz Rossi, who's an old rival of our A&R girl, Rowena Gordon – the woman who gave us a record deal. Rowena's working in New York now, and Topaz Rossi is determined to give her a really hard time. So she gets at us. There's hardly been one article published by magazines in that company that don't slag us off. So we ignore it.'

'Are you sure?' Oprah asked, scenting something interesting. Like a high-profile libel case, for a start.

Joe shrugged. 'Barbara Lincoln, our manager, went through all the American Magazines articles with us. They're all the same. Maybe it's coincidence, but I don't think so.'

'And how do you feel about that?'

Hunter leant forward and looked straight into the camera, his brown eyes angry. He knew this girl Rossi would be watching.

'It's what you expect, right?' he replied. 'Rowena Gordon's a doer. Rowena participates, and Topaz commentates. It don't mean nothing to Atomic Mass.'

With her perfect sense of timing, Oprah let the tension hang in the air for just long enough. Then she waded in to break it up.

'A female talent scout, a female manager – we don't think of Atomic Mass as exactly leading the feminist charge,' she remarked to loud laughter. The first album wasn't even out yet, and already the stories of what they got up to on the road were being printed in the *National Enquirer*. 'Do you like working with women?'

Joe gave the camera a wink.

'We like doing *everything* with women,' he replied.

'It reflects badly on the company,' Matt Gowers said. 'I take on board what you're saying, Topaz – and we all know your work on *Girlfriend* is terrific and your journalistic contributions to *US Woman* are invaluable.'

Joe Goldstein kept his face impassive as he watched Rossi burning up with humiliation. She was obviously itching to defend herself, but he'd noticed Nathan Rosen kick her under the table, and she was now biting her lips in order to force herself to keep quiet.

'And we couldn't be happier with the way *Economic Monthly* is selling,' Gowers added.

For once, the reference to his recent defeat didn't hit Joe in the solar plexus. No, it was Rossi's turn to try to hold her head up in front of her colleagues. *Don't smile, don't smile, don't smile*, thought Joe. Topaz had gloated when she surprised everybody by beating him out of the new glossy. She'd lost a lot of friends that way.

He glanced round the editors' meeting. A number of them were looking down and smirking. This was the first real setback Topaz had had since she joined the company, and many of them weren't sorry. The girl had started to act like she was the Queen of Sheba. Like she was invincible.

Well, that long-haired English boy had had other ideas.

Not that this was a threat to Topaz's career, as the

chairman was making clear. But it was her first fuck-up. Rap-on-the-knuckles time.

Joe Goldstein was enjoying himself.

'But even if, as you say, you didn't bring pressure to bear on Josie or Tiz or Jason, Topaz, it looks bad. Our lawyers have told us we'd have a tough time bringing a case. So unless there's a real story, lay off this band, OK?'

'Yes, sir,' said Topaz, ashamed and enraged. The fact that Gowers was obviously right only made it worse. She could feel the eyes of her co-workers crawling over her skin.

Topaz glanced at Joe Goldstein, who wasn't looking at her. Apparently he was fascinated by the meeting agenda. She knew that it was an act, he was faking it to be polite.

Self-righteous jerk! she thought.

Rowena Gordon watched the sun sinking over Central Park from her luxurious apartment window, and felt her heart sinking with it. Another night of futile talent-hunting. Another night when she didn't want the acts that were prepared to sign with Luther Records, and the ones she did want wouldn't sign.

She pulled on her clothes. Tailored black slacks by Ralph Lauren. Long-sleeved Soundgarden shirt. Ankleboots by Manolo Blahnik.

That day at work, the Luther offices had been almost silent. Lucy, her secretary, had taken exactly four calls; three of them from Josh Oberman about work on the new Roxana Perdita record back home – Jack Reich was supervising her career now, but Rowena liked to keep in touch with her other two acts – and one from Matthew Stevenson, sneeringly asking when they might see a New York band in exchange for their investment. He'd pretended it was a joke, but Rowena knew better.

It wasn't as if she was in danger of getting fired. As long as Roxana, Bitter Spice and of course Atomic Mass kept selling records, she was safe. Even without the protection of Joshua Oberman and Michael Krebs.

But there was a timebomb under her, and she knew it. Oberman had been given leave to develop an American operation over the objections of other board members, and there was a time limit on her bringing home some bacon. Three months. After that, they'd close the American company and bring her back to run Atomic's career in Europe.

She was one month down.

Rowena walked into the bedroom to grab her bag, and was greeted with the sight of her rumpled bed, the Irish linen sheets tumbled from her sex with Michael Krebs that afternoon. A mixed-up pang of lust and longing ran through her, and she buried her face in the bedclothes, drinking in the scent of him. She felt like crying. Michael had been so detached this afternoon, so cold. When he was dressed, he'd turned to her and said, 'I'm just gonna call my wife and then I'm gonna get back to the studio,' and when he'd seen her stricken expression, Krebs had added, annoyed, 'Come on, Rowena. I'm not rubbing it in your face. We're friends and that's it.'

She could still feel the inexpressible chill that had run through her. *My wife. My sons. My family, which is a tight little club from which* you *are excluded.*

And even worse, the subtext. *I love my wife. I don't love you. I'll never love you.*

Why was he so bloody honest about it? Rowena thought bitterly. At least if he lied, she could hate him. She could blame him. She could say she was tricked, deceived like all the other mistresses from time immemorial with promises that he loved her, he'd leave his wife for her. But Michael Krebs was a stand-up guy. He followed his own rules and he wouldn't lie to her. In fact, he preferred almost anything to discussing their relationship.

'Let's talk about us,' Rowena would say. If she was feeling brave.

'Us? There is no *us*,' Michael would answer with displeasure. 'We're *friends*. I've said it before.'

'I try to measure what I do by whether you would do it,' Rowena said to him, as they stood together in a private box at Madison Square Gardens, waiting for Atomic Mass to come on and play their support set.

Michael gave her an affectionate smile. 'Except that you should try to be the most moral and ethical person you can be.'

She felt a great sense of distress. 'But Michael, you are, totally moral and ethical,' she said.

'Except in one respect.'

'That's my fault,' Rowena said.

'No, it's my fault,' he replied, also sadly.

She hated to hear him say he felt guilty, when guilt was eating her alive. She hated to think of herself as a mistress, but was furious when he refused even to call her that. She could see, quite clearly, as though she were watching someone else, how hopeless and destructive this affair was for both of them, but especially her. After all, Michael wasn't in love.

Rowena Gordon had decided – a cold, academic, intelligent decision – that she was not going to end up like all those other women. Abandoned by a lover who ran back to his wife, frozen out of the society of mutual friends, begging the guy to call her again. She'd seen it happen to girlfriends of the band. All of a sudden you were out of the charmed circle, doors shut, access revoked. Well, *she* was a career girl, even if her progress was a little slow right now. She was young, beautiful, well-bred and self-reliant. She wasn't about to immolate herself on the altar of a married man twice her age – even if he was a musical genius, frighteningly intelligent, ferociously intelligent, devastatingly handsome, one of her all-time heroes, spectacular in bed . . . *oh, Christ Almighty. Oh, dear God*, Rowena thought, forcing herself to pull her face out of the sheets. She'd have to tell him to get lost. At least as far as sex went.

But in her heart she knew they were empty words. Rowena was so in love with Michael Krebs she couldn't see straight.

'Come on,' she said aloud. 'Let's go to work.'

The *Girlfriend* offices were busy as hell. Phones were ringing off the hook, the staff writers were yelling at each other, teen models in Gap outfits traipsed round the desks, waiting for Sasha Stone or Alex Waters to call them into the photo room for that week's fashion layout. In one corner, the sales and advertising team were busiest of all, sitting in almost permanent crouches over their desks, either dealing with desperate make-up companies, fighting over the last square inches of ad space, or logging yet more orders from new retailers, mom-and-pop stores outside the national loop.

Success, success, success. It was only the editor's insistence that stopped them from doubling the thickness of each issue with glossy ads, or raising the cover price by ten cents. Topaz let nothing interfere with the magazine itself. *Girlfriend* was a sensation, and she planned on keeping it that way.

'Where's the editor? I need to speak to the editor,' a stylist begged Tiz Correy, the talented twenty-year-old features editor.

Topaz had hired her own crew, and she'd hired

carefully: young, gifted kids barely older than their target readers. The strategy had proved brilliant, and Rossi had repeated it over at *Economic Monthly*, where the most media-friendly Harvard experts had columns next to guest industrialists, powerful figures who wrote every month on their personal rules for profitability – Ross Perot, Rupert Murdoch, Michael Eisner. With both her titles, Topaz followed her gut instincts. With both of them, she followed what she thought was a fundamental trait in the American psyche – the need to hero-worship. For teenage girls, that meant Madonna. For businessmen, that meant Bill Gates. But the rule was the same.

'American Magazines' new flagship comes across as *Vanity Fair* meets *The Economist*,' sneered the *Wall Street Journal*, but as far as Topaz was concerned, the only good title was one that sold.

Economic Monthly was selling.

'The boss is busy,' Tiz shrugged, gesturing to the editor's office, the door of which was firmly shut. Even over the din of the offices, the sound of raised voices – a man's and a woman's – could be heard.

'But Sasha won't let me dress Jolene in her Jean-Paul Gaultier jacket. And it would look *divine*,' the little man pouted. 'Who's she talking to, anyway?'

'Mr Rosen. He's a director of the board,' Tiz answered firmly, hoping to shut him up. 'And Jolene will wear the Gap like everyone else. *Girlfriend* readers can't afford Jean-Paul Gaultier.'

'How could you not let me know? I am so goddamn embarrassed!' Nathan shouted. '*White Light. Westside.* Fucking *Girlfriend* magazine. Article after article on this goddamn band! We look so stupid, Topaz! And I get it shoved in my face on fucking *Oprah*!'

'I didn't write them all,' Topaz said sullenly. Couldn't he give it a break? She'd had the lecture this morning.

'Yeah, but you let your feelings be known to the people whose pay cheques you sign. In no uncertain terms. Am I right?' demanded Nathan, stalking round her office. The blue vein at the side of his grey temple was pulsing, and he looked awkward in the tailored suit.

'Can't we talk about it later?' Topaz asked.

Rosen felt anger rise up in his throat, half choking him. He felt so stressed-out, his blood pressure must be off the scale. First that damn *Oprah* show airs yesterday, and no one has the guts to mention it to him because the girl he's living with is the one being criticized. Then Topaz and he had a fight last night because she wanted to make love again, and he didn't. Who did she think he was? Superman? And to cap it all, Matt Gowers had called him into his office this morning and fucking carpeted him.

As director of the East Coast, he was responsible for editorial policy. As Topaz Rossi's line manager, he was responsible for her actions. And as a board member living with one of the staff, he'd better be damn sure he didn't get any wires crossed.

'I value you and I value Topaz,' Gowers had said dryly. 'And what you do in your spare time is nobody's business but yours. *Except* when it interferes in our affairs. You should have seen this and stopped it, Rosen. Don't let it happen again.'

'No, sir,' Nathan said, nodding.

It was his textbook nightmare, come to life.

'No we *cannot* talk about it later!' he roared, suddenly *Westside*'s editor again, faced with an impertinent junior. 'Later is *personal*! This is *business*!'

He wrenched open the door. 'I hope to hell you can separate the two of them, Topaz,' he said. 'Because we don't have a future if you can't.'

Rowena threaded her way through the crowd to Joe, precariously balancing two large vodkas on the rocks. CBGBs was only half full, the narrow corridor of the club still giving her space to breathe. Not like a week ago, when Atomic had played a warm-up gig to start the tour. Tonight she could actually see Velocity, the new band, onstage, as well as hear the dark, brittle frenzy of their movement. It pounded through the club, hard as diamonds, heavy as lead.

Joe was slouching against one of the far walls, which was papered with flyers. She could see the intent expression on his face as he watched the band, carefully, the way one musician watches another. Rowena felt happiness wash through her. This was what made it all worthwhile. A dark club, a great band, optimism, music. To the kids in the crowd she was just another girl, a pretty student type from NYU. They accepted her as one of them, without comment, and she loved that.

'What do you reckon?' she asked Joe, handing him his drink.

'I think you should go for it,' he replied, not taking his eyes off the stage.

'That's what I think, too,' Rowena said happily.

They were both too engrossed with Velocity to notice the short, unassuming brunette a few paces behind them, watching them both and making notes.

On his way home – he and Topaz never left the office together – Nate Rosen was struck by a pang of remorse. Topaz's stricken face when he threatened to break up with her had been on his mind all day. He saw something that had been absent from her personality almost as long as he'd known her.

Fear.

The Topaz Rossi he knew was not about fear. She was about stupid risks, naked aggression and brilliant journalism. She was about imagination and a refusal to give up. The Topaz who'd shot down David Levine. Who'd surprised the whole board by creaming Joe Goldstein for *Economic Monthly*.

That vote, he remembered guiltily, had been unanimous, not just cast by him. And the sales figures on the title showed what a great job she was doing. True, maybe Joe could have done better, but it would be close.

Topaz had changed from the pushy kid he'd first hired. No doubt about it. Ever since 'NY Scene' had been syndicated, she'd grabbed her success and hung on to it with both hands. It was like the eighties had never finished: Chanel, St-Laurent, Dior. Bright colours, high heels and lots of jewellery. Interior-designed apartment. Joy perfume. A black Porsche 911 Turbo. Rolex. Patek Philippe, and dinners for two at 21 and the Four Seasons.

She was different in the office, too. At first she'd settled in slowly to her role as editor of *Girlfriend*, testing the waters, being cautious and polite to the staff. But as it became clear that Topaz's ideas in the dummy she'd produced were good ones, ones that worked in practice, she started to change. Overriding the old features editor. Personally designing new layouts. Sometimes even yelling at the staff writers.

The approach had caused outrage. Who was this Italian kid in her early twenties who thought she could show them how to run *their* magazine? With her colourful clothes and her board director boyfriend, the girl had had one scoop and thought she was Si

Newhouse. Resentment was high, but so was the new circulation. Topaz, finding herself in charge for the first time in her life, had apparently turned into Attila the Hun in couture. She stuck rigidly to her guns and if her authority was challenged she fired the challenger. After the third month, she started firing people anyway and replacing them with younger, hipper, more talented journalists and photographers. Topaz Rossi was intent on making *Girlfriend* the best and when staff called her a loudmouthed Italian bitch she just shrugged.

'Whatever it takes,' was her attitude.

Nobody interfered. Topaz was selling magazines and she was selling ads and she was keeping down costs. It had been her idea to use teenage models for the cover, and from the second she'd sat down in the editor's office, *Girlfriend* had never employed another super-model.

'They cost too much. They're too thin, too famous and a bad role model for the American teenager,' she told the editors' meeting. '*Girlfriend* readers like Janet Reno, Nancy Kerrigan and Winona Ryder.'

Nathan remembered it now, the sensation of pride and lust he'd had watching her give it to them, standing there in a dark green tunic by Gianfranco Ferre, the simplicity of the dress countered by an armful of glittering glass bracelets from Butler & Wilson. Amongst the army of sombre dark suits and the occasional neutral dress, Topaz had stood out like a sore thumb encrusted with rubies. Joe Goldstein had remarked to Nathan later – apparently forgetting their relationship – that Topaz used her beauty like an offensive weapon.

'And we will never run another advert featuring Kate Moss,' Topaz went on, daring anybody to contradict. 'Anorexia isn't glamorous.'

At which point every man in the room had

involuntarily looked up and down her own incredible curves until Nathan had hastily thanked her for her presentation, and called on Richard Gibson at *White Light* to give his report.

Rosen shifted in his seat, feeling his anger dissolve and the first stirrings of desire take its place. Every guy at American would give a month's wages to trade places with him for five minutes, and he knew it. But Topaz was his. She wanted him. Not only that, but she'd pursued him relentlessly. It was flattering.

And he'd been in therapy long enough to see some of what was causing this heady materialism, this need for display and aggression. Topaz was nervous and scared. It was a classic reaction; the girl was hiding her insecurity behind fitted Versace, and her terror behind naked aggression. She was worst of all with Joe Goldstein; Jesus, those two were such competitors now it was almost a joke. The unstoppable force and the immovable object.

The gaudy clothes? That was simpler still. Not that she didn't look great in them – a girl like Topaz Rossi could carry that look with ease. But she used to dress in a far simpler, less attention-grabbing style and he could date the change exactly from the night of Elizabeth Martin's party: when Topaz had worn a Chanel sheath and that Rowena Gordon girl, the record executive, had turned up in a huge sweeping ballgown, with spectacular ruby earrings.

Which also explained her fury over the way Atomic Mass had shot to stardom. And her pain this morning when he'd threatened to break it off with her.

Topaz Rossi had been rejected by her father and betrayed by her best friend. No wonder the poor kid was bruised. It was insensitive of him not to remember that.

Rosen picked up the car phone and dialled

Mellenick's, the exclusive Fifth Avenue florist. Fuck business. Fuck Matt Gowers. Topaz was his girl, and he was happy about that. Still.

'If you want them, go get them.'

'I can't, Josh. I don't have a budget authorized yet,' Rowena said, shivering. The heating in Luther's offices had given up the ghost, and she was beginning to feel like her American career was, too. How could I have been this disorganized? Rowena thought. First I can't find a band. Then I get sick with worry over finding a band and now, because I neglected to hire a good accountant, I can't *sign* the fucking band.

She felt totally incompetent. Jesus, maybe she was just a talent scout. Obviously there was more to running even a small company than that and she wasn't sure she had what it took.

'The money I've been allocated so far was for leasing space, hiring an assistant, basic overheads . . . I don't get any more until there's a solid financial plan with sales projections.'

'You should have completed that by now, Rowena.'

She was silent.

'I might have known it wouldn't be a social call. OK, Gordon, I'll see what I can do.'

Her boss sighed; she could hear the faint scratching of his pen, making notes.

'Hans Bauer hated giving you this job in the first place, you know. He'll really love me for insisting on an emergency A&R budget for you.'

'If we want Velocity, we've got to move,' she said. 'They won't stay secret for ever.'

'Goddamnit, I'll go as fast as I can!' Oberman growled. 'Just make sure you don't lose the act. I don't want you making a fool of me.'

'I'll get them,' Rowena promised him. 'You just get me a budget.'

He grunted. 'By the way, I saw a tape of the *Oprah* show. Pretty funny. Did you put him up to that?'

'No, it was a surprise,' Rowena answered, smiling a little. She'd enjoyed Joe doing that for her. Topaz could see where her pathetic attempts at revenge would get her. From what little she knew about journalism, that would have caused her some embarrassment. Good. Pushy bitch, the English girl thought, glad to have someone she could openly dislike.

'Has that girl been causing you problems?' Oberman asked.

Rowena drew herself up a little in the shabby room. Embattled, ignored and struggling in Manhattan, her sense of class superiority came right back to her.

'She's nothing. Topaz Rossi is the least of my problems,' she said with contempt.

Nathan Rosen thrust again, savouring Topaz's low moans. His hands moved gently over her swollen nipples, and he lapped at them softly with his tongue, tugging them and pulling them into full erection. Her hands were all over him, stroking, clutching, sometimes reaching under him to trail her fingers gently over his balls, in that way that drove him crazy. He refused to be hurried, and for once she wasn't rushing him. They both enjoyed slow, bridge-building sex like this that lasted for hours and ended in long-drawn-out orgasms as relaxing as a scented bath. This was Nathan's pace, not Topaz's. But she was happy to give in to him tonight.

Topaz moved under her partner, her supple body keeping pace with his rhythm. She smiled into his eyes, feeling tenderness, mild arousal and the relaxation of tension. She hadn't wanted to lose Nate. He was her family, and family was important. He was the first person truly to care for her and not just lust after her. That was worth a little sexual incompatibility. She kissed his shoulder, remembering yesterday, when flowers from Mellenick's, chocolates from Godiva and vintage champagne had all been delivered to the house and they'd made love on the kitchen floor to celebrate.

'I love you, Topaz,' Nathan gasped, feeling his whole body bathed in a pre-orgasm sweat. He glanced down at her superb breasts, pressed hard against him. 'Oh, God, I love you. I love you,' and she murmured, 'I love you too,' knowing that he was coming, nowhere near climax herself, but wanting him to come, wanting him to be pleased, wanting him to love her.

'Ohhhh,' Rosen groaned, erupting inside her with a surge of white-hot bliss. Topaz put her arms round him, holding him to her, kissing the handsome line of his jaw, until he eventually, reluctantly, pulled out of her. He rolled off her and lay in the bed next to her, feeling like a young lion.

She was so giving, so generous in bed. Compared with Marissa's tight-assed sufferance of his pleasure, Topaz was Mother Earth and Venus rolled into one.

Her only fault is to want too much of me, Rosen told himself, with a flash of vanity. The idea pleased him. Put like that, her overdemanding attitude to sex – as he saw it – wasn't so bad after all.

'Will you marry me?' Rosen asked suddenly.

'Do you want to?' Topaz asked, surprised, propping herself up on one elbow to look at him. Her red hair tumbled down her back and her breasts thrust themselves towards his face. Incredibly, Nathan sensed the renewed stirring of desire.

He suppressed his misgivings. 'Yes I do,' he said. 'Absolutely.'

Topaz felt her eyes fill with tears. She'd never expected him to ask her so soon; to have a successful career, be a wife with a loving husband, maybe even a mother – it was exactly what she'd dreamt of.

Now all she had to do was to find some way of dealing with the two things that still bothered her. Joe Goldstein, her newest rival, still with one more magazine than she had and still determined to block her career at American Magazines. And Rowena Gordon.

Maybe her recent humiliation *had* been her own fault, but then she'd been careless. And unsubtle. Flinging insults at a band that were already on their way was futile, as well as obvious. No, she wanted to really do Rowena some harm. Topaz had done a fair amount of research on her situation at Musica and she knew that it wasn't as secure as it looked. She also knew that Rowena was having trouble signing a band. And that Atomic Mass were getting pretty wild on tour. There had to be some possibilities there. Topaz didn't want Rowena to just fail to make it and go home – she had to *help* her to fail. Yeah, sure, she knew nice girls didn't pursue revenge. They forgave and forgot.

Fuck that. She betrayed me.

Topaz smiled at Nathan, putting Rowena from her mind.

'The answer is yes,' she whispered, and kissed him.

Chapter Eighteen

'Married?' demanded Joe Goldstein. He pushed back his chair and stood up, black eyes luminous with anger. 'Married? To Topaz Rossi?'

'Who else?' Nathan replied coolly. He hadn't expected this reaction from Joe. *American Scientist, Week in Review* and *Executive Officer* were all flourishing now that Goldstein had moved to New York, and he had taken good care to see that Topaz was never unduly favoured over Joe. Goldstein was still favourite to succeed Nathan to the board. He thought he'd made that clear.

'Is that what she wants?' Joe asked. He was struggling to contain himself, so great was the rage sweeping through him. Topaz Rossi *marrying* Nathan Rosen? It was all wrong, totally wrong. His old mentor was thinking with his dick and Rossi was just a stupid child. Either that or climbing the ladder horizontally.

'I guess so,' Rosen answered.

'Well, I hope you'll be happy,' Goldstein said shortly.

'Thank you,' Nathan Rosen said, looking at his protégé with a new wariness.

'Married! *Now* you tell me!' Gino Rossi said, his disapproval echoing down the phone. 'Is he Catholic?'

Amazing, thought Topaz, how much this still hurt.

She called her father for the first time in years, to tell him she was getting married, and all he could say was 'Is he Catholic?' No 'How are you, where have you been?' Even fury would have been preferable to this total lack of interest in her life – anger would have meant he gave a damn.

'No, Poppa, he's Jewish,' she replied.

'A Jew! My daughter is marrying a fucking Jew? How did we bring you up, for you to be–'

Topaz slammed the phone down, feeling the shame and rejection all over again.

Thank God I got away from them, she told herself fiercely, determined to ignore the dull ache in her heart. Nate Rosen was marrying her and *he* hadn't seen anything to despise. She glanced at her reflection in the door of her office: a pretty blue dress, elegant shoes, ethnic bangles. Good enough for Nathan, good enough for anybody.

Her assistant buzzed her. 'It's John Aitken.'

'Show him in,' Topaz ordered, her mind switching gears. If John had come through the way she hoped, the scores would be settled and there'd be one less thing on her mind.

'Well?' she asked, as the journalist walked into her office. His Rage Against the Machine T-shirt was crumpled and his eyes were bloodshot, as though he'd been up all night.

'I've got something,' Aitken said, handing her a sheaf of dirty notes.

Topaz tore through them, her mind racing. When she'd finished, she looked up at him with an expression of pure triumph. 'Can we run with this now?' she asked.

'There's a launch party for the album in a fortnight, at Madison Square Gardens,' John told her. 'If I were you I'd wait. This is a real killer.'

*

Topaz thought about it. Maybe she *could* wait. This would be the second punch in a one-two jab at Rowena that would put an end to her unfinished business with that woman.

She'd had the first real break yesterday night.

'Can you see what I'm getting at?' Tiz Correy had yelled in her ear.

Tiz was setting up the October issue, and wanted her boss to come with her and check out a scene – the new industrial music in New York, epitomized by bands like Cop Shoot Cop, which was attracting a new wave of young, pissed-off female punks, art students and assorted misfits. Topaz had vetoed the idea at once. She didn't think that was what *Girlfriend* readers were looking for – more like lipstick, fashion and *Beverly Hills 90210*.

'It will made a great feature,' her staffer repeated angrily. 'You should trust me, Topaz. I haven't been wrong before. All you think about these days is impressing the guys over at *Economic*.'

Topaz flinched. 'That's not fair.'

'It is. OK, look: you come check out one of the bands, they're playing CBGB's tonight, have a look at what I'm talking about for yourself. If you want to kill the story after that, fair enough. Is it a deal?'

Topaz, trapped, nodded. 'What's the band?'

'Hot new group, no record deal. They're called Velocity.'

'Never heard of them.'

'You will.'

'Can you see what I'm getting at?' Tiz yelled in her ear. 'These girls are wild! We run something like, "She's a

Rebel" and a few shots of this mayhem crowd stuff, a list of the bands, a picture of Axl Rose . . .'

'I like pictures of Axl Rose,' Topaz yelled back, knowing what was indisputably good for circulation. 'OK, Tiz, it's your call. Run whatever you want.'

She gestured at the stage, where Velocity's female bassist was hammering out a blitzkrieg run. 'Is this stuff popular?'

'What, are you kidding me? This band is the edge of the cutting-edge.'

'You were always the rock fan,' Topaz shrugged.

To her, it sounded like meaningless white noise designed to make the ears bleed. But that was why she'd given Tiz her head on the article. Tiz Correy was only twenty; she could remember what it was like to be fifteen. Topaz, on the other hand, was twenty-four and starting to forget; and anyway, even at fifteen, she would never have gone for this.

'The rumours about them are hot,' Tiz enthused.

'Really?' Topaz enquired politely, not giving a damn. She'd paid her dues, now she wanted to go home. Yes, the girls in the audience would take some interesting pictures. Yes, it might make a good feature. Enough! Do I have to endure the whole show? she wondered.

'Oh yeah. The guy behind the bar told me your Rowena Gordon was here last week. She's been to see them a few times now, and he noticed her talking to the manager last time she was here.'

Topaz turned to face her, slowly.

'Are you telling me Rowena Gordon wants to offer this band a record deal?'

'Does it matter?' Tiz asked, surprised at her boss's sudden intensity. 'Sure, I think she does. Like I told you, they're cutting-edge, real new and hot. I expect she wants to get them for Musica before that situation changes.'

'Can she do that?'

'I don't know, I'm not a record company executive. I guess so. Wasn't that how she got Atomic Mass, signing them up before word got out?'

'Tiz, you're a genius!' Topaz exclaimed.

'What? Are we doing a profile on Rowena Gordon?' Tiz asked, thoroughly confused. 'I thought you didn't like her. The female anarchy thing will make a better piece.'

Her boss ignored her. 'Will the manager be here tonight?'

'Probably. Do you want an introduction?'

'Yeah,' Topaz said, grinning. 'We can't have a cutting-edge band like Velocity snapped up for next to nothing, can we?'

She smiled at Tiz. 'You like the band, right? If I arrange for you to write a large guest feature in *White Light*, do you want to introduce them to Manhattan?'

'Of *course*!' said her features editor, excited. 'If I do it tonight, we could make their Thursday edition.'

She looked back at the stage. 'I could start a bidding war for these guys!'

'Exactly,' said Topaz.

'So did you get the tape?' Rowena asked Michael.

'Yeah,' he said. 'I got it this morning. I didn't get a chance to listen to it yet.'

'Well, hurry up,' she said. 'I want to know what you think.'

'What if I hate them?'

'I'm signing them anyway,' Rowena said firmly, 'because *I* think they kill. A bloke called Andrew Snelling manages them; he's a sharp guy, very good with money. We're exchanging contracts on Friday.'

'How did you come up with a budget?'

'I got Josh to wring some emergency funds out of the board.'

Krebs laughed. 'You must be everyone's favourite little girl.'

'Hey,' she said defiantly, 'I'll sign the act, they'll be a flagship band for this subsidiary, and Holland will stop concerning themselves with my ability.'

'Babe, you have nothing to prove to me . . . I'm sure you'll sign them, if you want them.'

'Of course I'll sign them,' she said. 'No one else has even heard of them.'

Joe Goldstein sat in his office at *American Scientist*, seemingly staring into space.

From time to time his secretary looked through the blinds, but knew better than to disturb him; when Mr Goldstein closed his door and stared at the air like that, it would take Wall Street crashing or a new cure for cancer to rouse him.

Joe was deep in thought. His office was situated high up in the building, and the gleaming skyscrapers of Seventh Avenue towered everywhere outside the three glass walls of the room, but he was impervious to urban beauty today. Today he was wondering about his future. He had made a grave error of judgment – underestimating a rival – and had, he felt, been humiliated in front of the entire company by failing to add *Economic Monthly* to his portfolio of business titles. Possibly for the first time in his life he was discovering what it felt like to fail. It was not an experience he wanted to repeat.

The worst thing, though, was that Nathan Rosen had voted for Topaz. That was something he just could not understand. It was Nate, after all, who'd brought him into the company in the first place, become his close friend, and eventually acted as his mentor. It was also Nathan who had engineered his transfer to New York, and considering that Rosen had become the director for the East Coast, he'd kind of counted on his vote.

In fact, forget 'kind of'.

And yet, and yet, and yet, Goldstein mused. Topaz had performed quite brilliantly. He remembered as if it had been yesterday the way his heart had sunk as he'd listened to her pitch, and if he was honest, he might have voted for her too.

But now Topaz was going to marry Nathan.

He couldn't work out why this annoyed him so much, but he'd found it hard even to be civil to Nathan this morning. In fact, since he'd found out when he first got here that the two of them were dating, Joe had seen his long-standing friendship with Nathan go down the tubes. And when they'd moved in together, a week before the *Economic Monthly* pitch, it had disappeared completely. He started turning down all Nathan's invitations to drinks or baseball games. He went with buddies from his own titles or he picked up women for company.

And he worked. He worked his balls off. For all Topaz Rossi's flamboyance, Joe Goldstein still edited one more magazine than she did and he still submitted business memos to the board. She wasn't the only one who could push up circulation. *American Scientist* and *Week in Review* had both posted record figures this month.

Joe knew he'd made a fundamental error with his pitch. It was readers and revenue that counted, not content – content of a magazine was the means, not the end. It was the bait. Topaz had demonstrated that and it was a lesson Joe was determined not to need twice.

The next time they set a title up, Goldstein thought darkly, there won't even be an open pitch.

His mind strayed back to Topaz Rossi. No male rival had ever got him going like this, but then no male rival had ever looked like that girl. Maybe that was it. It just didn't sit well with him to see an attractive woman so goddamn obsessed with the nine-to-five. Or the eight-to-ten, in her case. He'd heard that outside the office Nathan and she didn't have much of a life.

Not for one second did it occur to Joe that the same thing was said about him.

He flicked through yesterday's *Westside*, noting the article on some odious-looking band called Velocity – distinctly *not* Goldstein's speed. When he wanted to hear music he generally headed for the Lincoln Center. There was a pull-out quote by the writer, Tiz Correy, pointing out that Rowena Gordon, the girl behind Atomic Mass, was looking to sign them up.

Joe recognized a clarion call to every other player when he saw one. He wondered if Gordon had them inked on the dotted line yet, because if not, she didn't stand a prayer now. Assuming it was true, and she was interested in the first place. But he was inclined to believe it.

He scanned the article again. There was no mention of Topaz Rossi anywhere in it.

Joe smiled grimly. As if that mattered.

Nathan Rosen walked up the steps to his house at half-six, carrying a small package from Cartier. It was a cool evening, a light breeze rustling the tops of the trees in his street. You could almost call it quiet.

Topaz was waiting for him in the kitchen. There was a silver candlestick on the table, and the soft light from its flame was the only illumination in the room. Dinner for two was set with their best porcelain, a bottle of his favourite Perrier-Jouet champagne chilling in an ice bucket and small heaps of caviar glinting on their plates as a starter. She'd served it just the way he liked it: neat, no messing around with chopped egg or blinis. Perlman was playing Beethoven's Violin Concerto gently on the stereo.

Rosen stopped at the door, struck with the perfection of the moment.

His fiancée was wearing a muted, floating full-length gown in dusty blue chiffon, which flowed round her curves like cream. Her hair was pinned up in a formal style, swept back and secured with a tortoiseshell comb. She had no jewellery, nothing to spoil the line.

She took his breath away.

'I brought you something,' Rosen said, walking up to her and handing her the box.

She opened it, smiling at him. Inside was an engagement ring, a cluster of sapphires exquisitely set on a band of white gold.

'I love you,' Topaz told him, kissing his cheek, then his mouth. There were tears in her eyes as he slid the ring on to her finger.

'Are you sure you want to do this?' Rosen asked her. 'Be with me, I mean? Even though I'm so sedate, so laid-back? Are you sure I'm not too slow for you?'

She shook her head and kissed him again. 'Things are going to be different now,' she told him. 'I'm going to relax. Be less uptight.'

'You?' he repeated, smiling. 'Why?'

Topaz pictured the look on Rowena's face when she found out. The first blow would be bad. The second would finish her off.

They were quits.

She could forget about Rowena, and get on with her life.

'Just because,' she said.

*

'No, it's OK, Andrew,' Rowena said, 'I understand. Business is business.'

Her knuckles were white with fury, gripping the phone.

'I'm afraid not,' she replied. 'I called my chairman already. We can't match that kind of money. No, I have no hard feelings. 550 Music is a great label, you'll do fine, and I wish you well.'

It was true. She didn't blame the manager, not for a second. It was his job to get the best deal for the act and she knew she'd have done exactly the same thing.

'I should have moved faster,' she said.

Rowena replaced the receiver and stared towards Seventh Avenue. Topaz Rossi was in one of those buildings.

The phone went again. 'Gordon,' she said.

'Would you care to explain to me what the fucking hell is going on?' snapped Josh Oberman.

Chapter Nineteen

'I guess that's everything,' John Aitken said.

'Thanks,' his editor told him. 'Richard Gibson's real pleased with the story, John. There'll be a rise for you in this.'

'I hope so,' he replied with feeling.

'Fax me the final draft at home, could you?' she asked. 'I want to see it as soon as it's done.' Her long fingers were absentmindedly rolling a tennis ball round on her desk.

'OK,' he said, ringing off.

Topaz surveyed her empty office.

'Bullseye!' she said.

It was autumn in Manhattan, and Rowena was still surviving. Just. After the Velocity fiasco, only one thing had saved her from recall to London; Barbara Lincoln and Michael Krebs had both insisted she stay and be put in charge of the album launch for *Heat Street*. It might be a Warners record for North America, but it belonged to Musica for the rest of the world, as Krebs pointed out to Oberman.

'She needs to find a band, Michael,' Josh told him.

'I know,' Krebs said. 'She will.'

A week later, Rowena found Obsession, a talented rap

act from Brooklyn, and signed them, very quietly.

After the deal was done, she sent a tennis ball over to American Magazines, for the attention of Ms Topaz Rossi, with a note attached: 'Thirty-fifteen.'

'I'm impressed!' Barbara said.

'So you should be,' said Rowena.

Josh Oberman didn't say anything, as he was calculating the exchange rate of dollars to pounds and wondering if this would get him promoted. One more album like this, and they'd make him President for Life.

'Hi, this is Alex Isseult on MTV News,' said the stunning brunette on the limousine TV, smiling at them engagingly. 'Britain's newest supergroup Atomic Mass are rumoured to be planning a huge launch party for their debut album, *Heat Street*, at Madison Square Gardens in New York. A spokeswoman for Musica Records admitted that they were waiting for a go-ahead from city authorities. Atomic Mass, currently enjoying their second number one single with "Trapped", will be issuing free invitations at dates on their sold-out US tour, which follows earlier supports to the mighty Guns n' Roses.'

She paused to give them another dazzling smile.

'*Heat Street* will receive its first ever playback at the stadium, and fans attending will also be issued with vouchers entitling them to a discount when they buy the album . . .'

'Can I believe my ears?' asked Oberman in theatrical disgust as the car glided past a huge billboard proclaiming THE ATOMIC AGE BEGINS 2 NOVEMBER. 'You can't do that.'

'Why can't I?' asked his Managing Director defensively.

'Because it's a carbon copy of what Burnstein and Mensch did to launch Metallica's last record.'

'So?' said Barbara impudently. 'I've always believed in learning from the masters.'

'Look, Lincoln,' began Oberman, who'd gone pale, 'you –'

'Calm down, Josh, I asked for permission,' Rowena said soothingly.

The old man visibly relaxed.

'Mensch said, if I wanted to be totally fucking unoriginal it was fine by him.'

'*Metallica* didn't sell twenty trillion copies because they threw a launch party at Madison Square Gardens,' Barbara pointed out. 'It sold twenty trillion because it was a phenomenal album.'

'Absolutely,' said Josh and Rowena in unison.

'We've done two million in firm pre-sales, Josh,' said Rowena. 'Firm, not shipped. I have point-of-sale in stores across the country and two independent promoters on the album. I have radio promos and competitions in four key markets for November. We're taking print ads, radio ads, MTV ads . . . marketing spend is huge . . . the whole thing is huge. It has to launch in style, and that was still the best idea anyone ever had . . .'

'OK, OK,' said Josh, throwing his hands in the air. 'Do what you like.'

'This album will sell itself,' Barbara insisted.

'Fine. We'll cancel the marketing budget,' grinned Rowena as Barbara glared at her.

Rowena had Press type up a list of the international TV and radio stations and magazines that were being flown in for the *Heat Street* launch and faxed it to the Musica affiliates around the world. It was four pages long, excluding American media. She copied Michael on it; he called her back almost immediately.

'I want you to know that I'm proud of you,' he said. 'You really did good here, Rowena.'

'Thank you,' she replied, suffused with pleasure.

'I really mean it,' Krebs insisted. 'You're one of the best I've ever seen.'

'They wouldn't have happened without you.'

'Sure they would. Maybe not so big,' he conceded.

There was silence for a moment.

'I want to be with you,' Krebs said gently. 'Can I come round tomorrow?'

'I would love that,' said Rowena.

She stared at the phone for a few seconds, luxuriating in happiness. For these infinitely rare moments of tenderness and affection she lived and died. She loved him so hard, so fiercely, perfectly aware he didn't love her back. He had never pretended to. She ought to leave him. God only knew she'd tried.

The first time had been a big deal, maybe because Rowena assumed Krebs would respect her wishes. They'd been together in Dublin, checking out a new band, and after some of the hottest sex she could remember he'd started talking about his wife. Feeling his insensitivity like a kick to the stomach, Rowena stood there and told him it was over.

'We'll talk about it in the morning.'

'No we won't,' Rowena said, her voice thick with the pain gathering at the back of her throat. 'I never want to see you again.'

'Never?' Krebs asked, propping himself up in bed on one elbow.

Rowena felt as if some sadist was performing open-heart surgery on her without an anaesthetic.

'Never!' she managed, tears trickling down her cheeks.

'Come back here,' Krebs said, but she ran away from him, barely reaching her own room before collapsing on to the bed. It was anguish, it was torture. For all he was a sonofabitch, the thought of never being with Michael again was sheer agony. She had to sit on her hands to stop herself calling his room and telling him she'd changed her mind. She sobbed for three hours, and cried herself to sleep.

In the morning, she got up early and checked out. The stewardess on board the Aer Lingus flight asked her if she was feeling ill. Rowena said no and refused all food and drink. She thought about Michael Krebs every second of the five-hour flight home.

She'd lasted a week and lost half a stone, hardly eating, hardly sleeping. Getting through each day was like running a marathon. Krebs was her first thought in the morning, her last thought at night. After three days, relentless sexual longing started to mix with the misery.

And then he'd called.

'This has gone on long enough. You can't still be mad at me,' Michael said.

Rowena was dumbstruck. 'You think this is *funny*?'

'Absolutely,' Krebs said firmly. 'I'm just gonna laugh at you, Rowena. All this angst . . .'

'*Angst*?' she spluttered. 'I *hate* you!'

'You hate me now?'

'Yeah,' she said sullenly, trying to ignore the flood of limitless joy that had surged through her at the sound of his voice.

'And you're never gonna sleep with me again?'

'No I'm not.'

'That's a shame,' Krebs said softly.

Lust swept a long, lazy, feathery caress right across her body.

'Is it OK if I reminisce, then? Because I have to tell you, I've been thinking about it . . .'

'No . . .'

'About Sweden. Remember that? I enjoyed that, Rowena.'

Sweden. Christ. He'd grabbed her by the nape of the neck and shoved her, belly down, across the desk in the hotel room. The lamp and all his papers had gone crashing to the floor. She'd come so many times that night she'd lost count.

'Shut up, Michael . . .'

'How did my cock feel, Rowena? Do you remember that? Sliding into you? You were so hot it wasn't even funny.'

She stifled a gasp. 'Fucking shut *up*, Michael . . .'

'You're gonna have to hang up on me.'

'I can't hang up on you. You know that . . .'

'If I was there now, we wouldn't be talking. I don't know, I might start with your breasts this time. I keep thinking about your nipples. They're so sharp when you're turned on . . . You know what I'd like to do? I'd like to lick them for a couple of minutes and then put a hand in between your legs. Then you could tell me how much you hate me.'

'*No.*'

'Yes. Yes. You know, baby. You could tell me how you couldn't stand me while I was stroking you. I'd be real gentle, you wouldn't even know I was there. Probably wouldn't notice me lifting you up and pulling you down on my cock. I'd fuck you very, very slowly. Deepthrusts. Give you time to say whatever you've got on your mind. How about that? I mean, you hate me, right? Having me fuck you right in front of a mirror so you could watch it going in, that wouldn't make any difference . . .'

'Michael!'

'Don't tell me you *like* that idea.'

'Stop this.' Her stomach was contracted. Her whole body was shaking with desire.

'No. I won't. Because I know what's happening to you.'
She couldn't speak.

'I'll be there in five minutes,' Krebs said firmly, hanging up.

Rowena had never forgotten it. By the time he arrived, she was so racked with lust she couldn't stand up. When Krebs walked through the door and saw what he'd done to her, he pushed her up against the wall and took her where she stood, just unsnapping her jeans and shoving into her.

She'd tried to walk five or six times after that. But Michael wouldn't hear of it, and his sexual hold over her was absolute.

The American Magazines tower was buzzing. Gowers and the rest of the board had called an emergency editorial meeting.

'Are you sure we can run with this?' Jason Richman demanded.

'I'm sure. Our lawyers have gone through it with two fine-tooth combs,' Topaz assured him.

'How are you spreading it?' Joe Goldstein. Cold and businesslike.

'Over three issues initially. Maybe more to come, we're still digging.'

'Why don't you wait for the whole thing?'

She glared at him. Every damn meeting the guy tries to crucify me, she thought.

'Because I don't feel we can sit on this for even a day. It'll be leaked.'

'I agree completely,' Nathan snapped. Goldstein must be out of his mind. The story was so hot you could fry eggs on it.

'They're right,' Matt Gowers said, with an air of finality. Goldstein flushed slightly. Gowers added, 'We'll need a bigger print-run for the third and second issue.'

He turned to the meeting. 'It only remains for me to congratulate Topaz Rossi. You all know that most of the time American Magazines is in the business of great features, not breaking news, so it's good to see that we can handle that properly too, when the need arises. You also know that *White Light* has been lagging in the music press market. I think this could be the solution. So, Topaz, well done indeed.'

The meeting broke into applause, although she noticed angrily that Joe Goldstein just shuffled his notes instead. As everyone left to get back to their offices, she grabbed him by the arm.

'What?' he snapped, shaking her off with an expression of distaste.

'Look, Joe,' she said patiently, 'I know we've had our differences but –'

He cut her off. 'Oh, spare me the "can't we be friends" spiel,' he said coldly. 'We work for the same company. That's about the extent of it. Now if you'll excuse me –'

'What's your problem?' shouted Topaz, losing her temper.

He seemed to consider whether or not to reply. Then, regarding her, he said, 'The fact is, I don't have any respect for people who fuck their way to the top.'

As she stiffened in shock, he turned and walked out.

Nathan was cooking supper when she got home.

Topaz relaxed against the doorway and enjoyed the sight of him, carefully and methodically fiddling with the pan. He'd even put an apron on. How sweet, just like him. She could see it now: *no applesauce is going to get the better of Nathan Rosen!*

He was barechested, apart from the apron, just cooking in jeans. That did something to her, the sight of his broad back, the muscles shifting under the skin as he moved. Topaz looked appreciatively over his tight, lean ass. Lust began to tug at her, mingling with the overwhelming sensations of triumph she'd been feeling all day. She padded up behind him and slid her hands round his waist, kissing his shoulderblades, and then started to brush his crotch through the denim.

'Hey, cut it out,' he said. 'This has reached a delicate stage.'

Topaz ignored him and silently slipped out of her shirt and bra. She began to brush across his spine with her nipples.

He groaned, immediately becoming erect beneath her hands.

Topaz started to unbutton his fly and rubbed him gently through the silk of his boxers. He moved with her, trying to press himself against her hands. She tickled and stroked him lightly for a minute or so, and when she felt him thickening and distending under her touch smartly withdrew and backed towards the kitchen table. Then she unhooked her skirt and slowly wriggled out of her panties, starting to touch herself.

'Topaz,' Rosen breathed, his hard-on chafing against his pants. He wanted to be where her fingers were. To come where her fingers were. But he sensed she wanted something else first and he came towards her, ripping off his jeans to free his swollen cock, and dropped to his knees, burying his face in the tiny, wiry red hairs of her pussy, hearing her groan.

Nathan started to kiss her softly, marvelling at how wet she was, and when he felt her thighs relax slightly, he began to lick her, slow, sure strokes, aiming to please.

Oh God, thought Topaz.

She reached down and moved his head, arrogantly guiding him for her pleasure. When she thought she could sense orgasm, she grabbed his wrists and pinioned his arms behind his head, kissing him.

Nathan shivered with desire, watching this beautiful young girl astride him, her magnificent breasts swaying just out of reach, her soft mouth suddenly determined and lustful, crashing down on his.

Christ, what was she doing now . . .

Topaz had loosened her ponytail and was brushing his cock with her hair, in long, sweeping caresses, stroking him with a million feathery touches. He felt desire and surprise rip through him. Then she grabbed him with her right hand and positioned herself, slick and open, above him.

'Do you want it? Tell me how much you want it,' she whispered.

He stared up at her, aroused and amused.

'Or I guess I could just leave you here,' she teased.

'No! I want it, OK. Just fuck me, damn it,' Rosen gasped, and Topaz smiled and lowered herself on to his straining cock and flung her head back, her body arching, and he exploded inside her a second later.

She collapsed against him, panting.

'What was that all about?' Nathan murmured, stroking her hair.

Topaz smiled and kissed him.

'I think you burnt the applesauce,' she said.

Rowena stretched comfortably in bed and flicked on MTV. The morning sun streamed through the windows.

'This is Alex Isseult with MTV News,' said the TV excitedly. Rowena waved at her lazily, registering her constant little thrill of pleasure at seeing the Atomic Mass logo on MTV.

'British supergroup Atomic Mass look certain to run into trouble this morning, as the current issue of *White*

Light magazine, which hit the stands last night, reveals that two of the band members have previously undisclosed criminal records, including possession of drugs.'

'*What?*' Rowena screamed, sitting bolt upright.

'MTV News can exclusively confirm that New York authorities have already issued a statement banning the group from holding its planned launch party at Madison Square Gardens. The move is sure to cost Musica Records hundreds of thousands of dollars in wasted air fares and promotional costs. However, that may be the least of their problems: spokesmen for the DEA and the Justice Department have already said that they are actively considering deporting the band if the allegations are proven, meaning the cancellation of a sell-out tour and huge costs . . .'

'*What?*' she screamed again.

Downstairs, insistently, the phone began to ring.

Chapter Twenty

'How could you do this to me? I must have been insane to give you this label! Didn't you anticipate the press would dig around an act of this size?'

'Josh, I –'

'No!' he screamed. 'Don't give me excuses! I have Holland on the phone every five minutes! Our goddamned fax is jamming because the worldwide MDs are having a mass panic!'

Rowena passed her hand across her forehead, cursing technology. Oberman might be three thousand miles away but he sounded as though he was in the next room.

'Gordon, this is not a game!'

'I know that, Josh, I '

'You report to me, I look like a fool. And I can tell you right now that Hans Bauer wants you recalled.'

She went pale.

'I can't cover your ass for ever. If it ever happens again, you're through. This is a fucking fiasco.'

'Understood,' said Rowena faintly.

Oberman slammed the phone down.

It was the last call in a long, long day, most of which had been spent in trying, fruitlessly, to get hold of the band and repeating 'The allegations are being investigated. We have no further comment at this time,' over and over again.

She was totally shattered.

When Michael rang the apartment doorbell at nine, she was in floods of tears.

'I'm sorry,' she said, mortified. 'I forgot you were coming over – let me wash my face . . .'

'Ssh,' Krebs said, kissing her gently. 'It's OK, you go ahead and cry. I think it's kind of cute, actually, the great Rowena Gordon showing weakness.'

She fled to the bathroom and doused herself in cold water, blew her nose and slapped on some foundation. Amazing, pathetic really, how even in this state she couldn't bear him to see her looking less than beautiful.

'Get out here, Rowena,' Michael called.

She went back out to him, embarrassed by her appearance, her spectacular failure, forgetting he was coming over, everything. Also, the familiar sensation of desire was starting to crawl over her. Merely to be in the same room as him was usually enough.

He came towards her, sensing the shift in her mood immediately. His kiss this time was less consoling, harder, sexual. 'What shall I do with you this evening?' he said. 'I was going to take you out to dinner somewhere discreet, to celebrate, but I guess that's inappropriate now.'

She nodded mutely.

'Take off your shirt,' he said. 'I want to play with your breasts while I'm thinking about it.'

He started to lightly caress her, discussing various different positions he might take her in in a calm, detached tone of voice, as if talking to himself.

After two minutes she broke down, gasping.

'Can't hold it?' Michael asked, smiling. 'God, you're

really out of control today, Rowena, aren't you? I didn't even touch you between your legs yet.'

She started to unbutton his jeans, freeing his erection. He was red and swollen, and she wondered again how he managed to master his arousal so completely when she couldn't hide hers for a second. Krebs could often go from erection to ejaculation without making a single sound.

He spun her round so she was facing the wall, tugged down her skirt and panties and entered her, moving in aggressive, rhythmic strokes. As she shut her eyes in ecstasy he ran one hand across her groin, the other tracing a firm line up and down her spine possessively. She choked out his name as she came.

Michael tightened his grip on her shoulders and climaxed.

He held her firmly for a few seconds, just to make a point, and then kissed her affectionately. 'Always the best cure for stress,' he said.

She smiled ruefully. 'My problems are still there, though.'

'Come shower with me,' Krebs said. 'You have no problems. Let me explain something to you, Rowena: you're a friend of mine, and so are the band. When some little writer fucks with you, and fucks with Atomic Mass, they fuck with me.'

She glanced at him.

'Nothing has been proved, and nothing will be. There *are* other stadiums in America, and you should also bear in mind,' he added with heavy sarcasm, 'that I have produced for a few other companies besides Musica Records. I have a lot of favours coming to me.'

He paused. 'Do you know who's responsible for this?'

'I think so,' said Rowena.

'Good. Because you and I are going to talk to the press

in a language which they'll understand, believe me.'

'Michael!' said Rowena.

She was excited now. She believed he was going to get her out of this. Gratitude and relief and the giddy prospect of revenge surged through her; and then admiration; and then a slow, deep wave of almost violent desire.

He watched her redden. 'You can consider this a continuation of your education,' he said. God, how hot he could get her. She was the most passionate girl he'd ever seen in his life. He felt his erection returning.

'Come here and pay me for it,' he said.

The next day she was her old self. There was something great about dealing with a crisis of this size; Rowena kicked into action, pouncing on phones, yelling at reporters and faxing 'please await further information' messages to her affiliates around the world. Krebs, meanwhile, called Freddy deMann, Doug Goldstein and Warren Entner, and Madonna, Guns n' Roses and Faith No More all cancelled exclusive interviews with *White Light*. Historically, artists are not fond of people or publications that smear other artists.

Michael was enjoying himself. 'It's just something for them to think about,' he said. 'Wait till I find Paul McGuinness. Then they can forget their U2 Christmas issue, as well.'

Rowena's secretary stuck her head round the door. 'Sorry to interrupt,' she said, 'but I've got Barbara Lincoln on line one.'

'Put her through!' said Rowena. 'On the speakerphone!'

'Why the fuck haven't you called?' Krebs demanded.

'We had the phones disconnected while I talked to the band,' Barbara explained. 'Sorry, you guys.'

'Sorry!' Rowena exploded, furious. 'Do you have *any idea* what it's been like in New York? Christ, Barbara –'

'Look, most of it's not true –'

'Why don't you just tell me what's true and what isn't,' Krebs said calmly.

'I want to speak to the band,' Rowena demanded, still furious.

'Hey, this is me, Rowena!' Barbara protested. 'Me, your best friend, remember? Now take a deep breath, and listen to this.'

'I don't understand it.'

Richard Gibson, *White Light*'s editor, was presenting to the editors' meeting.

'I mean I really do not get this. The Atomic Mass issue quadrupled our circulation, I have extra print-runs for the next three issues. I mean these magazines are just flying out of the stores and everybody knows it.'

'So what's the problem?' Nathan asked.

'I can't sell advertising space. I mean not at all. Musica Records pulled their ads, OK, this I understand. But now Geffen is pulling, Mercury is pulling, Epic pulled a whole page ad for Screaming Trees this morning. Said they decided to run it in *Spin* magazine instead.'

'Anything else?' asked Topaz.

'Yeah. All our cover stories are cancelling interviews.'

'Like who?' Joe Goldstein asked, making notes.

'Ever heard of U2?' Richard replied, with the withering sarcasm music journalists reserve for money men. 'Suddenly they can no longer fit us into their press schedule. Bang goes my Christmas double issue.'

'Madonna?' Topaz probed gently.

'Gone. Out of here,' Gibson snapped. 'I mean, this is *insane*. I have a music magazine which, right now, has triple the circulation of *Rolling Stone*, and I can't get an interview or sell an ad.'

Joe Goldstein shot a baleful look at Topaz. 'Richard, my friend,' he said, 'they're going to shut you down.'

Gibson considered it. 'No,' he said. 'It did cross my mind, OK. But the record business is highly competitive. Why would Geffen care if Musica screws up?'

'It's Rowena Gordon!' Topaz burst out.

Joe rounded on her. 'Gordon doesn't have that kind of reach, Rossi,' he said. 'If you could keep your little private vendetta out of this, you'd realize that. No; there's somebody else involved now, and whoever it is, they're going to shut you down.'

There was a silence.

'Joe's right,' Nathan said, eventually. 'There's no other explanation.'

Topaz and Nathan walked home at sunset, holding hands.

'Don't worry about Goldstein,' he said. 'He's just jealous of you. He'll come round.'

'He blames me for what's happening to *White Light*,' Topaz said, and then added, 'I guess they all do.'

'Hey,' Nathan told her, kissing her. 'It is absolutely not your fault. OK? There isn't one of them wouldn't have run that story, and there isn't one of them that wouldn't have used our only music magazine to run it in. So relax.'

She was quiet all the way home. Nathan led her to the sofa and they sat down, and he clasped both her hands in his.

'Tell me what's bothering you,' he murmured. 'I can't bear to see you like this.'

She looked at him, her eyes brimming. 'I don't know,' she said. A large tear rolled down her cheek, and then another.

'What is this?' asked Nathan, kissing her. 'This is not like my girl.'

'Do you think' – she faltered – 'do you think I fucked my way to the top?'

'What? No!' he said, almost laughing, but she looked so upset he stopped himself. 'Is that what this is about? Come on, Topaz! I didn't make you MD of *Girlfriend*, did I? And I voted for you for *Economic Monthly* because you gave the best presentation. You stupid woman, it was a unanimous decision by eight people.'

She was really crying now. 'Don't leave me, Nathan,' she sobbed.

'Who said anything about leaving you?' he said, bewildered. 'I *live* with you! I *love* you, for God's sake.'

She cried herself out for a couple of minutes, then wiped her eyes.

'Are we finished yet?' Rosen asked.

'Yeah,' Topaz snuffled. 'Sorry.'

'I'm not going to leave you, or reject you, like your dumb-ass parents or your college friend. You got that?'

'Yes,' said Topaz meekly, kissing him.

'Come to bed,' he said.

They lay entwined in each other's arms. 'What are you thinking about now?' Nathan asked her.

'Ice cream,' said Topaz, honestly. She smiled lazily at her lover, and added, 'Coffee ice cream.'

'If I go get you some coffee ice cream, what will you do for me then?' asked Nathan, looking down at her, wondering how he'd ever got this damn lucky. God, she was so beautiful.

'I'll marry you twice.'

'OK,' he said. 'I'll be right back.'

Topaz lay in bed and thought how gorgeous he was, and how smart, and played naming their kids again:

Nate and Louise and Nick and Rosie, she thought. After he'd been gone a quarter of an hour she started to worry, so when the bell buzzed she was relieved.

She opened the door.

There was a cop in the porch.

'Do you live here, ma'am?'

'Yes I do,' she said, clutching her robe around her. 'What's the problem?'

'Are you any relation to Nate Rosen?'

Topaz went cold. 'I'm his fiancée,' she whispered.

'I'm very sorry, ma'am,' the cop said.

Musica Records issued a press statement. The whole thing was an exaggeration. Mark Thomas, drummer for Atomic Mass, had been convicted of possession of two joints of marijuana at the age of sixteen and let off with a fine. Alex Sexton, the bassist, had borrowed his dad's car without permission, but that had been a mistake and no charges had ever been brought. Yes, it was true that the head of security hired for the tour had a criminal record for grievous bodily harm, but the band and their representatives had not been aware of it until now. The man had been dismissed and deported.

Rowena had rarely enjoyed a press conference so much.

'But dope is still a drug . . .' protested one journalist, desperate to keep some controversy alive.

'What can I tell you?' shrugged Rowena. 'He didn't inhale.'

There was laughter and applause.

The *Heat Street* launch was back on.

'I'm not risking more delay in New York,' Oberman insisted. 'You saved your ass this time, but who knows what that goddamn magazine will come up with next?'

'Nothing at all,' she assured him. 'We're closing them down.'

'Yeah, well. I heard you and Krebs were stirring things up for them.'

'I still think we should have it here or in LA.'

'I said *London*, and I was still your boss last time I looked,' snarled Oberman. 'The subject is closed. Oh, and kid –'

'Yes, commander?'

'Wear something nice.'

Two days later, a thick, stiff, expensive-looking cream envelope arrived for Richard Gibson at the *White Light* offices on Seventh Avenue, sent registered delivery and marked 'Personal'. Inside, to Gibson's blinding fury, were two invitations to the launch of the Atomic Mass album *Heat Street* at the Earl's Court Exhibition Centre in London, and a short handwritten note from the Managing Director of Luther Records.

Dear Mr Gibson,

I have great pleasure in enclosing an invitation to our launch party, and hope that your doubtless enormous advertising revenue will enable you to afford the air fare. You will be most welcome, although regrettably, due to the sheer volume of interview requests from TV, radio and major magazines –

Fuck you, thought Gibson furiously

– we will not be able to give interview time to White Light *on this occasion. I also enclose an invitation for Ms Topaz Rossi, who I gather has been advising you on your editorial policy. I'm sure her advice has greatly benefited your magazine. I am quite sure that you, as editor, are aware how useful she has been to you and will therefore want to pass on our invitation to her yourself.*

With best wishes.

Rowena Gordon.

Yeah. She's been real useful, Gibson thought bitterly. He tore the envelope up.

'I love it! I think it's fantastic,' Michael said. 'You're really coming on. I never knew you had this kind of a vindictive streak in you.'

'Normally I don't,' Rowena said, 'but Topaz Rossi and I have a long history. This was the closest she's come to screwing up my career. I want the guy we're putting out of business to know exactly who's responsible for this. I want her management to see she's unreliable, short-termist, lets personal stuff affect her business decisions.'

Krebs was not used to the edge in her voice.

'You look good,' he said, changing the subject.

'Thank you,' she smiled, instinctively tossing back her long blonde hair. It was an adolescent gesture, totally appealing. She's a hot little thing, he thought, pleased.

'I wanted to look good for the band,' she said. 'You should too. It's a moment of triumph for you. It's such a great record.'

'Thanks, babe,' Krebs said.

He wasn't listening; his eyes were still fixed on her dress. It was a long, sleeveless figure-hugging Dior creation in moss-green velvet, a classic, but cut to emphasize the small, inviting swell of her breasts, the soft, delicate line of her bare shoulders and her long, slim legs. Her hair, normally tied back in a ponytail for convenience, spilled down her shoulders and the bare skin of her back. Long diamond drop earrings dangled and glittered against it. She looked aristocratic, unattainable.

'How are you getting there?'

'I'm going on Concorde, tomorrow morning.'

'I'm flying out this evening, so I'll see you there,' he

said. 'Make sure you wear this outfit. And don't wear panties.'

'Why? Are you going to fuck me?' she asked, getting excited.

'Yes, I think so,' he said, getting up and coming behind her. He put one hand on the small of her back, just above the fabric of the skirt, and laid the other open on her stomach. 'I always want to fuck you when you look like this. Just to remind you that you belong to me.'

He could feel the heat begin to stir under her skin. She moved slightly under his hands.

'You can be as much of a hard-nosed bitch as you want with everyone else,' he said, speaking low and close to her ear, 'as long as you remember your place with me. On your knees, at my feet. Or bent over a flight case. Or spreadeagled on my bed . . .'

She gasped with desire.

'It's true, isn't it?' Krebs pressed her. 'Yes or no?'

'Yes!' she whispered. His hands were still on her. 'Now. Please, Michael. Now.'

He turned her head to face him, her pupils dilated with wanting.

'No,' he said. 'You'll wait my pleasure. Tomorrow.'

'OK,' she murmured, fighting to control herself.

He smiled and kissed her, a luxurious, possessive kiss, letting her press herself against his erection.

'I'm sorry, miss,' said the policeman. 'All the roads to Earl's Court are blocked. It's pandemonium down here.'

She leant out of the driving seat window. He was right. A mob of fans and photographers was blocking the way.

'I'm with Musica Records,' she said, showing him her company ID. 'Can you get me through to the reserved parking?'

'Certainly, madam,' said the policeman, with a friendly smile.

That's *one* thing I don't miss about New York, Rowena thought, grinning.

A police escort guided her through a crowd comprised mostly of screaming, hysterical girls to the backstage door.

'The pop group is going to play live, miss,' one of them explained, 'and Capital Radio gave tickets away on the air, so those as didn't manage to get in are going mad.'

'Sorry,' she sympathized. This was great; she'd had no idea the boys were so popular back home. She'd get a number one album on both sides of the Atlantic.

'Oh, I seen it before,' the policeman said with a worldly air. 'I done security at a U2 concert.'

This guy is equating my band with *U2*? she thought, delighted. Oh my God!

'This is worse, though,' he added.

'Rowena! Come over here,' Josh Oberman said as she stepped backstage, threading her way through a jungle undergrowth of camera leads, lighting cables and microphones. 'Come meet my head of Press, Rachel Robinson,' he added, without drawing pause for breath. 'She's desperate for someone to say something about Atomic Mass to a bunch of important press people who're having to wait their turn with the band – everyone's working flat out, we still can't meet demand. And make sure you *shout*,' he bellowed unnecessarily, waving a wrinkled hand at the auditorium behind them, which was packed out with yelling, whistling, clapping kids waiting for the band to come on.

'Did you have to have them play? I thought we were just going to put the CD on,' said Rowena.

'They wanted to play,' Oberman shrugged.

'Artists!' she said, using the same tone of voice women normally reserve for 'Men!'

Her boss laughed.

'Is Michael Krebs here?' Rowena asked casually.

'Yeah. He arrived four hours ago; Rachel's been setting him up for interviews with *Guitar World*, *Bassist Magazine*, *Drums Unlimited*, et cetera, et cetera.'

She looked to her right and saw Krebs standing against the stage scaffolding, surrounded by reporters, greatly enjoying himself.

'. . . so by the time we got to the drum fills stage, we had about seventy-five fills on this one song, and Mark also wanted a different sound on the hi-hat, so we . . .'

'Rowena? I'm Rachel,' said an incredibly slim woman who looked about nineteen.

She reluctantly dragged her gaze away from her lover.

'Could you come and talk to *Kerrang!*? They want the story of how you discovered Atomic. And when you're done, so do sixteen others . . .'

'Of course, I'll talk to *Kerrang!*. It's an honour to talk to *Kerrang!*!' she exclaimed, laughing. 'But why do people want to interview backroom boys?'

'Are you kidding?' Rachel exclaimed. 'The band is so hot right now their dustman could sell an exclusive to the *News of the World* on what they ate for breakfast this morning! The scandal in the States was pretty good for them, too.' She looked slyly at Rowena. 'Did you plant it?'

An hour later, she was finally allowed out of the press tent, if only because Atomic would be hitting the stage in fifteen minutes. They would play a four-song mini-concert, and then the *Heat Street* playback would start. Some teenage girls in the front row had become hysterical with anticipation and were being given first aid by medics. She wanted to go and say hi to Barbara and the boys, but was warned away from the dressing rooms by a burly security guard, and felt too exhausted from the flight and the interviews to argue.

'Where am I supposed to go now?' she asked him.

He examined her perfectly valid all-access laminate sourly.

'Well,' he conceded, 'it says here that you can go up on the stage.'

'Good,' she snapped, and stalked up the ramps to the wings of the stage, finding an amp she could hide behind to watch the show. Out in front of her, the exhibition centre stretched out, brilliant with lights and banners of *Heat Street* and the blue and gold Atomic Mass logo. Oh, Jesus, this was exciting. This was *her* little band that she'd found a few years ago in a Yorkshire club. All those people, just banks of people, kids all crushed and sweating and unbearably excited, fields of them right in front of her, jamming every inch of space in the arena until it had to shut the gates because of the fire risk – all these kids here for Atomic.

She was Mistress of the Universe tonight.

'Like the view?' Michael Krebs murmured in her ear, standing directly behind her.

He ran his hands over her ass, and smiled, satisfied. 'Good,' he said. 'I won't have to waste time taking your panties off.'

She blushed. He was feeling her naked under the dress, enjoying her obedience.

'We can't really do anything,' she objected softly. 'The whole record business is here.'

'I keep telling you, Rowena,' he said, 'that I will have you wherever I want, whenever I want. If I tell you to march out there and do it for the cameras, you will.'

He had pushed her legs apart, and was stroking her gently at the top of her thighs. She pressed slightly backwards, into his hands, staring straight ahead of her, trying to look as though she were having a normal conversation.

'Please don't do this,' she said.

'Don't do what? Don't get you hot? Don't turn you on?' he teased.

The arena lights dimmed. There was a huge roar of anticipation from the crowd, waves of sound sweeping over the stage.

'We did this, you and me,' he said in her ear, leaning in towards her to counteract the noise. 'This gig. This record. This launch. Your enemy, what's her name – Rossi? – we had total victory over her.'

As the boys hit the stage running, to screams of joy from the arena, Rowena Gordon felt a light, sweet, spontaneous orgasm rush across her groin. Krebs felt it, and thrust up the velvet of her dress in the darkness, brushing his thumb firmly against the slick nub of her clitoris.

She cried out, the noise drowned in howling guitars, and came again instantly, against his hand.

He spun her round to face him, tugging her dress back down. 'Come with me,' he said, hardly able to control himself. 'I told you you'd wait my pleasure. It's my pleasure right now.'

He led her to centre backstage, behind the drum riser, above a little stairway going downwards.

'There's a room under the riser,' he said. 'It's got a trapdoor which locks.'

'Right here?' she whispered.

'Right here,' he said. She put her hand on his cock, rock-solid through his jeans, and he grabbed it and held it there.

'Do you think I can wait?' he asked.

'No.'

'Can you wait?'

'No!' she gasped. 'Oh, Michael! Oh!'

He practically threw her down the stairs before they were interrupted by a stagehand, slamming the trapdoor under the base of the drumkit and bolting it. The little room was crammed with clean towels for the band, two guitars and a bass, flight cases, bottles of Gatorade and other musician clutter. They were swamped by music and the audience out front going crazy. The dull boom-boom-boom of the drums pulsed loudly above them.

Alone with him, Rowena couldn't look him in the face.

'Don't groupies usually end up down here?'

'Yes they do,' he said.

'Why don't you show me what happens to them?'

He came over towards her, twisting a piece of flex in his hands. 'Do managing directors and groupies fuck in the same way?' he said, teasing her again. 'Put your hands up by the crossbeam.'

He lashed her wrists to the ceiling, so she was perched on a case, helpless and aroused before him.

'That's tight,' she protested, tugging futilely at the cable.

Krebs looked her over, all velvet and pearls, her breasts unprotected beneath the fabric, her arms over her head.

'You can't touch me,' he said. 'You can't free yourself. You can't caress me, you can't brush my hand away. Do you understand? I can do whatever I like to you. You're at my mercy.'

'I know,' she whispered.

'Do you like it?'

'Yes,' she said. 'You know I do.'

For a moment he didn't move, just stood there looking at her.

She twisted impatiently. 'Do you want me to beg?'

Krebs reached forward and eased her dress away from her shoulders, kissing and licking the collarbone. She moaned, quietly. He unsnapped her bra in a practised movement, freeing her breasts, swollen with lust, the nipples red and erect with longing. As she gasped with pleasure, he started to lick slowly round the left aureole, flicking his tongue back and forwards across the peak, which was getting bigger and harder in his mouth.

'That's OK,' he said. 'Your body is begging for you.'

Then he moved to her right breast, and when she was practically incoherent, he took the whole thing in his mouth and sucked.

She screamed, little rivers of sensation coursing through her to her crotch, which was beating, throbbing with need. She tried to press herself against him but he held her back, smiling.

'What do you want?' he whispered. 'Tell me. Tell me exactly what you want me to do.'

'I want you to put your cock inside me!' she gasped. The sound of the band and the screaming fans was all around them; her triumph heightened his every touch. She had never in her wildest dreams thought her body capable of such feelings.

About to burst, he shoved up her dress and pulled her legs open, freeing himself and thrusting into her, hard, as far as he could go, grinding into her. Krebs had his hands on velvet and warm skin, feeling his woman clench around him like she wanted to milk him dry. Christ, she felt so good. He fucked her even harder. Oh, she was great. She was the best. Look at her bucking and writhing against him, pleading with him not to stop . . .

'I'm gonna come, Rowena,' he said thickly. She was

already there; he looked down and saw her stomach literally convulse beneath him, one, two, three times . . .

He called out her name over and over as he came.

'It was *amazing*! I've never seen a reaction like that,' gushed the *Music Week* reporter to her an hour later, at the glittering post-launch party at the Dorchester. 'I've never felt like that during a concert.'

'I felt good during that concert too,' Michael Krebs said, joining them with a glass of champagne for Rowena. She bit her lip to stop herself from laughing; Krebs winked at her.

The reporter looked from one to the other, bewildered. 'There's obviously a great friendship between you two,' he said.

'Not really,' Rowena grinned. 'Michael produces great records, so I just pretend to like him so he'll keep working with me.'

'Ha, ha, ha!' laughed the reporter sycophantically. 'But would you go on the record as saying you make a great team?'

'Yes, indeed,' said Michael.

'I'll go on the record too,' Rowena added, dropping her voice conspiratorially, 'as saying –'

The reporter hastily took out a biro and a scrap of paper.

'– Atomic Mass are a really, really great band.'

Krebs made a strangled coughing noise.

'– really great band,' the reporter wrote earnestly.

'Excuse us,' Krebs said, pulling her away to dance.

The hotel ballroom was full of media types, celebrities, musicians and executives from Musica and other record companies. Both Rowena and Michael had networked the place for hours, and finally wanted to relax. The playback had been another huge success; Michael's laborious, fat production had brought out the best in the band, who were fantastic to start off with, and it looked tonight as if *Heat Street* might become the bestselling album of his career. Rowena watched, burning with pride, as suit after suit came up to pay homage. She accepted her own tributes with one eye on him, absentmindedly spooned beluga caviar into her mouth while staring at him smiling and shaking hands across the room. Half the other women there were doing the same thing.

'I'm jealous,' she said lightly. She could feel the pressure of his hands, pulling her closer towards him. She loved the way the black dinner jacket picked out his eyes. 'All these other girls are looking at you.'

'Don't you think I see the guys stripping you with their eyes?' he smiled. 'But I know who you want. And I only want you.'

What about Debbie? she thought, but didn't say it.

'Come over tonight,' he said, '47 Park Street. We'll take up where we left off.'

'I'll check my diary,' she said, laughing.

God, I like this woman so much, Krebs thought affectionately, smiling at his friend.

As she was about to leave – ten minutes after Michael – a rough hand grabbed her shoulder.

'Rowena,' said Joe.

She looked at her singer, who was hoarse, sweating and exhausted.

He held out his hand for her to shake. 'Thank you,' he said. 'For everything.'

'Oh, Joe,' she said, clasping it, and her eyes filled with tears.

That night, Michael was tender and gentle with her.

'I love you,' said Rowena afterwards, and regretted it instantly.

'Come on, Rowena, don't spoil it,' he said, pulling his jeans back on. 'You're not my girlfriend.'

'What am I, then?' she asked, astonished.

'You're my friend,' Michael said breezily. 'You're my good friend, who I happen to enjoy having sex with. Debbie and I are absolutely secure in our relationship.'

He said this without a trace of irony.

Topaz organized the funeral. It was merciful that she had something to do, it took her mind off the loneliness and the loss.

Nathan had died instantly, hit by a drunk-driver, crossing the road. He'd been carrying coffee ice cream. When she saw it spattered over his shirt, mixed with dirt and blood, Topaz had felt grief so violent she'd fainted.

They held the service at Mt Hebron Synagogue, his favourite. She drove upfront in a long black limousine and stared out numbly at Fifth Avenue, at the cold sidewalks and crawling traffic. She thought about Nathan the whole time. The synagogue and the roads were jammed with his friends, the ones she knew and dozens she'd never met; a sister, a cousin; all weeping for him and praying for his soul.

Topaz felt her pain as if it were a great stone, physically blocking her breath and the tears that might clean her. She had loved Nathan and felt safe and comforted in his presence; her initial hot sexual crush had mellowed into friendship and alliance over the months. Up until now, she hadn't realized just how dependent on him she had been. Nathan had made all these friends; real friends, crying because he was dead. Topaz had companions, her buddies from the office, who'd all come round and been honestly sorry for her. But amongst them all, there was not one real friend. She had not one soul whom she could call on in the night, when she lay awake staring into space.

Nathan Rosen was the only person she'd allowed to truly befriend her since Rowena's betrayal.

His sister, Miriam, began the eulogy. Topaz crossed herself, and beseeched the Blessed Virgin to intercede for his soul.

'Thank you again, Miss Rossi,' Miriam Rosen said, kissing her on the cheek. 'I'll be thinking of you. You make sure and call me if there's anything you need.'

'I will, Miriam,' said Topaz. 'Goodbye now. Thank you.'

She shut the door on her and breathed out. That was the last guest gone; now she could clear up the wake and just sit and think. Maybe cry some.

Joe Goldstein cleared his throat.

She jumped and spun round.

'I'm sorry,' he said. He was standing in the kitchen doorway. 'I didn't mean to startle you.'

'It's OK,' she said.

'I–I wanted to wait until everyone else had gone,' he said. 'I have to say something to you.'

She gestured wearily at the sideboard and tables, covered with plates and glasses. 'Can it wait until Monday, Joe? I'm really busy.'

'It's not that, it's not work.' He shifted slightly, uncomfortable. 'I wanted to apologize to you. For the record, not just because Nathan . . .' He petered out.

'I know.'

'What I said about the two of you was unforgivable. And it wasn't true. I was just jealous, I guess I felt humiliated when you got *Economic*. You know Nathan was my mentor; I could see you meant more to him than I did.'

Topaz looked levelly at him. Man, it was really costing him something to come out with this stuff.

'OK, I accept your apology,' she said. 'It's decent of you to admit it.'

He nodded curtly, obviously debating with himself whether to say something more, decided against it and walked to the door.

'You make sure and –'

'– call you if I have any problems, OK, Joe,' finished Topaz, a shade sarcastically.

He smiled ruefully at her. 'You know, I do realize you're very talented,' he said, and let himself out.

The phone rang, shatteringly loud in the darkness.

Goldstein glanced wearily at his bedside clock. It was 3.30 a.m. 'Goldstein,' he said.

'Joe?'

'Topaz, is that you?' he asked, wide-awake. She was crying so hard he could barely make the words out, but it was her, definitely.

'Could you come over, please? I can't be alone . . .'

'I'm on my way, OK? Don't do anything,' said Joe, illogically, reaching for his slacks.

She opened the door for him, red-eyed and haggard.

'I'm sorry,' she said. 'I don't know what came over me.'

'It's OK,' said Joe. 'Honestly.'

'I know it's pathetic,' said Topaz, 'but I don't have anyone I can call,' and she started to cry again.

He shut the door and guided her into the kitchen, putting on the kettle.

'So I'm nobody, right? You never stop,' he said, and she made a weak attempt at a smile.

'Grief comes at bad hours for the people who really

care,' he said. 'You need to mourn him, and not just by yourself. You know what sitting shiva is?'

'I *am* a New Yorker,' said Topaz indignantly, through her tears.

'Oh, OK. Sorry.'

'Stop saying sorry.'

'OK.'

There was silence for a minute or so.

'I brought some cheese popcorn over,' said Joe.

'I love cheese popcorn.'

'Wanna talk about him?'

'Yes I do,' she sobbed.

Joe stayed with her till dawn.

Chapter Twenty-One

Nathan Rosen's death changed a lot of things.

In practical terms, it meant that Topaz Rossi, the main beneficiary of his will, became a very rich woman overnight, with a net worth of more than four million dollars. She was also that rarest of creatures in New York, a house owner.

It left a vacant seat on the American Magazines board. Joe Goldstein, in confident possession of his MBA – Topaz had given up on hers due to pressure of work – was determined to occupy it. He mourned his friend and bitterly regretted his behaviour towards him over the Rossi business. But he knew that Rosen was dead, no amount of sorrow could change it. And life – and business – went on.

Joe planned on being on the board by forty and president by fifty. Gowers wouldn't stay in the game for ever. He hoped Topaz Rossi would be content to consolidate and build on her three magazines – because he'd annihilate her if she went for this one, and he was beginning to enjoy her company.

Topaz grew up. She took a step back from her work, made time for her friends. She was appalled to discover how little she knew about the people she'd been working with for years. She had dinner with Elise and her husband, and baby-sat for her secretary. Josh Stein, who'd moved from *Westside* to be art director for *US Womam*, introduced her to his boyfriend. Socially, she was awkward and stilted, but people made allowances. She began to feel less alone.

She got herself an accountant and a lawyer and a realtor, who sold the house for a huge amount of money. Topaz didn't want to mess up her head any worse, thinking about Nathan promising to be right back. The realtor plunged all the money straight into a new apartment – a fashionable triplex on 5th Avenue, with lots of bare space and natural light.

Topaz spent the better part of half a million dollars redecorating it. It gave her something to do, and it seemed appropriate. After all, she was going to be the youngest board member of a major magazine group in history. She hoped Joe wouldn't fight on this one; she'd beaten him before and would do it again if she had to, but she was really getting fond of the guy.

Heat Street sold a million records in six months.

Michael Krebs made a fortune off the deal.

Joshua Oberman succeeded John Watson as the new chairman of Musica.

Rowena set up Luther as a full company. She found a building with a knockdown rent across the park and called it Musica Towers – not exactly Black Rock, but it'd do. She bought five pairs of jeans and twenty T-shirts and stopped caring what she looked like. She was in the office by eight every morning, fine-tuning Oberman's distribution deals, supervising computer systems and decorators and huge wall-mounted TVs that could blast out MTV and VH1 twenty-four hours a day. She stomped about in a cloud of dust and woodshavings, losing her temper. She started hiring, and that was the fun part;

there was so much talent going begging it wasn't true. She hired people like herself, young, clever hustlers who were also music junkies. Nobody older was going to work for a fledgling company anyway. She did try to recruit a few established names, and failed miserably. It didn't bother her superiors much, though; young hungry staff were more motivated – and they came cheaper.

There were plenty of role models in New York: André Harrell, ruling at Uptown; Richard Griffiths at Epic, another expat Brit and one whose roster made her sick with envy – Spin Doctors, Brad, Screaming Trees, Rage Against the Machine, Eve's Plum, etc, etc; Monica Lynch of Tommy Boy and countless others.

Obsession had a little success; the second act Rowena signed, Steamer, a thrash band, had more.

People started to fill offices, and Luther mixed the whine of chainsaws with whirring computer printouts and stereos pumping out Ice Cube and Sugar. Rowena filled one floor with phones and faxes and started the promotion department right away; Roxana was being worked at urban radio and Atomic Mass at Metal and CHR within a week.

In all her life, she'd never felt so alive.

She'd learnt her lesson and made sure they had good accountants and administrators as well as talented staff. By the end of the year Luther was a growing concern, and Josh Oberman finally thought that if they could just arrange to market more product, they could set up their own distribution.

Rowena was still obsessed with Michael, but slowly, painfully, from a lack of oxygen, hope was starting to die. Still, she just could not give him up, and Michael had no intention of letting her go. He liked her. He desired her. And though he would never admit it, Rowena was more to him than either a friend or a piece of ass.

Michael needed her admiration, he enjoyed her intelligence, and there was a part of him – the part whose parents had neglected him, whose first real girl-friend had cheated on him, whose wife was more interested in their children – that revelled in being the object of such blind, heedless, reckless love.

He wasn't an intentionally cruel man. He told Rowena, and he believed it when he said it, that he wanted her to have other lovers. To be happy. To find an available guy. But he knew her intimately, and he knew that there was never any real competition for him from the occasional dates that Rowena forced herself to go on for a week or so, something she hated doing, something she forced herself to do to prove to herself that she wasn't helpless.

Rowena met plenty of men, but so far she had been blind to them all. Krebs filled her dreams, her fantasies, her life.

It was true love.

It was terrible.

'I got some news for you,' Mary Cash, her assistant, smiled at Topaz as she handed her her coffee. 'Strictly gossip, though.'

'That's usually the most reliable source,' Topaz said. She meant it; not only was Mary a brilliant office man-ager, she was plugged into the nerve centre of the secretarial mafia.

'Well, word is that the boys upstairs are scouting to buy a sports property.'

'Really?' her boss asked. It made sense.

'Yeah, and when they've found one, they'll be picking some people to work on the buyout, monitoring the team . . .'

'And promoting the best person to the board?'

'You got it.'

Topaz felt a rush of pure adrenaline flood through her. She hadn't been this excited since before Nathan died.

'And for what it's worth,' added Mary, pleased to see her interested again, 'the same person who told me was talking privately with Linda this morning.'

Linda was Joe Goldstein's secretary.

'Aha,' said Topaz, thoughtfully.

'Aren't you guys going to another Mets game tonight?' asked Mary archly. 'Will this get in the way?'

'Yes we are, and maybe,' said Topaz. 'But you know what? If it does – tough!'

They laughed.

'Are you sure?' Joe pressed Linda.

'Mary Cash. I swear.'

'OK, thanks.'

He took his finger off the buzzer and stared out of the window. It was a spectacular view from the forty-third floor, the tops of the skyscrapers and the Hudson and the long, straight roads with their glittering little cars. That was the prize: New York. Nothing less, as far as he was concerned. New York was media city, and only two types of men really ruled here: media bigshots and the Wall Street crowd. It would have been television, if he had had his choice.

But even someone as driven as Joe couldn't complain about the speed of this rise.

The American Magazines board, before he was thirty-five!

It was a bright autumn day in Manhattan, the sun streaming weakly into the chill air, nothing but dry, crisp brilliance outside his warm office.

He truly hoped Topaz would not take it personally, but he wouldn't give this up. For anyone.

*

'Seeing much of David?' Rowena asked Barbara, cradling her phone with her shoulder as she studied the Bitter Spice sales figures.

'Not really,' Barbara said. David Hammond, head of A&R at Funhouse Records in the UK, had been dating her for years. 'He took up with some Central European girl and carried on with me at the same time.'

Rowena winced. 'That must've hurt.'

'Yeah it hurt. And you know I slept with someone else once, two years ago, when David and I had just broken up?'

'But he wasn't seeing you.'

'I know. But he keeps referring to it, every time. As if my seeing this guy once is the same thing as him taking Elvira to every bloody industry event . . .'

'And he's still sleeping with you?'

'I know.' Barbara sighed. 'It's pitiful. But I'm sexually addicted, and I love him, however much of a bastard he is. What women will do, how low women will sink when they're in love.'

'I know,' said Rowena, thinking about Michael.

'Your head can be fully aware that the guy's no good. It's all very well, magazines saying that if you can see what a jerk he is you'll be cured. That's bullshit.'

'Your heart rules.'

'Every time.'

'It's an occupational hazard of being female,' Rowena said.

'How's business? Apart from us.'

'Apart from you, pretty good; including you, sensational. I've been consolidating, building, nothing flashy. Oberman's looking to set up a soundtrack deal, a label/studio-type deal – an exclusive arrangement.'

'You'd do all the soundtracks for one movie studio?'

'Exactly. And they'd own a piece of the label.'

'Sounds interesting. It could kick you up the corporate ladder, too.'

'No one ever said you were dumb, honey.'

'Nice change-up,' said Topaz appreciatively. 'Maybe we have a chance in this one.'

'I wouldn't bet on it,' said Joe, demolishing the first third of his hotdog. He swallowed and added, 'Pitching's OK, just. Hitting sucks. Us and the Padres have the lowest hitting average in the league, remember.'

'Thanks for the recap,' said Topaz, glaring at him. She hated defeatists. 'I love sports,' she added.

Joe stared fixedly at the field.

'And I love magazines,' she added.

Joe turned to her, dragging his gaze away from the game. 'Look, Rossi,' he said, 'if this is your attempt at subtlety, it's not working. I take it you heard about the sports title.'

'Right.'

'And . . . will you be requesting an assignment to the takeover team?'

'You mean am I pitching for the board?'

'That's what I mean,' said Goldstein.

'Are you?'

They looked at each other for a long moment, regretfully.

'Let's make it a clean fight.'

'OK.'

'No resentment,' Topaz insisted. 'Either side.'

'Fine by me.'

'Let's make it a rule never to talk about business after hours.'

'Let's watch the damn game, Topaz.'

Gary Sheffield strode on to the field, pinch hitting for Pat Rapp.

'Oh no,' said Joe.

'That's never in the pitch zone! Oh, no!' said Topaz, jumping up in her seat. 'No!'

Sheffield swung and hit a low outside fastball in a soaring curve towards the leftfield stands.

'It's history,' moaned Goldstein, a man in pain. 'Oh God. I can't bear it.' Topaz covered her eyes with her hands to avoid the gruesome sight of another enemy home run.

'I want you to know that I'm not gonna back off or ease up in any way on this,' Joe said.

'No business.'

'OK.'

Topaz drove them to René Pujol's on West 51st Street for dinner. 'They have a melting chocolate cake that's the closest thing to heaven this side of a cemetery,' she said.

'French food. Makes a change,' Joe remarked.

'What do you normally eat?'

'Italian.'

She smiled at him.

They talked a lot at dinner, about politics, religion, music. Topaz discovered that Goldstein had been pretty lonely since transferring to the East Coast; he hadn't done as badly as her, but he still missed his friends.

'I gotta get back,' said Joe eventually, checking his watch. 'I got a girl waiting.'

'Oh, I'm sorry,' Topaz said. 'I didn't know you had a girlfriend.'

Joe laughed. 'She's not my girlfriend, she's just some girl. I told the porter to let her in at ten so I'd better not be much longer.'

'Some girl?' repeated Topaz.

'Yeah. Joanna or Joanie or something. I met her at a bar, arranged to see her tonight.'

'Just to get laid?'

'Right,' said Joe pleasantly.

'Does this woman realize you call her "some girl" and don't even know her name?'

'Don't preach at me, Topaz,' said Joe less pleasantly. 'She's going to get what she wants out of it. Girls who hang around that kind of pick-up joint aren't looking for a "meaningful relationship".' He put quotes around the phrase.

Topaz found herself getting angry. 'You were hanging around that kind of pick-up joint too, Joe. What does that make you? A gigolo?'

Goldstein flushed. 'It's different for men, and you know it.'

'Damn right it's different for men. Men don't get labelled as whores for having sexual desires.'

Joe flinched. 'I don't like hearing a lady talk dirty.'

Topaz paused, then reached for her wallet and threw two hundred-dollar bills on the table.

'Fuck you, Joe Goldstein. And fuck the double standard,' she said calmly, and walked out.

The team working on the buyout of *Athletic World* was announced internally. Only two people of the requisite seniority had applied: Joe Goldstein and Topaz Rossi. Employees graffitied notices with 'Round Two' and 'The Rematch'.

Topaz sent Joe a copy of *Backlash: The Undeclared War Against American Women* by Susan Faludi.

In return, he sent her a copy of *The Way Things Ought to Be* by Rush Limbaugh.

Athletic World proved a complicated deal. The magazine was still family-run, one of the only major sports magazines not part of a publishing conglomerate – 'yet,' as Matthew Gowers said. The trouble was that it didn't stand alone. *Athletic World* was part of a small group of sports companies – the middle-aged man who'd founded it had also acquired a gym and a company that made personalized shoelaces for trainers, in addition to a medium-sized operation selling *Athletic World* merchandise.

Joe suggested the board look for an easier target.

They turned him down, unanimously. American Magazines was tired of risky start-up ventures. American Magazines was shopping for a little goodwill, for a brandname.

Topaz played to her strengths and requested that she be assigned to profile the magazine, circulation and advertising, how it could be improved. Joe set to work with due diligence, finding an investment bank, finding buyers for the other parts of the group.

Both of them were in their element, completely. The chairman and the board kept close tabs, and were extremely impressed.

'Let me get this straight,' Kirk said. Kirk was Joe's closest friend; they jogged together before work. He swallowed a mouthful of doughnut.

'She's smart, she's funny, she has a great body –'

'Knockout. Absolutely knockout.'

'And she *likes baseball*?'

'Yup.'

'And you let her go? You really screwed up,' commented Kirk.

'Yeah, well,' said Joe. He pummelled the punchbag. 'That's the problem. She's too masculine.'

'Tomboys are usually great in bed,' said Kirk.

'I didn't fuck her, OK. I'm talking about losing a friend here.'

'But you guys were inseparable for the past six

months! You couldn't pull her in all that time?' Kirk
teased.

'Jesus, Kirk. I said it wasn't like that. We just talked,
about politics, art, you know.'

'Uh-huh.'

'Oh, please,' snapped Joe, exasperated. 'The goddamn
bitch is fighting me for the board. For the *board*. She
refuses to budge an inch. I mean I've had it with her.
She's too young and totally inexperienced and I am
going to *cream* her. *Fuck* her. I'm out.'

He savagely laid into the punchbag.

Kirk chuckled. 'Joe, my friend,' he said, 'you've got it
bad.'

It was 7 p.m. and the *Girlfriend* offices were emptying
out. Topaz wrapped up her discussion with Sue Chynow,
the editor-in-chief, and went to fix herself a fresh pot of
coffee.

It was going to be a long night.

'I got takeout,' Joe said as she appeared in his office five
minutes later. 'Chinese, is that good for you?'

'It's fine,' Topaz said coldly, drawing up a chair and
briskly opening a file. 'Coffee?'

'Yes, thank you. Black,' said Joe, equally briskly.

They both began to study cashflow charts in
aggressive silence.

An hour later, they were having what politicians term
'a free and frank discussion'.

'But women working out are *totally different* to women
sports fans!' roared Topaz. 'Just like men, you stupid
asshole! Working out is not a sport! It's exercise!'

'No. You're wrong,' Joe said, through clenched teeth.
'They're into Flo-Jo because she wears make-up, not
because of her speed.'

'No. *Men* are into Flo-Jo because she wears make-up.'

'Take women *out* of the goddamn reader profile!' yelled Joe.

'I will not. It alters the finance –'

'Don't tell me about financing, Rossi! What do you think I've been doing for the last month –?'

'Looking in the mirror and jerking off, probably,' said Topaz rudely.

Joe went white with anger. 'What did you say?'

'You heard.'

'If you were a man, I'd knock you out.'

'Oh! Big guy,' sneered Topaz contemptuously. Why was he so gorgeous and such an asshole? 'I want you to remember that I kicked your ass over *Economic Monthly*. Think about that, Joe. Consider it a dress rehearsal.'

Goldstein got up and came towards her. 'You just don't get it, do you, cutie? This job's mine already. You couldn't buy out a loaf of bread, and they know it. You'll be reporting to me, and I'm truly going to enjoy it.'

Topaz was an inch away from him. 'Who are you calling cutie?' she hissed.

'Who do you think, babe? What are you gonna do? Sue me for sexual harassment?'

She looked at him, black-haired, handsome, taunting her furiously. He was wearing jeans and an expensive-looking Oxford shirt.

'Oh, that's not sexual harassment, pretty boy,' Topaz said. '*This* is sexual harassment.'

And she grabbed the collar of his shirt and ripped it down the front, sending the little ivory buttons clattering on to the boardroom table.

His chest was strong, lean and covered in tiny wiry black curls. Topaz steadied herself. An incredible, overwhelming rush of desire surged through her.

'What the fuck?' said Joe softly. Oh God, he shouldn't

have brought up this sex-tension thing. The touch of her hand against his neck – even that sharp, angry touch – had set him off. He wondered if he dared kiss her. Damn, he was hard. He didn't dare look down in case he drew her attention to it.

'I'm sorry . . . I got carried away . . .' murmured Topaz. 'Maybe I can get a pin and fix it for this evening – I'll replace it, of course . . .'

She tried to pull his shirt together, her hands on his chest, his ribcage.

'Quit touching me, damn it,' growled Joe.

'Fine,' Topaz snapped back. 'I –'

She gasped. Goldstein grabbed her shoulders and pushed her back on the hard table.

'What are you doing?' whispered Topaz.

'Take an educated guess,' said Joe, and took her face in his two hands and kissed her impatiently, sucking on her top lip, thrusting his tongue into her mouth.

I shouldn't do this, thought Topaz.

Heat flooded her belly.

She kissed him back, hard.

'No! Go on,' said Marissa, utterly fascinated.

'Well, apparently,' said Lisa, 'the janitor heard screams at one in the morning, like woman's screams, upstairs in the boardroom, so he runs upstairs and Joe goes, "Everything's OK," but he insists on going in to check, and Topaz Rossi was sitting there all red-faced with her buttons done up wrong and her breath's coming short –'

'No!' said Marissa, trying to suppress a jealous rage. Joe Goldstein was the best-looking man in the company.

'– and Joe was tucking his shirt back into his pants,' finished Lisa triumphantly.

'What a tramp!' Marissa trilled. 'She let him do . . .

that with her in the *boardroom*? First Nathan, now this. Well, he'll want nothing more to do with her now, of course.'

Lisa wasn't so sure about that, but kept her counsel. Marissa Matthews was a powerful columnist.

'Topaz Rossi just preys on older, rich men. I shall tell everybody.'

'Everybody knows,' said Lisa, 'and he's not that much older.'

Joe called Topaz.

'Wanna go to the game on Saturday?'

'Sure,' she said, delighted.

Fernandez pitched some brilliant high-heat balls and struck out six enemy batsmen.

Chapter Twenty-Two

The flight from JFK to LAX takes five hours, and Rowena spent most of it working. Generally speaking, she loved to fly. She liked to have a few hours away from the phones to read a novel or daydream. She enjoyed the lift in her stomach at takeoff and landing, and even now she felt a small thrill of adventure at jetting from one city to another. But this time it was different.

She pencilled another note next to the paragraph on royalty breaks, wishing for the millionth time that she had a better grasp of maths. It was one hell of an important deal for her. Every per cent in every clause had to be exactly right.

'Champagne, Ms Gordon?' enquired the stewardess, hovering solicitously. So far this elegant businesswoman had refused the chocolates, cashew nuts, cocktails, and main meal of fillet of Dover sole, lobster or roast pheasant which was the envy of every other first-class service in America. She injected a pleading note into her voice.

Rowena relented. 'That would be lovely. Thank you.'

The attendant tilted her crystal glass slightly and filled it with the light golden nectar, which delicately spat and bubbled as it poured. Rowena smiled her thanks.

'Busy trip, ma'am?' She glanced at the pile of contracts on the empty seat.

'Just slightly,' Rowena said.

Interesting that she's English, the stewardess thought as she moved on. The Brits don't usually dress that well.

Rowena leant back to sip her champagne, glad of the break. She was wearing a soft Liz Claiborne pantsuit, flowing and loose, in a gentle fawn. She'd teamed it with chestnut shoes from Pied à Terre, and a crisp white shirt. Her make-up was equally subtle: buttery eyeshadow, matt bronze lips, the faintest hint of blusher. Her long blonde hair was gathered at the nape of the neck in a tortoiseshell clip. She looked every inch a nineties player: beautiful, casual, absolutely businesslike.

She allowed the drink to refresh her and ran over her schedule for the trip. She was staying in a house in the Hollywood hills, permanantly rented for visiting Musica executives. Lunch with John Metcalf was all set for noon tomorrow, and that, she reflected wryly, would be an all-mineral-water meal. That would be one conversation where she could *never* afford to drop her guard. Then the Coliseum, where Atomic Mass were headlining their first stadium gig. She felt proud and anxious all at once; no matter how many copies *Heat Street* had sold, this was the first date of the tour, and they'd never filled a venue of that size before.

Even Atomic Mass could run into problems.

The ticket printout she'd seen two days ago showed only a 75 per cent gate sale, and the world's journos were poised with sharpened pencils and unforgiving cameras, ready to label them an overblown hype.

She shuddered. In the music business, 'hasbeen' is a dangerous insult – it often became a self-fulfilling prophecy, and nobody, but nobody, was immune from media backlash – look what it did to Michael Jackson's last record!

Everyone's a critic, she thought furiously, and that bitch Topaz Rossi is the Queen Bee. Ever since Atomic Mass had launched the album in London, Topaz had done what she could to hurt the band, hurt Rowena, and hurt Luther.

She won't stop until she's brought me down, Rowena reflected. Venomous tramp. She wants her revenge.

She knew Rossi had primed at least three people in MTV and one at *Rolling Stone* to trash this gig, probably more. And anyone who worked for American Magazines knew what they thought of the show without turning up to see it, at least they did if they valued their jobs.

I won't dwell on it, Rowena told herself. The boys will be OK. They're the best band in the world. I have a deal to do here.

She wondered if Michael would find time to call her.

She was still working on release obligations when the plane banked into its descent. The ocean shone in the moonlight, and Los Angeles was spread out in the darkness like a sparkling, jewelled grid. Mercifully, for once VIP arrival service was fast and effortless, and her Gucci cases were amongst the first off the carousel.

In the limo she relaxed. She was pretty sure of what she wanted from Metcalf now.

And I'll get it, too, she thought. They say he's pretty tough. But I'm tougher. And I'm hungrier than he is for this thing.

The car took a left at the Hyatt on Sunset and snaked up the steep, winding hills. A little while later it stopped at the house, and Rowena let the chauffeur unlock the gates and carry her luggage into the porch. She tipped him twenty bucks. Why not? She was rich.

She flicked on the lights and took a look around,

interested in what the company provided for its top people – but you're not top people yet, she reminded herself. Maybe tomorrow you'll be top people.

There was a note for her from the maid on the kitchen table, propped against a huge vase full of orchids. Towels, cosmetics, toiletries, bathrobes and pyjamas had been provided for her convenience. There was food and drink in the refrigerator and cinnamon coffee on the stove. The office next to the bedroom was equipped with a computer and fax machine, and had a range of exercise equipment set up for her use. There was a selection of books and videos in the drawing room. The chauffeur and herself were on call twenty-four hours. She hoped everything was to Ms Gordon's satisfaction and that Ms Gordon would have a nice day.

Cinnamon coffee? Rowena wondered.

The phone rang.

'Rowena Gordon.'

'Miss Gordon?' asked a warm male voice.

'Yup, that's what I said,' said Rowena, slightly irritated.

'This is John Metcalf.'

'Oh,' said Rowena. 'Hi,' she added lamely.

'Did you have a good flight?' Metcalf asked, sounding amused at her discomfiture.

'Yes thanks,' said Rowena. 'Good of you to call.' She didn't ask how he got her number. I'll let him make the running, she thought.

'I got your number from Musica in New York,' he said. 'Thought I'd call and check you were OK in LA by yourself.'

'Hey, that's nice of you,' she said. 'But I'm a big girl, and I carry a gun at all times.'

Why am I snapping his head off? I'm supposed to be pitching this guy.

Metcalf chuckled. 'Point taken. Will the Ivy be good for you tomorrow?'

'It'll be fine. I hear they have amazing soft-shell crabs.'

'Rowena! You mean you've never tried them? You haven't lived until you've tasted those things,' he said.

Well, we've moved on from 'Miss Gordon' pretty quickly, Rowena thought. But she didn't really mind. He sounded so friendly and warm, not kissy and LA-insincere like she'd expected.

'I'll look forward to it, and I'll look forward to meeting you,' she said pleasantly.

'It goes double here – the legendary Rowena Gordon!' he said.

The legendary Rowena Gordon? OK, so it was just a line, but she liked the way it sounded. She liked it a *lot*.

'See you tomorrow, Mr Metcalf.'

'Please call me John. I hope you look as good as you sound,' he said, and rang off.

Cheeky bastard, Rowena thought. But she was grinning.

She flicked a switch on the stove to heat the coffee. When in LA, after all . . . the fridge was lavishly stocked with ham, chicken, ice cream, smoked salmon, olives; food enough for a starving army of gourmets. In the drinks door there was a pitcher of margaritas, a chilled magnum of champagne, and a bottle of Gordons next to three cans of Schweppes tonic water. *Nice touch!*

She fixed a weak G&T, clinking oversized ice cubes into a large frosted glass, and padded round the apartment. Everything was state-of-the-art, everything was the height of luxury. The drawing room projected on to the side of the hill and was three walls glass, so you could look out over Hollywood and the glittering city set at its feet, quiet from this height, moving calmly in rivers of light. In stark contrast to New York's concrete forest, there were only two clusters of skyscrapers visible on the horizon.

Rowena looked out over Los Angeles, towards Century City. John Metcalf might still be in his office there, making deals, rubbishing scripts, green-lighting pictures. He held sway over the destinies of hundreds of directors, actors, producers, agents. And right now, one record company executive.

Michael rang the next morning.

'I was thinking about you last night,' he said. 'I was having sex with someone else, and I was thinking about you going down on me.'

Rowena couldn't help herself. She felt her nipples stiffen in response to his lust.

'I put my cock inside her,' he said, 'and I fucked her, and I thought about you sucking me. You want to do that right now, don't you?'

'Yes,' whispered Rowena, wet for him already.

'Are you playing with yourself?'

'Yes.' She was.

'I can hear it in your voice,' Michael said, satisfied. 'You can't come unless I say so. If you were here I'd come in your mouth, and I wouldn't let you touch yourself.'

Rowena moaned.

'If you're sucking my cock, I expect it done properly,' he said. 'You have to lick my balls, and swirl your tongue over my cock, and suck me real, real slow, and make me come. I haven't got time for you to touch yourself. It's not my problem.'

She shuddered, uncontrollably aroused.

'I'm gonna make you beg for it,' he said. 'I'm going to take my cock out and rub it over your cheeks and lips until you beg me to put it back in your mouth.'

'Please,' Rowena sobbed. 'Please.'

'Have some control,' Michael teased her. 'You can't come yet. Then I'm going to shove it back in your mouth, right down the back of your throat. I'm going to grab the back of your head with my hands and push you down on my cock. I'm going to fuck your mouth . . . maybe I'll have you stop in the middle and tell me how much you love it, what I taste like . . .'

Her breathing was ragged and strained.

'You'll give me head whenever I ask for it,' he said harshly.

'Yes,' she managed.

'I can have you at my whim.'

'Yes.'

'Now come for me,' Michael ordered.

She gasped as she climaxed, her body arching, her splayed fingers soaked in her own juices.

Michael's voice came smiling down the phone. 'Good girl,' he said. 'I have to go now.'

'Goodbye,' she whispered. She put the phone down and wondered if she had ever felt cheaper. But she still longed for him. God, how she longed for him.

I'm a junkie, thought Rowena. *I'm addicted to Michael Krebs.*

She stepped out on to the patio, wet and silken from her shower, swathed in a huge white towelling bathrobe, a mug of very delicious cinnamon coffee steaming in her hand. The warm scent of hundreds of flowers hit her straight away. She settled into a green wicker chair, breathing in the gentle humid morning air, birds singing all around her.

'Bloody hell,' she remarked to a starling. 'I could get used to this.'

Work, work, work, her New York brain screamed at her.

What do you think you're doing? You're supposed to be setting up a soundtrack deal with the third-biggest studio in the world! Whole record companies have been established on less. This is a deal that could push Musica one, maybe two places up the world rankings, and as for your own position . . . bottom line, you want to wind up president, or not? You think Ahmet Ertegun would be out here drinking coffee? Haul ass, woman!

Rowena sighed.

Now! it added.

Reluctantly, she drained the mug and went off to study the diagrams of unit sales in relation to box-office takings.

By lunchtime she was sick with nerves. She changed her outfit four times, eventually settling on loafers, black Calvin Klein jeans, a Def American T-shirt, and a very, very expensive pair of sunglasses. She wanted to look Californian and give the impression that she was too important to bother with dress codes. Damn it! I am important! she told herself. I'm Rowena Gordon, MD of Luther Records and the hottest music business executive in New York!

He was just a studio head. That was all. Right?

The limo glided through LA. Rowena stared out of the windows, mirrored from the outside, watching the landmarks of Sunset Boulevard slip past her . . . the Rainbow, the Roxy, Geffen Records . . . it was a city designed only for drivers. She stepped out at the Ivy looking sleek and confident, trying to feel the same way.

Relax! It's a breeze. It's a done deal.

'Rowena Gordon for John Metcalf,' she announced to the maître d'.

'Of course, ma'am. This way,' he said cheerfully, leading her through the packed restaurant to the best and most secluded table in the place. 15–0 to Metcalf,

Rowena thought, using her metaphor for the war with Topaz Rossi. He was studying a wine list as she approached, immaculately dressed in a dark suit by Hugo Boss with discreet gold cufflinks. She pulled at her T-shirt and felt like an idiot. 30–0.

'Mr Metcalf,' she said, extending her hand. 'I'm Rowena Gordon.'

She was shocked, and tried not to show it. She was so used to being the youngest player in any deal. But he couldn't be more than a few years older than her; he was smooth-skinned, he had a large, taut, muscular body, and thick hazel hair with just the faintest grey flecking the sides. Christ, he was gorgeous, and what astonishing eyes. Thirty-five, tops.

'Good to see you, Rowena. Have a seat, please. And the name's John.'

She wanted to reply that he could call her Rowena, but forced herself to swallow the rebuke. It was his show.

'Please, indulge me, don't insist on sticking to the mineral water,' he said. 'The kir royales here are exquisite. I'll order for us both, so you won't be at any negotiating disadvantage. Please. I beg you.'

She looked at the handsome man smiling opposite her, who then batted his eyelids in a theatrical gesture of persuasion.

What a character, she thought with complete approval. The kind of guy you'd call a record man. Except that he's in movies.

She decided to throw away the script.

'OK, you win,' she said. 'I hate to see a grown man cry.'

The two-hour lunch turned into a three-hour lunch, and a three-hour lunch turned into tea, complete with china cups and a fake Georgian silver teapot.

'Cucumber sandwiches! Bring me cucumber sandwiches,' Metcalf demanded. 'I have an English lady here.'

'You're a jerk, John,' said Rowena, grinning. 'No one in England eats cucumber sandwiches. And no one eats muffins either. And we don't all know Princess Diana.'

'Next thing you'll be telling me there's no Victoria's Secret in England,' Metcalf protested.

'There isn't.'

'No Victoria's Secret, English lingerie, in England?' he asked.

'None,' said Rowena mercilessly.

Metcalf considered this disconsolately. 'What about the tooth fairy?'

'Oh, she's real,' she reassured him, and they both started to laugh.

'Twelve per cent rising one per cent, point five, point five, point five in the four years.'

'Get out of my face,' she said.

'That's the deal, take it or leave it,' John insisted. 'I can take it to PolyGram tomorrow.'

'They'll leave it too,' she said. 'I won't make this deal unless the numbers are right. And you can forget about reversion of rights. Musica does not surrender its masters. We're only in the market to buy, we're not interested in renting.'

'You're a tough bitch, Ms Gordon, anyone ever tell you that?'

'Frequently, Mr Metcalf. Frequently.'

'So I hope I can tempt you along to the gig tomorrow,' Rowena said.

'What, go see the hottest band in the world with the best-looking woman in the universe? I'll have to check my diary,' Metcalf teased her, shaking her hand.

Rowena opened the door of the limo and gave him what she hoped was a businesslike smile. 'I feel like I just went nine rounds with Mike Tyson,' she said.

He gave her a quick, intelligent glance. 'You did,' he said.

'But I'm still standing.'

'For now,' said John Metcalf. 'For now.'

Chapter Twenty-Three

'. . . And this is Gloria Roberts, *live* from 105.5, KNAC, always there at all the really *big* concerts, and we are *backstage* at the Coliseum and Joe Hunter of British rock sensations Atomic Mass is here with me! Welcome back, Joe.'

'This lady I am talking to,' said Hunter, in his rich Lancashire burr, 'was one of the first people *ever* in America to play Atomic Mass on the radio! Can you remember?'

'I *do* remember!' said the DJ, immensely flattered.

John Metcalf spun the steering wheel lightly with one hand, cruising down the Santa Monica freeway towards the Coliseum, listening to the band on KNAC, where Joe, the singer, was playing the interviewer like a guitar. He flicked a few buttons on the multi-play sound system, trying to find a Top 40 station that wasn't wall-to-wall Atomic Mass. He failed.

'And this is "Big Cat" from *Animal Instinct* . . .'

'. . . That was "Frozen Gold", a little Atomic Mass for ya there . . .'

'. . . from a record which just sold and sold and *sold*.'

'. . . making the British rock combo only the third act ever to sell out the Coliseum . . .'

'. . . *live* from Venice Beach, where our "what would

you do for a pair of tickets for Atomic Mass" contest is reaching its climax.'

'And that was "Sea Diver" by Mott the Hoople . . .'

John rolled his eyes in mock relief.

' . . . who, by the way, are cited as one of the biggest influences on *the* band of the moment, Atomic Mass, headlining the Coliseum tonight on the *very first show* of the *Animal Instinct* world tour 1995 . . .'

He groaned in delighted defeat. He couldn't get away from them, which meant he couldn't get away from her. At least his baby label was in good hands. What a woman! What an executive! What a . . . what a *babe*!

She had sat in his office, commandeered a spare telephone and fixed the problem.

'OK. This is how it is,' she had said briskly, slapping a sheet of ticket sales in front of him. 'Gate is eighty-five per cent. And that's not good enough. I need a hundred per cent.'

'But why do you care?' he'd asked, amused. 'You're fine at eighty-five. They'll make money!'

'That's not the point. It's how the band are perceived. We open at the Coliseum, we sell out the Coliseum. That's it. No argument. I want people clamouring for tickets they can't buy.'

'Otherwise what? They look bad?'

'Congratulations, you win a cigar,' said Rowena, as if to a particularly stupid child. 'The boys are hot property today and I want them to be hot property tomorrow and the day after that.'

'But the gig is tomorrow,' he pointed out, admiring the silver-blonde cascade of hair tumbling to her slender waist. Her iced-mint eyes were sparkling with the challenge.

'That gives me three hours,' said Rowena.

'You can't do anything in three hours!' laughed John.

'Oh yeah?' she said. 'Watch me.'

And he'd watched her. He'd watched the elegant turn of her calf in her tight jeans, the tight sweet swell of her small breasts under her bodystocking, the way she sat with her legs apart like a man, tapping her knee with one beautiful, unpainted hand. He'd tried not to stare too hard at her crotch, gently outlined under the protecting denim. He wanted to undo the buttons of her fly and slide his hand in there, and guide her slowly, slowly, to spasm, till she was whimpering and begging, and maybe he'd take a couple of handfuls of that fountain of blonde hair and twist her head roughly about while she squirmed against his palm . . . God, he'd be patient with her, and when he put his cock in that soft silver wetness he'd take her with a slow intensity, deep, long strokes, ignoring her pleas to fuck her brains out. He'd teach her what sex was really about, and she'd come like it was the end of the world, and then . . . and then . . . and then he'd marry her, the gorgeous fucking creature.

And occasionally he'd watched how goddamn great she was at her job.

'So can I speak to the PD? Hey, Ken? Rowena Gordon! Uh-huh? You too, up book *again* I see . . . Look, I got a trade for you . . . stick on the Catch-22 single. No, listen, you play it, I got five hundred tickets for Atomic Mass at the Coliseum tomorrow . . . that's right, completely sold out . . . great.'

'Sam Goody in Sacramento please – Richard Brown? Rowena Gordon – you got a nice Mass display up there, babe? Cause I'm thinking maybe the boys might drop in on their way out to the plane . . . shit, you know I can't guarantee it . . . No, the show's totally sold out, but you wanna run a promotion I can cut you a deal – a hundred, two hundred? two fifty? I don't know, it's tough – call Simon at TicketMaster and tell him it's on Musica corporate rate. Anything for my favourite store manager.'

'Joseph Moretti. This is Rowena Gordon. Of course top brass work the promo phones! This is Musica, not MCA! Here it is. Show is totally sold out. I want tomorrow to be Atomic Mass day on KXDA – you get one thousand tickets and ten pairs of all-access passes, I get three tracks an hour every hour minimum – I can fix interviews – no, that's fine! I don't know, what are the three most beautiful words in the English language? A done deal? Ha ha ha! You got it . . .'

She put the phone down on Tower on Sunset two and a half hours later, and Atomic Mass had an exclusive franchise on every major radio station and record store in southern California.

'You're just a show-off,' said John, shaking his head.

Rowena lit a cigarette and took a deep pull, satisfied. He noticed she neither asked for permission to smoke nor apologized for it.

'What now?'

'Now I fax Musica's head of PR in New York with a press release.'

'Which says what?' he asked, completely fascinated.

'Which says,' she grinned, 'that the show is sold out, the only way to get tickets is through radio and in-store competitions, and that police have been warned of possible riots by crowds of disappointed fans unable to get in.'

He laughed. 'Woman, you are incredible. I can't believe it. I gave you a phone, and you delivered Los Angeles.'

'With red ribbons and a cherry on top,' Rowena agreed.

'So modest.'

'Fuck modest!' she said, feeling powerfully happy. 'I'm the best.'

He drove her to Morton's for dinner, and the night air was charged with jasmine and sex. She was wearing a grey dress, a little silken thing that poured over her slim body like water. Her long legs were naked down to the designer sandals. He wanted her so badly it ached.

John Metcalf was a studio president, and attractive in his own right. He was rich, he was powerful, and he was straight, in one of the most hedonistic cities in the world. There had been a lot of women, not all of them stupid.

But he knew within days of meeting her that Rowena Gordon was quite different from all of them. It wasn't a blinding revelation, the flash of light and cosmic neon arrows and everything else an Angeleno expects.

It was just a quiet certainty that this girl was the one.

He wanted to own her and possess her. He wanted to put his ring glittering on her finger and scream to the world that she was his alone. The contradictions of her entranced him – that cool, ladylike English voice wheeling and dealing with the appetite of a Brooklyn hustler; that delicate rosy beauty throwing itself into brutal male music like heavy metal and hardcore rap; her classically educated brain focusing its laser intelligence with total absorption on music he didn't understand and names he didn't recognize – techno, glam, swingbeat. She seemed interested in making money, even greedy, and yet completely uninterested in making it anywhere other than the record business. The day after the soundtrack deal was finalized, he'd offered her a vice-presidency at the studio, with stock options, at triple what she was making at Musica. She'd smiled and asked him to explain to her why she should trade down.

He wondered about her sexuality as his dark eyes

swept over her lithe athletic body. He wondered if she realized how obvious she was about what she wanted. She flung her success down like a sexual gauntlet. She couldn't have made it clearer if she'd gone out in a T-shirt saying DOMINATE ME in big black letters. And she evidently had some lover, some man who was giving her what she thought she wanted.

John Metcalf pressed his foot on the accelerator, thinking murderous, aroused thoughts. The cool night air rushed past them, lifting Rowena's blonde hair like a golden banner streaming in the darkness. That made it worse. *Whoever he is, he's history*, Metcalf thought grimly. *I wonder what he made her do for him. I wonder if he made her swallow. I wonder if he put her on her hands and knees and screwed her from behind. Jesus! If he touches her again, he's a dead man.*

Rowena stretched in the seat, lifting her arms above her head. Her body bent into a slight bow, and he could see her delicate little nipples, hardened by the cold, push slightly against her dress.

I'm going to have you, Rowena Gordon, he said to himself. *I'm going to make you come so hard you weep. I'm not just going to shove it into you the way you think you like it. I'm going to make love to you an inch at a time, until you're so sensitive to my touch you get wet when my fingers brush your elbow. If you think about me when you're walking down the street, the friction of your legs will make you come . . .*

Rowena sipped her champagne, frustrated. Was it possible he didn't find her attractive? Maybe he was gay.

'Well, it's fifty million dollars' worth of business,' she said. 'That's worth getting excited about in my book.'

John Metcalf smiled, indulgent and infuriating. 'Maybe so, for music,' he said. 'If I could bring a movie in so cheap, I'd be a happy guy.'

'Oh, these numbers are chickenfeed to you,' she snapped sarcastically.

'Yes they are,' he said. 'Absolutely.'

She felt a rush of lust. Damn, he was good-looking. Well-muscled, confident, masculine. His jaw was hard-set and his lips fairly unremarkable. But there was something about him, she wasn't sure . . . she didn't know . . .

Rowena felt a disturbing confusion. She'd spent only a few days with John Metcalf. She didn't even know him. He wasn't *Michael*, was he? Michael was who she loved. Always and for ever and no matter what.

John Metcalf knew nothing about music, nothing about her, nothing about all the ties that bound her to Krebs. And he was an arrogant sonofabitch, sitting here telling her the most important deal of her life was chopped liver!

'I bet you're really selfish in bed,' she said, furious.

There was a pause. Metcalf looked at her over the table, slowly swallowing his steak.

'Selfish?' he asked.

Silence.

'I have a boyfriend,' Rowena whispered, suddenly frightened.

'Oh?' Metcalf enquired politely. 'That's nice.'

'I love him,' she insisted.

He tilted his glass towards her, courteously. 'Congratulations.'

'I must go,' said Rowena, flustered. 'I have to see to the arrangements for soundcheck. I'll get a cab.'

'Sorry you have to go,' he said, completely at his ease. 'I'll walk you to the car.'

He opened the cab door for her and stood aside so she could get in. Rowena turned round to thank him, intensely disturbed by how close together they were standing.

'It was good of you to take me to dinner, John,' she said.

'Thank you for coming,' he replied. With a barely perceptible movement, he took hold of her waist, thumbs in the hollows of her hipbones, his fingers resting on the top of her ass.

His touch changed everything.

The electricity was instantaneous.

Rowena stared at him, her groin dissolving with pleasure and panic.

'I'm not going to do anything to you that you don't want,' he said. 'And when we go to bed, you'll be mine. And there won't be any going back.'

Chapter Twenty-Four

All Rowena's worlds exploded at once.

Everything, suddenly, was falling into place, and everything was being decided tonight.

She looked out over the ocean of people before her and below her, stretching out into the night as far as she could see, small points of light filling the stadium as the fans clicked their lighters and held them above their heads. The gig wasn't due to start for twenty minutes yet, but the band, eager to amplify the already intense atmosphere, had dimmed the stadium floodlights, pumped up the huge house PA system to blare music into the darkened arena, and turned one brilliant light on the vast curtains sealing off the stage.

The Atomic Mass logo – a spinning molecule in gold on blue – shone like a massive raised beacon above the audience, demanding homage. Rowena could make out waves in the crowd, as people started to slam to Guns n' Roses 'Paradise City'. She paced, alone in the executive box. Michael Krebs was locked in Mirror, Mirror, recording with another huge band. Rowena had asked him to come, but he was adamant – nothing took Krebs away from a record. She'd resented it; for Atomic Mass, he might have made an exception. If she'd played mother to their careers, Michael Krebs had played father.

Can't we be together in anything?

The Musica board should have been here an hour ago.

Atomic Mass, her band, her boys. They were poised on a knife-edge between 'major act' and 'legend'. It had taken everything she had to sell out this gig, and Musica would have to grin and bear an unprecedented promotional cost. The world was watching this evening. I can't help you now, she thought. Do or die, lads. Do or die.

Then, Musica. Everything she'd struggled for all her adult life. Luther was profitable; Atomic were the biggest band on the planet, at least for the next five minutes; and Picture This was a movie/music deal even Peter Paterno might have been proud to sign.

One thing's for certain, Rowena admitted to herself. That's it. That's the best I can do.

If they didn't give her North America now, they never would. It was that simple. And when – if? – Joshua Oberman finally made it to the gig, he'd tell her in person. She didn't know if that was good or bad.

The tension mounted in the Coliseum. The slow, heavy chords of Metallica's 'Enter Sandman' filled the night air, and Rowena shivered with joy as tens of thousands of voices took up the anthem:

Exit light
Enter night

What an awesome lyric, she thought. She swayed to the grind of the bass, her long legs taking up the beat, her golden hair sweeping from side to side. The excitement in the air was so strong you could taste it. Where was Oberman? And where, she wondered with a strange ache of longing, was John?

The final song blasted out of the PA. It was AC/DC. She couldn't help laughing at the irony.

> *It's a long way*
> *Such a long way*
> *It's a long way*
> *To the top*
> *If you wanna rock 'n' roll . . .*

Topaz leant back in her chair and tried not to cry. *Damn it, take it like a man. I mean take it like a woman! Do some work or go for a walk. I mean do* something, *just don't sit here moping . . . just don't . . .*

It was no use. A large tear trickled down her cheek, and then another, and another . . .

She put a hand over her mouth to stifle a great wrenching sob. Embarrassed by her own reaction, and frightened one of the assistants stationed outside her office might see her, she rose from her desk and went to stand by the window, and then, with her back to the door, she leant wearily against the sill and wept.

Ten minutes later she wiped her face clumsily, pulled on a pair of shades and rang for a cab.

So I'll take the rest of the day off, she thought grimly, and I'll cry or whatever and I will deal with this. I'll congratulate Joe like a professional. OK, it hurts like hell. Big fucking deal. Mama always said I had eyes bigger than my belly . . . Bottom line, if I don't have what it takes, it's better to find that out now than when I'm fifty.

The phone buzzed. *Oh Jesus Christ, get lost.*

'Hey, Topaz.' Marissa's jealous, smarmy voice greased its way down the line. 'I heard. You must be devastated.'

Topaz glanced out of the window at the tiny yellow ladybug cabs, crawling along Seventh Avenue in the impersonal sunshine. She felt a little welcome steel creep back into her soul.

'What can I tell you, Marissa? Shit happens. I'll get another chance.'

'Well, I wouldn't count on that, honey. American Magazines moves on real fast . . . Joe Goldstein calls the shots now.'

'And he's a great man to do it,' Topaz said firmly. 'I'm looking forward to being a part of his team.'

Marissa sighed theatrically. 'Oh, Topaz. I don't think you should rely on . . . how shall I put it? A *close* working relationship that you had in the past . . .'

Topaz's knuckles were white as she gripped the phone.

'Past, present and future, sugar,' she said sweetly. 'In fact, as the second most senior MD, Joe's asked me to look at redefining the roles for our star reporters. We both think that your talents are just wasted on the society circuit, babe . . . Joe thought you'd be ideal for a major series in *Economic Monthly*, something serious you could get your teeth into.'

'Like what?' asked Marissa warily.

'Like six months covering the Midwest farming depression,' spat Topaz. 'That way you could report on things closer to your own level. Such as pig sewage.'

She slammed the receiver down, feeling a little better. The phone rang again.

'Look, whoever you are, just fuck off, OK?' she shouted. 'I'm not in the goddamned mood!'

'That's a nice way to greet an old friend,' said Joe mildly.

'Oh, shit,' said Topaz, blushing. 'I'm sorry, Joe. I didn't know it was you.'

'Evidently,' he said.

Topaz bit the bullet. 'Congratulations, Joe. Really. I

mean it. The best man won, and all that stuff . . . you'll do a great job . . . obviously you'll have my resignation by the end of the week, and no hard feelings.'

Joe chuckled. Topaz flushed a deeper red, this time from resentment. *There's no need to laugh at me on top of everything else. Winner's privilege, I guess.*

'Of course you're not going to resign, Rossi,' he said.

'Oh yes, I am,' said Topaz stubbornly. It'll be a cold day in hell before I report to you, Joe Goldstein, she thought.

'Topaz Rossi,' Joe insisted, 'I do not accept, and American Magazines will not accept, the resignation of the best print woman in the country.'

'If I was the best, I'd have got the job,' snarled Topaz, ashamed of herself but unable to be gracious.

'However,' Joe continued, ignoring her completely, 'we do need to talk about your future role. Why don't you come over to my place tonight? I'll cook something and we can discuss it over dinner.'

With a herculean effort, she swallowed a hundred smart-ass replies.

'Good idea. I'll be there at eight thirty,' she said.

'I look forward to it,' Joe said, and rang off.

Oh Joe, Topaz thought miserably. My best friend and worst enemy. I wish you were here. Then I could cry on your shoulder and kick you in the balls at the same time.

The phone rang again.

'What? *What?*' she shrieked.

'Uh, cab, Ms Rossi,' whispered a terrified receptionist.

'Oh. Cool,' said Topaz, a little gruffly. 'I'll be right down.'

The private jet was halfway from Stockholm to Los Angeles, and the four men were still arguing.

'But that was your point six months ago, Hans,' said

Joshua Oberman. 'And Luther's already turning a profit. Not only that, but she's got three or four baby acts that are selling albums, not singles. I wanted a presence in domestic repertoire, and she is delivering.'

The president of Musica Holland and new group director of Finance glowered at him with all the anger fifty-three years and a red moustache could muster.

'It's insanity, putting an A & R man in a senior corporate job, Joshua. Name me one example where it's worked out.'

'Roger Ames at PolyGram.'

'Apart from Roger Ames.'

'Clive Davis at Arista.'

'Those are two freak instances,' said Hans Bauer.

'David Geffen,' said Josh Oberman. 'Rick Rubin. Russell Simmons. Charles Koppleman . . .'

'You can't put a *woman* in charge of North America!' Maurice LeBec objected.

The old man glared at his executive committee.

'Well, by my watch, you have three hours to persuade me not to, gentlemen,' he said.

It was early evening in Manhattan, and the summer air was balmy and cool, rustling the branches of the trees in Central Park. As far as the city ever feels relaxed, it was relaxed in New York that May. Topaz watched little children sucking noisily at their ice creams, and the horses trotting alongside the park, uncomplainingly hauling their carriages full of tourists.

She felt *weird*.

She sat on her apartment balcony, sipping Cristal. She was wearing a dark green dress by Ann Klein, which fell invitingly in folds of soft cotton round her magnificently curvy body, and then cut sharply off at the knees to reveal a pair of heart-stopping calves. She'd done her hair Renaissance-style, half of it piled on top of her head in a luxuriant coil, half tumbling down the sides of her face in long ruby curls. There was a thick gold bracelet on her left wrist, and jet-black mules from Chanel framed the sexy turn of her ankle.

She felt rich, and stunningly beautiful.

She felt like a wretched failure.

She hated Joe Goldstein. He'd beaten her hands down.

She wanted to fuck his brains out.

Mind you, I always wanted to do that, from the first moment I laid eyes on him, she reminded herself. But now, now I should hate him! He cost me my seat on the board, the bastard . . . Marissa was right about that one . . . American Magazines, like the rest of this town, doesn't cut losers a lot of slack.

Rowena Gordon, of course, had the world at her aristocratic feet.

Topaz felt little prickles of hatred crawl across her skin at the thought of it. The bitch had done everything right. She'd been born to the right parents, for a start. She'd gone to a prestigious school. And she'd betrayed her best friend, who loved her like a sister, at the first opportunity . . . At least you can't write 'President of the Union' in that sparkling biography, she thought with satisfaction.

Across the park, Musica Towers glinted in the sun.

The satisfaction evaporated.

She'd come home, flicked on her wide-screen TV and been confronted by some inane MTV VJ getting orgasmic over Atomic Mass. What had the bitch done to sell out the Coliseum? She was damn sure it had been a quarter empty on Monday. Just wait for the reviews, Rowena. Your band will be about as hip as Whitesnake.

It was a small measure of comfort, and Topaz took a

slow sip of champagne, trying to banish the vision of her enemy's triumph. I don't need this, she thought. I won't give her that final victory. I won't let her sour my life.

She got up and strolled to the fridge, checking her reflection in the wall mirror. She was a knockout. 'Better than Joe Goldstein deserves,' she said, smiling. Well, she'd do it in style, at least. She'd bought two sensational bottles of wine to congratulate him: vintage Moët et Chandon champagne and a Château Lafite 1953. Maybe she'd take off the bracelet and wear her diamond necklace instead. After all, she still ran two of the most profitable magazines in the United States.

When the chauffeur buzzed up to the apartment, Topaz was ready for him.

She blew a kiss at her exquisite reflection, clutching a bottle in each hand. Wow! The original playgirl of the Western World. Joe would be blown away.

Oh, face one more thing while you're at it, Rossi. You're head over heels in love with your boss. Again.

The curtain was ripped away from the front of the stage and hundreds of lasers spun into the sky, crossing and recrossing in spectacular webs. The ecstatic screams of about 80,000 girls rent the California skyline. They stayed screaming.

Rowena Gordon, twenty-seven years old, label boss, businesswoman, A&R goddess, rammed her knuckles into her mouth to stop herself doing the same thing.

It was absolute, total, mass hysteria.

And then the band came on.

'I'm telling you, the men won't work with her,' Maurice said, purple with rage and struggling to control himself. Unbelievable. A woman had never sat on the board of a major label, never in the whole history of the record business. It was farcical. The old idiot would make fools of them all.

'She's not even thirty years old,' moaned Hans, reading his thoughts.

'She's got no experience in classical,' said Jakob van Rees, clutching at straws.

Josh Oberman looked at them all, whining, whingeing, carping. Pathetic. He remembered Rowena storming into his office five years ago, hurling an armful of CDs on to his desk, passionate and furious. What were these snivelling Eurotrash? Glorified fucking accountants.

'If people won't work with her, we'll just have to replace them, won't we?' he said with deadly calm.

Maurice and Hans swallowed nervously.

'You'll be able to work with her though, won't you?' he wondered aloud.

'Oh yes,' said all three men, hastily.

'What do you see in her, Joshua?' asked Jakob miserably.

He fixed the three group presidents with a contemptuous glance.

'She's the son I never had,' he said.

Joe Hunter stood centre stage, Zach's guitar howling beauty into the blackness. Alex was running over to the left-hand monitors, his bass swinging against his body, greeting the sea of crazed fans on that side of the stadium. He felt the glory of it course through his veins. It was better than power. Better than riches. Better than sex.

He started to sing.

> *Why don't we start at the end*
> *It's great to see you again*
> *Have you heard anything new . . .*

*

The answering roar shook the foundations of the building.

'Hi Rowena,' John Metcalf said.

Just when she'd thought it couldn't get any better.

'John!' she exclaimed, shocked at how pleased she was to see him. 'Oh, it's so good to see you, it's so good that you're here!'

This might possibly be the best moment of her life, and she found she was delighted to have him there to share it with her. He was wearing jeans and a white T-shirt, which threw his large, tanned body into sharp relief. An all-access crew laminate hung on his muscled chest.

Rowena smiled at the thought of a movie mogul humping flight cases around; although, if circumstances were different, he'd be big enough and strong enough for the job . . .

'Quite a show, young lady,' John congratulated her. 'Makes me tempted to try music for a couple of years.'

'Maybe I can find a place for you somewhere,' said Rowena.

John shook his head. 'Are you kidding? I couldn't take the cut in salary.'

'God, you *asshole*,' said Rowena, livid. 'You fucking . . .'

'Oh, shut up,' said John Metcalf gently, and gathered her into his arms and kissed her.

She didn't even bother with a token protesting squirm.

Atomic Mass were blasting through 'Karla' when the Musica board finally made it to the executive box, panting from the effort of climbing so many stairs, even though hordes of respectful security guards had shown them every short cut in the book. The group presidents were all wincing from the violent music and the delirious screams of the fans; Jakob was trying to hide an unimpressive hard-on which he'd got on passing two teenage girls, who, mad with worship, had torn at their shirts so much that they'd exposed their breasts, bouncing around in time to the beat. Josh Oberman noticed them too, and wished he was forty years younger. He was ecstatic with the job his protégée had done; the scene reminded him of the Beatles at Shea Stadium.

'*It's getting closer, It's getting clearer, I don't believe you, I'm getting out of here,*' soared Joe's spectacular voice.

The board stopped dead in their tracks. Maurice, Hans and Jakob were overjoyed. Surely now he would see reason.

Rowena Gordon, managing director of Luther Records, lay flat on her back, stretched underneath John Peter Metcalf III, chairman of Metropolis Studios, kissing him wildly, pressing herself into his caressing hands. Metcalf had thrust her skirt up almost to her panties, exposing her magnificent right thigh.

Joshua roared with laughter. 'How's it going, John?' he bellowed. 'I see you've met the president of our North American operations!'

Joe Goldstein liked to think he had the best apartment in TriBeCa. It was basically one huge room, with a separate bathroom. He had stripped the pine floorboards himself and painstakingly coated them with a dark varnish. The gentle light from his soft red lamps gleamed on the wood. He sat on the couch, underneath his poster of Sid Fernandez, pitcher for the Mets and all-time Goldstein hero. Northwards outside his window the spires of the Empire State Building stared back at him.

Good, he thought. I'm going to enjoy this.

The bell rang, and he went to open the door. He was wearing a flannel shirt, beat-up jeans and sneakers.

Topaz stood there in full evening dress, defiant and nervous and utterly beautiful. Diamonds glittered on her throat and ears, sending little points of light dancing over her blue eyes and red hair. Her deep green gown hugged her bosom and ass provocatively, taunting him. She was without question the most attractive woman he'd ever seen.

'Jesus Christ,' he said, staggered.

'Don't say that! You're not a Christian,' snapped Topaz, weak with longing for him. *Oh my God, you beautiful bastard.*

She pushed her way past him into the apartment, trying to catch her breath from the sudden rush of desire.

'I brought you a congratulations present,' she said, roughly thrusting the two bottles at him. 'Well done.'

She sounded nearly as awkward as she felt. But what could she say? *It should've been me! Damn you to all hell for ruining my life! Let's go to bed?*

'Come on, Topaz. You're hardly the good Catholic girl, now are you?' demanded Joe, opening the Moët and wondering how long he should let her stew before he told her.

'Don't you insult my fucking religion,' said Topaz, perhaps not as piously as she might have done.

Joe courteously pulled out a chair for her, and they sat down.

The mahogany table was covered with silver candlesticks and pink and white roses, and Joe had set out fresh mango slices as a starter. He poured champagne into two Lalique crystal glasses.

'To the director of American Magazines, East Coast,' said Joe, raising his glass.

Topaz swallowed her anger. Once, just once, she'd allow him to gloat over her. 'To Joe Goldstein,' she said, saluting him.

Joe regarded her across the table. Unless he was very much mistaken, her nipples were erect. All this battling must be getting to her, he thought. He remembered how much he'd hated the pushy, masculine bitch that night, and how furious he'd been when his cock seemed to have other ideas . . . and how she'd hated him right back . . . until that one touch had set everything off . . . and he remembered screwing her so hard on that desk, their mutual need so urgent and demanding that it blocked out all reason . . .

Topaz licked a drop of mango juice off her lips.

That's it, Joe thought. Forget about teasing her. If I get any more turned on, this table is going to lift an inch from the ground.

'I wasn't toasting myself,' he said shortly. 'That's your title now. I'm not taking the job.'

'What?' gasped Topaz.

'Don't you understand English? I've been offered a programming position at NBC. I'll have to drop a rung to do it, but that gets me into television, which is where I've always wanted to go.'

Topaz took an unladylike slug of her drink. The room was spinning.

'So! You just reckoned you'd let me stew for a day, did you, you asshole?' she demanded, trying to hide her joy. *Poor Marissa*, she thought bitchily.

'Why don't you shut up,' said Joe thickly, 'and ask me nicely if I'll fuck you, like you want me to.'

'I do not,' denied Topaz, unconvincingly.

'Yes you do, Rossi,' said Joe, rising from his chair and walking round the table towards her. 'Yes you do. You've been hot for me all day. You're wet for me now. Did you fantasize about it? Huh? Did you wonder if I'd sit in that big black chair in the director's office and make you kneel under my desk and suck me off?'

Topaz was so aroused she could hardly breathe. She sat transfixed in her chair, watching Joe come slowly towards her, a colossal erection straining under his jeans.

'Why should I bother fucking you?' she asked dismissively. 'You're not even a print man any more.'

Joe towered over her, his crotch right next to her face. 'I'll enjoy making you pay for that,' he said.

Topaz stared at the outline of his cock, and was seized with a paralysing longing to have it inside her.

'Beg me to fuck you,' said Joe.

'Please fuck me, Joe,' whispered Topaz, dying of lust.

'Louder,' Joe demanded, trying to control the urge to jump her bones immediately.

'Please fuck me,' she said, shaking with need.

'I'll fuck you when I'm good and ready,' Joe said, and then he knelt down and seized her left ankle in a vicelike grip, and slowly licked the tender hollow under the anklebone.

Topaz moaned.

Joe worked his way up her legs inch by inch, refusing to hurry his pace, holding her down if she tried to shove herself against him. Eventually he reached the top of her thighs, and roughly pulled down her panties.

Topaz tensed. 'Joe . . . I've never . . .'

But he could smell the beautiful thick musk of her desire.

'I'm going to give you what you want, Topaz Rossi,' he growled. Then, as she was shuddering with longing, he languidly trailed the tip of his tongue back and forward over her clitoris.

'Oh, Jesus!' Topaz screamed. 'Oh, my God!'

'Don't blaspheme,' Joe teased her. Then he licked her some more.

'Oh, Joe! I love you! I love you! Oh, Jesus! Please fuck me! Fuck me!' Topaz begged, insane with pleasure.

Joe's erection was swollen almost to the point of pain. Continuing to lick Topaz out, he kicked off his shoes and pants. 'You do want it, don't you,' he said. 'Catholic girl. You want my Jewish cock in your pussy. Isn't that right?'

Topaz writhed against his tongue, completely incapable of speech.

Joe pulled her roughly off the chair, and, unable to wait a second longer, shoved himself inside her, losing himself in the pleasure of her tight wet heat around him.

They moved together.

'I love you,' said Joe.

'I love you too,' said Topaz.

'You're going to get me pregnant,' said Topaz.

'I know that,' said Joe.

'Will you marry me?' asked Topaz.

'Oh yeah,' said Joe Goldstein, entering her for the fourth time. 'Yeah.'

Chapter Twenty-Five

Once again, Elizabeth Martin was throwing a party.

Once again, both Topaz Rossi and Rowena Gordon were invited.

And this time, *everyone* was watching them.

'You can't get an invite. Nobody can,' Rowena told John. 'If you lived in New York she'd have chosen you like a shot, but you're from LA. Elizabeth isn't David Geffen or Mike Ovitz. Running a movie studio won't give you any clout with her.'

'I'll get an invite,' Metcalf told her with supreme confidence, and he had.

'How did you manage that?' Rowena asked, surprised, when he rang her a week before the bash. 'That's impossible.'

'Nothing's impossible,' John teased, refusing to say. 'I'll pick you up at eight.'

'What are you going to wear?' Joe asked Topaz. Since they'd been living together, Goldstein had developed an intense interest in women's fashion, as far as it related to Topaz. The style and boldness with which she wore clothes used to infuriate him, but now he adored it. So what if the look disturbed her co-workers? Topaz was answerable to nobody. Topaz was a free spirit. That was exactly why he hadn't been able to forget her.

'You can wait and see,' she replied.

'You'll be the most beautiful woman in the place,' Joe said, coming up to her and taking her in his arms.

'I haven't told you what I'm wearing yet,' she pointed out.

'You'll be the most beautiful woman there if you turn up in a sack,' he said, kissing her.

'You can't avoid me for ever,' Michael Krebs said. 'We'll both be at Elizabeth's party.'

His tone was taut with what Rowena knew to be controlled anger. For a month now she'd been communicating with him by fax, talking to Barbara or letting a deputy negotiate for her. When he called her at home, she had the answering service take a message. She wanted to let her relationship with John develop, and that meant not talking to Michael.

Eventually she'd called him back, in his office, at 11.45 a.m. A nice, safe time when others of his staff might be there.

She took a deep breath. 'And so will John Metcalf,' she said. 'Who I'm going out with.'

There was a pause at the other end.

'Good!' said Michael, brightly. 'Congratulations, Rowena, that's great. But what does that have to do with us?'

'I can't do anything with you any more, Krebs,' said Rowena, with a slight smile. Some things never changed.

'Of course you can,' he said simply. 'You always did before.'

'John's different.'

Krebs gripped the phone, his knuckles white around

the handset. He couldn't believe how angry he felt. Insulted. Cheated. Rejected. Of course John Metcalf was different – a young, attractive man, single, president of a movie studio, rich. A guy who made the 'America's Most Eligible Bachelors' list every summer.

A man richer and more powerful than him.

A *younger* man.

'Well, it's your choice,' he told her, as casually as he could manage. 'But I think you're being dumb. We had a lot of fun.'

Unexpectedly, Rowena found her eyes had filled with tears. 'Yes, we did,' she admitted.

Both of them had an instantaneous vision of the last time they'd had sex – in a hotel in Munich on the European leg of the *Heat Street* tour, when they'd barely been able to make it inside before ripping their clothes off and grabbing at each other. Krebs had fucked Rowena standing up, her back to the wall, while she was still half-dressed.

'Rowena –' Michael began.

'I have to go,' she said hurriedly, and replaced the receiver.

It had to end some time, Krebs told himself. I don't give a damn. It was fun while it lasted, that was all.

Rowena was the one who'd stressed out about it all the time. He, Michael, had been totally consistent in his attitude. Debbie was his wife and he loved her. Rowena – well – he shouldn't have done it, but she was so *good*. And he enjoyed her company, when she wasn't moaning and complaining and getting weepy on him.

John Metcalf, eh? Well, he was pleased for her.

'Eli, goddamnit!' Krebs roared. 'Where the fuck are my notes?'

*

Sometimes you work through a day and don't realize how tired you are until you sit down. And sometimes you can work through several years and not realize how lonely you are until you meet a guy. It had happened to Rowena Gordon in Los Angeles; first, the nervousness she'd felt around John Metcalf that none of her other lovers had provoked; then the simple happiness at finding her body responding to a man who didn't dominate her; and finally, the surprise at seeing him at her door every evening, the flowers that arrived every morning, the endless compliments and proclamations of love. She'd found herself extending her time in LA indefinitely, and then, one morning, Rowena Gordon had woken up in a beautiful bedroom in Beverly Hills, in her lover's arms, and decided that John made her happy.

Being with him made her happy. Being paraded in public made her happy. Getting complimented made her happy and making love to him made her happy. He couldn't drive her to the sexual nirvana that Michael could, but then again, John wasn't married and he was offering her love.

And she wasn't twenty-two any more. She was kissing thirty, and she hadn't had a serious relationship since the day she met Michael Krebs.

Yeah, she was a high achiever. She'd struggled in London, struggled in New York, and come through both times. She was the president of Musica North America and a powerful figure in her chosen industry. Of course, there was still a long way to go, but she was well on target. Rich in her own right. Famous amongst her peers. Music business magazines referred to her by her first name alone – now *there* was a sign of making it.

But she was unmarried and childless. Another New York career girl, alone and unhappily attached to a man who didn't love her back and didn't even pretend to.

No! I have choices! Rowena told herself that morning, looking at Metcalf's handsome face on the pillow beside her. There was nothing great about being a victim, a role-reversed Lancelot sighing for an unattainable Guinevere.

She would choose happiness. She chose John.

Topaz selected her outfit with great attention. She'd always cared about her looks, but this time it was important. She had to dress appropriately to her new position as director of American Magazines, East Coast – the youngest in the company's history and only the third woman to rank so highly. Last month *People* had called her 'the new Tina Brown' and Topaz had been completely thrilled. Shamelessly thrilled. If she got another chance to meet Tina Brown, she wanted to look dynamite for the photo. Rowena would call that shallow. *She* called it honest.

Also, she had to be a knockout for Joe. It was the first time they'd have been out socially since they got engaged.

Give Marissa something to write about.

And then she had to look better than Rowena Gordon.

Topaz still burned with resentment whenever she thought about that woman. The pain of her first betrayal had faded with time, but the cold arrogance of her attitude hadn't. She *had* taken a band from under Rowena's nose, but after that all the scoring was on the other woman's side. Musica's success, Atomic Mass, surviving that drugs story – *Jesus, how I hate writers that don't check their sources* – and selling out the Coliseum.

She'd wanted to get even, that was all. She was an Italian. Nobody spurned her and got away with it.

Yet Topaz might have let it go, all the same. She

hadn't been *in* love with Nate Rosen – though only since she'd known Joe had she realized that – but she had loved him, and his death had changed her frantic attitude to life. And with Joe Goldstein, she was a woman blissfully in love, with a great career.

But Rowena Gordon had pushed her over the edge again.

It was the day after Joe had proposed to her. The day after Atomic Mass had played the Coliseum to wild reviews. Topaz had just got into the office, ready for a very pleasant meeting with Matt Gowers. After all, Joe had just resigned and would formally appoint Topaz to the board that morning. What with Joe, and the job, she was so happy that day that not even the sight of a triumphant Joe Hunter on *Good Morning America* had been able to dent her mood.

But then her assistant had come in with a large parcel. 'This came from Luther Records, this morning,' she said. 'I had to sign for it. Do you want me to send it right back?'

'No. I'll open it,' Topaz answered, curious.

She'd torn off the brown paper and felt a shock of rage.

It was a Dunlop tennis racket, with a small typed note attached. The note read: 'Advantage Miss Gordon.'

She picked it up, almost disbelievingly. Three years in the United States, and Rowena's fucking blue limey blood hadn't warmed up one degree. She'd never apologized, never explained, and she treated the whole thing like a game. She was fucking *laughing* at her.

That day she decided it was war. She was going to destroy Rowena Gordon, however long it took her.

You want to play this out? You got it.

Topaz twisted round, checking herself out in the full-length wall mirror. The dress was her first piece of fitted haute couture, a one-off original, with a price tag to match – but right now, she thought it had been worth every cent.

It was a sweeping ballgown in oyster-pink satin, the fitted bodice dusted over with hand-embroidered tiny gold beads, the skirt ruched over folds of stiff gold brocade. Watching her reflection carefully in the huge mirror, Topaz took out her favourite ebony combs and caught her hair up in a silken pile on the crown of her head, pinning it securely in place and then fixing it with a burst of Elnett hairspray, a regal style which exposed her long, elegant neck. She added dangling coral earrings and a ruby necklace, a magnificent piece from Cartier which Joe had bought her two weeks after they got engaged.

'What's this for?' Topaz had asked in delight, when he'd presented her with the box over dinner at Elaine's. A woman at the next table had given an involuntary gasp when Topaz, stunned, held up the perfect string of rubies to the light.

'Just for being alive,' Joe answered, feeling his heart almost burst with love at the sight of the tears in her eyes.

Being apart was torture. Every day, when they kissed each other goodbye, they took too long about it, not wanting to let go. They met each other for lunch, and one was always waiting to pick the other up after work. They walked everywhere holding hands like teenagers. Topaz sometimes called Joe on his direct line at NBC and told him in detail what she wished she were doing to him, so that he couldn't get up for fifteen minutes because of the erection surging in his pants. Nate would never have allowed it; Joe revelled in it. When he got home those evenings, if Topaz wanted to make love three times, Joe wanted to do it five. Where Nathan would have pushed her away, Joe asked for more. And where Nathan had made her feel good, Joe made her scream.

'I want to have your children,' she'd whispered to him in the restaurant, and Goldstein, feeling choked up himself, replied, 'I think that can be arranged.'

They hadn't even made it through the starter before Topaz called for the check.

'Can I come in now?' Joe yelled from the kitchen.

'Yeah,' she yelled back, spraying on a burst of Joy. She turned round as he appeared in the doorway, holding up her skirt with one hand as she slipped into her shoes, a pair of gold heels from Kurt Geiger.

'Do you like it?' she asked nervously.

Joe Goldstein looked his fiancée up and down, slowly, taking in the delicate pink and gold satin, the sexy earrings, and the way his rubies sparkled against the creamy back-drop of her full breasts, pushed up even further by the clever corsetry of the bodice. Her blue eyes looked anxiously at him, fringed with those delicate red lashes, and her hair gleamed softly in the light.

'It's beautiful,' he said neutrally, 'but there's something missing.'

'What? You think I should take a purse? A purse would be all wrong with this gown . . .'

'No. Not a purse.' He handed her a small jeweller's box with 'Asprey & Co' written on the top. 'I've been waiting for the right moment to actually give you this.'

Her heart hammering, Topaz opened the box, and was confronted with an exquisite engagement ring, a dark emerald set in diamonds. When she could drag her eyes away, she saw that Joe had sunk to one knee before her.

'I know you asked me,' he said, 'but I'm a traditionalist . . . Topaz Rossi, will you marry me?'

'Yes,' Topaz said, 'oh yes, oh, Joe, I love you.'

*

'You look good,' John said, when Rowena showed him in. He glanced round her apartment. 'Very New York.'

Rowena had chosen a long slip dress, a narrow silhouette in silver silk by Isaac Mizrahi. She had matched it with silver leather sandals from Jimmy Choo, a white Hermès scarf and a silver cross on a simple thong. Her hair was loose, hanging down her back in a curtain of pale gold. It was a look she preferred these days, slim and minimalist. A year ago she'd had her apartment redesigned to match – the Georgian furniture and English watercolours had given way to spare Japanese tables, a low couch and rice matting – all the hitech paraphernalia of a busy executive taking up the least space possible.

John noticed the fax machine and phone by the bed, the slimline stereo speakers on the walls.

'Never stop working, right?'

She took a slim clutch bag from the dresser and slipped her arm through his.

'What else is there?' she asked, and he thought for a second he heard a touch of regret.

Flashbulbs popped around them like out-of-control fire-crackers.

Rowena, conscious of the press, nodded at Topaz Rossi with an icy smile. John was already off, working the room like a pro, but Joe Goldstein was at his girl-friend's side. Rowena recognized his picture from the LA trades – the new VP programming over at NBC, right?

Well, yet again, I outranked you, she thought triumphantly.

She looked at Goldstein with frank curiosity. He was very attractive, not Topaz's type, she thought. Rossi was looking sensational; Rowena was childishly jealous of the stunning gown, the womanly figure and the breathtaking necklace. Next to Topaz, her stylish simplicity was just outgunned.

'Good evening, Rowena,' Topaz said pleasantly.

That accent's got thicker since she's been in New York, Rowena decided, not bothering to answer.

'Have you met my fiancé, Joe Goldstein?' Topaz continued. 'Joe left American Magazines to work in television. I guess you've heard that I'm the new director for New York.'

'Yes,' Rowena replied, her tone contemptuous.

Topaz felt her anger bubbling up like oil. Same old Rowena Gordon, for whom friendship was a matter of convenience, and low-rent girls stayed low-rent girls, however far up the greasy pole they climbed.

'You're not concerned,' she said.

Rowena looked at Topaz, standing in front of her with Joe's hand circling protectively round her waist, her engagement ring glinting on her hand, looking beautiful and triumphant. She was radiant with happiness, but at the same time, bristling with defiance. And the older, colder side of Rowena, the one she thought she had buried, the one that refused to face up to her first betrayal, the one that had been prepared to win at all costs, the one that still knew exactly how to hurt, surfaced, longing to wound.

'Why should I be concerned with *you*, Ms Rossi?' she replied, emphasizing the American prefix. 'You mean less than nothing to me. You're just a journalist, and your efforts to stop me so far have come to precisely nothing. It's just like the girl I remember at Oxford to get obsessed by some insignificant quarrel.'

She opened her clutch bag and took out a small spray of Chanel No. 5, casually scenting her wrists in an aristocratic gesture.

'Sticks and stones may break my bones, but words will never hurt me,' she said with a smile, and then turned away from them, walking across to John Metcalf and kissing him on the cheek.

Topaz stared after her for a long moment.

'What a bitch,' Goldstein said.

'Is Josh here?' Barbara Lincoln asked, sweeping up to them in a barebacked white organza dress which looked stunning against her black skin. She embraced Rowena on the cheeks and added, 'You look like you've seen a ghost.'

'I'm fine,' Rowena told her. 'He couldn't make it, he's getting a little old to be shuttling across the Atlantic.'

'Is it true that they're restructuring the board? Hi, John, baby, how are you?' she added, leaning forward and kissing him on the cheek. 'Still looking after my best friend?' She gave Rowena an approving wink over Metcalf's shoulder. Barbara was still the only girl she knew who sized men up as if they were livestock.

'I'm still getting looked after,' John answered. 'Rowena and I are trying to figure out how to make as much money as you.'

'That's a tough one,' Barbara said, her every movement sending little showers of light out from the diamonds that sparkled at her throat, wrists and ears. 'I have twenty per cent of the biggest band in the world and the second record is out in a month. I'm shopping for my own country right now. Something modest, like Malta or St Kitts . . . but the board, Rowena. You didn't answer my question.'

Her friend jumped, taking her gaze off the man who had just entered the ballroom and was standing talking to Rudolph Giuliani.

'What? Oh, yeah,' she confirmed. 'It's true. Oberman

could be outvoted now, not that the new members are likely to want to . . . it's some lawyer from France and an English management consultant.'

'Should we be worried?' Barbara asked, watching the new guest detach himself from the ex-mayor and wander towards them. She knew there had been objections to Rowena's promotion.

'Not since you signed Atomic Mass direct to Luther for the second album,' John pointed out. 'Rowena would have to be a mass murderer to get fired now.'

'Hello, Michael,' Barbara said, greeting her friend as he walked up to them.

Krebs kissed her on the cheek.

Rowena stiffened.

'Hey, honey, how's it going?' he asked pleasantly, adding, 'Hi, Rowena.'

'Oh, the usual,' Barbara smiled. 'Sold-out stadiums, promoters on their knees begging for multiple dates.'

Michael chuckled. 'Who's tour managing this time? Still Will Macleod?'

'The one and only,' Barbara agreed. 'Who else? Are we sitting together at dinner, Rowena?'

'No, she's next to Jake Williams,' John said, checking the seating plan.

Rowena was looking at Michael Krebs, feeling her heart thudding against her chest. It was the first time she'd seen him since before she left for LA. He was wearing a dark suit by Gieves and Hawkes; again, the ebony cloth picked out those awesome black eyes. The grey hair was a little thinner at his temples, but it made no difference to Rowena. Michael Krebs was like Sean Connery, she thought, one of those men who got more attractive as they got older.

Krebs had barely acknowledged her, and hadn't looked at her blond escort at all.

I hope he's not going to make a scene, she thought.

'You'll have to excuse him if he gets up to powder his nose,' Barbara said, grimly.

'Is there a problem?' Rowena asked, worried about her rhythm guitarist. She knew what *that* meant.

'Yeah, I'd say so,' the manager replied, giving Rowena a tiny glance that said, *Not here*.

'You're the producer, Michael, right?' Metcalf asked. 'You must be working very closely with Rowena on this.'

Krebs turned to face the younger man, his movement deliberate. 'That's right,' he said, neutrally. 'We've known each for a while. John Metcalf, isn't it? She told me about you.'

Rowena looked from one man to the other, her smile fixed on her face. Out of the corner of one eye she could see the gossip columnist, Marissa Matthews, hovering ominously.

'Anyway, it was nice to meet you,' Michael said politely. 'I should go and talk to the band. Barbara, Rowena,' and to her amazement he shook John's hand and walked away, without so much as a backward glance.

Rowena couldn't believe it. No anger, no hostility, nothing.

'My lords, ladies and gentlemen,' announced a footman loudly. 'Dinner is served.'

'You can't let her get away with that,' Joe muttered to Topaz as they sat down.

'Don't worry,' she said, settling into her mahogany chair in a rustle of satin and gold brocade. 'This thing will be finished tonight.'

'Tonight? How are you going to manage that?'

'Just something she said about how I hadn't changed,' she replied. 'It gave me an idea. Back to basics.'

'What? Tell me,' Joe asked, intrigued.

Topaz shook her head. 'That would spoil the surprise.' She smiled at him, and added, 'Lovely flowers, don't you think?'

Goldstein, mystified, glanced at the arrangements of orchids and tiger lilies placed on every table. 'What the hell have flowers got to do with it?' he asked.

'You'll find out,' she said.

This year's surprise wasn't in the form of gifts; tonight it was the food. Liz Martin's chefs had prepared dishes of such shameless opulence that every fresh course brought gasps of appreciation and amazement from the guests. The starter was a large mound of beluga caviar, served neat to each guest with a wedge of lemon in individual ice sculptures, six hundred fantastic mini-masterpieces, each different, little gleaming fragments of art destined for just a few minutes of display. Rowena's was a transparent ballerina, supporting the delicious black pearls over her head in an intricate basket. Joe Goldstein's was a crouching baseball player, cupping caviar in his catcher's mitt. It was followed by hen lobsters in a sorrel sauce, served with piles of real truffles; a warm salad of pheasant and grouse; impeccable grapefruit sorbet, to clear the palate; and finally a luscious dish of vanilla ice cream, served with a bitter chocolate sauce and tiny, perfect martins, the birds that were the corporate logo for Martin Oil, created out of glazed spun sugar.

Jake Williams, apparently, had lost his appetite.

'Try it,' Rowena prompted him, spearing some pheasant salad and proffering it to her rhythm guitarist.

He shook his head. 'Not hungry.'

Rowena was concerned. In the space of a couple of months, Jake had lost over a stone. He was frowning and tense, he'd snapped at her all evening, and he'd turned up to the most exclusive party of the year in one of Atomic's own T-shirts. Totally out of character.

'I suppose you're gonna tell me that I shouldn't do drugs,' he added nastily, rounding on her.

She shrugged, sending ripples of silver silk across her dress. 'Do drugs if you want to, man. I mean, I've had a few tabs of E in my time. It's a perk of the job, everybody does it. The trick is not to let drugs do you.'

Michael found Rowena at the end of the party, while John was deep in conversation with George Stephanopolous.

'If you come over next week I'll play you the roughs of the new record,' he said. '*Zenith* they're calling it.'

'*Zenith*. OK, I will,' she replied, waiting for him to say something else, to tell her he couldn't leave his wife, to tell her John Metcalf was a *putz*, to order her back to his bed. She would turn him down flat.

'Great,' Michael said, his dark eyes expressionless. 'I'll see you then. You have a good night,' and he walked off to the cloakroom.

She watched him go, cursing herself for being so hurt.

'Are we done?' asked John, coming up behind her and scooping her into his arms. Rowena pressed back against his chest, grateful for his familiar warmth, for the comfort, for the fact that someone she cared about would make love to her tonight.

I wonder if Debbie Krebs sees it like that.

Topaz Rossi and Joe Goldstein were among the last to leave. Joe couldn't remember when he'd had so much fun outside of a huge Mets victory; he'd spent a golden night being congratulated by New York's best and brightest on the NBC job, and then recongratulated as word of his engagement spread through the room. Topaz had her fair share of corporate homage, too, and the dress was a genuine sensation; in a party crammed full of designer labels, she'd been photographed for *Vanity Fair*, *GQ*, *Vogue* and *Women's Wear Daily*, and Liz Smith had asked her for details of her couturier. Goldstein had fairly burst with pride.

'You'll make a pretty good trophy wife,' he said.

'You'll make an adequate trophy husband,' she shot back, and they'd stared into each other's eyes for a second, wanting to kiss, not able to in such a crowd, luxuriating in the sexual tension.

'Later,' Joe whispered in her ear.

She had been fairly sizzling all night, her smile effortlessly charming, her laughter genuine and relaxed, enjoying every introduction, savouring the food, joking with all their friends.

'What got into you?' Goldstein demanded as they came to leave, taking his fiancée in his arms and kissing her lightly on the bridge of the nose.

'You did. About four hours ago,' Topaz teased.

'Nothing else?'

'Well, maybe there was *one* other consideration,' she admitted, beckoning to him to follow her over to a table in the centre of the room.

'That's where Rowena Gordon was sitting,' Joe exclaimed. 'Topaz, what the hell have you done?'

Grinning at him, Topaz reached down into her cleavage, fiddled about a little, and pulled out a small tape recorder.

'Remember that David Levine interview?'

'Of course,' he answered.

'Well, this hasn't been clasped to my bosom all night, but –'

'The *flowers*! You're telling me you hid a tape recorder in the vase?'

'That's what I'm telling you,' said Topaz, and she smiled.

Chapter Twenty-Six

Will Macleod, Atomic Mass's tour manager, strode around backstage, looking ferocious as usual, and people didn't mess with him. He was constantly in motion, searching for something that might go wrong before it happened, checking the band were OK, sorting out a billion problems a night ranging from water in the PA to trucking permits to landing schedules for the private jet, and always, incessantly, checking and rechecking the guest list. His all-access tour personnel laminate bounced against his chest as he ran, but guards across Europe, America and the Far East rarely demanded to see it. Basically, you took one look at Will and you did not get in his way. Not if you valued your mobility.

It's something of a rule, especially in hard rock, that the crew's tough exterior conceals warm-hearted family men who are constantly dreaming of their wives and baby daughters back home in Alabama. In Will Macleod's case, the tough exterior concealed a tough interior. He was single, Glaswegian, and hard as all hell. He cared about running a good show, he cared about getting paid, getting laid and getting drunk. He also cared about his mates. Macleod had no family and didn't want one, he was completely addicted to life on the road, but when he did make a friend, he stayed loyal to them for life.

Over the course of three world tours, Atomic Mass, and to an extent their wives and girlfriends, had become his friends. And so had their manager, Barbara Lincoln.

Macleod was slightly surprised to find himself in this position. Barbara was about as likely to wind up a friend of his as a gay rights activist. She was, to say the least, not his style. For a start, she was a woman, which under most circumstances would have knocked her right out of the running. Second, she was a woman who was also his boss. That stretched the bounds of credibility, as far as Will was concerned. Third, she was about a million miles away from being 'one of the boys'. On the (very) rare occasions when he had the misfortune to encounter a woman on the road – no, scrap that, to encounter a woman *working* on the road – a catering girl, a wardrobe assistant, the rarer-than-hens'-teeth instance of a female truck driver or rigger or something – at the very least, he expected the lass to bend over backwards to fit in with the lads, to laugh the loudest at all the dirty jokes, turn a blind eye if one of the roadies wanted to 'entertain' a groupie behind the generator trucks, swear like a squaddie and generally do her best to blend into the wallpaper.

Barbara, inexplicably, had refused to do any such thing.

She showed up on the road dressed in Chanel or Armani, full make-up and often wearing jewellery. She didn't joke around with the crew, and if the boys were reading porn magazines when Ms Lincoln showed up, they had to stuff them under sofa cushions. Not that she wasted much time socializing. Normally, she'd go and see that the band were happy, then find the promoter and the local record company rep, introduce herself and get straight down to business. She would be in total command of the production office from five minutes after she hit a venue. Watching her, Macleod was surprised that the phone wasn't surgically attached to her ear.

He asked the band about it once.

'What you gotta understand about Barbara,' Joe told him, 'is that she's clever. I mean she is *really* smart. And she can make sure that we're not getting screwed financially, with the promoters and the agents and stuff, and on the record side – she used to work for the company. So she understands exactly what's going on, and she also knows them all. We got a perfect relationship with them, y'know? She takes care of everything, and she lets you take care of the road.'

Will took a lot of convincing. He finally became a fan on the one hundred and third show of the *Heat Street* tour, in Rio. He'd come into the production office to find Barbara, dressed in delicate black silk, arguing with the promoter.

'Not very practical,' Will said, looking disapprovingly at her outfit. It was in the nineties out there, it was total chaos setting up the stage and supervising the dodgy electrical systems, and most of Macleod's boys had sweat pouring down their backs. Barbara, barely pausing in her yelling at Vasquelez, the promoter, turned round to Will, screamed, 'You can keep your fucking mouth shut, I wear what I fucking like,' and went back on the attack. Somewhat taken aback, Macleod started to listen to what she was saying.

'I can no afford it,' the guy was whining. 'It is inflation.'

'It is theft,' Barbara snarled, 'and you will refund what you overcharged, my friend, or we are not going on.'

'You cannot do that, you have contract –'

'Yeah, so do you. And the contract says ten bucks a head. Not seventeen.'

'You, also, you get more money,' wheedled Vasquelez, spreading his hands in a gesture of powerlessness. 'I have more, band has more, everybody is happy, I am an honest man, I will pay you also –'

'Our *fans* are not happy, you little fuck,' screamed Barbara. 'I don't give a damn about more money for the band! We came out here to play for everybody, not for the fucking rich kids with swimming pools! You go out there and you announce that anyone with a seventeen-dollar ticket can show the stub at the back gate for a cash refund, right now, and every new ticket sells for the equivalent of ten dollars or we are not going on. And don't try anything on, because I checked the exchange rate before I left the hotel this morning.'

'Is impossible,' shrugged the guy. 'I cannot do this.'

Barbara turned round to Macleod. 'Will,' she said, 'how long will it take the boys to get everything packed away?'

'Two hours, tops,' he said, smiling broadly.

'Great,' she said. 'Have them make a start, will you?'

'No problem, boss,' Macleod said, nodding.

The promoter stared at him wildly. 'No! You cannot do this thing! There is hundred thousand people waiting! There will be a riot!'

Macleod looked at the manager, questioningly.

'Will,' she said, 'you saw the ticket price agreement, right?'

'Yeah,' he said.

'Tell me something,' Barbara said. 'It seems to have slipped my mind. We'd agreed a special ticket price for the poorer territories, right?'

'That's right,' Macleod said, glaring down at the promoter.

'Uh-huh. I thought so. Could you remind me what it was?'

'Ten dollars in local money,' growled Macleod, enjoying himself.

'*Ten* dollars. Not seventeen.'

'Definitely not seventeen.'

'Absolutely, definitely not seventeen.'

'Ten dollars.'

'Well, you know what?' Barbara said. 'Amazingly, some kids in Brazil are being charged seventeen dollars to see Atomic Mass.'

'By ticket touts?'

'By the promoter. What do you think we should do about that, Will?'

Vasquelez glanced nervously at Macleod. The Scotsman towered over him.

'I think we should go on home,' said Will, airily. 'And make sure to let other bands know about the promoter.'

'Pack up our gear, Will.'

'No! No!' pleaded the little man. 'They will riot! They will kill me!'

'Really?' asked Barbara, not sounding remotely interested.

Vasquelez gave a wail of despair. 'OK, OK. I give the seven dollars back . . .'

Barbara shoved her face into his. 'You do that,' she hissed. 'Exactly the way I said. You give that money back now, not tomorrow, not next week, right now. And I'll tell you what else. My tour manager here is going to supervise it, in case you have any more last-minute problems with your arithmetic. If you make any mistakes,' she said, with icy calm, 'he's gonna rip your balls off and shove them down your throat. Do I make myself clear?'

Vasquelez gulped. 'Yes, señora,' he said.

Macleod was beside himself. 'She's fantastic,' he said to Mark Thomas, when they were packing away the kit that night.

'Oh, she's the business,' the drummer agreed. 'Best female manager since Sharon Osbourne.'

Will Macleod became a good friend to his boss and a trusted ally. They didn't have deep conversations all that often, mainly because he knew nothing about designer clothes, million-dollar deals or two-timing lovers, and she knew nothing about football. On the other hand, when they did talk, they usually agreed about the important stuff – the band, the show, the venue and the travel arrangements. Barbara Lincoln left him to get on with his job. Right up until this summer, it had been a solid partnership.

This summer, Jake Williams started taking cocaine.

At first, Will didn't comment. If Jake had been on the crew Will would have bawled him out the first time and sacked him the second time. But he wasn't on the crew, he was the rhythm guitarist.

'Is Jake out of control?' Barbara asked Macleod.

Will hesitated. He knew that as the album was exploding worldwide, Barbara was less and less able to get out on the road. Will had become her eyes and ears. She trusted him. She believed him.

He thought about every beer he'd ever had with Jake Williams, every football game they'd played, and the fundamental, basic code of the road. Which includes the commandment, *Thou shalt not get thy mates fired*.

'No, he's fine,' Macleod answered, and started avoiding her calls.

Of course, he faxed in gate reports regularly and called the office, picking times when she'd be busiest and one of her associates would deal with him. It was a betrayal of trust.

But what the fuck can I do? Macleod thought.

And the band weren't stupid, either. They recognized the signs, and Macleod knew they didn't like it. At first, it looked under control: Jake never indulged in front of Atomic, he rarely indulged at a show, and he didn't talk about it at all. You could almost ignore it. Almost, but not quite.

The *Heat Street* tour wound on and on, moving from the big arenas to headlining the Monsters of Rock that summer, to filling stadiums to capacity. As the album sold and sold around the world, Barbara's office multiplied dates, booking four nights in cities that had originally asked for one, and added further legs to the tour as new territories got in on the game; now they were heading for New Zealand and Australia, then he had to make room for Japan, Hong Kong, Taiwan and Thailand, and finally the hot areas newly added to the international touring map – Jakarta, Indonesia and Singapore, as well as the Indian subcontinent.

One year turned into eighteen months, eighteen months became two years, and still there was no sign of stopping. The crew were now working in shifts, staggering the three-week vacation periods, except Will who couldn't and didn't want to go home. The adrenaline rush kept him hooked. He was chief of the Mongol hordes, in complete control of this vast juggernaut crisscrossing the world.

Apart from the band and a handful of others, the tour manager rules over *everybody* on a tour. His authority is absolute. His word is law.

And Will Macleod was good at his job. He was a fair guy to work for, and the crew rspected him. He made sure that everyone got paid in full and on time, but if he caught somebody slacking or committing an unforgivable breach of etiquette, he docked their wages or sacked them. (Selling your allocation of tickets was unforgivable; getting a groupie to give you head in exchange for some fifth-rate, no-access pass was not. Feminism had pretty much passed Will by.) Macleod ran a smooth ship, and he got off on the adventure and the atmosphere and the camaraderie of the band and crew.

He also got off on the money. Atomic Mass were generous, and as the stadiums sold out and the CDs flew off the shelves, there was suddenly a lot of serious cash flying around. Merchandizing broke sales records across America, and Brockum, their T-shirt manufacturers, could hardly keep up with the demand. Will noticed it everywhere, in bars, in airports, in newsagents. Wherever he went there was somebody wearing an Atomic shirt. The gold molecule on the blue background was becoming as popular as Metallica's grinning skulls or the Guns n' Roses logo.

Everybody was getting rich. Even on the road, away from the obvious symbols like houses and cars, you could see that. One tour accountant turned into three. The singer's wife was dripping in diamonds. Alex, the bassist, started wearing a gold Rolex. Zach, the lead guitarist, routinely ordered bottles of champagne for the whole crew when one leg was finished, and that ran into hundreds of people. The band stopped leasing a private jet and bought one of their own.

And Jake Williams took more cocaine.

Will knew now he'd made a mistake. He shouldn't have deferred to him, he shouldn't have been too embarrassed to interfere. The lad was getting sick. He wasn't careful any more, he kept coming out of the loos with an ugly white smudge on his pallid skin. If Macleod pointed it out, he'd curse at him and wipe it away. He was getting painfully thin; he'd always been slender but nowadays he just looked anorexic. His clothes hung off him. He would become mean, nasty and petty when he was high, traits which Will knew weren't part of his personality. And furthermore, he had no reason to stop.

Jake Williams had no boss and he was making hundreds of thousands of dollars a month. He could run a full-on addiction to every drug known to man and service his habit to his heart's content without even noticing the cost.

For another two months, he still played OK.

Then he started to miss rehearsals.

Then he started to fuck up onstage.

Yesterday, for the first time since Macleod began working with him, Jake missed a flight. Will sent the band on ahead and booked two first-class seats on the next plane to Rome. Then he tore back to the hotel and only managed to get into Jake's room by a succession of lavish bribes and heavyhanded threats. He found his guitarist passed out on the bed, his gaunt body half dressed, a syringe jutting out of his arm. Macleod pulled it out as gingerly as he could.

Smack. Jesus, it was heroin now . . .

The local doctor, called and even more lavishly bribed to keep his mouth shut, roused him and gave him an emetic to make him throw up.

'You can thank whichever god it is you worship that he's alive,' he told Will, who'd seen this story before and had never known a happy ending.

At least it wasn't an overdose. Macleod dressed Jake himself and dragged him half-conscious to the plane, got him strapped in and told the stewardess he was sick.

He had to *do* something. Fast.

His heart in his mouth, Macleod called Barbara Lincoln at home.

*

'Can I speak to Joshua Oberman, please?' Topaz Rossi said, politely. In front of her, the huge glass windows of the sixtieth floor revealed the island of Manhattan, spread out below her. If she turned to her right, she could see Musica Towers, the tall building by Central Park glinting in the light of the sun.

It looks so tranquil.

Not for long.

'Yeah?'

Topaz smiled at the gruff voice, intrigued to hear what Rowena's boss sounded like. Old, crabby, intelligent.

'Mr Oberman, this is Topaz Rossi at American Magazines.'

'I know exactly who you are,' Oberman said coldly. 'And I presume you have a good reason for making this call.'

She smiled. 'Yes, sir, I think I do. We've had a reporter out on the first leg of Atomic Mass's *Zenith* tour for a month, and we plan to run a big story in next week's *Westside* magazine on Jake Williams' addiction to heroin and cocaine.'

There was a pause.

'No comment.'

'I understand that, Mr Oberman. I'm just calling for the record as to Musica Entertainment's official policy on the use of illegal narcotic drugs.'

'Policy? We don't permit it or condone it. Obviously,' Oberman snapped.

'So if an employee of your company was encouraging a musician to take illegal narcotics, that would be grounds for instant dismissal?'

'Yes, but none of my employees would ever do any such thing,' Oberman barked. 'Is that all, Ms Rossi? I'm a busy man.'

'Thank you, Mr Oberman; you've been most helpful,' said Topaz sweetly.

She hung up, grinning.

Barbara walked the last hundred yards or so along the Paseo Virgin del Puerto, where the cab had been forced to drop her because of police barriers, towards the Vicente Calderon Stadium, looming huge in the deepening twilight, floodlit from all sides. Music was blasting into the street from the PA, the earth-shaking rap/rock of House of Pain at the moment. Fans were out in their thousands, clogging the streets, crowding the various entrances to different sides of the stadium, sitting on the concrete with beer and hotdogs and joints, swarming round the bootleg merchandizing stalls, yelling in Spanish and various other languages. She had her laminate, hanging round her neck on an inconspicuous black cord, tucked safely inside her shirt. In fact, she'd tugged the little plastic square down between her breasts and was using her bra to clip the cord against her chest, so it wouldn't flap. If one of these kids saw she was wearing a laminate, they might very well rip it off her and that would be it. She'd never get backstage without a pass. She spoke no Spanish and security at an Atomic Mass gig these days would be adequate for the average head of state.

Barbara threaded her way through the fans around the side of the stadium; backstage had to be over there because she could see all the generator trucks parked in a monolithic cluster, thick powercords and rubber-insulated pipes running from them into the back entrance of the arena. She loosened her laminate as she got further away from the crowd, pulling it out of her shirt when she got to the first row of security guards.

They glanced at it and hundreds of pounds of

forbidding muscle just melted away. Fans crowding round the security cordon gazed at her in awe and shouted pleadingly at her in Spanish. Barbara strode into the tunnel leading to the backstage area, looking for someone she recognized, perhaps a sign to the dressing rooms or production office. Crew members scurried about with guitar stands and extra drumsticks, making little finishing touches to the Atomic stage set and taking support band gear away. She wondered how the Knuckleheads, a newish act on as support, had gone over with the crowd. She'd have liked to see them, too, but had decided it was best to keep away from the venue until showtime; any earlier and somebody would have noticed her and told Macleod, or told Jake, and she didn't want to give them time to hide him. Nobody knew she was here. She wanted it to stay that way.

She rounded a corner and emerged into catering. Long trestle tables were set at the back of the amphitheatre, with a buffet of hot and cold food, huge steaming urns of tea and coffee, and an icebox with Cokes and beer and mineral water. Roadies were serving themselves and bantering with the catering girls as Barbara walked in.

She strode up to the main table and addressed the biggest guy she could see. 'Will Macleod in here?'

'Not in catering, sweetheart,' he replied, not recognizing her. 'You can try the production office, about a hundred yards ahead and to your left, right under the stairs. If he ain't there, the dressing rooms are on the first landing just up those same stairs. You can find that OK?'

'Sure,' Barbara said. Score one, she thought. 'I guess . . . Jake Williams isn't around, is he?'

'Don't waste your time,' the big guy grunted, not unkindly. 'He's here. But he's not available for business. He's seen his connection already this evening, you know what I mean? Will Macleod takes care of his shit.'

'Do you guys mind?' Barbara asked, controlling her voice.

General shrugs. 'Will keeps him out of our faces mostly,' the big guy said. 'Yeah, he can be a grade-A bitch, but that's the drugs talking.'

'Well, that ain't *my* fucking problem,' said his neighbour.

'He used to be a real sweet guy,' the big man said angrily. 'And he's dying, so make some fucking allowances, would you?'

'Thanks, I appreciate it,' said Barbara, walking away.

The sky was darkening out front, she could see it behind the stage scaffolding. She'd never been to this venue before, but most backs of stadiums are the same: expanses of concrete, the constant smell of petrol, people rushing about, groups of roadies manhandling huge flight cases so heavy they need wheels.

A roadcrew in operation is an impressive sight, like a colony of strong worker ants with beer-guts. They can raise a vast stage set in an afternoon and tear it down in two hours. You don't get in their way when they're moving gear. Barbara scattered out of the path of several guys and thus got slightly lost, but eventually found the production office without too much hassle. To her left, the way out to front of house was being illuminated by coloured spotlights, racing round the stadium. They'd stopped piping music to the PA.

Her watch showed thirty minutes to showtime.

Barbara took a deep breath. Then she flung the door open.

Macleod was bent over a prostrate figure, sprawled on the couch. Barbara had to look twice to see that it was Jake. He was wearing his normal T-shirt and jeans, but they hung off him obscenely, in loose, flapping folds, his ribs poking through his skin. His emaciated chest heaved spasmodically as though it was an effort for him to breathe.

One skeletal hand was clasped round a small vial which Macleod was trying to prise loose; she could see grains of white powder dusting his hands.

Barbara's hand flew to her mouth in horror.

'Jake's sick,' Macleod growled without turning round. 'Whoever you are, get lost.'

Barbara, shocked rigid, burst into tears.

Chapter Twenty-Seven

For the first time since she'd started working, Rowena Gordon was an unmitigated success.

It hadn't been easy. Finding her first band had been tough, getting Michael Krebs involved had been tough, signing an American act had been tough, doing the Picture This deal had been tough.

But finally she'd come through. She was the first woman to run the North American division of a major label, many of her discoveries had reached stardom, and one had reached the true superstardom that founds empires, something that happens to one band in a million. She had power, money and a good-looking boyfriend even more successful than herself.

But like thousands of men before her, Rowena was finding that achievement brought its own set of problems.

'I'm so tired, I can't think straight,' she complained to John.

'You should move down to LA,' he suggested. 'It's just as good as New York for the record business and at least you could cut out the shuttle flights every other weekend.'

'I can't do that. All the good bands are up here.'

'You're not a talent scout any more, babe. Since when did you last have time to go to a club?'

'That's true,' she admitted, feeling old. Luther Records had a bunch of teenagers finding bands for it now.

'Think of the sunshine. Think of the jacuzzis,' John tempted her. 'You know what we'd be doing if you were here this evening? We'd be out at my house in the hills, naked, in a warm hot tub in the open air, looking at the stars and sipping champagne.'

Rowena tried to imagine it. Her first three months as division head had been more physically and emotionally taxing than she could possibly have imagined. Running Luther as a one-man outpost, and even heading up a small team that shovelled product into somebody else's pipeline, was a whole different ballgame to this.

She was supervising the birth of a seventh major American label. That meant having to make decisions every minute of every day, about things she'd never have dreamt of dealing with before. At Luther her only concern had been music. At Musica North America, her job involved marketing, promotion, budgeting, tax structures and distribution.

Rowena found herself picking between haulage systems, flying to Detroit and Minnesota to meet with truck companies. She had to set whole days aside to talk to investment bankers and accountants. She had to become competent to judge advertising agencies and indie promotion. Her days seemed to melt one into the other, in a sense of urgency and unremitting rush. If John hadn't insisted they spend time together at weekends, she wouldn't have had any free time at all.

And now, Atomic Mass's second album, *Zenith*, was nearly finished.

'Feeling warmed up, kid?' Josh Oberman cackled, in

town on a flying visit. 'Because the fun's just about to start.'

Initially he'd wondered whether to mention Topaz Rossi's call to Rowena, but decided against it. No point in bothering her with that venomous little journo now, when they were under such pressure. She was only trying to stir things up, and Joshua Oberman never went for hype.

Rowena groaned. 'Don't you think Frank Willis should handle it? He's in charge of Marketing.'

Oberman shook his head. 'No way. After what you did with that Coliseum gig? Nobody handles this record but you.'

'Christ,' she muttered, pushing a hand through her hair.

'You haven't been talking to Michael Krebs much these days,' her chairman added shrewdly. 'That has to stop. I've heard the final mixes, and they're terrific – they make *Heat Street* sound like it was recorded in Joe's bedroom in a couple of weeks. I want Michael involved in strategy for radio promotion and tour support.'

'But that's not a producer's job.'

'Krebs isn't just a producer.'

She didn't want to do this.

She didn't want to see him.

It was unavoidable.

What could she say? 'Boss, I'm uncomfortable with Michael because I used to sleep with him'? 'I think Krebs would prefer working with someone who hasn't dumped him'? 'I never want to see him again'?

But she *did* want to see him.

And that was the problem.

America the beautiful. America the free, Rowena thought as she dressed for her meeting. America, where the national pastime is reinventing yourself and taking control of your own life.

Hadn't she done that? Hadn't she walked away from one way of life and carved herself a place in another? She had all the accoutrements of the modern American woman. An apartment of her own, with furniture pared down to the bare essentials. A regular gym class, where she worked out in Lycra and Nike. A smart wardrobe of classic basics. A refrigerator stocked with lots of mineral water, fruit and vegetables. Everything designed for the Manhattan way of life; maximum style, maximum efficiency.

Yet Rowena failed the test in one respect. In the most important respect. Her love life had been screwed up from the word go. Until she was twenty-two, she'd had a few boyfriends, a handful of lovers, nice unthreatening boys whose names she could hardly even recall now. The boyfriends had often complained that she was driven, she never made time for herself, she'd never love anyone. Rowena had laughed and kissed them, but her heart was an impregnable fortress. Not one of them could get through.

But when I fell, I fell hard.

Michael Krebs. Everything a first love should not be. Twice her age. A different religion. A different background. A different country. The father of three sons. The husband of his high-school sweetheart.

And the other strikes against him? He was a close colleague. He was in a position of power over her. He was insensitive. He was domineering. But they had been good friends. He had been her mentor. All of which, of course, had evaporated into thin air when Rowena met somebody else, because the only way to eliminate Michael Krebs was to cut him off, cut him out.

Rowena wondered what the hell to wear. Something

plain, but flattering, she decided; if she dressed deliberately frumpy, Krebs would think she was sending him a signal. She had to look like this was no big deal. He was married, she had a terrific partner, and they worked together.

What was in the past will stay there.

She picked a loose Armani sweater dress in buttery cashmere and teamed it with sandals and a thick wooden bangle, brushing her hair to one side and choosing a bare foundation with a muted berry lipstick; a natural, stylish look, nothing too provocative. She finished it off with a spritz of scent: 360°, by Perry Ellis, a clean, fresh fragrance.

Yeah. That's perfect, Rowena told herself, heading out of the door.

She looked put-together and in control.

She could handle this.

'Hey, it's good to see you again,' beamed Amy Tritten, the Mirror, Mirror receptionist, with complete insincerity when Rowena's white Lotus Esprit pulled into the parking lot. She was walking across to the main studio with a sheaf of papers, immaculate in a navy Adrienne Vittadini suit. None of the women who worked with Krebs had ever been glad to see Rowena Gordon.

'Did you want Ms Lincoln? Because she called to say she needed to see Michael right away, but she can't get here for a couple of hours.'

'No,' Rowena answered, wondering why Barbara needed to see Krebs so urgently. 'I have an appointment with Michael to discuss the new record.'

Amy smiled slightly. 'He's in the office. I'll take you.'

Rowena followed the younger woman through the studio complex, trying to calm her nerves, smiling brightly at all the engineers and technicians who waved hello. This was going to be OK. Actually, it was a good thing that they have this discussion. She could use some help with the *Zenith* launch right now, and Michael was an expert on radio. He seemed to be able to tell what programmers would go for merely by *looking* at a CD.

She was shown into the office. Krebs was drinking a cup of coffee, talking animatedly to a pretty woman in her late thirties, her sleek brown hair cut in a neat bob. As Rowena walked in, she gave her a friendly smile.

'Rowena, I'm glad you could make it,' Michael said. 'Have you met my wife?'

How she got through that day, Rowena could never figure out.

Deborah Krebs was just the start. Not a bimbo, not a frump, not a bitch; an attractive, intelligent, pleasant woman, who took an interest in Rowena's career, and who obviously loved her husband. She had one hand in his throughout their conversation; less a signal of ownership than the relaxed, natural posture of a woman completely at ease with her partner.

Rowena had felt a fist of jealousy clutch at her stomach with almost physical force. She felt her legs tremble. For a second, she couldn't breathe.

'Debbie, right? It's nice to meet you,' she said.

And at that moment she blessed every unhappy moment she'd spent at an English boarding school. The old reflexes snapped into focus: *composure, composure, composure*. She told his wife how much she'd heard about her. She asked meaningless questions about the health of her boys. She rhapsodized about John Metcalf.

And she avoided Michael's eyes.

When they moved on to *Zenith*, Rowena took notes, knowing that Oberman would ask her about the meeting and she wasn't registering a single word

Michael said. She didn't hurry, she didn't rush, and when she got up to leave she shook both their hands and told them that they must all have dinner when John was next in New York. All the way across the complex to her car, she had a happy, contented expression on her face, like someone who's just finished a production meeting with an old friend. And when she finally, blessedly, pulled out of the parking lot, she still didn't cry. The pain was far too deep for that.

But there was worse to come.

She knew something was wrong the moment she walked through the doors.

At 11 a.m. on a Wednesday morning, Musica Towers should be buzzing – job candidates waiting anxiously in the foyer, bikers dropping off DATs and artwork, visitors being shown up to offices and her motley crew of staffers running everywhere. But today there was nothing. The lobby was completely empty, the black polished marble of the walls and floor ominously silent. Not even the duty receptionist was at the front desk.

Has there been a fire or something? What the hell's going on? Rowena thought.

At that moment, a security guard in the Musica Entertainment uniform, accompanied by a short man in a dark suit, marched into the lobby from the ground-floor corridors. She didn't recognize either one of them.

'Ms Gordon?' asked the man.

'Yes,' she replied, suddenly scared.

'My name is Johnson. I'm with Harman, Kennedy and Co.'

Her heart contracted. What in God's name did that mean? Harman, Kennedy & Co represented the parent company's legal affairs.

'I am here to inform you that your employment with

Musica Entertainment has been terminated with immediate effect.' He walked forward and handed her a small sealed envelope. 'Furthermore, this letter notifies you of a breach-of-contract suit being brought against you by the company. The guard and I are to supervise your removal of any personal effects you may wish to take from your office.'

'What?' Rowena gasped.

'I am furthermore required to inform you that you are to cease and desist from claiming to represent the company in any way whatsoever. Your security classification and system password have been revoked. Any papers pertaining to company business which may be at your home or elsewhere in your possession must be returned to Musica Entertainment forthwith, or the company will take legal action to recover them.'

'I want to speak to Joshua Oberman,' Rowena said.

She was standing paralysed. This could not be happening, it just *couldn't*. What the hell was the reason for it? She'd spoken to Josh two days ago and he'd been fine. God in heaven, her boss was one of her closest friends!

'I am acting under direct instructions from Mr Oberman,' the lawyer replied. 'If you care to open that letter, Ms Gordon, you can check his signature yourself.'

With trembling fingers, Rowena ripped it open. She couldn't take in the official-looking type, but Oberman's spidery hand was unmistakable at the bottom of the page.

'I see,' she managed. Then she lifted her head. 'I do have some things I want to remove from my office,' she told them in a clear voice. 'If you could take me up there, please.'

Thank God for the executive elevator, she told herself as they stepped out on to the twenty-fourth floor. She knew instinctively that she had to behave with dignity right now; whatever the fuck had happened, she, Rowena Gordon, was not about to run sobbing from her own company like a postroom boy caught stealing stamps. Nevertheless, only shock was keeping her upright. The humiliation of being frogmarched upstairs in front of the rest of the staff would have overwhelmed her.

As it was, when she reached her own office and saw her secretary, Tamara, standing weeping outside, she barely retained control.

'It's OK, Tammy. Nobody died,' Rowena told her.

She wanted to ask the girl if she knew what was happening, but there was no way she'd do it in front of these men. While they watched, Rowena took a plastic crate and packed up all her personal stuff: the printed note that came with Michael's flowers the day she'd arrived in New York; her personal platinum records, presented to her by Musica for Roxana, Bitter Spice, Steamer and Atomic Mass; a photo of herself and Joe Hunter at the launch of *Heat Street*, a cartoon Barbara had clipped for her. Nothing much.

Christ Almighty.

She felt Tammy thrust something into her hand. A sheet of newsprint. Without looking at it, Rowena folded it up and put it inside her desk diary.

'You have my home number, honey, right?' she asked her loudly.

Weeping, Tammy nodded. Rowena put a hand on her shoulder. 'It'll work out,' she said gently, and turned to the two men.

'Right, gentlemen,' she said. 'I'm ready if you are.'

The sense of unreality stayed with Rowena all the way home as she threaded her way through the midday traffic on Broadway up to West 67th Street. The doorman touched his cap to her as she entered her apartment building and handed her a small parcel, neatly wrapped in brown paper. When she unlocked her door and shut it behind her, she was still half dazed from shock.

Automatically she put down the orange plastic crate, thinking how strange it was to be in her apartment in the middle of a weekday. She reached for her diary and took out the piece of paper Tammy had slipped her. It was the cover of the new issue of *Westside*. Rowena unfolded it, and started to read.

As she did so, she felt herself swaying. The whole room seemed to go dark.

DETONATION: HOW ATOMIC MASS BLEW UP JAKE WILLIAMS, read the headline. Underneath was a picture of the guitarist, obviously taken illicitly, slumped on the side of a flight-case, his eyes wild, his body skeletally thin. Next to that, she saw with dawning horror, was a picture of herself, looking poised and relaxed in the silver dress she'd worn to the Martins' party. There were several pull-out quotes in the middle of the text, but the one that screamed up at her said, *Do drugs if you want to . . . it's a perk of the job*.

Unsteadily, Rowena took the small parcel the doorman had given her and opened it.

Inside was a small silver cup, a replica of a sports trophy, and a note.

It read: 'Game, set, match and championship.'

PART THREE
WAR

In the Wall Street offices of Maughan Macaskill, the prestigious investment bankers, Gerald Quin stared at his Quotron screen. It was flashing up a takeover: Mansion Industries had bought out Pitt Group, a small magazine company based in Minneapolis. The deal was a tiny one, scarcely worthy of the market's notice. But it interested Gerry.

Everything Mansion did interested Gerry.

Quin was twenty-six, happily married, a *cum laude* graduate of Wharton Business School and a skilled analyst. He was a rising star at Maughan Macaskill, and his specialization was tracking the movements of big conglomerates, predicting what they might do next. Months of harrowing research hell in the company library, grunt work on structuring deals and an instinctive feel for what makes a great entrepreneur tick had paid off, and Gerald was very, very good at his job.

He watched Lords Hanson and White. He watched Sir James Goldsmith. He watched Barry Diller. He watched Rupert Murdoch. And he watched Connor Miles of Mansion House.

Gerald took a sip of coffee from the plastic beaker on his desk. The takeover had been hostile, but Pitt hadn't put up much of a fight. Who could blame them? David and Goliath wasn't in it. Pitt Group was an old family company, running two local papers and a sports magazine. Three years ago they'd gone public, and recently a stock flotation meant that the family had – just – lost control. And Mansion's all-encompassing, predatory eye saw that as an open invitation.

Mansion Industries. A monolith so vast it crisscrossed the entire globe, and yet most people had never heard of it. Of course they knew about the individual companies it owned: Pemberton Diamonds in South Africa; Freyja Timber in Sweden; Natural Foods in France. Connor Miles was a bottom-fisher, like Larry Tisch, which was to say he bought undervalued companies cheap, then broke them down and sold them off or merged them into each other for economies of scale. Tradition, staff policy, product quality – all these meant nothing to Miles. Money was the only bottom line. On every company he took over he imposed his own supervisors, and in ninety per cent of cases fired the incumbent management. Who cared if they'd been there for generations? If they couldn't give Mansion the profits they demanded, they were *out*. End of story.

In the business community, Connor Miles was feared.

In the banking community, he was admired. And Gerald Quin was his number one fan. To watch Connor Miles at work, he thought, was to watch the shift in world profit centres: after the war, Mansion had been heavily into construction; in the sixties, pharmaceuticals; in the seventies, computing; in the eighties, any upmarket quality product – God, the eighties was a great decade, you made money just breathing – and in the nineties, entertainment and leisure.

He knew their big shopping spree wouldn't start for a few months. But Pitt Group was one of the first symptoms, although it was too small for most analysts to notice.

But Maughan Macaskill noticed, Quin thought, and he smiled.

Chapter Twenty-Eight

As far as Topaz was concerned, it was over. She put Rowena Gordon out of her mind. There were a million other things to think about.

'Temple wedding,' Joe said. 'We're getting married under a wedding canopy and that's it.'

'But you haven't been to a synagogue for years. You're not religious,' Topaz retorted, outraged. 'We're getting married in St Patrick's Cathedral.'

'No way.'

'*Yes* way.'

They settled on a justice of the peace, with a rabbi and a priest blessing them afterwards.

'Have you got any plans for restructuring the division?' Matt Gowers asked his new director.

'How long have you got?' she replied, crossing a terrific pair of ankles in Ann Klein heels.

Gowers mentally cursed the fashion for long skirts, but part of him was relieved to see Rossi bang up-to-date as usual. Her flair for fashion had pushed American's women's titles to the front of the newsracks; refusing to use editorial space on see-through bras, designer grunge or thigh-high minis designed with an anorexic teenager in mind had won them a lot of friends amongst American women, who'd had it with being told to aspire to a body shape biologically impossible for most of them.

'Try me,' he offered.

'OK,' Topaz said. 'I want to rehaul *US Woman*, close down *White Light* altogether, take *Westside* national and start an entertainment glossy to rival *Vanity Fair*, except we won't bother with stories about businessmen – ours will be wall-to-wall stars.'

'Nate Rosen never tried anything so radical,' her boss commented.

Topaz shrugged. 'I'll need your support, Matt.'

'You have it,' said Gowers, mildly amused at her boldness. 'Aren't you getting married soon? You're going to be pretty busy.'

'Ain't that the truth,' his director answered with feeling.

'I've moved house so many times I can't do it again,' Topaz complained. 'What's wrong with your place?'

'It's not big enough. Neither is yours.'

'They were big enough for us before.'

Joe pulled her to him, running a large tanned hand across her stomach. 'They're not big enough for children,' he said.

'Children?' she repeated.

'Yeah,' Joe said, grinning at her. 'You know, sons, daughters. The indispensable accessory for the modern married couple.'

She picked up a beanbag and threw it at him, and Goldstein reached forward with a lightning thrust, grabbed her wrist and twisted her underneath him. Topaz felt him hardening on top of her as they stared breathlessly at each other, smiling, eyes alight with desire.

'Let's practise,' Joe murmured, hands reaching down to unbutton her silk cardigan.

She remembered that summer as one of the hottest, stickiest, busiest, most terrifying, aggravating, exhilarating, passionate times she'd ever spent in her life.

Work exploded. Financial projections, design reworks, marketing changes – it was a miracle she ever got out of the building. But the restructuring was screaming to be done and Topaz had decided to do it. She was the boss now, with no one but Matt able to countermand her, and at twenty-eight she'd learnt to trust her own instincts.

Some things were painful, like making the staff on *White Light* redundant. But the magazine had never recovered from the Atomic Mass fiasco, and it was better to cut the company's losses. Topaz made as much effort as she could to place employees elsewhere in American and see that the journalists got good settlements, but she was determined to act like a businesswoman. The decision was final.

Some things were difficult, like rehauling *US Woman* over the strenuous objections of the editorial team. But Topaz fired the editor himself and talked most of his colleagues round, with demonstrations and presentations. By the time she was through, they thought it had been their idea in the first place.

And some things were your basic nightmare. Like starting a new glossy from scratch and changing *Westside* to a national. The new title was called *Stateside* and Topaz envisaged it as a *Village Voice* for the entire country, encompassing radical views and underground culture from San Francisco to Dallas, Pittsburgh to Detroit, as well as New York. For both these projects, Topaz took over three empty offices on the thirtieth floor and converted them into a war room, where a crowd of writers and executives could be found any given hour of the day, brainstorming. The best ideas were chalked up on blackboards and left standing around the room, and the atmosphere was so inspirational that editors from existing magazines wandered in to steal ideas.

Josie Simons came up with the best one. A major feature in every issue of the new title, *Impact* – 'Not Size Eight' – which profiled women who didn't fit the supermodel straitjacket, or were older than twenty-five, or came from ethnic backgrounds; strong, beautiful women from all over the world and lots of them.

'Unadulterated sex bombs,' Jason Richman was heard to remark, and there were sighs of satisfaction from every girl in the room.

'We'll give real women something to aim at,' Josie said, underlining *How Diana Looks Better When She Puts ON Weight*, and placing a picture of Drew Barrymore next to ones of Felicia Rashad from *The Cosby Show* and Sharon Stone at her fortieth birthday party.

'That,' said Matt Gowers when he saw it, 'will sell *millions*.'

Her home life exploded too.

Joe and she seemed to fight about everything. The wedding. The reception. The honeymoon. Where to buy a house.

'I've got a lot of friends. I want them to share this with us,' Joe said.

'So do I, but I don't want a circus,' Topaz insisted.

'Let's go skiing in the Alps,' Joe suggested, bringing home a sheaf of travel brochures.

'That's about as romantic as root-canal work,' replied Topaz angrily. 'How could you think of sports on our *honeymoon*?'

'Yeah? What do you want to do? Europe and museums all day?'

'I like SoHo. We could get something really cool down there,' Topaz said. 'It's a great area.'

'You're joking, right? I want a penthouse on Fifth,' Goldstein replied. 'We can easily afford it.'

Jesus, the stubborn sonofabitch, Topaz thought furiously as Joe vetoed another idea.

She'll drive me nuts in six months. Tops, thought Joe, glaring at his betrothed's obstinate expression.

But they couldn't stay mad for long. The heady swell of love would overcome Joe or Topaz and the other would instantly sense it and get turned on, and then nobody talked for a while. They could hardly keep their hands off each other; they made slow, gentle love, they played games, they screwed each other senseless over tables and on the floor and up against the walls.

'All the therapists say this is the worst way to resolve a dispute,' Topaz managed, as Joe slipped two fingers inside her, pleasuring her most intimate places.

'Fuck the therapists,' Joe growled, aroused to boiling point by her heat, thrusting himself inside her.

'Oh, I love you, I love you so much,' she gasped.

'So I see,' he teased her.

They picked a large reception, a honeymoon in Venice and an eighteenth-century house on Beekman Place.

'I hate him,' Topaz said, slamming the phone down. Her hands were balled at her sides in tight fists. 'I *hate* him and I'm not going through with it.'

'Yes you are,' said Tiz Correy calmly, leafing through the dummy for *Impact*. The spacious director's office was a mess, the immaculate caramel carpet covered with photographs, clippings and colour charts, and Topaz's kidney-shaped desk piled high with articles, memos and financial data. For a week now she'd refused to let the cleaning staff in, because, as Jason Richman pointed out, 'Who the hell knows what you'll be throwing away?'

The launch was less than a month away and operations had moved into Topaz's office. Some of her fellow directors were more than a little bothered by this, but Gowers made it clear that she was to be given a free hand. Rossi was doing major work, however unorthodox a method she was choosing, and her reports to the board already showed improvements in operating costs.

Back in the fifties, when he'd borrowed three thousand dollars to start *Week in Review*, Gowers reflected, he'd been pretty hands-on himself. And he hadn't done badly.

'Leave Rossi be,' he commanded. 'It's only another month,' and Topaz's office descended into a malestrom of creative chaos.

'Do you know what he just said? He said he can't believe I'm not taking his name. All this time and he never mentioned it! He just assumed I'd take his name! He can go straight to hell,' Topaz exclaimed tearfully.

Tiz tried to keep a straight face. Every week there was a new crisis, every week the wedding was off, and every week Topaz skipped back into the office like a schoolgirl, glowing from head to foot with pure happiness.

'And you assumed he'd be happy that you wouldn't,' she said reasonably. 'You know you should both have discussed this before.'

'I'm giving him back his ring,' Topaz snapped. She felt giddy and miserable. The stress must be making her ill; she'd thrown up every morning this week, almost as soon as she'd got into the office.

'Call him back, tell him you love him and you're proud to be his wife, but you want to keep your own name. Ask him how he'd feel if you wanted him to become Joe Rossi.'

Her boss gave a weak smile at the thought.

'And if he say's it's traditional, tell him he knows you're not a traditional girl.'

'Topaz, have you approved the amethyst headlines for "Not Size Eight"? Production are crawling up my ass about it,' said Tristam Drummond, *Impact*'s art director, marching into the room. 'We're two days after their final deadline already.'

'Jack Levinson in Sales wants to see you about the Revlon ads,' her secretary announced.

'Thanks, I'll be ten minutes,' Topaz promised. She passed a hand across her forehead. 'Amethyst headlines . . .'

'We thought burnt gold worked better,' Tiz reminded her.

'Henri Bendel are on line two,' her secretary said. 'About the fitting. They can't do this afternoon, would tonight suit you?'

Patrick Mahoney, *Economic Monthly*'s new editor, walked in looking harassed.

'Alan Greenspan just cancelled on me,' he told her. 'I need a replacement right away. Do you think Joe could find me someone at NBC?'

Impact and the new look *US Woman* were previewed to the trade with great fanfare. They were an instant hit. The first issue of *Impact* sold out across the country in forty-eight hours.

Joe Goldstein and Topaz Rossi were married in a private room at the Pierre, in front of a hundred guests. They held hands throughout the ceremony.

The bride wore a cream gown shot through with

delicate gold thread and glittering with tiny seedpearls. Her deep red hair was caught in ropes of gold beads and hung warm and lovely down her back, under a long, romantic veil of antique English lace, secured at the top with a coronet of white rosebuds. Tiz Correy and Elise DeLuca, her maids of honour, were dressed in pink Chanel suits. Joe Goldstein and his younger brother and best man, Martin, wore traditional black tie and for once Joe looked completely comfortable in it.

The reception was a riot: their buddies from NBC, Harvard, American Magazines and Oxford downed a lot of champagne, ate a lot of smoked salmon and danced into the early evening. The speeches got bluer and bluer as the evening progressed, but most people agreed with Jason Richman, who called it 'Not so much a marriage as a merger.'

That night, when they got into the honeymoon suite at the Ritz Carlton, Joe handed Topaz a large square box.

'Your wedding gift,' he said.

Glancing up at him she opened it. Inside was a long necklace, a beautiful piece set with fifteen carat diamonds and exquisite polished beads of topaz.

'I'm sorry it's always necklaces,' Joe said awkwardly.

Topaz reached up and stroked his cheek, her eyes wet with tears. 'I love it nearly as much as I love you,' she said.

They kissed. 'You've got two wedding presents from me,' she said. 'One I couldn't bring, because it's in the garage at home. But I have the other one.'

She reached into her purse and handed him a crumpled scrap of paper with their doctor's letterhead.

Puzzled, Joe unfolded it and read it. Then he smoothed it out, looked wildly at his wife, and read it again, carefully, just to make sure.

'You don't mean –'

'I'm pregnant,' Topaz said, smiling at her husband.

For a moment they just stood there, almost drunk with happiness. Then Joe gathered Topaz into his arms, as gently as if she were made of fragile glass.

'We'll be together till we die,' he said. 'Nothing can go wrong now.'

Chapter Twenty-Nine

As far as Rowena was concerned, it was over.

Only pressure from Barbara Lincoln staved off a lawsuit, and she was finished in the record business. All her success as a talent scout, all her achievements as a businesswoman, were swept aside in a second. She was publicly associated with drugs, and no record company would touch her.

'I tried to stop them but I was outvoted,' Josh Oberman said, calling her the day after. 'These new fucking board rules. How could you have been so *careless*?'

'Are you crying, Josh?' she asked.

'Of course I'm not fucking crying,' he sniffed. 'You fucking moron.'

'Come and work for me,' Barbara said, anxious about her friend. Rowena had lost half a stone and sunk into total lethargy. She had her groceries delivered and she rarely left the apartment.

'You must be joking. After what I said to Jake?'

'You can't blame yourself for that. As if he paid any attention to any of us,' the manager replied. 'Look, Will Macleod decided not to tell me until the lad was half-dead, but I'm not blaming him, either. What can the crew do if the band go off the rails? Jake's in rehab and we're looking for a new guitarist. The band have had it with him, Michael can't work with him . . . *you* didn't pass him a syringe, Rowena.'

'Thanks, but I can't work with you,' Rowena told her. 'I can't face any of it.'

Her friend shrugged. 'Any time you change your mind.'

'Come and work with me,' Michael said. 'You can help me choose my projects and negotiate my deals. I'll give you ten per cent of my company.'

The offer was worth millions.

'I can't ever work with you again,' she said flatly.

'Why not? We're good friends. We think the same way. I don't give a fuck what drugs you did, and I don't have shareholders.'

'It wouldn't work,' she replied. 'It's over.'

'I want you back. I miss you,' Krebs said.

For a second she closed her eyes, longing for it all to be different, longing for the blank ache in her heart to go away, for a return of the hot, passionate joy that had filled every waking second when they'd started this affair.

'We can't go back,' she said. 'Thank you for everything you did for me, Michael. Goodbye.'

She put down the receiver.

John Metcalf could only guess what she must be feeling. It happened all the time in his business, of course: scandals, resignations, corporate coups. He'd been a teenager at the time of the Begelman affair; on his first steps up the ladder when Dawn Steel was ousted whilst giving birth. Hollywood was a monster, and the only emotions worth jack were fear and greed.

The trouble was that Rowena was guilty. Undeniably so. If it had been libellous, the paper would have been sued to kingdom come by Musica's lawyers. He very much doubted whether some flippant remark by Rowena would have pushed her young guitarist down the road to addiction, but that wasn't the point. She'd condoned the use of drugs and she'd been caught doing it.

She was right, of course. Everybody *did* do it, especially in LA, and he doubted the music moguls in New York were any better. Like she said, you experimented and gave up, or you didn't give up and you screwed up your life. So she'd taken Ecstasy in the past, well, so had he. But for years they'd both been clean.

What was she supposed to say to a young rock star? 'Just say no'? And the boy would *listen* to that? 'Don't let drugs do you' was a better way of putting it, in Metcalf's opinion. If a blockbusting Metropolis star had that conversation with him he'd probably say the same thing.

It was going to be difficult, though. Metcalf knew that. As the youngest studio head in town, he'd made a lot of enemies just by having hits. What was it Shakespeare wrote? *Uneasy lies the head that wears a crown*. Right. And the shark pool circling constantly beneath him would drool at the scent of anything they could use against him. Like a girlfriend who was blackballed by her entire industry.

Fuck them all, Metcalf told himself. The closest they've come to love is Heidi Fleiss.

There was no decision to make.

'Book my table at Spago's,' Metcalf told his secretary loudly after the Metropolis production meeting, while all his VPs of Production and other development people were gathering their papers. 'I'm having dinner with Rowena Gordon. Thursday at nine.'

The VPs all studiously avoided his gaze, but John wasn't fooled for a second. Within ten minutes the word would be out round Hollywood that whatever else had happened, John Metcalf and Rowena Gordon were still an item.

He called her. 'How are you feeling?'

'I've been better,' she said. Her voice was flat and listless. 'I'm finished, John. I just don't know what to do. I can't do anything in the music business any more.'

'You can't do anything the way you did it before,' he corrected her. 'That's not the same thing.'

'I'm a non-person,' Rowena said.

'Bullshit. I won't allow you to give up like this,' he answered sharply. The resignation in her tone shocked him. She sounded as though life itself had ground to a halt. 'We've having dinner at Spago's on Thursday, and if you're not in town by Wednesday morning I'm flying up to get you.'

For the first time in a week Rowena found she actually wanted to do something. She wanted to see John.

'OK,' she said.

Was that a faint spark of animation? Metcalf wondered.

'Do yourself one other favour,' he cajoled her. 'Sort out your finances. Make sure you know where you stand.'

'I can't be bothered,' she said.

'You can and you will,' Metcalf told her. 'Do you want all those guys blanking you right now to watch you just fade to black? What would your jerk-off father say, "I always knew she wouldn't last the course"? You hold your head up, Rowena Gordon. Don't you dare let me down.'

'You're telling me I have no money,' Rowena said three days later.

She sat opposite Peter Weiss, her accountant, in the

oak-panelled offices of Weiss, Fletcher and Baum, waring a short brown suit and pumps. Her hair was neatly brushed and tied back in a ponytail, and she'd put on a little foundation. She was perfectly presentable, but that was about it.

Weiss had never seen Rowena Gordon look so unattractive. Her slender frame was now gaunt, her normally healthy skin pallid, and the sparkle in her green eyes had totally vanished.

'Not exactly,' he replied cautiously. 'Under the settlement with Musica, you lost your pension funds and received no compensation, as well as having surrendered the Lotus. The financial plans we made for you' – he cleared his throat – 'didn't take account of the possibility of, uh, what happened. Which means we have to rework your numbers. Now your apartment will have to be sold because Musica Entertainment part-funded the original deal.'

'They own the apartment?'

'No, you have a share in the freehold,' he replied hastily. 'Part of the proceeds belong to you. You also have fairly substantial monies that you could realize from selling your Musica stock.'

She shook her head. 'I want to keep the stock.'

Weiss shuffled his papers nervously. 'Ms Gordon, I would have to advise you against that course of action,' he said. 'Your actual monetary savings are limited. You, uh, you've tended to live at the top of your budgeted bracket.'

'If we sold the apartment and my other stocks, and with what savings there are, how much would I have altogether?'

'I can't be exact,' Weiss replied, 'but I believe that such a sale would only realize a little over a million dollars. And with the need to find a new apartment, Ms

Gordon, you couldn't live in the style to which you've become accustomed.'

'Thank you, Mr Weiss,' Rowena said. 'I'd be obliged if you could send me your final bill.'

'This firm will be happy to represent you for a reduced retainer, Ms Gordon,' Weiss said impulsively, moved by the calm dignity she was showing. 'We are sure you will make a success of whatever you next decide to pursue.'

She offered him her hand, touched. It was the first sign of confidence that anyone outside her immediate group of friends had shown in her. Record executives and promoters who had kissed her ass till it turned blue would no longer even take her calls.

'I must decline, Mr Weiss, but I shan't forget your kindness,' Rowena said.

'Why, Ms Gordon?' he asked, surprised to find he was disappointed.

'I'm leaving New York,' she replied. 'There's nothing here for me now.'

Chapter Thirty

It was all she could do to get up in the mornings.

To begin with it was easy by comparison, because at least she had things to do. The apartment was sold. She found a relatively cheap house in the Hollywood hills above the Château Marmont; after the earthquakes in '94, prices for property on the slopes had plunged. Then there was the liquidation of her stocks and arranging for the packing up and delivery of her personal effects.

Peter Weiss had been right on the money. The value of her entire estate, without selling her Musica stock, came to $1,100,000.

For most people, a fortune. By Rowena's standards, failure.

Every single person she'd had close dealings with was worth at least ten times that amount. John, Josh, Barbara, Michael, the band. She'd been too busy flying first class, designer shopping and looking after other people's business to take care of her personal funds.

And now it was too late.

She had plenty of time to look back over things, and she knew it had been her own fault. She'd betrayed someone who trusted in her, and then refused to admit any guilt. She'd taunted Topaz again and again because she'd hated her for being her own victim, and despised her because of her own success. A flimsy enough success, as she was just finding out. As if a veil had been lifted, Rowena could suddenly see what Topaz must have seen: a haughty, arrogant bitch who cared for nobody but herself.

After Rossi's attempt to screw up the launch of *Heat Street* failed, Rowena had thought she was invincible. Never mind that it was Michael Krebs, not her, who'd turned that one around. And when she'd managed to sign Obsession and Steamer, she'd thought she was immortal.

Her comments to Jake had been just another symptom. It wasn't what she'd said, it was where she'd said it. *At Elizabeth Martin's party*. With practically every important man and woman in New York in attendance, including at least fifty of the top investigative reporters in the city.

Sticks and stones may break my bones, but words will never hurt me.

Oh yeah?

She'd been in the record business since she'd started working. She had no skills for doing anything else, and there was no way any record company would have her back.

I'll never work again, she thought blankly. Feelings of shame and catastrophe drifted through the house like black fog.

Rowena had coped with everything. Her father's rejection. Squalor in London. The struggle to find a job, and the struggle to keep it. Setting up on her own in a foreign country. Building a major new company. Deliberately walking away from the love of her life.

She had coped with everything. Except failure.

*

It was John Metcalf who saved her from complete collapse.

At the start he stayed away, just calling now and then to see if she was OK.

'She's hurting now. She needs a mourning period,' his therapist said.

'But she won't even go out with me any more,' Metcalf protested.

'You have to respect her space. It's a difficult time for her.'

Finally, John Metcalf handed his house keys over to a buddy, packed up a suitcase and simply drove over to her house.

'What the hell are you doing here?' Rowena demanded when he turned up at her gate. It was a cool winter's morning, the type Metcalf particularly enjoyed; a mild breeze, the flowers in Rowena's small garden faintly scenting the air. She was dressed appropriately: a dark blue pantsuit in crisp linen by Michael Kors and fawn pumps from Chanel. In the doorway behind her he could see the main room of the house, immaculately neat and tidy. *Too* neat and tidy. The place looked like a museum. And for all Rowena's careful outfit, she looked utterly lifeless. She had on no make-up, no jewellery, not even a watch.

'Can I come in?' he returned.

She unlatched the door and stood aside for him. John seemed like a refugee from another world. Someone she had known a million lifetimes ago, when she was working, when she was able to use her brain.

'It's a nice place,' Metcalf said. He glanced round at the modest reception room, the orderly kitchen and the glimpse of Rowena's bedroom and bathroom to his left. She had set up a television and stereo and there was everything you might actually need in a home – a microwave, refrigerator and coffee percolator, but that was it. She'd hung none of her paintings, unpacked none of her bonsai trees, laid out no ornaments.

'Thanks,' she replied automatically.

Metcalf hefted up his suitcase and carried it through to her bedroom. Then he picked up the remote and switched off the TV, flickering brightly in the corner. 'You shouldn't be watching that at ten in the morning,' he reproved her gently.

'Why have you brought a case?' she asked, looking at Metcalf's tanned body and luxuriant hazel hair. Almost despite herself, she was glad he was there. In fact, she was *surprised* he was there. Taken aback that someone was still interested.

'Because I'm staying for a while,' Metcalf answered impudently.

'I can look after myself.'

'I don't think so,' he replied, reaching out and loosening her ponytail. A blonde shower fell about her shoulders.

'Don't do that!' she snapped.

He grinned at her. 'At least you can still get mad.'

'Go home, John,' Rowena said. 'You can't stay. I need to be by myself.'

'You've been by yourself for too long.'

'I want to be alone.'

I can't make her accept me, Metcalf realized.

'OK, I'll go, if that's what you want,' he told her. 'But first I need your help. I've run into a problem with Picture This and we have the divisional meeting coming up – it's in San Antonio and everyone in the company's gonna be there. Including Nick Large.'

Large was his boss, a redheaded industry veteran who controlled Cage Entertainment, the company that owned Metropolis.

'So get Sam Neil to look into it,' Rowena shrugged. Sam was her successor at Musica North America and the soundtrack label was his responsibility now.

He shook his head. 'Won't work. If this was easy I'd have fixed it myself. I need you because you structured the original deal.' He gestured towards his briefcase. 'I've brought the papers with me. Please, Rowena, I know you feel lousy but I'm stuck. We have a picture opening soon with a dynamite soundtrack –'

'*My Heart Belongs to Dallas*,' Rowena agreed, with just the faintest glimmer of interest.

'Right. Anyway, word is that our numbers are gonna be just OK, but the merchandizing could turn it into a very profitable picture. The success of the record is crucial to that –'

'MTV, radio tie-ins, press,' she cut in.

'Exactly. Now we have a situation where the management for Black Ice – one of the bands featured – are insisting that the studio percentages must exclude their cut because of their original deal with Musica. They're threatening litigation and that could delay the launch of the record, which probably won't hurt the album too much but its knock-on effects for our T-shirts and sunglasses and stuff could be disastrous . . .'

As John explained the problem, Rowena began to turn the situation over in her mind, taking a pen from the sideboard and making notes. When he sat down she didn't stop him, and when he opened up his case and handed her the thick sheaf of notes Rowena took them eagerly and paced through them intently.

Half an hour later she looked up, triumphant, her face flushed with effort.

'I've got it,' she said. 'It's clause 16b. The rolling break-even states that –'

John's face stopped her in mid-sentence. He was

leaning against the kitchen table, smiling gently. She realized with a start that he'd been watching her silently for the last twenty minutes.

'Welcome back,' he said.

He took her to dinner at the Ivy, where they'd first met.

'You can't understand what it's like,' Rowena said. 'When you've fought for a dream all your life, and as soon as you get it, it's taken from you.'

John kissed her hand. He wanted to let her talk, to help her admit her feelings to somebody else. He was overjoyed it was him she was confiding in.

'Everything you hated before becomes precious. Like phones ringing all the time, like the travel – God, John, I missed getting woken up at six to go to the airport every month because Atomic Mass were playing somewhere.'

She gave him a tiny smile.

'You could have done that any time you wanted,' he told her. 'Atomic Mass are on a stadium tour of Europe. It's a complete sell-out.'

'It is? How's the record doing?'

John leant towards her. 'Haven't you even been listening to the radio? Didn't you put on MTV?'

'My radio's tuned to a classical station,' she replied, the soft candlelight glinting on her gold earrings. 'And I couldn't bear to look at MTV. I knew I'd see Musica acts – *my* acts – and it was too painful. Like watching all the other kids at a party you weren't invited to.'

Metcalf shook his head in wonderment. 'I guess you're about the only person on the planet who doesn't know, then. *Zenith* is busting sales records across America. Atomic Mass have turned into U2.'

Rowena digested the news in silence. Then she said, 'Maybe I should tell you the whole story.'

Starting at the beginning, she recounted all of it. Her parents' coldness and her own independence. Oxford, and meeting Topaz Rossi. Peter Kennedy and the Union. Soho. The fruitless hunt for a band. And Topaz in America, from the launch of *Heat Street* to Velocity and finally the *Westside* story that destroyed her career.

'So don't you want to get this Rossi girl back?' he asked when she'd finished, looking at the shadows under her beautiful eyes, the tiny lines that had appeared around her mouth and forehead for the first time.

Rowena shook her head. 'Absolutely not. In Topaz's place I'd have done the same thing.' She paused, then added, 'I told myself that one day she'd give up and let it go . . . I couldn't resist taunting her. I forgot what she was like. Topaz was always passionate, always hot-blooded. What we'd consider a grudge, she'd think of as a score that needed settling.'

'Why did you make such a friend of her in the first place?'

She thought about it. 'You know what it was? We both had something to prove.'

'Because your fathers wanted boys?'

She nodded, a lovely, graceful movement. John admired her dress again, a fitted gown in moss-green velvet that picked out her eyes.

'Your fathers were morons,' he said.

'Perhaps. I've sometimes longed to be a man,' she answered. 'It would have cut down on some heartache.'

'Do you miss Topaz Rossi?' John asked.

'No,' Rowena said slowly. 'Certain things can't be undone. I miss my job. I miss Barbara and Josh and Atomic . . .'

And I miss Michael Krebs, she finished silently.

'So what are you going to do about it?' John asked.

His liquid blue eyes were intent. He was going to get her back in the game, whatever it took – pleading, bullying, threats.

He ticked the points off on his fingers. 'You used to run a record company, and that option's closed to you now. You've always worked in the record business. It's unlikely that any big corporation would be in a position to hire you right now, because you're too high-profile to be hired quietly. Those are your disadvantages.'

She looked at him as he bent over and refilled her glass with champagne; a vintage Dom Perignon, one of her favourites.

'You built up a company from scratch, so you acquired general business skills. You have intelligence and guts. You have a million dollars of your own which you could borrow against. And you will have a lot of key players in your corner – Joshua Oberman, Michael Krebs, Barbara Lincoln, Steamer, Roxana, Atomic Mass, and me. Those are your advantages. Now the question is, what are you going to do with them?'

She sipped at her drink, considering it. 'What do you think I should do?'

'I think you should set up in business. Be your own boss,' he replied. 'But I don't know *which* business. And it's not my job to find out.'

'I could, couldn't I?' Rowena asked, and with a rush of joy Metcalf saw that her eyes were sparkling again.

'Your hero David Geffen walked away from his brilliant career because they told him he had terminal cancer. A year later they say it's the wrong diagnosis and he had a load of money and nothing to do. Did he turn into a zombie? No, he went and founded Geffen Records.'

She speared a forkful of Caesar salad.

'You can do anything you want,' he said. 'Real glory

isn't about a smooth ride to the top. It's about picking yourself up when you fall and building it all again.'

'John, I could fall in love with you,' Rowena said.

'That's what I'm counting on,' he replied.

Chapter Thirty-One

Three weeks later Rowena Gordon was back in business.

It could hardly have been more different to her last office. No expensive carpets and designer window space. No Eames chairs. Not even a filter coffee machine.

She set up in a cheap lot on Melrose with two phones, a fax machine and an eighteen-year-old secretary. Things were different when you paid the overheads bills yourself.

John Metcalf offered her anything she wanted – start-up capital, the use of an office in the Metropolis lot. Rowena thanked him but refused. 'This is something I have to do myself,' she said. 'Taking help from anyone just wouldn't be right.'

'At least move in with me. Then you could sell your place and use the funds from that.'

She kissed him, a soft, wet kiss that stirred his groin. 'I can't. I nearly gave my independence up before. You helped me out of that, remember?'

'This isn't just for you,' he admitted, an erection growing in his pants. She saw it and pressed her hand between his legs, caressing his hardness through the cloth. He groaned. 'Please. I want you near me.'

'You're near me now,' Rowena said, reaching behind her and unzipping her slip dress. The silk slid off her like water, and with a shock of lust he saw she was naked underneath it. The long slender legs had tanned to the colour of butter-milk, and her nipples were a beautiful pink against the golden skin of her small breasts. She leant back, displaying the blonde triangle between her supple thighs. 'Want to get closer?'

Without a word he unbuttoned his jeans and kicked them off, taking her in his arms. His cock pressed against the flat of her stomach, hard and swollen with wanting.

'It's been a long time,' he said.

'Too long,' Rowena answered. She thought of the last time she'd made love to John, a week after the Martins' party, and then, unbidden, a vision of the last time she'd touched Michael like this swam into her mind.

John felt heat flood her belly. He pushed a finger into her, probing. She was already, instantly wet.

'Do you wanna fool around?' he whispered in her ear. 'Or do you wanna go right to it?'

For answer she smiled at him and spread her legs, an insolent, sensual movement.

John felt the urgency in his cock take over and he guided himself to the quick of her, pushing inside her, inch by inch, until he was sunk in right up to the hilt. She moved with him, pressing down, as though she wanted him to thrust even deeper, to fill her even more.

'You feel so good,' he said. Her eyes were shut tight and he could see her nipples harden and erect in front of his eyes. Metcalf bent to suck them, tugging at them lightly with his lips like a greedy child. Pleasure stabbed through her, and she felt herself getting hotter, needing a man's touch, loving the strong grip of his arms and the muscled torso, which she could feel through the thin cotton T-shirt he hadn't bothered to take off.

Eagerly he started to thrust, finding his rhythm, maddened by the feel of her tight, slippery clinch around his cock. As he got faster and faster her own body responded, until she blocked out everything except the sweet ripples spreading through her and his driving, relentless cock, and white-hot release came in a violent spasm which physically shook her.

John erupted inside her, held her for a second, and then pulled out of her sweating, trembling body. He put up his hands and tilted her face towards him. 'Like I told you,' he said, 'there's no going back.'

She took his right hand and pressed her lips to it, kissing him gently, gratefully. 'Only forward,' she replied. 'Which is why I can't move in.'

Nothing he could do or say would move her. She was with him almost every night, but she refused to sell her house. She was going to do all this by herself, and be beholden to nobody.

The choice of business was difficult.

She could work for a production company, or manage a band – not Michael or Atomic Mass, but others. However, that would mean working for somebody else and it would also mean she was on a percentage.

No. I never want to be in a position where I could be fired. And I want to own stock; not take a salary.

She could start a record company of her own. But any act she signed as a tiny independent would leave her for a major at the first taste of success. That was always the way. Recording costs had soared since David Geffen had founded his labels, and while it could still be done, it was much more difficult . . .

But that's not the real reason, is it? she asked herself. The fact is that Atomic Mass and Josh and Barbara and all the rest of it meant *everything* to me. When it was taken away I was devastated. Music is my life. Music is too much to risk.

No emotional capital. She would start again as a business-woman, and keep her passions separate.

She would be in control.

Rowena settled on the best compromise she could come up with. It had to involve music, because that was her area of expertise, but it also had to be as dry as dust. Something that would let her work to live, not live to work.

She got a piece of paper and listed her main talents.

1. *A&R*. Well, that one was pretty useless now.

2. *Promotion*.

Rowena scored a line under this and sat staring into space. *Promotion* . . . now there was an idea. Hadn't she pulled off the marketing rescue of the century when Atomic Mass booked the Coliseum too early in the US tour for *Heat Street*? And that was one thing Krebs hadn't done for her.

All my own work, she thought with a smile. Damn, that had felt so good.

But unforeseen disasters didn't happen every day, and the major companies had in-house marketing experts, as did the big promoters and agents.

So who needed help?

Wasn't it obvious? Everybody who couldn't afford to hire marketing specialists. Indie labels. College promoters. Small clubs around the country.

Couldn't afford them, though, that was the point. How could one of them afford her?

The answer came back instantly: *one of them couldn't. But a lot of them could*.

That evening, Rowena drove up to John's weekend beach house in Malibu to tell him her plans. After she'd taken a long, refreshing shower, washed her hair and pulled on one of his huge paisley Turnbull & Asser bathrobes, he joined her on the terrace, carrying two frosted glasses and a pitcher of margaritas.

'Do you still have that conference in San Antonio coming up?'

He nodded, a shadow crossing his face. 'Yeah. And I still have problems with the record. The plan you dreamt up stopped the lawsuit, but now the act is refusing to help promote it. And "Face Up" is the first single.'

Rowena sipped her drink. Black Ice were one of the toughest groups to deal with, she knew that. They hated big companies on principle and nothing was good enough for them: not enough posters in the stores, not enough radio play, not enough MTV. They raised objections at every stage from artwork to distribution. She remembered them and their stubborn manager, Ali Kahed, only too well.

Black Ice also sold a lot of records. They'd been the first big act on Musica North America that she hadn't signed herself, and they made the reputation of Steve Goldman, the young scout who'd risen to become her head of A & R. Their last album had debuted at number four in the *Billboard* charts.

Properly handled, 'Face Up' could sell a lot of records for Picture This, and a lot of T-shirts for *My Heart Belongs to Dallas*.

'I can tell you what to do,' she said.

'Really? Jesus, I hope so,' Metcalf said, pushing a hand through his hair. 'Because this is a total fucking mess. The new Musica guys are terrified of Kahed and they won't lift a finger to help out.'

Rowena lifted her glass to him. 'Congratulations,' she said. 'You've just become my first client.'

When Metropolis biked round the contract the next day, Rowena signed on the dotted line in front of Joanne, her secretary, and the guy who sold leather boots in the store opposite.

'They've left a space for us to include the company name,' said Joanne.

Rowena shrugged. 'Any ideas?'

'Call it Cowhide,' suggested the bootseller, 'can't have rock 'n' roll without leather,' and the Cowhide Consultancy was born.

For the first two hours Joanne just sat at her desk reading *Impact*. Her boss worked in silence, spreading large sheets of paper over her desk and writing down names, phone numbers and lists of stores, radio stations and music magazines with large coloured pens, occasionally doodling lines from one to another. Eventually she came out, her hands covered with bright inkstains, and handed Joanne a small list with seventy names and numbers on it.

Joanne raised an eyebrow.

'Oh, that's just the first batch,' Rowena told her. 'Think you're ready for this?'

'I'm ready if you are,' Joanne said, smiling.

Maybe this job wouldn't be such a dead loss after all.

Once Rowena got started there was no stopping her. Carefully she'd picked out her target audience: maverick programmers, store managers who owed her favours, and writers and TV execs who'd been closely involved with her work on Atomic Mass.

'Christ, Rowena! How are you? Where the fuck have you been?' asked Jack Fleming at *Rolling Stone*.

'Black Ice? Yeah, they'll play,' said Joe Moretti at KXDA. 'They're on. My pleasure. When are you coming by?'

'I'll do what I can,' Pete Meyer at MTV promised. 'It's good to have you back.'

At lunch Joanne ordered them a pizza and a couple of Diet Cokes, and Rowena called John and listed all the stations and papers she'd delivered so far.

'I don't believe it. How the hell did you pull that off?' he asked, amazed.

'Oh, I'm not through,' she replied. 'That was the warm-up. Now, how much money would you be willing to give me for an advertising budget?'

'Advertising? Isn't that Musica's job?'

'Depends what you want. If you want to sell a few albums, we already have. If you want to help your film merchandizing . . .'

'How much do you need?' John asked, struck by the briskness of her tone. She was using his private line, but she was all business.

Jesus, we were making love on the beach this morning.

She named a figure.

'OK,' he said. '*My Heart Belongs to Dallas* is opening two weeks after this single is commercially released. Do you think you can get publicity for the movie out of this as well?'

'That's the idea,' Rowena said. 'I have something in mind, but I need an ad budget to do it.'

'All right, Rowena,' John said. 'You got it. Surprise me.'

'I will,' she said.

That afternoon Rowena gave Joanne the second list. This contained the names of programme directors and editors in the key markets whom she couldn't count on personally; men that were still friendly to her, though. The trick was to spend a little money where it would buy the most exposure; she knew better than to simply go for the magazines and stations with the biggest readership or catchment areas. Influence meant everything. That was what working with Michael Krebs had taught her.

She knew all about *My Heart Belongs to Dallas*. It was a bittersweet modern romance, the story of a woman torn between a Texan lawyer, the love of her life, and a doctor who'd fathered her child and would make the better parent for him. She chooses the doctor for her boy's sake, and then to her surprise finds herself falling in love with him after all.

Rowena didn't think it was a bad film, it just wasn't what Metropolis had expected. They'd wanted a very dramatic, highly charged Oscar winner. They'd got a wry, sexy comedy with a few tear-jerking scenes.

Personally, she thought that everyone who loved *When Harry Met Sally* would love this one too, but the Metropolis marketing guys felt differently. They'd pitched it as a classy weepy, *Kramer vs. Kramer* or *Terms of Endearment*. Rowena guessed that the reason the numbers were so low was that the *Kramer vs. Kramer* types at the previews were disappointed.

She hadn't said a word. Films were John's business, not hers. If John had offered her advice on Atomic Mass when she was at Musica, she'd have yelled at him to butt out.

But the 'Face Up' single gave her an idea.

A week before the record went to radio, huge billboards appeared in New York, LA, and Dallas, plain black backgrounds with foot-high white lettering: FACE UP TO YOUR CHOICES.

Two days later, full-page ads ran in the *New York Times*, the *LA Times* and other big papers, all with the same plain message. There was no mention of the movie, album or single.

The campaign was an instant hit. People started ringing radio talk shows to ask what the ads meant. At one intersection in Manhattan there was a logjam as drivers craned their necks up to look.

Then 'Face Up' was released.

The original work with her extensive network kicked in, and astonished Musica promo men found their brand-new single had already been plastered across the airwaves in key cities – by, get this, *Rowena Gordon*.

Then the competitions Rowena had set up started running on the other stations and in the magazines.

'What's the hardest choice you ever faced up to?'

'What would you do for love?'

It was pop psychology at the simplest level. Everyone's given something up, Rowena figured, everyone's been in love, and she was proved right as switchboards jammed coast-to-coast.

Finally there was the video. Black Ice had refused point-blank to shoot one, and the guys at Metropolis wanted to string old footage together and use that, but Rowena had a better idea. 'We won't show the act at all. We'll show the movie,' she suggested, and the result was a terrific promo, the best moments from *Dallas* segued together and laid over the funky, aggressive pop of the song.

MTV loved it.

The last calls Rowena made were to old friends of hers who worked in the industry tipsheets, both film and music-*Variety, The Hollywood Reporter, HITS* magazine and the like, and every one of them ran an article along the lines of 'Just when you thought it was safe . . .'

'Face Up' hit number one in the Hot 100 the week it was released, and a fortnight later *My Heart Belongs to Dallas* opened to packed theatres.

Ali Kahed, astonished to find his act had the biggest hit of their career, called Sam Neil and told him that they might consider doing a little soundtrack promotion.

Nick Large called John Metcalf and dryly congratulated him.

And late one evening Rowena's phone rang in her bedroom.

'Hello?' she asked, surprised. The number was unlisted, John was on a plane to San Antonio, and the only other person she'd given it to was Joanne.

'Hello, kid,' said Josh Oberman. 'What the hell took you so long?'

Chapter Thirty-Two

Peter Weiss stared at the young woman sitting opposite him with something approaching astonishment.

She no longer looked emaciated, listless and pale. On the contrary, she was a tanned, slender thirty-year-old woman in an elegant pink Chanel suit that fitted her to perfection. Her right wrist sported a platinum Rolex, and a sapphire engagement ring glinted on her left hand. Her blonde hair had been feather-cut to add body and movement. Her long legs were covered by the sheerest nylon stockings, and her shoes were stack heels by Azzedine Alaïa. She was lightly made-up, just enough to perfect the delicate beauty of her skin, and she wore a delightful scent – which one, Weiss had no idea, but it smelt vaguely of sandalwood. And jasmine.

It had been barely a few months since he'd seen her last, but Rowena Gordon looked like a different person.

That was partly to be expected, of course. After the Jake Williams scandal and her summary expulsion from Musica North America, Rowena had come to his offices with the weight of public humiliation and the loss of her livelihood on her young shoulders.

He recalled their meeting clearly. As the first woman to be president of a major US record label, Ms Gordon had been one of their most high-profile clients, and his partners had been insistent that, after laying out for her the sorry state of her financial affairs – relatively speaking – he let her know that Weiss, Fletcher & Baum would no longer represent her. Instead, he'd been so shocked by her emaciated body and so impressed by the quiet dignity with which she bore herself that he'd wound up offering to reduce the fee so she could keep her accountants.

It had been an impulsive offer. Completely out of character.

But now Rowena Gordon was back in his office. And this time she wasn't a private client in severe trouble, she was the chairman of her own company. Cowhide, Inc had customers all over the entertainment business – film studios, TV stations, rock bands, sports teams. They picked their events and records and shows very selectively, choosing only assignments that were both difficult and high-profile. That way, with every successive coup, Rowena's company got more famous – and more pricey.

Weiss knew that the pressure on Cowhide to expand was immense. Rowena employed sixteen people, when she could have had sixty. She took on three projects a month when thirty more were desperately trying to secure her services.

Cowhide Goes Hell for Leather, screamed *Variety*.

Rowena rules! proclaimed *HITS*.

Bullish Cowhide Wins Raiders Contract, announced *Billboard*.

They'd had offers from every conceivable source, wanting to buy them out – CAA, William Morris, ICM, Turner Entertainment, you name it. Rowena had turned them all down, as far as he knew. Certainly, she looked like a young woman who knew exactly what she was doing.

And yet he could scarcely believe what he was hearing.

'Are you sure about this, Ms Gordon?'

'I'm quite sure, Mr Weiss, I want your firm to represent Cowhide, both in general terms, for a retainer, and specifically, for – for any financial work that may arise,' she finished vaguely.

'But we handle private individuals, Ms Gordon. We're just a small firm. For a company like Cowhide, you'd be better off with a big name – Coopers and Lybrand or the like.' Weiss coughed, embarrassed. 'I would be derelict in my duty not to advise you of it.'

She smiled, a serious, courteous smile. 'And you *have* advised me of it, Mr Weiss. Nonetheless, Weiss, Fletcher and Baum is the firm I want. If you think you need more associates to handle our business, by all means hire them.'

She fished about in her purse and drew out a neat folded piece of paper. 'I hope you'll forgive the liberty,' she said charmingly, 'but I have brought a certified cheque with me for a year's retainer in advance. Assuming your partners will be willing to take on our account.'

Mesmerized, Peter Weiss unfolded the cheque. It was made out to his firm in the amount of one million dollars.

'You told me a few months ago that you had confidence in me, Mr Weiss, when circumstances were rather different,' Rowena continued, seeing he was too stunned to reply. 'Cowhide returns the compliment.'

He couldn't believe it. Jack Fletcher was going to have a heart attack.

Rowena stood up and shook his hand in a firm, dry grip.

'Nice doing business with you, Mr Weiss,' she said, and walked out of his office, leaving the old man staring after her.

*

In the taxi on the way to the Regent, Rowena permitted herself a small smile. The meeting at Weiss, Fletcher & Baum had been something she'd been looking forward to; it was one of the pleasures of a second wind of success to reward your friends and snub your enemies.

Well, maybe enemies was too strong a word. They existed in every business; as a new Angeleno she should be aware of that. Cowardly, greedy little types that kicked you when you were down and kissed your ass like mad if you happened to get up again. The record company execs who'd blanked her when she got fired by Musica. The promoters and agents who'd refused to take her calls. Recently, every single one of them had called up, or sent flowers, watches, other such peacemaking tokens. She had taken great delight in telling Joanne how to answer the phone to those jackals: 'Ms Gordon is not available to you, Mr X, now or at any time up to and including the Day of Judgment.'

She stirred in her seat, looking forward to her lunch meeting. First of all, it would be great to see Oberman again. For all the talking they'd done, she hadn't actually laid eyes on the old buzzard since she'd got canned. And second, meeting the chairman of Musica Entertainment at such a powerbroker venue was the best way to announce that the exile was over.

Rowena Gordon was well and truly back.

As night was deepening, the electric floodlights grew more brilliant by the minute. Barbara could smell the acrid smoke from the dry ice drifting out from the venue; the sound of the people inside was a low rumbling noise, punctuated by sharp football whistles and interwoven with the pumping blast of the sound system.

On her way out of the arena, Atomic Mass's manager sighed with satisfaction. Another sell-out, and here in

Barcelona the T-shirt stall was doing even brisker business than when they'd played Florence the previous night. Jim Xanthos, the new guitarist, was settling in great – there was no more sniping and secrecy among the boys, and Jim fitted in like he'd been there for ever. A happier band paid off both in better shows and more creativity; Michael Krebs had loved the demos they'd written on the road.

Jesus, that's a good sign, Barbara thought, as the limo spun out on to the main city road. Two hit albums is good, but there is better . . . we could still gain a little ground in Australasia.

She smiled faintly, catching herself plotting. God, how she'd changed in the past few years; from a cool, impersonal lawyer to a kick-ass manager with the best of them. And if you'd told her when she first saw this act that they represented the rest of her life, she'd have laughed in your face. Even when she started out with Atomic Mass, she couldn't tell Van Halen from Van Morrison.

The quiet streets slipped past her, a huge medieval cathedral at the city's centre, not much traffic in the early evening. She had time for a good two hours with Michael before they went back to watch the boys.

Imagine me wanting to see a hard rock show! Oberman never lets up about it . . . I wonder what Rowena will say when we get her back out on the road.

Rowena. Her most constant friend; they'd been as close as two of the busiest women in music could be, and Barbara had been appalled by what had happened to her. For the sake of that useless junkie Jake Williams, too. She hated it when Rowena went into hiding and didn't give a soul her LA number, but she understood. If somebody took this life away from her now – if Atomic Mass split up tomorrow . . .

Barbara shuddered. It didn't bear thinking about.

She knew what it was like, when you were a woman in business. You made sacrifices. If you were lucky, you had some joy out of your work. For both herself and Rowena, work and life had become inseparable.

Rowena always loved the record business, and I came to love it, Barbara thought, pulling up in the hotel forecourt. But at least I had a lover, too.

She'd met Jake Barber a week before the *Zenith* release. It was love, if not at first, then certainly at third sight. Jake worked at a cool independent record label, and they were married after five weeks at Chelsea registry office in London, with all their friends warning that it would never last. It was their eighteen-month anniversary next week.

Rowena, on the other hand . . .

Barbara got out of the car, her light Armani dress rippling in the warm breeze, and stepped into the hotel. The receptionist nodded at her and told her Mr Krebs was waiting.

On the surface it all looked wonderful. The wild success of *My Heart Belongs to Dallas* followed by the world beating a path to Rowena's door. She was her own boss now, and any corporate misgivings about ill-advised remarks had been drowned in the heavenly sound of cash tills chiming. Even *Vanity Fair* had done a profile on her – 'The Rise, Fall and Rise of the Hit Woman'. And then, on her thirtieth birthday, her engagement to John Peter Metcalf III, the brilliant young president of Metropolis Studios, had been announced. The happy couple were photographed together at the wrap party for *Steven*, the big Metropolis weepie for autumn, looking impossibly rich, powerful and glamorous. Truly two of the 'beautiful people'.

And yet, and yet.

She knocked loudly on the door of Krebs's suite and walked in.

'Barbara, you look great,' Michael said, greeting her warmly.

'So do you,' his friend replied. Krebs was wearing his usual T-shirt and jeans and still managed to look gorgeous – the muscled torso rippling under the thin cotton, the stomach trim and lean, the wiry hair at the side of his head giving him an unmistakable aura of intelligence and power.

He's not my type, but I understand what she saw in him.

'Yeah, but I have to work at it. How's Jake?'

'Wonderful. How are Debbie and the boys?'

'They're great,' Michael said.

There was always just a slight edge to this ritual exchange between the two of them. Krebs didn't know whether Rowena had ever told Barbara about their affair, and the doubt hung in the air whenever they spoke.

Since Rowena fled New York for LA, that edge had got keener. It was an unspoken bargain between the manager and the producer that her name be mentioned as little as possible, and only ever in a business sense. For after Cowhide had catapulted her back into the industry spotlight, Rowena had recontacted Barbara, the band and all her old friends – except Michael.

In interviews and on television she'd repeatedly called him a genius, her mentor, the sixth member of Atomic Mass. Rowena made it perfectly clear that she was a big fan of Michael Krebs, both as a producer and a human being.

But she didn't call.

Well, Barbara reflected, if I'm right, that's all about to change.

'Michael, when did you last speak to Joshua

Oberman?' she asked him, sitting down and lighting up a St Moritz.

'About a month ago. Why?'

'Did he mention Rowena Gordon to you?'

Krebs stiffened imperceptibly. 'No, I don't think so.'

'OK,' Barbara said, taking a long, satisfying drag. 'I'm gonna tell you something, but it's totally confidential.'

'Shoot,' he said, watching her through narrowed eyes.

'Josh rang me in Florence last night. He asked Rowena to meet him for lunch at the Regent Hotel in New York this afternoon, and he's going to offer her a newly created post at Musica. They've changed the make-up of the board again, and Oberman has an absolute majority now.'

Michael leant back in his armchair. 'What new post, exactly?'

'President of the worldwide company. She'd report directly to him, but Josh is basically retiring from active involvement.'

'Holy shit,' Krebs said softly.

'We don't know if she'll take it. It would mean giving up Cowhide, and that's something of her own.'

He shook his head. 'She'll take it,' he said, and there was an expression glittering in his dark eyes that Barbara couldn't decipher.

'Maybe. Anyway, that's not all, which is why I thought we should talk,' she said. 'Oberman told me something else. One of the reasons he wants to hand over to Rowena Gordon now is that he doesn't think he'll have the opportunity in a year's time.'

'Why not?' Michael asked.

'Because he thinks Musica Entertainment is the target of a hostile takeover bid.'

'Who from?' Krebs demanded. 'Musica is a major

record company. They've got the clout to hire the best investment banking in the world. Who the hell would try to swallow them?'

'Try Mansion Industries,' Barbara replied.

Rowena leant forward, trying to take in what she'd just heard. She was careful not to let her surprise show. Oberman had taken a centre table, right in the middle of the dining room, the most blatant position of all. The two of them – old corporate warrior and his young entrepreneur protégée – were on display to the business elite of Manhattan, and she knew they were being watched.

'Let me tick these points off,' she said. 'Number one, despite the fact that the company had me fired in the most ostentatious way, you now want to make me president.'

'Spoken to my lawyers,' said Oberman testily, 'and you haven't been convicted of any wrongdoing. Even if *Westside* kept the tape, it doesn't prove you did what you said you did. You might have been trying to talk Jake out of it. And if the industry thinks it's weird, so what? Everyone's read *Hit Men*. We *are* weird. I don't explain myself to them.'

'Number two, you expect me to give up Cowhide. Which is totally successful, Josh, and which I own privately.'

'So sell it. You'll be rich. And you'll be the first woman ever to make president of a major and that's your goddamn life's ambition, Gordon, so don't try and snow *me*.'

'Number three, according to you I'll only have this job for a matter of months, because Mansion Industries are going to take us over and ruin our artists' careers.'

Joshua Oberman fixed her with a watery eye. 'Listen up, princess,' he said. 'I've been working at Musica since your mom was a teenager. After my wife died, records were my whole life. I was there for the Rolling Stones and I was there for Led Zeppelin and I was there for Metallica and I was there for Atomic Mass. Now in nineteen seventy-one management, including me, took the company public, and as you may be realizing with Cowhide, that means a lot more money but the loss of your control.'

He paused, shaking his head. 'Finally, I made chairman. I'm running the whole show now. Took me long enough. Even a year ago, I couldn't stop you getting fired. But right now I have control of Musica as it stands and I'm not prepared to give it up without a fight.'

Oberman grabbed his napkin and coughed into it. 'I'm not a fool, Gordon. I know perfectly well that we may not be able to withstand Mansion Industries. But I also know that you've got the best chance of anybody around. Which is why you have to accept this job.'

'Are you asking me or telling me?'

'I'm telling you,' he said.

She nodded, blonde hair lustrous in the morning light. 'All right, Josh. I can't promise anything, though.'

The old guy smiled slightly. 'Admit it, Rowena. You missed it like hell. You want to get back to *Zenith* and all the rest of it. You want to be dealing with Barbara and the boys again and,' he added slyly, 'Michael Krebs.'

'How is Michael?' Rowena asked casually.

'Still married,' Oberman said mischievously.

'Josh,' she protested. 'It wasn't like that. There was nothing going on. Anyway, I'm engaged to John Metcalf. See?' She held up her left hand, letting her new sapphire sparkle in the sun.

The old man speared a forkful of omelette and winked at her infuriatingly.

'Sure, kid,' he said.

*

Knowing that word would be leaking out around the record business, Rowena got in a cab to JFK the moment she left the Regent. She called John from the first-class cabin and asked him to meet her at the house at six.

This was going to be difficult. How could she tell him that she was going back to Musica Records? It would mean giving up Cowhide, which John had helped her to build. And it would also mean moving back to New York. John ran Metropolis, he could hardly come with her. Maybe one day she'd be able to engineer a transfer of the company down to LA, or set up another branch there, but at the moment taking this job involved a return to their weekend relationship.

Lots of couples live like that, Rowena reasoned. Plus, how many couples both run big companies? It'll mean that we can get on with our work in the week and enjoy each other on Saturday and Sunday . . .

'Champagne, ma'am?' the steward asked, filling her glass to the brim.

She sipped thoughtfully. *But will John see it like that? After all, we're engaged.*

And yet Oberman had been right. Amazing how well the old guy knew her. As soon as he'd offered her the job she'd known she would accept, for all her pretended outrage. She shifted a little in her roomy seat, feeling pure adrenaline pump through her veins. First woman in history to run a major record label! It *was* her dream come true. She couldn't deny it. And however mad her boyfriend got, there was no way she was walking away from it.

John was waiting for her in the garden when she got home, standing under the orange tree, a glass of iced mineral water in his hand.

Rowena fixed herself a grapefruit juice and walked out to join him. After the dirt and cold of Manhattan, the warm fragrant air of the Hollywood hills seemed especially welcoming.

I'm gonna miss this, she decided with a pang of regret.

'I had lunch with Josh Oberman today. He offered me the presidency of Musica Worldwide, with complete power to run the company. He reckons Mansion Industries is going to try a hostile takeover.'

Metcalf stared at her and Rowena felt her heart sink. His handsome face had gone tight with anger.

'Don't tell me. You accepted.'

'Yes, I did,' she replied, trying to sound confident. 'It's everything I ever wanted, John. I can't pass it up.'

'Why?' he demanded. 'So you can be the CEO who hands it over to Mansion? Don't you read the *Wall Street Journal* or *Economic Monthly*, for Christ's sake? Conrad Miles can't be stopped. If he wants Musica, he can buy Musica twenty times over. Meanwhile, you're prepared to sacrifice our relationship for the sake of an empty title and a corporation that threw you out on your ass.'

'It wouldn't be sacrificing our relationship, darling,' she pleaded, walking over to him and putting a hand gently on his arm. 'It'll just be for a few months until I can open a Los Angeles office . . . I could fly down here at weekends.'

'Weekends! Jesus!' John exclaimed, pushing her away. His blue eyes were icy with fury. 'I'm not some puppy you can treat however you want.'

'That's not fair.'

'Isn't it? After the way you were when they sacked you? Is your memory so short?' he demanded, cupping her chin in his hand and tilting her face up to his. 'Rowena, you were a recluse. I had to personally go over to your house and kick your butt. And I took risks for you then. I was the president of Metropolis and you were in the middle of a drugs scandal –'

'– and I'm grateful,' she interrupted. 'But that can't change this! Please try to understand.'

'Oh, I understand,' he said savagely. 'Just like I understood when you were working day and night at Cowhide. When you couldn't make time for me then, either. Christ, I'm such an idiot. I thought that when you agreed to marry me things might be different.'

He stroked her cheek, but it was a rough, almost desperate caress. 'Your heart's a fucking fortress, Rowena, you know that?' he demanded. 'I love you. What the hell is it going to take?'

'I love you too,' she said, grabbing his hand and pressing it to her skin. 'That's why I agreed to marry you.'

'Is it?' he asked. 'Or is it just part of the masterplan?'

'John!'

'Do what you have to do,' he snarled. 'Try and remember to book some space in your fucking diary for our wedding,' and he stormed off into the house.

For a second she stared after him, and then she put down her juice and ran inside.

'Hey, hey,' she murmured, putting her arms around him. 'John. Sweetheart. Please, I'm sorry . . . I should have asked you first. I swear it'll only be for a few months. We'll open an office in LA.'

Metcalf tried to brush her away, but there was just something about the insistent press of her body, the catch in her tone, the scent of her hair. Despite himself, he weakened.

'It's OK,' he said, 'it's OK, baby,' and he scooped her up in his arms, as lightly as if she were a doll, and carried her through to their bedroom, letting her cover his chest with little breathless kisses, tiny butterfly caresses, that drove out his anger and sparked his desire.

He laid her down on the Pratesi sheets, slipping off her jacket, unbuttoning her silk chemise, his thumbs clumsy with excitement as he unhooked the lacy La Perla bra and felt his breath catch in this throat at the sight of her pink nipples, half stiffened in anticipation. His left hand slipped up her smooth thigh, a new rush of passion surging through him as it met the delicate wisp of her panties.

'I can't do without you for long,' he murmured, but then her arm snaked round his neck and her hand reached down to unzip his pants, and all protest was silenced in another hot kiss, a tangle of clothes, a liquid melting of flesh.

'Oberman? it's Rowena,' she said.

Thank Christ we bought a pied-à-terre in Manhattan, she thought, as she looked round the smart apartment John and she had picked out together last Christmas. It was a light, roomy place on Mercer Street in SoHo, with a huge window Rowena had fallen in love with and a polished wood floor. Neither John nor she had had much time to use it up until now, so her cases sat in an almost empty bedroom, with just one change of clothes for each of them hanging in the closet. A few of her files relating to the various offers she'd had for Cowhide, and her lawyers' cast-iron employment contract with Musica were strewn over the bed.

'Good, I'm glad I caught you.' Oberman's crabby voice crackled down the lines. 'I've just spoken to Barbara Lincoln and she has some ideas about the Atomic Mass contract. Like a keyman clause relating to you. Know what that means?'

'Nice to speak to you too,' she replied, laughing. 'And

of course I know what it means. If I leave the company for any reason, their contract would be null and void – they could walk out of Musica and sign to PolyGram. Clive David and Whitney Houston have the same –'

'Exactly. It would be a first step in persuading Mansion not to bother,' the chairman cut in. 'So be a good girl and hop out to Spain. They're playing Barcelona.'

'But I've just got into New York this morning.'

'So take a shower,' Oberman snapped. 'You can play with your new office tomorrow.'

'Well, yes, sir,' Rowena said, smiling, and put down the phone. *Plus ça change* . . .

She opened the wardrobe. *Thank God for one sensible habit I've got into.*

She kept a small case of essentials packed and ready to go – jeans, white shirt, Nikes, two pairs of panties and bras and a nightgown, along with toiletries and her passport. Next to this case were two smaller ones with extras according to the climate: sweaters for Moscow, sunblock for the Caribbean. She picked the 'hot' case and got on the phone to Continental airlines, then booked herself in at the Meridian. Atomic Mass would be playing the Olympic Stadium tomorrow, two nights there and then up to Paris.

At least she'd get to see the lads play Europe. The last time she'd been able to get away to go to one of their concerts had been the night they stormed the Meadowlands, New Jersey, at the start of the US leg of the *Questions* tour. And that was so long ago she didn't want to think about it.

Rowena faxed John a short note, telling him she'd be back in a couple of days, and started to get undressed, deciding on a comfortable Perry Ellis suit for the flight. It was navy blue, a simple cut that flattered her figure and let her move about easily – perfect airport gear. She kicked off her beautiful, impractical Italian high heels and went for a smart pair of navy flats, taking no jewellery and snatching her purse from the dresser. She could make up on the way to the plane.

Continental Airlines flight 18635 for Spain swung slowly round on its heavy axis and prepared to head down the runway for takeoff.

Rowena Gordon, seated comfortably in first class with a blanket draped across her knees for the long night flight, was deep in thought.

Well, she told herself, you're the Chief Executive Officer of Musica Entertainment. The first woman to run a major label. Congratulations. Not quite what you expected, is it? How long do you think you'll last?

Barcelona slipped by her, neon and beautiful in the darkness. She hadn't been here for years, she'd forgotten how openly the city was laid out towards the edges, all wide roads and tree-lined spaces. Her cab driver, mercifully, did not speak English so she was able to appreciate the winding streets as they tore into the centre of town, hundreds of fly-posters lit up by their headlights. She found she was twisting and turning, looking for Atomic Mass spots. There were plenty of them, luckily for Musica Spain. The gig had sold out within hours of being announced five months ago, but that was no excuse not to promote it. If most people in Barcelona that bought records already had a copy of *Zenith*, they could get *Heat Street* too. And besides, the Knuckleheads, on as support, needed the exposure.

The Olympic Stadium was an impressive sight, floodlit towers jabbing into the sky. As Rowena stepped out of her limo, the sound of a roaring crowd drifted towards her. She felt a quick, adolescent thrill of excitement. Christ, it had been a long time since she'd seen a band.

She walked up to a security guard, flashed her laminate and was immediately ushered inside the barriers. One of the crew took her up to the production office.

Will Macleod was sitting perched on a table, yelling into a phone. When he caught sight of Rowena, he shouted, 'I'll fookin' deal with it later,' and slammed down the receiver.

'Who the hell are you?' he barked, obviously unimpressed with the all-access laminate swinging ostentatiously on her T-shirt.

'I'm Rowena Gordon, president of Musica Records,' she said hastily. Being mistaken for a groupie or a gatecrasher by this guy looked as though it could cause problems. 'To see Barbara Lincoln?' she finished, wondering why it came out as a nervous request.

'Aye. Well, you've missed her,' growled Macleod. 'She went back to the hotel. I'm sorry I cannae help, but the boys are onstage – in five minutes,' he added menacingly.

As if to confirm his words, the sound of Steppenwolf's 'Born to Be Wild', their intro tape, flooded the air at maximum volume. A huge howl of approval tore from the crowd.

Rowena involuntarily turned towards the stage. Exhilaration ripped through her.

Jesus! she thought. I really want to see this! And why shouldn't I? Barbara won't mind, we could talk tomorrow . . . I never *did* get to see the *Zenith* set . . .

'Would you take me up onstage, Will?' she asked.

He looked at her for a second, then nodded briskly.

Rowena followed the tour manager through the labyrinthine corridor out to the back of the stage. The ramp leading up through the scaffolding to the onstage viewing area beside the wings was directly ahead of them. The sound of Atomic's bass-driven raw harmonies was bleeding into the warm night sky, mixing with the violently loud roar of the crowd. It was deafening. She loved it.

'Sixty thousand capacity here,' Macleod yelled in her ear. 'Sold out.'

The sky was misting with smoke from the stage, pierced by their trademark green lasers, caging the amphitheatre in bars of light, panning out in front of her as she followed Will up the ramp. Now she could see glimpses of the crowd, a few sweating, crushed faces in the front row picked out by the red, blue and golden spotlights that circled the packed audience as well as catching each member of the band. Giant video screens, the standard accessory for arena and stadium shows these days, were mounted at the sides of the stage so that the crowd could see the expressions on their heroes' faces, blown up to thousands of times lifesize. The fans were roaring as though Spain had just scored in a World Cup final.

She felt her exhausted body spring back into life.

'We've got a box at the side of the stage where we sit VIPs,' Will yelled. 'You can watch from there wi' the other guest.'

'Who do you have visiting tonight, then?' Rowena asked.

Will guided her along the back of the stage towards the box.

'Their producer,' he said. 'Michael Krebs.'

He pushed the little door open.

From the second she laid eyes on him, Rowena knew she was lost.

She was weakened, physically drained from the

flight. And the instant she let go of all her stress, just gave up and allowed the music and the passion of the crowd to sweep into her bloodstream, she'd been shut alone in a box, onstage, in the dark, thousands of miles away from anyone either of them knew, with the man she most desired in the world.

'What are you doing here?' she said.

'I came to talk to Barbara in Modena last night,' he said, staring at her. 'Thought I'd stay for Barcelona and check out the show. It's not a crime, is it?'

She shook her head, mutely.

'What about you?'

Rowena shrugged, and gave him a simplified version. That provided a little breathing space; they talked about Josh for a few minutes.

The slow, sensual intro to 'Karla' spilled through the amps around them.

'Why didn't you tell me?' Michael said.

'Tell you what?' asked Rowena, trying not to look at him.

He grabbed her shoulders angrily and spun her round to face him.

'Don't play games with me,' he said, lifting her left hand to expose the engagement ring. 'You never told me. You never called me at all.'

'I didn't know how to,' Rowena said.

'You hurt me,' Krebs said furiously. 'I had to find out from Barbara Lincoln.'

Rowena, starved for him, raked his face with her eyes, that close-shaven grey hair, the deep black irises, his thick, beautiful eyelashes. She wanted to remember it always, to keep it clearly etched in her mind. He was challenging her, he was angry. Now that it was too late, she realized how wise she'd been to keep away from him. Love welled up in her like a flooded river.

'How do you think I felt?' she said. 'Why did you do that to me with Debbie? Do you have any idea what that was like?'

Krebs stared at her. 'Do you love him?'

'Of course.'

He shook his head. 'Don't lie to me.'

'Please, Michael, let it go,' Rowena said. She was near breaking. It was torment to be so close, and not to be able to touch him. 'This is the best way for everybody.'

'No it isn't,' Krebs said.

He moved closer, till he could hear her breathing, till there were only millimetres of space between them.

'I didn't like to see him touching you at that party,' Michael said. 'You thought I couldn't see that? He had his hand on your breasts, right in front of me.'

Rowena bit her lip. 'He can do what he likes, Michael. I'm going to marry him.'

'Look at me,' Krebs said. 'Do it, Rowena.'

She turned her head and looked at him, and felt her stomach cave in with lust. Her control evaporated. She moaned, she couldn't help it.

'I don't give a fuck what's right or not right,' Krebs said harshly. 'I won't let you go,' and he cupped her head in his hands, twisting his fingers in her long hair, and pulled her to him and kissed her.

Rowena collapsed against him, kissing him back wildly, feeling shame at the weakness and sexual heat that rushed through her. She pressed her thighs together, she was already wet, and it was getting worse. His cock was swollen and hard against her.

Krebs put his hands on her shirt, feeling her breasts through the fabric, her nipples erect, distended with desire for him. He'd never forgotten how Rowena felt to hold. Whenever he touched her, she was passionate and eager. But this time, after an absence of months, it was like the first. He felt a surge of wanting explode in his chest. She was his. He had to have her.

'We can't do it here,' Rowena gasped, pulling away.

Goddamn it, every second he had to wait now was an eternity.

'Come on,' Krebs said, and tore out of the box, grabbing her hand. She followed him, hoping her legs would still work OK. Maybe people would see them.

She didn't care. She didn't care about anything. She could only feel the blood throbbing in her legs, only hear her heart crashing against her ribcage.

They ran down the ramp and into the backstage area. Michael took a right up some deserted stairs and they found themselves in a maze of corridors on the first level, above the ground floor where the crew were working. Krebs tried some doors; they were all locked. They went round a corner, right, left, and then he suddenly stopped running and she stumbled against him.

'Now,' he said. 'Here.'

'What if somebody comes?' Rowena panted.

Krebs looked her over, pleasurably, luxuriating in her desire for him. She moved uncontrollably under his gaze, feeling it as though it were a physical caress.

'Stand against the wall,' he said, thick-voiced.

She moved back, feeling the rough brick grate against her skin through her shirt, now soaked in sweat. All her clothes were clinging to her. Her jeans felt heavy and awkward on her flesh.

'If somebody comes, they'll see us,' Krebs said, reaching for her waistband and snapping open the buttons of her jeans in one impatient movement. Rowena gasped with excitement, squirming against the wall. Michael smiled and moved closer, standing to face her, and then yanked down her jeans and panties until they were below her knees.

'They'll see you like this,' he said, and put his right hand over her pussy, lightly, feeling her heat and moisture for himself. 'They'll see you waiting for me.'

'Please, Michael,' Rowena managed. 'Please.'

He shook his head, barely controlling himself. 'I want to see you,' he said. 'Standing out here, in the light. Take your top off. Show me your breasts.'

Her fingers were clumsy, shaking as she undid her buttons and ripped at the clasp of her bra. It was sweet, protracted torture for both of them, and when she was topless, standing against the wall in the full glare of the striplights, her nipples sharp and full of blood, her flat stomach tapering down to her damp sex, displayed for him, whilst he stayed fully clothed, Michael could no longer hold back. He rammed himself against her, kissing her mouth and neck, one hand grabbing her breasts while the other loosened his pants, letting his cock spring free against her groin, and Rowena moved under his touch in ecstasy, absolutely out of control, mad for him, parting her legs as widely as she could. She'd dreamt of this, even with John she'd dreamt of it, and now he was going to fuck her and take her again, she couldn't live without it, and Michael had his fingers in between her legs, feeling his fingertips get slick with the wetness of her, feeling her move and buck under his touch, and then he found her, open and ready, and he shoved himself into her, all the way up to the hilt.

'Michael!' she gasped.

'Rowena,' he said. 'Oh, baby,' and he started to fuck her, up against the wall, and she felt him hard and thick inside her, stroking her with his cock, like he was nailing her to the wall with his cock, and she loved it, she moved with him, and Krebs felt how totally he had mastered her now, how completely she was his, and it made him harder, and he wanted to tease her some more but he couldn't speak, it was too good to speak, and he just thrust, and thrust, and thrust, deeper and harder, and she screamed a small strangled scream, gasping her ecstasy, and he burst inside her like a dam, feeling the wave of his orgasm consume him utterly, pleasuring every inch of his skin, from his toes to the crown of his skull, and he growled out her name, gripping her to him.

Chapter Thirty-Three

'Excuse me, gentlemen,' said Topaz, hefting herself from her chair with as much dignity as she could muster.

God, sometimes I hate being pregnant, she thought, covered with embarrassment as she waddled off to the john. What asshole invented the radiant, glowing mother-to-be? Obviously a bachelor. And a misogynist. Christ!

There were eight men and two women in that meeting, and the other woman didn't count because she was the director of Personnel. So she, Topaz, sole representative of the sisterhood – *ha*! – in the upper echelons of power at American Magazines, was soundly impressing everybody by having to rush off to pee three times an hour. Wonderful.

She glowered at her reflection in the bathroom mirror. She'd put on ten pounds apart from the weight of her lump, her face was flushed, her ankles were swollen and the pull of the child was straining her back. Her normally elegant feet were strapped into wide Dr Scholl sandals, and the only dresses she could wear were goddamn maternity tents, the ones they made in foul shades of 'feminine' pink or covered with iddy-biddy flowers. Topaz had her own made up, the best she could do: ankle-length smocks in navy, with thick white bands at the collar and cuffs, or just plain black or dark green. It was the navy today, the most businesslike outfit in her wardrobe.

Yeah, right. I look like an executive elephant, she told herself, suddenly irritated beyond belief by the sight of her red curls snaking over her shoulders. She took a velvet tie from her pocket and pulled her hair into a severe ponytail, then waddled back out to the meeting.

Harvey Smith, American's director, West Coast, was giving a short statement on the Los Angeles view of the threat they were facing. Around the table, the others listening attentively were Matt Gowers, chairman; Eli Leber, of Leber, Jason & Miller, the company's attorneys; Damian Hart, chief financial officer; Nick Edward and Gerald Quin, investment bankers from Maughan Macaskill, the firm hired to advise American Magazines; Ed Lazar, director of Sales; Neil Bradbury, director of International; Nick Thomson, director of Marketing; Louise Patton, director of Personnel; and Topaz Rossi, director, East Coast.

In other words, the board of American Magazines and their closest advisers. Matt Gowers had refused to allow anyone else to attend; even the notes were being taken by Louise, as the least senior person in the room.

This was a small meeting, but a vital one.

The company was in play.

'We've got serious concerns,' Harvey was saying as she sat down. 'The West Coast is afraid that Mansion Industries will change the entire nature of American Magazines. From what we've been told' – he waved at Gerald Quin – 'Connor Miles is only concerned with raising profits. We believe he'll close all our books that aren't making a profit yet, lower quality and ban expensive photographers and writers. The question is, how we can persuade him that magazine publishing works on different economic rules to timber-felling or food retail.'

There were nods around the table.

'What do you think, Topaz?' Gowers asked.

'I think we should fight it,' she said. 'If Nick and Gerry are right, we've got no chance of *persuading* Mansion of anything. No senior management has survived for more than a year after Mansion Industries took over their company.'

'We can't fight Mansion. We have to be realists about this,' Bradbury replied.

'American's a large corporation,' Lazar agreed, 'but Mansion Industries is a huge conglomerate.'

'Who have never lost a takeover yet,' Damian reminded them.

Topaz knew the tide of opinion was running against her, but she couldn't let it go and bow to the majority. To come so near to power, and then have it snatched away by a greedy conglomerate? Maybe she could get another job somewhere else – her record was exemplary – but she'd put a lot of work into *Impact* and *Economic Monthly* and all of them, and she was damned if she'd just walk away. Who could tell if she'd get as many chances at Condé Nast?

The boys were taking the ostrich approach. *If I stick my head in the sand, maybe the monster won't see me since I can't see him. If I'm nice to Mr Miles, maybe I can persuade him to leave me alone.*

But executive elephant or no, she knew they were wrong. When American was bought out by Mansion Industries, every board member here was history. That was obvious. But they didn't want to recognize it.

Topaz had caught that Quin boy looking at her when she spoke up to object. He sounded like he knew his stuff, and it made her even more certain she was right.

'Look, you're all way off-beam,' she burst out impatiently. 'OK, so they've never lost a takeover. Then by the law of averages, it's about time they did.'

'Really, Topaz,' muttered Louise, in a tone that clearly said *Hormones*.

'You're in Personnel. You don't know jack,' Topaz rounded on her, infuriated by the obvious glance at her swollen stomach. 'I run six magazines and that's what I intend to go on doing. If everybody else is happy to kiss up to Connor Miles and kiss their job goodbye, I'm not.'

Gowers, who had been watching her with narrowed eyes, turned to their lawyer. 'Eli, what can we do in the first instance?'

The older man spread his hands. 'Blocking petitions, ownership of magazines by a non-American citizen, the usual delaying tactics.'

'Do it. Immediately,' the chairman ordered. He gestured at the investment bankers. 'We'll hire Maughan Macaskill to represent us in a defence, as we've discussed. Topaz, Damian and myself will be your main liaisons at the company. Harvey, you, Ed and Neil are to prepare statistics and presentations that would try to persuade any predator or due diligence shark that we work best the way we are.'

'I don't get it,' Neil said. 'Which approach are we taking? Fighting or talking?'

'Both,' Gowers answered grimly. 'In this situation, we have to try everything.'

Topaz gazed out of her window at the Manhattan skyline, sparkling in the sun. She was sitting in a new orthopaedic chair she'd had installed as her pregnancy advanced – or rather, which Joe had insisted she get installed. Next to her was a small device for monitoring her blood pressure, which she was supposed to do every other day but couldn't bear to. Pregnancy was one thing, stress was another, and the combination of the two . . . well, Joe would have a fit.

He should try being pregnant in the middle of a hostile takeover. Now there's a double whammy, Topaz thought, staring out towards the Hudson.

Summer was coming to the city . . . she could see it, from this air-conditioned eyrie, the sunlight flashing on the tiny cars racing through the gridlike streets, glittering on the river. She loved summer. Even when it was too hot. And this August, of course, she'd be a mother . . .

Topaz felt her mood soar. A baby . . . my baby! she thought, with a rush of utter bliss. She placed her hands tenderly on her stomach, hoping to feel it move, and was overwhelmed by an intense surge of love and happiness. Joe's child, *our* child . . .

What would it look like? Black hair, she sincerely hoped; maybe blue eyes . . . would it be a boy or a girl? Joe had been desperate to find out, but she'd put her foot down.

'No, I want to be surprised,' she insisted, when Dr Martinez had put the question to them.

'But we could decorate the room the right colour,' Joe begged.

Topaz had shaken her head, smiling. 'Nice try.'

They'd had the ultrasound at just three months, because Topaz didn't want Joe to be able to cheat – '*Is he waving?*' '*Yes she is, Mr Goldstein.*'

When Dr Martinez had put the stethoscope down on her stomach and they'd heard the muffled, pumping little heartbeat, Topaz remembered with another rush of affection, Joe – that great hulking guy – had burst into tears. Afterwards he'd been so ashamed of this slip from macho grace that he'd watched four solid hours of football and snapped at her if she teased him about it.

Overall, though, he couldn't be more solicitous. Opening every door, refusing to let her lift so much as a coffee cup. Treating her like she was made of the finest porcelain. At first it was annoying, but as the months wore on she'd been glad of it; her stomach seemed incredibly heavy, like a dragging weight on her back and feet. She was sure a baby didn't weigh that much when you just picked it up.

The phone rang on her desk, an outside call. Topaz smiled; Joe always called her around this time of day. Every day.

'How's it going?'

'Fine,' Topaz replied, staring out at the bright blue sky. 'I can tell you more tonight.'

They had Lamaze class at eight, right after Lisa Martinez palpated Topaz's stomach at seven, and it would take some doing to make that appointment. But there was no way to cancel it. They'd had the bare minimum of checkups since the ultrasound; amniocentesis had already given the pregnancy a clean bill of health, and Topaz was a very busy woman.

'Too much for the phone?' he asked, then grunted when Topaz didn't reply. 'I hate it when they stress you out over there. Can't they see you're pregnant?'

'Joe, *everyone* can see I'm pregnant,' Topaz teased him, amused by a sudden vision of her husband calling up Connor Miles and yelling at him to lay off for another three months.

'OK, well, don't work too hard,' he said gruffly. 'I love you.'

'Love you too,' she replied cheerfully.

'Topaz,' said Matt Gowers, sticking his head round the door. 'In my office, please. Five minutes.'

She nodded at him. 'Joe, I'll see you tonight.'

*

If Matt Gowers noticed that his youngest director was looking extremely happy all of a sudden, he knew better than to say so. Rossi had made it quite clear that she didn't want special treatment; hormones, unruly bladders and sore feet notwithstanding, she was clinging on to her position with both hands. He knew some of their colleagues considered it perverse, but Gowers wasn't so sure. Topaz had only just completed her restructuring programme, and late nineties or no, motherhood was still a dangerous occupation for an ambitious female.

It's tough to look tough when you're expecting, the old man thought to himself as Topaz walked carefully into his office. He'd known exactly what Louise Patton had been trying to pull when she lost her temper at the board meeting, and he admired Rossi for refusing to take it . . .

She's got a good attitude, Gowers thought. Because frankly, right now we can't afford passengers.

'Have a seat,' he offered.

Topaz drew up a chair at the walnut table in the middle of Gowers' luxurious office. Sitting with their backs to the glass walls were Quin, Edward and Hart, each with several sheets of financial data spread out in front of them.

'Basic defence work, Topaz,' Damian Hart told her, passing across a sheaf of papers. 'Numbers, poison-pill safeguards, stock issues . . .'

'We've just heard that you're not alone in this,' Edward added. 'They've bid for a group of radio stations in California and a major record label.'

'Radio stations . . .' Topaz mused aloud. 'Aren't they going to run into FCC regulations about owning radio stations and a print group? Are they after any other magazine houses?'

'Small ones,' Quin replied.

'Yeah, but how many small ones?' Gowers asked, getting his subordinate's drift. 'Can we do them for antitrust?'

'Which record label?' Topaz suddenly asked in a small voice. The banker's words had just washed over her at first.

It can't be. It can't be. Can it?

'Musica Entertainment. But they don't have any interests in print,' Quin told her. 'If we're going for antitrust, they aren't much help to you.'

Topaz took a slow sip of her coffee.

'That's where you're wrong,' she said.

The sun was setting over Fifth Avenue when Topaz and Joe arrived at Dr Martinez's clinic. They held hands in the elevator, kissing and stroking each other whenever the car was empty. Joe kept his right arm circled protectively around her, not wanting to let her go for a second.

It had been like this since the honeymoon. They still fought like cats every other day, and they still couldn't bear to be apart. Joe arrived at American Magazines the second Topaz said she'd be off work. Topaz cancelled lunch appointments, jumped in a cab and raced across town to NBC to be with him. He sent her flowers for no reason. She browsed in antique shops for hours, looking for baseball memorabilia he might like. They were so in love they were drunk on each other; Topaz had spent her first month back at the office in a haze of eroticism, walking around thinking about Joe all the time. She kept wondering if anybody guessed; somehow the sexual hunger beating between her legs seemed too powerful to be invisible, as if it could burn right through her Ann Klein suit, display her nakedness to the whole office.

The least thing could set her off. Walking past a

doorway where she'd yelled at him. Walking into the *Week in Review* offices. And once, she'd arrived at a board meeting first and been so struck by the memory of making love to Joe on that table that she had to sit down, bright red and weak with desire.

Another time Goldstein called her up. 'Hi,' he said.

'Hi,' she answered, feeling herself go wet at the mere sound of his voice. The way they'd said goodbye to each other that morning ran through her mind like a dirty movie.

'How are you?' he asked inconsequentially.

'Fine,' she said, only trusting herself enough for monosyllables.

'Topaz, you're turning to jello,' Joe observed, mocksternly.

'Yeah,' she said, glancing round the office to see if anyone could see her.

'Should I get off the phone?'

'Yeah.'

That night when they got home, Joe had ordered takeout jello and ice cream and proceeded to eat it off the flat of her stomach.

Their fights had also been epic. Over how hard they both worked. Over whether Topaz should drive herself to the office any more. Over maternity leave, paternity leave, and hiring a nanny.

'Six weeks is not enough,' Goldstein maintained. 'You'll need at least three months to bond.'

'Don't you dare tell *me* how to bond with *my* baby!' Topaz spat, furious. 'I'm the one that's carrying it for nine months. I feel it every time it kicks. If you want to stay home and bond for three months go right ahead. Just don't expect me to turn into Marilyn Quayle.'

'Don't be ridiculous,' Joe returned angrily. 'I can't stay home. I run programming for NBC.'

'And I run the East Coast for American Magazines.'

'Really? I'd never have guessed,' he snapped.

But the next day a huge bouquet of white roses turned up at her office with a small rectangular package, and when she ripped it open Topaz found a video of *Mrs Doubtfire*.

Elise DeLuca, watching the expression on her boss's face, had shaken her head in affectionate envy. 'The rollercoaster marriage to end them all,' she said.

Work got tougher, Topaz got larger, and Joe got gentler. Paradoxically, it made her feel more vulnerable; when her love started backing off, she couldn't help sensing his desire to shield her and protect her, which meant she needed shielding. Also, at around six months, they had to stop making love, and that made her frustrated and anxious.

'Jesus, how many times!' Goldstein told her, finding her sobbing in the bathroom one morning. 'I – don't – mind. I'd wait for you until the end of time. Three months is nothing.'

'What about Jane? She's so pretty and so thin,' Topaz sobbed.

'Jane, my assistant?' Joe repeated, trying not to laugh. His secretary was a small, mousy girl with neat brown hair cut very short, a wife and mother of three. 'Are you jealous of *Jane*?'

'Yes,' sobbed Topaz, inconsolable. She remembered every touch of her husband on her skin, every thrust of him inside her, all the fevered eroticism that had consumed them both since the first time they'd made love. Joe was more man than anyone she'd ever known. How could he be satisfied without sex? How could he stay faithful to a woman who looked like a beachball?

'Remember Thanksgiving?' he whispered, gathering her into his arms.

Topaz nodded. Last November, when they'd driven to his parents' house in Connecticut, they'd had to pull over three times because Topaz kept teasing Joe, trying to go down on him while he was driving. In the end they'd parked by the side of a cornfield, spread out her coat and made love in the stubble, kissing and tumbling and screwing each other blind. It had taken another half-hour to pick the straw out of their clothes and to Jean Goldstein's fury they'd turned up very late.

'Traffic was murder, Mom,' Joe explained, kissing the old lady on the cheek and hoping she wouldn't notice the scratches on his neck.

'I remember,' Topaz choked.

Joe kissed her on the temple, a soft, sexual kiss, pressing his lips to her skin. She felt his real desire behind the gesture.

'No woman can stack up to you,' he said. 'Ever. Nobody even comes close. Even if I didn't love you more than life, I could never settle for a substitute,' and at that moment she thought herself the happiest wife alive.

And troubles temporarily forgotten, Topaz felt pretty much like that right now.

'Come in,' Dr Martinez said pleasantly, waving them to a seat. She glanced at Topaz, briskly assessing her size and general state of health. 'How's it going? Any problems?'

'None,' Topaz lied, slipping off her dress and clambering on to the raised examining couch.

The doctor raised an eyebrow. 'No back strain? You're getting pretty large.'

'Well, maybe a little,' she admitted.

'It's a stressful time for my wife at work,' Goldstein

said firmly. 'She's a key person in a reorganization which is going on at the moment, and I'm wondering if she should relax more.'

Dr Martinez suppressed a smile. Joe Goldstein and Topaz Rossi were two of her most celebrated clients, a real Manhattan 'power couple'. They were also her favourites. Topaz used to ring her up and ask her not to tell Joe if her blood pressure was too high. Joe used to ring her up and ask her to bully Topaz into taking each Monday off.

'If he knows what it's really like he'll freak,' Topaz begged.

'She thinks I'm being sexist,' Goldstein sputtered. 'You have to help me out, Lisa.'

'Let's have a look at you, Ms Rossi,' Martinez said calmly. 'You were last palpated at three months, right? That's a bit of a gap. I'd rather you increased checkups now.'

She placed a cool hand on Topaz's swollen stomach and started to press it gently. After a few seconds she stopped dead still, looked at Topaz, and repeated the process, more slowly.

Joe went white. 'What's the matter? Is something wrong with the baby? Is something wrong with Topaz?'

'Not exactly,' replied Lisa Martinez. 'But I think you should have another ultrasound.'

'Why?' Topaz asked. A wave of anxiety spread through her. 'What can you feel?'

'This reorganization, is it vital?' the doctor asked her patient.

'No,' said Joe.

'Absolutely,' said Topaz. 'There's no question of me taking time off unless it's a medical necessity.'

'No, it's not a medical necessity. But I do advise you to rest as much as you can and to avoid arguments,' she added, looking sternly at Joe. 'You'll need as much rest as you can get.'

Lisa Martinez smiled at the young couple. 'Congratulations,' she said. 'You're having twins.'

After her husband had fallen asleep, Topaz Rossi lay quietly on her black silk sheets, staring into space.

She was tired, but she couldn't stop her mind racing.

Twins. Eleanor and Maria. Joe junior and Marco. Eleanor and Joe.

Connor Miles. No one has ever stopped him before and the guys want to hand him American on a silver platter. Is having two babies gonna hurt more? Should I cut down? I can't *cut down . . . Jesus, why now? Gowers won't like it, he'll reckon I'm about to walk out. Maybe he won't. He's seen what we did with* Impact *. . . maybe if I could get the data and work from home . . .*

Antitrust. Has to be. I mean, we're not a small company, we're not Pitt Group. We can afford Maughan Macaskill . . . but we need help.

I'm not fucking Superwoman, I'm tired . . .

She's a goddamn bitch . . .

If I can save the company maybe I could succeed Matt. Harvey wants the job but he's ready to give in and Gowers hates that attitude.

Why should she help me? She hates me.

Look at the way she jumped at it when she got a second chance . . . they need us. Tradeoff. Strictly business . . .

I want to keep my job. I love my work.

Can a woman really have it all?

Topaz swung her legs carefully over the side of the bed, grabbed her satin robe and padded across to her study, flicking on the Apple. The digits on the radio glowed 12.45 a.m.

She paged through her private addresses file, found

the number she was looking for and punched it into the phone.

A voice answered, not sleepily. 'Hello?'

'Hello, Rowena,' said Topaz.

Chapter Thirty-Four

Rowena Gordon had never been so powerful, celebrated and rich.

She was president of Musica Worldwide, the first woman to hold such high office in the record business. She was one half of a glittering Hollywood couple. She had liquidated her own consultancy for a personal profit of $6,000,000. She was profiled in *Newsweek* and *Forbes*. Her social appearances with John Metcalf were reported by Marissa Matthews and Liz Smith.

Rowena Gordon had never been so pressured.

Day and night she found herself struggling to make sense of financial data, company histories, legal defences for her company. Rowena, Sam Ncil and a bitter Hans Bauer arranged for as many big acts as possible to include 'keyman' provisions in their contracts, making Musica a less attractive target. It was a losing battle. Connor Miles bought parcels of stock wherever he could find them, hiding his interest behind webs of holding companies and fake subsidiaries.

Rowena Gordon had never been so unhappy.

'What are you thinking about?' John would ask her after they finished making love, and she would turn aside, kiss him and whisper, 'Nothing.'

Michael. Michael. Michael.

*

'Spain was a mistake.'

Rowena Gordon sat opposite Michael Krebs in the Oak Room at the Plaza, sipping a fine cognac and trying to sound as confident as she looked. She was wearing an Adrienne Vittadini dress in fluid peach chiffon, Stuart Weitzman mules and a sapphire bracelet, intentionally chosen to match her engagement ring.

Michael wore jeans and a black sweatshirt and beat-up sneakers, and he radiated authority and intensity. She had to use every inch of her self-assurance to prevent her response to his mere presence showing up in her face.

'No it wasn't,' he said flatly.

Oh, this was hard, Rowena thought. It truly was hard. Michael was fifty now, still with those knockout black eyes, still with that salt-and-pepper hair, still with that muscled torso that paid tribute to a lifetime of taking care of himself. Still, to her – she tried unsuccessfully to suppress the thought even as it surfaced – the most desirable man in the world. In terms of classic good looks, Michael couldn't hold a candle to John Metcalf. She knew that. She'd never, as she had with John, had her breath taken away by his pure beauty in certain positions, under certain lights.

But Michael's sexuality hung about him like perfume.

She saw he was staring at her.

'What is it?' she demanded.

'I was thinking how proud you've made me,' Krebs said.

'Thanks,' she smiled, angry with herself for being disappointed with that reply.

Come on, Rowena. He never lied to you. He was never a jerk about it. He said straight out that he didn't love you and never would, he said he was your friend and that was it. He doesn't want you.

'And I was thinking how much I want you back,' he added, not looking at her.

'Come on, Michael. You really don't mean that,' Rowena said calmly.

'Oh, I really do,' Krebs said. 'I really do.'

'Do you love me?' Rowena asked, despising herself for her weakness.

Michael battled with himself. It would be so easy just to say yes to that, and then she'd never deny him again.

'No,' he said. 'I don't love you. But I do want you. I miss you around in my life. I miss watching you have those Richter-scale orgasms.'

'I'm with somebody else now,' she said.

'But you enjoyed it. We had fun together.'

'We had a lot of fun together,' she agreed, determined to stay composed. 'But now I'm with John.'

'So what?' demanded Krebs.

'What do you mean, *so what*?' Rowena shot back. 'So I'm not gonna cheat on him.'

'You can't even meet my eyes,' Michael said, and started to look her over, slowly, a sexual, assessing look.

Rowena could feel his gaze, and blushed scarlet. He was right, she didn't dare look up.

'So tell me about John,' Krebs said conversationally. 'Is it good, with him?'

'Yes it is. It's very good, OK? Enough, Michael. I don't want to talk about this with you.'

'Does he satisfy you?'

'Yes, he does,' said Rowena defiantly. He was still looking at her like that. 'And cut it out.'

'So look at me,' Michael said. 'Come on, Rowena. I mean, your boyfriend satisfies you, so you shouldn't be afraid to look me in the face.'

She looked up and glanced at him. 'OK? Now let it go.'

She was so wet and aroused for him. *Jesus. This is killing me.*

'He must be quite a man, if he can satisfy you,' Michael said, adding mercilessly, 'so you come for him like you came for me.'

Rowena stared straight ahead of her, stony-faced.

'That is true, right?' Michael pressed her. 'You come as hard for him as you came for me.'

'Yes!' Rowena snapped. 'That's *right*. Now shut the fuck up.'

Michael put his hand under her chin, and turned her face sharply towards him. His touch on her skin was electric.

'That's the second time you've lied to me,' he said. 'I don't like it.'

'It's *over*,' she said.

'I could get us a room here, right now,' Michael said, as if she hadn't spoken. 'I could take you upstairs and push you across the desk. I could fuck you on your hands and knees on the floor.'

Rowena looked down at her untouched fruit salad, aware that she was flushing bright red with longing.

Please. You have to let me go,' she whispered.

'I will not,' he said.

'What do you want?' she demanded, raising her head and staring him in the face. 'What do you want of me? I've had success and a good relationship without you. Now you want me to come back to you and screw it all up for myself. Why? For *what*? Isn't it just sex? Isn't that what you always said?'

'You fascinate me,' he said.

Rowena closed her eyes for a split second. The force of his personality radiated across the table like heat from an open oven.

'You love me, Michael,' she said.

'No.'

'Yes, you do. You love me,' she said.

Then she stood up and walked out.

Michael. Michael. Michael.

It had become an obsession.

Even as she organized her own wedding, posed for the society photographers and worried herself sick about Musica, his name beat in the back of her mind like a drum. After the blinding, intense, wonderful ecstasy of what had happened to her in Barcelona, she was incapable of shoving him into the background of her mind.

When she'd left New York, she had left him behind her. The combination of failure in business and the sudden awareness of Michael's wife had been a double whammy that had utterly destroyed her.

Cowhide gave her back her control. Cowhide let her work day and night. It gave her something to fight for. It let her forget Michael Krebs, and gave her a little space to grow fond of John, to rediscover pleasure in sex with someone else.

But now she was back in New York, in his city, with his band, working with him every day, and resistance was futile.

She loved him so fiercely it hurt.

She wanted him so much she could scream.

One morning, on the way to work, she had found herself driving miles out of her way, to Turtle Bay where he lived. She'd parked the Mercedes a few yards down the street from the Krebses' house and just stared at it. It had been six o'clock in the morning, and the tree-lined streets were empty in the predawn darkness.

She had just stared at the front of the house for twenty minutes and then driven away.

She knew it was unhealthy. Dumb, narrow and faithless to her own partner.

Krebs had never even admitted he was *having* an affair. 'Just two friends who have great sex,' he told her.

She'd asked about everything. His brothers. His unemotional parents. High school. College. How he'd lost his virginity. Everything remotely connected with him was endlessly intriguing to her.

Now she began to dream up ridiculous ideas. Like finding where his father had his medical practice and booking an appointment, just to see what David Krebs looked like. Of finding the art gallery where Debbie worked and going to have another look at her.

Rowena did none of these things. She flew out to LA every week, avoided Michael, and worked on the defence of Josh Oberman's company. At least staying at the top was something she cared about passionately.

Because what can you do when the fairytale goes wrong? When you find the love of your life, and he belongs to someone else?

'I think we have a problem.' Hans Bauer's voice was gravelly with concern.

'No shit, Miss Marple,' snapped Joshua Oberman. He sat at the head of the Musica boardroom table, staring down at a photocopy of a letter addressed to Rowena Gordon from Waddington, Edwards & Harris, Mansion Industries' lawyers.

Central Park was bathed in the setting sun outside their windows, and the rays were reflecting off the presentation trophies hanging all over the walls, so that at certain angles Rowena was dazzled. She loved this time of day; Roxana Perdita's *Holding Out* sparkling gold across the polished mahogany floors, Black Ice's *Cry Wolf and Run* shimmering silver, and the huge Atomic Mass displays for *Heat Street* and *Zenith* glittering light back from twenty platinum discs.

'We've got a bunch of fucking problems. Like our fucking company's going up in smoke. Jesus Christ, I'm gonna have to sit here and *watch* while it slips into the hands of a bunch of fucking accountants,' Oberman cursed. He looked older and greyer than Rowena had ever seen him.

'There has to be something we can do,' she muttered.

'Actually, I don't think there is,' said Hans Bauer, sounding almost pleased about it. 'The terms of this letter are clear. If we keep on spinning keyman clauses into our artists' contracts, they're going to sue for dilution of assets. They own shares, so they have every right to do it. And our lawyers think they will win.'

'They won't win over Atomic Mass,' Rowena said, with some sharpness. 'I found them, I've been their manager's closest friend for years and I've been involved in every aspect of their career, production and touring included. If Musica wanted me back, I can legitimately say I demanded a keyman clause.'

'You might be right. But the case could take years. They could put an injunction on the release of their third album,' Maurice LeBec pointed out.

'We have clout.'

'Mansion has more.'

'Then *we* should have more! Why do they want a record company, Maurice? Who else are they targeting? Can we get some kind of common defence?' Rowena demanded.

Jesus Christ! Like these jerks give a damn about the artists! They've all got stock and they want to be rich. Well, fuck that, I just got here, she thought furiously.

'It's a good point. We know Connor Miles is South African,' Oberman interjected. 'There are laws about foreign nationals owning media companies.'

'Communications media. Not records,' said Jakob van Rees.

'So we buy a fucking radio station. We buy three,' shrugged Rowena.

'They'll sue,' objected LeBec.

'Who are the other targets, Hans? Didn't you tell me there were others?' Josh asked.

The senior executive group president, Finance, gave a petulant shrug. 'Prime Radio in California. Four or five small print companies, a daily newspaper in Chicago and American Magazines.'

'The guy thinks the United States is his fucking supermarket,' Oberman said outraged. 'He's trying to buy Prime Radio and us and American Magazines at the *same time*? How much money does he have, anyway?'

'Enough,' said Bauer and LeBec together.

'I would like to point out that Musica Entertainment is not an American company,' van Rees added, with a sour look at Rowena. 'Madam President may have forgotten it, working in New York for all this time, but Musica is incorporated in Holland.'

'Will that make a difference?' Oberman asked her, his brown eyes ignoring the rest of the executive committee. 'Antitrust, I mean?'

'Ask a lawyer,' his president replied. 'And ask an investment banker.'

Oberman nodded, and winced.

'Are you OK?' Rowena asked.

'Sure,' the old man said, grimacing a little. 'Heartburn. I'm fine.' He turned to the men around the table and waved them away in a crabby gesture of dismissal. 'We're done for now, people.'

With a few ugly glances at their new president, Maurice LeBec, Hans Bauer and Jakob van Rees left the room.

'Rowena, can I see you for a second?' Oberman asked, putting a withered hand on her arm.

'Sure,' she said.

Josh glanced at the heavy, gleaming doors of the board-room, waiting until LeBec had completely shut them behind him. Then he said sharply, 'Gordon, I don't want those guys within ten feet of our investment bankers.'

Rowena nodded, her shimmering hair swinging against the burgundy collar of the Hervé Leger dress she'd picked for this meeting. They called Leger 'the king of cling' in Paris, and the crossover number that hugged her handspan waist and accentuated her small breasts and the slight swell of her ass was no exception. Teamed with Versacc slingbacks and a thick gold bangle, the outfit was theoretically suitable for work, but it threw off a disturbing sense of sexuality behind the neat tailoring and expensive fabric. Oberman had managed a faint smile when he saw it; he knew Rowena inside out and he knew it was a deliberate dig at the other directors, who'd made it obvious how unhappy they were at having to report to a female, especially one who was younger than they were.

The sensible female executive would have gone for ultra-conservative suits, boxy jackets and neutral colours. Rowena made a point of exaggerating her femininity – *deal with it, boys*. Oberman liked that; the kid had never been one to kiss ass.

'I was thinking the exact same thing,' she agreed. 'They *want* to get bought out. Hans Bauer hates my guts.'

'Yeah, well. He's not gonna vote me Prom King either. Who are we hiring? Maughan Macaskill?'

'They've been stalling me. I think someone else got in there first,' Rowena answered.

He noticed she seemed preoccupied, the elegant fingers tapping aimlessly on the table, the green eyes clouded.

'Spit it out, babe,' Oberman ordered, wincing again.

'It's just something Hans said about the other targets,'

Rowena said. She pushed her chair back. 'I think I should make a few calls.'

'Let me know as soon as you've decided on the investment bank,' he said.

It wasn't till Oberman got back to his suite at the Pierre and found his copy of *Economic Monthly* waiting for him on his desk that he realized, with a stab of apprehension, exactly what she'd meant.

American Magazines. They're trying to buy American Magazines, Rowena thought, as she spun her Mercedes down Second Avenue.

It was late at night, and the city was melting into the bright lights of the traffic and neon billboards. She'd just come from a long dinner meeting with Barbara Lincoln, and it hadn't been encouraging.

'We want you to have that keyman clause. We don't want Josh Oberman to have to watch Musica go down the drain,' her friend had told her over grilled pheasant at Lutèce. 'But the boys are having their moment in the sun right now. I can't guarantee it'll last for ever and I have to put them first. If Mansion Industries buy you out we are *walking*. Even if I have to split them up and re-form with a different name and a keyboard player.'

Rowena had shuddered. Musica without Atomic Mass was unthinkable.

I have to stop this from happening.

With a boss who's too old to know what he's doing, a board who are probably on Connor Miles's payroll right now, and a company too small to resist this predator.

They're trying to buy out American Magazines.

She just launched Impact *there . . . she's not gonna be happy about it . . .*

She'll tell me to go to hell.

I'd deserve it.

By the time Rowena had picked up her mail from the doorman, though, her mind was made up.

John loved her, and that was good. And she was fond of him. It wasn't such a disaster.

But there had to be some passion in life. Something you love so intensely you would suffer any humiliation to hold on to it. Something that meant you were alive, not merely living.

And without Michael Krebs, Musica was all she had left.

Rowena strode through the door of her apartment, hung up her coat and leafed through her messages. John. Josh, twice. She could call him in the morning. Zach Freeman called from Berlin to say hi. That was sweet, Rowena thought, walking across the room to pick up the phone which had started trilling on her desk.

Who the hell would call me at half-midnight? Not Oberman again . . . that guy doesn't know the meaning of 'unavailable'.

'Hello?' she said.

There was a split second pause, and in that instant Rowena suddenly knew exactly whom she was speaking to.

'Hello, Rowena,' said Topaz Rossi.

Chapter Thirty-Five

Nobody in the White Horse Tavern took any notice of them. Why should they? A mother-to-be and her friend sipping fruit juices in the village on a summer afternoon.

Which was exactly how they both wanted it.

'Grill Room at the Four Seasons,' Rowena had suggested.

'You have to be kidding! Entertainment industry and Wall Street – we might as well put an ad in the *Times*,' Topaz scoffed. 'How about the River Café?'

'I know too many people who lunch there,' Rowena said. 'Maybe we should go somewhere a little less obvious.'

'Fine,' her rival answered coolly. 'I know the closest thing to a pub in the United States. In the Village. White Horse Tavern on Hudson Street.'

'Tomorrow at three,' Rowena agreed, and they hung up.

It was the first private conversation the two women had had for a decade.

Rowena dressed casually: black jeans, a white Donna Karan shirt, tan cowboy boots. She wondered whether or not to take her notes on Mansion House but decided against – if they *didn't* wind up working together, Christ only knew what Rossi might do with the information.

In the cab on the way there she wondered about Topaz; it was amazing how their minds still worked the same way. She would have called American Magazines the next day if Topaz hadn't reached her first. It was surely the only way. Musica Entertainment on its own couldn't withstand a raider with such a huge capital base, and neither could American Magazines. But trying to buy both at the same time must be stretching Mansion. Maybe together they could work something out.

Maybe.

Rowena couldn't count on any more than that: a gut feeling that Topaz Rossi would fight as hard for her slice of American Magazines as she would for Musica. It wasn't an ideal set of circumstances.

Two rivals who'd been publicly scrapping for years.

Two women only recently promoted to the tops of their respective trees.

Two executives with just a heartbeat's really senior experience between them.

They might both be past thirty but in financial terms they were still kids. Green, wet behind the ears, whatever. No knowledge of investment banking. Diehard specialists in their own industries.

Creatives, for God's sake. In a situation like this, that was a dirty word.

Topaz stepped carefully out of the cab, tipped the guy ten bucks and sat down at the first table she could see. She'd deliberately arrived early; being there when Gordon arrived was just one more way of establishing primacy.

Weird, Topaz thought. I could have sworn Rowena was expecting that call.

But how could she?

Unless she was thinking the same thing. Unless she was planning to call me.

Topaz ordered a Caesar salad and fresh orange juice and considered American's position. Sales were up, profits were up, market share was up. Under her personal scheme for the East Coast, they'd closed down three poor performers, including *White Light*, totally revamped a fourth – *US Woman*, now second only to *Homes and Gardens* in its market – taken *Westside* national and, of course, launched *Impact* – the debut of the decade, the reason Matt Gowers let her get away with so much.

She shook her head, wooden bead earrings swinging in the light breeze. *No way Mansion House can outmanage us. This board knows exactly what it's doing.*

Santa Maria, she hated having to do this, *hated* it! As if twins and a takeover wasn't enough! Now she had to arrange meetings with Rowena Gordon, too. A woman whose career she, Topaz, had personally blown away.

That had made them quits. She'd hoped that was an end of it. Yeah, of course she'd read about some consultancy in California, and of course she'd seen Rowena make president of Musica last month. But it hadn't mattered to her, why should it? Rowena had got hers, and if she'd managed another resurrection more power to her. Topaz had other things to occupy her mind: marriage, the new directorship, the pregnancy, the takeover . . .

Past history. It had an annoying way of refusing to stay past.

With a slight intake of breath, she saw her old rival walking down the street towards her. Topaz waved; a short, tight movement, enough to show Rowena where she was. The other woman saw her and threaded her way through the wooden tables.

Christ! Rowena thought. Look at that!

Envy flashed through her. Topaz was hugely pregnant, beautiful in a plain black maternity smock that reached down to her ankles and bared her toned, tanned upper arms. She had her mass of red curls elegantly pinned on top of her head, sexy earrings dangling round her neck and a radiant complexion. As she shook hands briskly Rowena saw the two rings, engagement and wedding, glint on Topaz's left hand. She flashed back to that handsome NBC exec, standing with his arm round Topaz at the Martins' party, and the sense of her own loneliness was crushing.

No time for that now, Rowena told herself.

'I'm glad you came. I think American and Musica can be of use to each other,' Topaz said briskly.

'I agree,' Rowena said instantly.

For a second the two women looked at each other, and a thousand questions, remarks, accusations hung in the air.

Rowena Gordon looked away first. Obviously it would be best if their business could be conducted without personal remarks of any kind, but Topaz was so magnificently, unignorably pregnant that she just had to say something.

She nodded at Topaz's swollen stomach. 'Congratulations. When is it due?'

'Two months. Twins,' she replied coldly, acknowledging Rowena's comment with the briefest inclination of the head.

'What do you think we can do about this?' Rowena asked, beckoning a waiter over. 'The chicken salad and a glass of white wine, please. My guess is that we have roughly three weeks to put something together before our lawyers get thrown out of court.'

Topaz nodded. 'We're in the same position.' She gave Rowena a hard look, as if assessing something, and then said, 'I have a different take on Mansion to some of my colleagues.'

Rowena smiled. 'Me too. Like you believe surrender isn't the only option?'

'Exactly like that.'

'OK.' Rowena ticked off the possibilities on her fingers. 'Off the top of my head: we could merge; we could form a loose holding company for the purposes of this takeover, and buy enough communications companies to stop him buying us, because he's a foreigner –'

Like you, limey, Topaz thought but didn't say so.

'– or we could do something like pooling our capital and implementing a stock repurchase.' She speared a forkful of crunchy lettuce and croutons.

'Merger doesn't make much sense. We've got nothing in common.'

'We've got Connor Miles in common,' Rowena answered rather sharply.

'You will never sell a merger to your board, Rowena, and I know I won't. Trust me on this. But financial partnership makes more sense.'

'You've got something in mind,' said Rowena.

It wasn't a question, it was a statement. She knew that look on Rossi's face only too well – the exact same look she'd had as a student when she was about to nail some poor sonofabitch to the wall in *Cherwell*.

'Ever heard of the Pac-man defence?' Topaz asked shrewdly.

Rowena's wine glass halted in mid-air. 'You are fucking kidding,' she said slowly.

Of *course* she knew what the Pac-man defence was – the prey turns round and swallows the predator. It had happened a few times in the billion-dollar-deal explosion of '81 and more often in the takeover frenzy that had gripped Wall Street in the heady madness of the Reagan boom.

Take Mansion Industries over?

'I'm not kidding. We don't have time for jokes,' Topaz said impatiently. 'I think it could be done. They're getting greedy, they haven't thought this one through. Entertainment might be a growth sector but they're rushing into it; we're two big organizations.'

'And you think they've been neglecting their other businesses?' Rowena asked, food and drink completely forgotten.

My God. What if it is possible? What if we could pull that off?

'Totally. This will be a disaster for them. Like Sony and Columbia Pictures; they reckoned they knew how to run *any* industry, but films is too human, it has too many variables. Just like magazines,' Topaz replied.

'Numbers. Financing. Secrecy,' Rowena interrupted, her green eyes alight. 'How can we do this and contain it in the time?'

'Maughan Macaskill are our investment bankers –'

'Goddamn it, I've been trying to hire them.'

'I know,' said Topaz, with a slight smile. 'They have a specialist analyst who's been following Mansion for years. He thinks he can put together a proposal for breaking it down and selling it off that would make all the buyers rich. If we banded together to buy it and provided cash and equity, a number of buyout firms would come in with bonds –'

'Junk bonds?'

'It's not like it used to be, OK,' Topaz said. 'They'd be providing debt. But we'd obviously need to work out the numbers very, very carefully.'

'I'd have to sell it to Joshua Oberman, our CEO. And you'd need to sell it to your board.'

Topaz shook her head. 'Our chairman Matthew Gowers has absolute control, but I would need to sell it to him.'

The two women held each other's eyes for a long moment.

'Are you in?' Topaz demanded.

Rowena nodded. 'I'm in,' she said.

'. . . and now we have the fourth top ten smash from *Zenith*, another Atomic album that just can't be stopped! This is "Sweet Savage", right here on K –'

John Metcalf flicked off the radio and spun his Maserati up Sunset. Jesus, he thought. I can't stand to hear that fucking band.

He was as mad as hell. He couldn't believe it. His fiancée had woken him up this morning to tell him she'd be stuck in New York for the next three weeks. *Three weeks!*

'Rowena, this is getting ridiculous,' he snapped. 'We had an agreement and it involved you coming down here on Friday nights.'

'I know, I know,' she pleaded. 'But this is the last time. Either it works or it doesn't, but I'll need this time –'

'For *what? For what*? Mansion's damn takeover? Can't you see it's a lost cause? Ask a fucking banker, for Christ's sake!'

'John. You can come up here –'

'You run the company on your own, Supergirl? Uh? What about your division heads and your board and your boss? Can't they help? Musica has you Monday through Friday day and night! Since when does it need your weekends too?' he yelled, pushing his hand through his hair.

She hung up on him.

She fucking hung up on me! Metcalf thought, incensed. My own wife! Or at least about to be my own wife. I don't *need* this shit. I don't need to be fighting about work every damn day of the week!

Was it going to be like this for the rest of his life?

Unlike just about any other man in LA in his position, John Metcalf was a feminist. He always had been; it was no big deal, it seemed natural to him. He believed in the free market and that meant giving everyone a fair break . . . there was no racism or sexism at Metropolis, because top management thought it was bad business.

He'd found Rowena Gordon totally attractive from the first moment he saw her and a big part of that was due to her hunger, her ambition. She was himself reflected. Metcalf saw himself in a skirt – whizz-kid, kick-ass little maverick carving out an empire in a tiny outpost of a big company. Hadn't he done the same thing? When he'd been assigned to Metropolis, it was making thirty-second commercials for dog foods. He'd started with one shoestring picture and built the first movie studio to qualify as a major since Orion. No wonder Cage Entertainment had been pleased with him. No wonder he was the youngest baby mogul to hit town.

But ambition was one thing. Obsession was another. What kind of workaholic put her life on hold?

Metcalf pressed his foot on the gas. He was getting frustrated. He couldn't stop thinking about her. About that lithe, naked body leaping in his arms. About her long, feathery hair brushing his cock. About the way she moaned deep in the back of her throat when she was getting close to orgasm.

Jesus Christ!

There had been that new girl at Jack's party last week. The compliant little brunette, stacked, tanned and stupid. A *Playboy* fantasy in the flesh.

The kind of girl he'd always steered clear of.
He wondered if he still had her number.

'Really?' asked Matt Gowers.

'Yes,' said Topaz, intently.

She was sitting in the chairman's office and it was
nine at night; the only time he'd had available all day.
Normal defence work had started at 7 a.m. with a review
of their legal position, broken at lunch for half an hour,
and carried right through till half-eight. Topaz had been
hunched over her computer till her eyes ached and she
hated it. Maths was never her strong suit.

Still, she couldn't complain. As the hours wore on,
the facts became clearer. Costs had been squeezed as
tight as possible without hurting the papers; after her
own revamp of the East Coast, Harvey had followed suit
in LA.

'I can't get one extra dime out of these, and Mansion
couldn't either,' Damian Hart asserted, and the bankers
seemed to agree.

Topaz had also managed to talk a little more to Gerald
Quin about their own idea. 'Are we totally leftfield with
this?' she'd asked quietly.

The young man shook his head. 'Nothing's leftfield if
it can be done.'

So she'd summoned up her courage and asked to speak
to Gowers alone after work; if I can ring up Rowena
Gordon I can go pitch my own supervisor, she told herself.

Outside his thick glass walls Manhattan was a carpet
of electric light, sparkling and moving; the cars seemed
to race faster, the skyscrapers to jab higher, pounding
along with her heartbeat. What if he thought she was
way off-base? What if he thought she was blinded by
personal ambition? That she was a hysterical pregnant
woman?

But Gowers hadn't thrown her out. He was listening.

'Gerald Quin has been analysing this company for years and he swears the deal finances itself,' Topaz insisted. 'Look, boss. If Connor Miles gets hold of this company we're all history.'

'We've got a duty to the stockholders,' the older man warned her.

'I realize that,' Topaz replied, trying to cool her impatience. 'But our duty is long-term, right? For all the stock might rise fifteen per cent from a takeover bid it'll have fallen thirty per cent when he publishes his first set of results.'

She leant forward, the edge of her stomach resting against Gowers' mahogany desk. 'Matt, you wanna retire?' she asked softly. 'Because there aren't that many spots open for unemployed CEOs at the other big magazine houses.'

Matthew Gowers looked down at the breakdown of Mansion Industries she'd put on his desk.

'All right, let's do it,' he said. 'And Rossi – *keep it quiet*.'

Rowena Gordon spent a couple of hours wondering how to broach the subject, then called Josh Oberman at home.

'Gordon, know what the time is?' Oberman snapped. 'This better be good. Found me an investment bank?'

'Topaz Rossi at American Magazines called me,' Rowena said. 'She wants to form a consortium with us, get some debt backing and take over Mansion Industries. They already hired Maughan Macaskill and there's a guy there, a specialist in conglomerates, who knows Mansion backwards. He reckons we'd have a good chance of doing it.'

There was a pause.

'Let me get this right,' Oberman repeated. 'Musica

Records and American Magazines team up and buy out Connor Miles. In a hostile deal.'

'You got it,' said Rowena.

Oberman cackled, a great rasping laugh sputtering across the Atlantic.

'Gordon, you are one insane girl. But why the fuck not? I've got nothing better to do.'

'Are you serious?' Rowena demanded.

'If you are,' he said, his tone suddenly changing. 'And you *are* serious, Rowena, right?'

'Yes, sir. It's difficult but not impossible and it's the only chance we have.'

'Then we'll try it. I'm old, but I'm not dead,' Oberman said. 'And Rowena – I don't want the executive committee involved.'

Gerry Quin was running on high octane.

He wanted this deal so bad he could taste it. A win fee would net millions for Maughan Macaskill.

More to the point, it would make his reputation. Forget Kravis. Forget Wasserstein. He, Quin, would be Wall Street's new boy wonder – David slaying the mighty Goliath of Mansion Industries. It was the deal of the century and owing to one stupid, overconfident mistake – thinking he could have American and Musica at the same time – Connor Miles had set him up for it.

Practically an engraved invitation.

American and Musica. Big corporations, but not big enough to stand up to the conglomerate. Companies who'd only recently reshuffled their boards. Executives ready to try anything to hang on to their first taste of real power.

They were cornered.

They were desperate.

They would fight.

Nick Edward and he drew up a quick fee agreement and advised on the deal team. It had to be kept from as many people as possible; surprise was going to be key. Topaz Rossi offered the use of her house on Beekman Place, and they arranged to meet there on Friday morning at 7 a.m.

From American Magazines, Gowers took Rossi, Harvey Smith, Damian Hart and Eli Leber. From Musica, Joshua Oberman took Rowena Gordon and James Harton, the company lawyer. He also invited, at Gerry's suggestion, the producer Michael Krebs, who worked on most of Musica's star acts, and finally Barbara Lincoln, the manager of Atomic Mass.

Both these last two would be needed for public relations purposes – if he could threaten the stockholders with a talent walkout if Mansion got hold of Musica, that would be effective. Anyway, Oberman told the bankers that Barbara Lincoln was a trained entertainment lawyer and had run his Business Affairs and Legal Department for years.

'Woman's forgotten more about our contracts than I ever knew,' he said gruffly.

They'd start work tomorrow morning.

Gerry Quin could hardly wait.

It was only seven in the morning, and limos were piling up along the tree-lined street. If anybody noticed anything, though, they weren't about to say. In this part of town, most of the neighbours would die rather than admit to curiosity about a thing like that.

Topaz was ready for them.

'We have to do this, right?' Joe had asked weakly the night before, lugging in armfuls of frozen pizzas and a case of mixed Häagen-Dazs.

'Right,' Topaz answered, hardly looking up from her figures. 'You're not going to try and stop me, baby, are you? Because that would be bad for my blood pressure.' She patted her stomach gently.

'No, no, you do what you want,' said Goldstein hastily, recoiling from the threat.

Topaz smiled to herself. Who'd ever believe she'd resort to feminine wiles?

Joe had the last laugh, though. When their alarm rang at six on Friday he got up, showered as normal, and wandered off to dress.

'What are you wearing?' his wife asked, propping herself up on one elbow and sleepily pushing away a mass of crimson curls.

Her husband was pulling a Mets T-shirt over black Levi's and his favourite pair of beat-up sneakers. 'What does it look like?' he asked.

'It's *Friday*.'

'It is,' Joe agreed amiably, 'and I'm staying here with you. I've taken the day off.'

'You've done *what*! You can't do that!' Topaz protested. 'Everyone'll be here in forty minutes.'

'Try and stop me. There's no way I'm letting you run this one on your own,' he said, grinning. 'Anyway, you seem to forget that I do know a little about American Magazines.'

'No outsiders,' Topaz objected feebly.

'I'm not an outsider. I'm your husband,' Joe said, coming back to the bed and pressing her head to him in a leisurely kiss.

Matt Gowers was the first to arrive and Barbara Lincoln – resplendent in the smoothest cream cashmere by Nicole Farhi – the last, but by seven fifteen everyone had assembled. Introductions were brisk and unsociable, Joe poured out coffee, and they started right in.

'Partners,' Joshua Oberman began. 'What are the possibilities?'

Instant pandemonium. The bankers and the lawyers all started talking at once. Topaz started flicking on various computers brought over from the office, and Matthew Gowers and Josh Oberman veered off on a tangent, discussing debt ratios between themselves.

Michael glanced over at Rowena. It was Josh Oberman who'd insisted he be here, and Krebs had sensed her effort not to look at him as soon as he'd walked through the door. Her handshake and her greeting had been as dry as dust. She'd been about that cordial to Topaz Rossi.

What a weird atmosphere, Michael thought, scoping the room. All these people with nothing in common, except this deal. The lawyers – and Barbara, holy shit, I never saw that girl as a lawyer – sniping at each other. The merchant bankers doing figures with the finance guys. The CEOs obviously at the start of a beautiful friendship.

And Rowena with Ms Rossi.

'Interesting, isn't it?'

Krebs looked up to see Joe Goldstein standing in front of him with a mug of black coffee.

'Thanks,' he said. 'I'm Michael Krebs. I produce records for Josh Oberman.'

Joe nodded. 'Atomic Mass, Roxana, Black Ice. And you did *The Salute* by Three Legions. Right?'

'That's right,' said Michael, surprised. *The Salute* had been his first really big hit, out on CBS more than fifteen years ago. 'You're well informed.'

'It pays,' Joe said, shrugging.

Both men watched Rowena and Topaz. They were deep in discussion with Harvey Smith about something, but their body language ignored Smith completely. Rowena's eyes kept sliding across to Topaz while her colleague was talking. When Rowena turned to Harvey, they saw Topaz shift on her seat, watching the other woman intently.

'Yeah, it is interesting,' Krebs agreed.

'You know Rowena Gordon well?' Joe asked.

He couldn't suppress a smile. 'For years.'

'What's she like?' Goldstein asked, surprised at his own curiosity. After he'd met Rowena at Liz Martin's party he'd hated her guts. Stuck-up English bitch! No wonder she'd given his baby a rejection complex, she was as cold as liquid hydrogen. But Topaz had torpedoed her career in retaliation and when she told him she'd called Rowena about Mansion, Goldstein had been stunned that the woman even agreed to a meeting.

And now here they were, in his house, in partnership. Business is business, but still . . . there was something strange about it.

'She's intense,' Michael said, and Joe watched a strange expression come over his face.

Check it out! This guy is her lover! he realized, in a sudden flash of insight. But Rowena Gordon was in the middle of the media romance of the year! Wasn't she?

'What's Topaz Rossi like?' Krebs was asking him, equally curious.

'She's intense,' Joe replied, and they exchanged glances.

'Have you got croissants cooking through there?'

'Uh-huh. Let's go eat.'

It was impossible to remain brisk and businesslike when you were working eighteen-hour days. Something they all discovered over the first weekend, when the place was covered with empty pizza cartons and beer cans, and

Matt Gowers was discovered with Josh Oberman cracking up to *Beavis and Butt-head* on the kitchen TV.

Edward had his Quotron terminal delivered to the house and hooked up. Harvey Smith started to take meetings by conference call in a spare bedroom. Rowena called Sam Neil and asked him to take over for a week. Josh and Matt worked by fax.

'There's a kind of sick pleasure in pushing yourself this hard,' Topaz remarked at eleven thirty one evening, as Goldstein's PowerMacintosh ran off yet another colour chart for Freyja Timber.

'Yeah. It's like Mods. Remember that? A huge pile of books, a huge pot of coffee and three packs of Pro-Plus,' Rowena said to her.

There was a second's complete silence.

'Let's get another pizza. I'm starving,' Eli Leber butted in hastily.

Then there was the time that Joe had been mixing Bloody Marys and Topaz said automatically, 'Rowena likes a lot of Worcester sauce, sweetheart.'

'You haven't changed at all, you know that?' Rowena told Topaz one night when she was tapping away at the IBM. 'You always used to crouch like that. Exactly like that.'

'That's right. And you always bugged the hell out of me by reading over my shoulder. The way you are right now,' Topaz replied, and they actually laughed.

'You know, I think this deal might work. Did you hear that Steel, Roven bought in?'

'For an equity stake, too. Not just debt,' Topaz agreed.

'What sex are your children going to be?' Rowena asked suddenly.

'No idea,' Topaz replied, looking round. 'Why?'

'Nothing,' Rowena said, and wondered why she was so close to tears.

*

Once the final break-up analysis had been completed, Gerald Quin pushed away his charts with an exhausted sigh.

'The numbers work,' he said. 'We need to find three billion dollars.'

There was an awed hush as the deal team tried to get their heads round that amount of money.

'Great,' Damian Hart said, with perfect deadpan humour. 'Now for the good part.'

Chapter Thirty-Six

It wasn't quite that simple.

Maughan Macaskill, the lawyers and the two chief executives finally had some numbers worked out and an idea of who might want to come in with them. They still had to hammer out a million little variables – tax problems, ownership regulations, SECC disclosures – and they also needed a creative plan that would sell Wall Street on the idea that Mansion House couldn't be trusted. Only Musica management could run Musica. Only the present board could run American Magazines.

'We have to split the team,' Gowers said wearily at half-eleven that night. 'There's just no other way to get this done in time.'

Oberman nodded. 'Rowena, you and Michael should put some kind of document together for Musica. I don't know who American want . . .'

'Topaz Rossi,' Gowers said instantly. 'Harvey Smith. Damian should work with us.'

'Am I needed?' Smith asked, annoyed. He wanted to be in the real action. 'LA can send up all the data through here by fax and I know some guys at RJR Nabisco we should pitch Natural Foods to.'

'Topaz?' Gowers asked.

'Fine,' she shrugged, seeing her colleagues' eyes upon

her. *Why don't you just say it? No way is she professional enough to work with Rowena Gordon?* 'It's no problem,' Topaz added, her face set in a mask of perfect indifference.

'Rowena, is that OK for you?' Oberman asked his president. 'We really only have a few days on this.'

'Absolutely,' Rowena confirmed.

Oh, bloody marvellous. Michael Krebs and Topaz Rossi. Just the two people I really want to be close to at the moment.

'So that's settled,' Eli Leber said, his eyes sweeping the room cautiously. Rossi and Gordon both looked as uptight as Tipper Gore at a strippers' conference, Gowers and Oberman were watching them with slightly nervous expressions, and the only person that seemed totally at his ease was Michael Krebs.

'That's settled,' Krebs agreed, smiling.

Musica Towers was electric with rumours.

Rowena Gordon could feel it in the air every day when she walked through the doors, striding through the marble lobby where she'd been served her termination notice, walking up the stairs to a marketing meeting, dropping in on a sales presentation . . . as soon as she appeared, staff ceased talking, studied their shoes or picked up the nearest phone.

Not that it was easy to tell. With Roxana's *Race Game* crashing to the *Billboard* Hot 100 at number one and the next Black Ice album due in a week, the entire building was frying ice in the rush. Sam Neil had been running the place for the year of her exile and he was in total control of the organized madness; suppliers were getting served, campaigns were being run, tours were being supported – so what if the new C.O.O. wasn't in her office all the time? What was there to talk about?

Plenty, Rowena thought furiously. Evidently.

'Sam, what's going on?' she demanded. 'I can't walk

in on a meeting without feeling like the elephant woman. I'm the class freak here. What's the score?'

Neil loosened his collar, sweating slightly, and looked his boss over with a wary eye. Rowena Gordon mad would give a charging rhino pause, even without those short black suits she'd taken to wearing – little Richard Tyler skirts in snug wool, DKNY fitted tops, her long blonde hair swept back in a schoolgirl's ponytail. That was Rowena's idea of dressing down. It was Sam's idea of a heart attack.

'Nothing's going on,' her division president replied, cautiously. 'Maybe some people are a little curious about you, that's all.'

Rowena fixed him with a steely glare.

'OK, OK,' he added hastily, 'I guess – uh – it's just that you haven't actually been around much since you took over, and, uh, the staff are wondering why not.'

'Go on,' she said.

Sam Neil felt himself start to sweat uncomfortably. Hell, he'd taken great trouble not to show even a flicker of curiosity. If the new head of the company didn't want to show up in the office, his not to reason why. But he suddenly had the sense that he was on very thin ground indeed.

'I guess they're wondering what you and Josh and Krebs are working on,' he finished lamely.

Rowena nodded. 'I see,' she said. 'What you're trying to tell me, Sam, is that the whole building wants to know if we're off devising some kind of secret buyout defence against Mansion Industries?'

'Yeah,' said Neil, squirming slightly.

'Is the whole company talking about this, Sam?'

He shrugged. 'I don't know, Rowena, I mean, I don't have that much contact with the junior staff . . . OK, all right, I suppose they are.'

Rowena pushed a wisp of blonde hair away from her forehead, feeling the tension crunch round her skull like a vice. She simply couldn't let this happen. If the staff in the New York office started to gossip about it, it was only a matter of time before her absence leaked to the trades. And if the same thing was going on over at American Magazines, it would take just one business reporter to put two and two together, and weeks of patient work would be blown sky-high.

The whole deal depended on secrecy.

She had to get back to her office, and she had to come up with the creative plan.

There was only one thing for it . . .

'Well, they can lay that one to rest,' she said firmly. 'Our legal defences are in place, you know that. I'll be back in the building from today . . . we just had some problems to do with the new Atomic Mass record, and you know Barbara and Krebs will only deal with Josh and myself on stuff like that.'

'Do you want me to tell people that?' Sam Neil asked, surprised. Atomic Mass were the Holy Grail around Musica Records. Even to *imagine* a problem with them was blasphemy.

'Sure,' his president said, expansively. 'We have no secrets at Musica Records.'

'OK,' Sam said, leaving her office with some relief.

Rowena Gordon watched him go. Then she picked up her phone and dialled Topaz Rossi's private line.

'Topaz, we have another problem,' she said.

American Magazines was just as busy and the rumours were just as wild. In fact they were worse. After all, investigation and exposure was what everybody in the building did for a living.

Topaz found that out the first day she came back to

work. Sauntering into the *Impact* offices and feeling twelve pairs of eyes crawling over the nape of her neck. Dropping in on *Girlfriend* to find herself as out of place as a high-school teacher at a slumber party.

'It's what I'd expect,' Joe told her when she rang up to complain. 'At least over at Musica only the chairman and the president took off. You guys had half the board playing hookey. Of course they're talking.'

'But we can't let everybody gossip about this! It'll leak!' Topaz protested.

'Which is why you're all back in the office, honey,' Joe pointed out.

'I can't stay in the office! When am I gonna work on the creative plan? I have to present Rowena Gordon with something in the next few days!'

'I don't know,' Goldstein said as calmly as he could. *Jesus Christ, she's eight months pregnant!* 'Just try not to stress yourself out, sweetheart. If I were you I'd talk to Rowena. It would be dangerous to be away from the office now.'

'OK, OK,' his wife soothed him. *Try not to stress myself out? That's real funny.*

'Topaz, Rowena Gordon is on the line,' her assistant said.

'Joe, I have to go,' she told him. 'I'll call you later.'

Christ Almighty, Topaz thought, glancing down at the frantic rush of lunchtime traffic pouring along Seventh Avenue, sixty storeys below her. Compared with her own life, it seemed as calm as a monastic retreat. She hoped that bitch Rowena Gordon was taking at least a little of the same heat.

'This is me,' she snapped.

'Topaz, we have another problem,' Rowena said coldly, trying to hide her panic. 'I don't think I can get away from my building. The staff here are beginning to talk.'

479

'Me either,' her rival replied. 'And we just can't risk it getting out.'

'Nobody can do a creative plan for Musica Records but me,' Rowena said flatly. It wasn't a boast, it was a statement of fact. She knew that it was her ideas about the kind of acts they should go for, her take on marketing and distribution, and her plans for buying smaller labels that made Josh Oberman give her her job back in the first place.

'Yeah. I'm sure that's true,' Topaz said, forgetting to be icy. 'I feel the same way about American. You know? Joe thinks I should delegate this plan, but I just can't do it – it's not about the nuts and bolts of the business, it's about –'

'Vision?' Rowena suggested.

'Exactly,' the other woman said.

'So what do we do?' Rowena asked. 'We have to get this done –'

'– and we can't do it in our offices because we have to go back in to all the meetings –'

There was a pause.

'So I guess we're gonna have to work together at nights and over the weekend,' Rowena said eventually. 'We could do it separately, but then how would we check with each other over wording, the general lines of the document . . .'

'Come round at nine,' Topaz said shortly.

So it was the only way. Well, she had to do it. But she didn't have to like it.

'And Michael Krebs?' Rowena forced herself to ask.

'If your Mr Oberman thinks you need him, bring him along too,' Topaz replied.

There was another moment's awkward silence, and then both women hung up, without further pleasantries.

*

Michael Krebs drove his black Ferrari Testarossa up to the Musica Towers executive car park and was instantly waved in by the guard. It was an early summer evening and Krebs was enjoying everything about it. The way the golden light fell over the trees and the sidewalks. The way the Tom Petty CD sounded in his top-of-the-range in-car system. The way Rowena Gordon had sounded to him on the phone.

'Michael? It's Rowena.'

'I know who it is,' Krebs had said dryly.

'There's been a change of plan,' she went on nervously, obviously trying to get off the phone as soon as she could. 'We have to meet tonight, not this afternoon. Can you be at Beekman Place at nine?'

'I don't know. What's in it for me?'

'Michael, for Christ's sake!'

'I have some ideas I want to discuss with you,' Krebs said, oblivious. 'If we have to be there at nine, I'll pick you up at eight.'

'OK,' Rowena said, tensely.

Krebs smiled. He knew every intonation of Rowena Gordon's voice, knew it like his own. So she'd wanted to object, but she couldn't – couldn't admit that she didn't want to be alone with him.

She wants to be all business, but she's as scared as hell.

He was looking forward to this.

Rowena had just sent her assistant home when Michael arrived.

She'd spent the last two hours trying to reach John Metcalf in LA and getting the brush-off from his assistant.

'The president's in a meeting, ma'am.'

'Yes, ma'am, I know who you are.'

'Yes, ma'am, I gave him *all* your messages.'

'Uh, he went straight into a new meeting, Ms Gordon. Yes, ma'am, I know, but we're extremely busy . . .'

'Well, thanks for your help,' Rowena said as Michael walked in, replacing the receiver with a bang.

Krebs took in her lean, elegant silhouette against the windows, the last light of day catching her blonde hair so it shimmered and gleamed, her tight black outfit hugging every slender curve and her long legs seeming to stretch down for ever in sheer black pantyhose.

He felt an instant twitch of lust. 'Who were you calling?'

'Oh, nobody special,' she said defensively.

'Was that your fiancé?'

'No,' said Rowena, blushing. She grew angrier with John. Why did he have to be so childish about her staying in New York for a few weeks? Now she was embarrassed in front of Michael Krebs. The last guy in the world she wanted to know about her relationship problems.

'Well, I guess that is nobody special,' Krebs commented shrewdly, giving her an infuriatingly knowing grin.

'Do you want to work this through here, or should we go over to Mirror, Mirror?' Rowena asked, determinedly ignoring him.

'Nether. I've booked us a table at LeCirque,' he told her, 'and don't look like that, Rowena, if we're gonna work all night I have to eat first.'

Rowena glanced at him, wanting to object but not daring to. If it was anybody else, of course they'd need dinner before working all night . . .

But it wasn't anybody else. It was Michael Krebs.

'Are you coming, or what?' he demanded, turning to go. His expression was one of complete indifference.

Pull yourself together, Rowena, she told herself severely, and grabbed her sheaf of notes and contracts.

'I'm right behind you,' she said.

They drove uptown through the twilight, talking business, watching each other. Rowena leant back against the supple leather of her seat and tried to listen to what Krebs was suggesting: buying a couple of hardcore labels, trimming the European roster, expanding the licensing division. She needed to concentrate. This stuff was important. And yet she just couldn't stop watching the way his mouth moved when he spoke, the way his large hands gripped the wheel, the sexy grey hair at the side of his head. She didn't want him to come on to her, but she was somehow resentful that he was being so goddamn professional . . . why didn't he push her like he used to? Has he given up on me? Rowena wondered, instantly ashamed to find herself dismayed at the thought.

Krebs stared at the traffic ahead of him, seeing Rowena out of the corner of his eye, talking on autopilot. This deal was Josh and Rowena's future, and he'd done a lot of work on it; besides, personally, professionally, it would be catastrophic for him to have Mansion House take Musica over. Krebs had his own proposals off by heart, which meant he could reel them off to Rowena without thinking. Leaving his mind free to consider those schoolgirl panty-hose. The clinging cut of her dress. The way her slim little body curled round in her seat. Jesus, but the way she moved drove him crazy. He remembered the tiny catlike curl she'd done on that studio chair in London, the night they'd first had sex.

I want you, I want you, Rowena thought fiercely.

She's so far under my skin, Krebs thought, heady with a sudden urge to just pull over and reach for her. He fought back the impulse and kept talking, but he was enraged. Rowena Gordon was his! She had always been his! Who was this little kid John Metcalf? Some jerk-off Angeleno who knew absolutely nothing about music, absolutely nothing about what fired Rowena's passions . . .

At the elegant restaurant on East 65th they were ushered to a secluded table, and Michael ordered champagne.

'Le Cirque is my favourite, these days,' Rowena said to him, searching for some safe ground for small talk. In the cool shadows and soft lights she felt Krebs's presence as a real threat. He'd put on a dark jacket and tie to eat here, something he never wore; it amplified his natural air of power. His charcoal eyes, fringed with those jet-black lashes, looked into hers with an easygoing interest that maddened her.

She wanted him to leave her alone.

She wanted him to forget her.

She wanted him to just be her friend.

Yeah, right.

'It's got the best diet menu in Manhattan,' she added hastily, suddenly aware that she'd been staring at him. 'I'm past thirty. I have to watch my weight.'

'Don't be ridiculous. You're perfect as you are,' Michael said, watching her drop her gaze. 'And what is this past-thirty bullshit? You're just a child, Gordon.'

Rowena laughed, and the long sweep of her hair caught the candlelight. He felt his left hand clench under the tablecloth.

'I'll always be a child to you, Michael.'

'You're a lot of things to me,' he said softly, 'but a child isn't one of them.'

He stared at her, and Rowena sensed the deep, familiar well of heat starting to pulse in her groin. Under the taut fabric of her sweater, quite noticeably her nipples tightened, swelling with blood. Lust strong enough to match his own started to trawl across her skin, digging little teasing hooks of pleasure into her groin. She felt a wave of panic, aware that her desire for him was written in bright letters across her face.

'I'm going to have you again,' Krebs said quietly, never taking his eyes from her. 'It's what you want and it's what I want.'

'No it's not,' Rowena answered sharply, reaching blindly for her wine glass. Michael lunged across the table and caught her hand in his, gripping it, his fingers pushing against the soft flesh at the base of the thumb.

His touch was like flicking on a switch. Rowena's stomach dissolved in longing and she flooded with wetness. Involuntarily she gave a little shudder of need, her whole body shaking on the chair.

'Isn't it?' Krebs insisted.

'Are you ready to order?' enquired a waiter politely.

Krebs felt the moment shatter and glared at the poor man with a look that could have melted steel.

'Thank you, yes. I'd like the monkfish with sorrel leaves,' Rowena said hastily, pressing her hot palm against the glittering coolness of her engagement ring.

She discussed contracts briskly for the entire rest of the meal.

They drew up at Beekman Place at nine exactly. Topaz Rossi let them in, elegant in an empire-waisted dress of dark blue velvet that cut off just below the knee, flowing over her round stomach and contrasting beautifully with her red curls, shiny and lustrous from her pregnancy.

'You look terrific,' Rowena told her, forgetting her reserve of that morning. 'That dress really picks out your eyes.'

'You think so? I hate it,' Topaz said. 'I hate everything in my wardrobe at the moment though. I can't find one thing that will make me look less fat.'

'Oh, you don't look fat, you look pregnant,' Rowena protested. 'Look at your arms and legs, Topaz. Look at your chin.'

'Hello, Michael,' Joe Goldstein said, appearing behind his wife. He put a protective hand on her shoulder and added somewhat coldly, 'Hi, Rowena.'

'Hey, Goldstein,' Krebs answered, feeling the renewed chill settle between the two women. Not that he would ever understand their relationship; he still remembered the unusual venom that had crept into Rowena's voice when she talked about Topaz; he could hardly forget all the barbs this cute-looking redhead had thrown at them, the sniping at Atomic Mass when they were just starting out, the way she'd blown out the Madison Square Gardens launch of *Heat Street*, the way she'd taken Velocity from under Rowena's nose, and the final damning *Westside* cover story that finished Rowena Gordon's meteoric career off in one fell swoop. And on their side? Joe Hunter publicly embarrassing Rossi on *Oprah*, closing *White Light* down with a few phonecalls, and the inexorable rise of Rowena and her band, right up until that final blow.

There has to be more to it than that, Krebs thought, watching Topaz Rossi's back as she led them through to the office. I know they had a history . . . it's like they know each other backwards. Half of the time they would act like sisters, fixing each other's coffee without asking how they took it, finishing off each other's sentences, complaining about the traffic. Then they would catch themselves doing it, and suddenly, instantly, snap back into the two bitter rivals who'd been forced to do business together.

But she keeps glancing over at Goldstein, keeps looking around the house, Michael thought, interested. It's like she's incredibly curious but doesn't want to show it . . . and Topaz, too, that girl's always checking me out, always striking up conversations with Oberman . . .

Of course, over the last few weeks there'd been a crowd of people around them. Now they were practically on their own.

Krebs grinned as he pulled the Atomic Mass contract out of his briefcase. This was going to be hard work, but it might be fun to watch.

Topaz shook her head, trying to clear the fumes of exhaustion and fatigue. It was ten to three in the morning, and they were still at work. Despairing of her stubbornness, Joe had long since turned in – he liked to be at NBC before seven – and Michael Krebs, who'd been up until five the night before mixing the latest Black Ice album, had passed out on the sofa.

'Do you want to call it a night?' Rowena asked, seeing her check her watch.

Topaz took another gulp of her industrial-strength coffee and shook her head. 'If we can work through this joint statement about artistic commitment we'll be finished. I'd rather do it that way, I gotta say. I don't want to have to go back to it.'

Rowena nodded. 'We did pretty well. Check this out,' and she reached down to Topaz's laser printer and pulled off thirty sheets of paper. 'Creative planning, sell-offs, the human resource factor –'

'Translation: all my writers and all your bands will be out the door in a heartbeat,' Topaz butted in, grinning.

'Exactly. Plus, detailed expansion plans, distribution details, licensing deals –'

'Translation: we know how to run these babies and Connor Miles knows jack,' added Topaz.

'Plus five-year plans for the core businesses –'

'Translation: if you sell this stock you're as dumb as Dan fucking Quayle,' said Topaz elegantly. 'Hey, Rowena, let's just be straight with this statement. Type this up – The boards of American Magazines and Musica Records –'

'Musica Records and American Magazines,' said Rowena loudly.

'– state that they have complete commitment to all their artistic principles, as long as they're making money –'

'– and if they stop making money, we'll drop them right away –'

'– and if Connor Miles buys us out we're walking –'

'– and everybody's coming with us –'

'– and your shares will be worth one-tenth of what you paid for them –'

'so don't fuck with us!' Rowena finished triumphantly.

The two women collapsed in a fit of laughter, clutching each other for support, then shushing each other as Michael Krebs turned fitfully on the sofa.

'Oh, I'm sorry,' Topaz whispered. 'I shouldn't wake Michael. He was really cool on all that licensing stuff.'

'Yeah,' Rowena agreed, turning her head to look at the producer. Topaz watched her gazing at him, her face suddenly softened and tender.

'What's the deal? You love him?' she asked.

Rowena jumped out of her skin. 'Of course not,' she said instantly. Even in the dull flickering glow of the Mac, the only light in the room, Topaz could see her old rival blushing scarlet. 'Whatever gave you that idea?'

'*Whatever gave you that idea?*' mimicked Topaz quietly.

'Oh please. How long have I known you?'

There was a pause, as the rhetorical question brought it all flooding back.

'A long time,' Rowena replied slowly.

There was another pause. Both women felt their heart-beats speed up a little. Over the course of the deal, and especially tonight, they'd been able to work together because they had to. Because there was no other way. Because they were career girls with their careers at stake.

And the unspoken, unwritten, unbreakable rule was: *Say nothing. Confront nothing. Resolve nothing.*

A temporary truce. No more than that.

And now . . .

Topaz Rossi looked at Rowena Gordon.

'Why did you do it?' she asked softly. 'We were so close.'

Rowena felt as though a fist of mixed emotions was closing around her heart.

'I was young, and dumb, and selfish,' she said eventually. 'I wanted him and he was with you. You were so . . . sexy and outrageous, and I was a virgin . . . it was just another guy rejecting me, I suppose.'

Imperceptibly, Topaz leant forward on her seat.

'And then I started to resent you, because you had him,' Rowena went on, unable to look the other woman in the face, 'and the more I was jealous of you the guiltier I felt, and I kept on wanting him but in reality, I think it was only because you had him.'

'And you were with him alone such a lot,' Topaz said, with the beginnings of understanding.

Rowena nodded. 'So I tried to justify it to myself, when there was no justification . . . I started thinking all these snobby thoughts . . . it was like all the establishment values I'd been hurt by myself I used against you. And I was ashamed of myself, so I focused all that on you. And then you blew me out for the Union Presidency, so I could kid myself that it was all your fault . . . you'd pushed me at him . . . and I hated you, because I just couldn't admit that what I'd actually done was trample all over the first person in the world who had ever cared about me for who I was. I am so, so sorry, Topaz,' Rowena finished weakly. 'I just hope you can forgive me.'

Topaz stared at her for a long moment. Then she broke into a slow smile.

'You know, if you'd said that before it would have saved us both a lot of trouble. All you English guys are such emotional cripples.'

'I'm not English. I'm Scottish,' said Rowena with dignity.

'Same difference.'

'Only a dumb-ass Yank would say something like that.'

They grinned at each other.

'Come on, Goldilocks. Let's put this thing to bed,' Topaz said, 'and you can tell me all about Daddy Bear over there while we're at it.'

Chapter Thirty-Seven

The main conference chambcr of Maughan Macaskill was packed out. Quotron screens had been installed along the length of the walnut table, and there were so many phones and fax machines positioned round the room that it looked like the Starship Enterprise. Nick Edward had also ordered up a couple of wide-screen TVs, so they could watch reactions to this deal as it broke.

The place was thronging with more millionaires than a Hamptons country club: investment bankers, debt financiers, lawyers, industrialists from eight of America and Canada's biggest conglomerates, and representatives from six banks. Twelve storeys below them, CNN reporters and *Journal* photographers were already jockeying for place on the sidewalk. There was a general sense of disbelief – *Barbarians at the Gate* Mark II and everyone had missed it! How in God's name was this bid put together without anybody finding out about it?

'Where the hell is Topaz Rossi? All hell's breaking loose up here and I can't find my fucking director!' Matthew Gowers fumed to Josh Oberman. 'Her assistant's not at her desk, Harvey hasn't seen her since lunch . . . she hasn't left any message with my secretary.'

'Rowena had a meeting with her at three,' the Musica

chairman told him. 'I called her in the car on the way over. They must have left the building together for some reason, because Gordon's not answering her mobile phone. Tammy Limmon told me she cancelled Hans Bauer to go see Michael Krebs, then went straight over to American . . .'

'Yeah, but it's four thirty. They should be here! Where's Rossi's goddamn secretary?' Gowers demanded.

Oberman snorted. The bid was announced now. If Gordon was dumb enough to miss *this* party, that was her problem. 'They've probably got some excuse,' he said.

Matt Gowers looked out of the window at the crowd of business journos below him. He was annoyed; he'd been looking forward to a triumphant photoshoot of himself and Topaz as his nominated successor. Surely it wasn't asking too much for just a *little* glamour at the end of his executive career?

'Well, it better be a good one,' he said darkly.

'*Hurry*,' urged Rowena. 'For Christ's sake! Is this the best we can do?'

'I can't go any faster without breaking the law, ma'am,' the chauffeur said imperturbably.

'Then *break* the fucking law!' she snapped. 'Or do you feel like becoming an instant midwife?'

The guy blenched visibly and pressed his foot to the floor.

'It hurts,' Topaz whimpered, her right hand clutching Rowena's in a pincer-like grip. 'Ohhhh . . .'

Her face twisted with pain as another violent contraction shuddered through her. Rowena watched it in an agony of sympathy. She estimated they were about five minutes apart now.

'You're doing great,' she said, as calmly as she could.

'Hang in there. We'll be at Mt Sinai real soon.'

A quick, pained grin came over Topaz's sweating face. ' "Real soon"? You're becoming an American, Rowena.'

'Am I hell,' she retorted, smiling at the woman in her lap.

'Are so.'

'Am not.'

'Are so. Jesus! *Jesus! Aaah!*'

'It's OK, Topaz. We're nearly there. They have some of the best anaesthetists in the city,' Rowena said, stroking her hair. 'Try and breathe. Don't they teach you to breathe specially, or something?'

'It's bullshit,' Topaz said through gritted teeth.

'It is?' Rowena asked, trying to take her mind off the pain. *Keep her talking, just keep it going . . .*

'Probably. I skipped most of the classes,' Topaz admitted.

'You always did,' Rowena reminded her.

Topaz managed a grimace. 'Like you were such a dutiful student.'

Rowena kept going as Topaz's grip tightened in anguish round her fist. 'Lectures weren't important. The Union was important,' she said. 'I had my priorities right.'

'Oh! *Santa Maria! Aaah, God.*'

'It's OK, sweetheart. It's OK,' Rowena said, watching her stomach convulse with yet another contraction.

God in heaven, she's gonna give birth on the back seat of this car!

'Run every fucking light! Just get us there!' she yelled at the driver.

'Rowena!' Topaz gasped. 'I'm having twins! I'm having two babies!'

'I know, honey,' Rowena said, holding her as tight as she could. 'I know.'

*

Michael Krebs heard the news on his car stereo.

'The Wall Street shock of the hour has to be the surprise hostile bid for the South African conglomerate Mansion Industries, owned by the notorious raider Connor Miles,' the DJ said. 'The bid, announced at four dollars thirty per ordinary share, is the work of a complex consortium of investment banks and firms operating in fields where Mansion has interests. It sets a total value of five billion dollars on the deal. So far, Mr Miles himself has refused to comment, but his board has convened an emergency meeting in Manhattan to consider the offer. In a strange twist to the sage, the two largest players in the consortium appear to be American Magazines and Musica Records, both companies recently thought to be targets of Mansion's drive into the media industry. If this is the case, we could be looking at the biggest Pac-man defence in American financial history.'

Without a word Krebs spun the wheel round, took a left, and headed downtown to Maughan Macaskill.

As with every other big moment in his career for the last nine years, he wanted to be with Rowena when this came through.

Backstage at the Globen Arena in Stockholm, Sweden, the Atomic Mass production office was hyping up for the show; Neil George, the tour accountant, was sitting down with the gate receipts, Jack Halpern, the stage manager, was yelling at a bunch of local crew guys who weren't getting the gear up quick enough, and Will Macleod was striding around looking for his boss. Eventually he found her at the main entrance to the venue, negotiating some extra Scandinavian dates with a desperate promoter.

'Four dollars and thirty cents,' Macleod said.

'I was talking,' the promoter said, pissed off that some great hulking ape was interrupting his urgent pleas to be allowed to schedule even one more gig in the summer break.

'Oh aye?' Macleod replied, with a glare of such ferocity that the promoter physically shrank away from him. 'Well, if we *want* to play a fokkin' giant golfball in July we'll let you know.'

'Will,' reproved Barbara halfheartedly, smoothing down her Norma Kamali pantsuit in an attempt not to laugh. The spherical dome of the Globen did look kind of like a golfball . . . Lord, look at Dolph Lystrom's face.

'Four dollars thirty, Barbara,' Macleod said again. 'Josh Oberman just rang the production office and said to tell you right away.'

She looked at him blankly.

'The *price*. Four dollars thirty,' he repeated. 'He said you'd know what he meant –'

'My God! They've actually done it!' the manager exclaimed. 'Didn't Rowena Gordon call?'

'Done what?' Macleod asked.

'Five-billion-dollar deal – I have to get to a phone,' Barbara said, looking about her wildly. *Had they tendered yet?* 'We have millions riding on this.'

'July eighteenth?' offered the promoter, hopefully.

'I don't care if it's Al Pacino. I'm not taking *any* calls, understand?' John Metcalf barked at his secretary. 'I'm in a meeting and I *cannot be disturbed*. The only person I want to speak to is my fiancée.'

'Yes, sir,' she said hastily, closing the door behind her.

The president of Metropolis Studios stared out of his window at the polished Century City offices gleaming in the LA sun. He was almost lightheaded with anger.

No wonder she had to have those three weeks . . . Mansion

Industries! Five billion dollars! An alliance with American Magazines!

The biggest deal this decade and she tells me nothing!

He recalled with perfect clarity every time he'd sworn at her that there was nothing she could do to save Musica. That resisting Connor Miles was a waste of time.

She must have been laughing her head off. Nothing she could do? They've only blown the guy off the face of the planet . . .

If this buyout came off, John realized with an unpleasant jolt, his wife would be more powerful than he was.

All along he'd encouraged her, been a cheerleader for her, and been happy to have a beautiful woman on his arm who was a success in her own right. But somehow that equation had always included the given fact that he, John Peter Metcalf III, the youngest-ever head of a major studio, would be the really important half of the couple.

What am I gonna be? Trophy husband to a female Rupert Murdoch?

He couldn't even get in contact with her. Rowena's assistant had no idea where she was. Josh Oberman could tell him nothing. And her mobile and car phones were both switched off.

Meanwhile, a hundred calls an hour were coming through to his office from West Coast players who all assumed he knew what the score was.

We're gonna have to talk, Metcalf thought grimly. We are really gonna have to talk . . .

'Any response?' Gowers asked Gerald Quin. The activity level in the dealing room seemed to have gone up several notches; traders were screaming into the phones, the fax machines were spewing paper faster than receipts from a supermarket till, and the Quotron screens were going crazy.

'Very little. Miles is on his way to JFK in his private jet,' the young analyst told him. 'He's saying that he wants time to counter.'

'Does that make a difference?'

'The longer he has to stall, the worse it is for us,' Nick Edward replied.

'We should turn the heat up,' interjected a gravelly voice. Joshua Oberman had wandered over from the end of the room, frustrated at not being able to reach Rowena Gordon. She wasn't answering in her apartment, either. 'We *know* this is a generous price for Mansion. It's only worth it to *us* because everyone in the buying group has space for a piece of them.'

'True,' Eli Leber agreed. 'There's no way any bank would support Miles bidding at that price.'

'So what do you suggest?' Quin enquired, humouring the old goat.

'I suggest we call Mansion and tell their board that if we don't have signatures by close of business today, the price becomes four twenty-five dollars. And four twenty at close Monday,' Oberman snapped.

'We can't do that,' Gowers said uncertainly.

'Why not?' Josh Oberman demanded.

Gerry Quin glanced at his boss, feeling the adrenaline crackle around them.

'Why not indeed?' Edward said. 'Gentlemen, let's apply a little pressure.'

Rowena and the terrified driver supported Topaz through the front doors of Mt Sinai, where she was immediately lifted on to a stretcher and rushed off to the maternity ward.

'Don't leave me!' Topaz choked, clutching Rowena's arm as she ran alongside her.

'I'm not going anywhere. I'm staying right here,' she promised, turning to the orderly. 'This is Topaz Rossi. She was planning to have her babies here ... it's twins ... her contractions are about five minuts apart, I think.'

'Who's the husband?' somebody asked.

'Joe –' Topaz moaned.

'Joe Goldstein at NBC,' Rowena said. 'I asked her office to call him but I don't know if he's here . . .'

'We'll get in touch,' the nurse said.

'I don't want Rowena to go!' Topaz gasped as they turned into the private maternity wing.

'Can you get her something for the pain?' Rowena asked.

'What the fuck are *you* crying for? *You're* not giving birth,' Topaz said gruffly.

'Try and relax,' the nurse soothed them. 'Everything's gonna be just fine.'

'Want a burger?' Josh Oberman offered Michael Krebs. 'Pizza, Bud, Chinese takeout?'

'No, thanks,' Krebs said, distracted. He looked around him at the chaotic scene in the meeting room. 'What the hell is this?'

'A consortium that's just issued an ultimatum,' Nick Edward told him. 'Welcome to wheeler-dealing.'

'And I thought the record business was full of slobs,' Michael commented. 'Did you get the number of the bus that drove through here?'

'What's the press like outside?' Matt Gowers asked.

'It's a total madhouse,' Krebs replied, grinning. 'Last time I got that much attention I was coming out of a party with Joe Hunter and Cindy Crawford.'

'Where the hell is Topaz Rossi? seethed the American Magazines chairman.

'Where's Rowena?' Michael asked Josh.

'That's the sixty-four-thousand-dollar question,' Oberman said.

Joe Goldstein's heart had never beaten faster. Not when he was a quarterback in school. Not when he was up for his first major job interview. Not even when he'd lost his virginity.

We're having twins! I'm gonna be a father! My god, what if she's already there . . .

'I'm having twins,' he said breathlessly to the receptionist. The cab had got stuck in traffic so Goldstein had jumped out and run the last six blocks.

'You are?' he replied, suppressing the laugh. 'Yes, sir. What's your partner's name?'

'Rossi. Topaz Rossi, my wife – I'm Joe Goldstein,' he said.

'Yes, Mr Goldstein, we've been expecting you,' a nurse told him, smiling. 'If you'd just like to follow me.'

'Graham Hackston is on the phone!' somebody yelled.

Instant silence in the dealing room. Hackston was the chairman of the board of Mansion Industries.

An assistant held out the phone towards Matt Gowers and Joshua Oberman, uncertainly.

'Age before beauty,' Oberman said to Matt, grabbing it.

He listened to the voice at the other end for a few seconds. 'In that case, our lawyers will be in touch,' he said calmly. 'Thank you, Graham.'

He hung up and turned to the crowd of businessmen, holding their collective breath like kids on Christmas Eve.

'We nailed the sonofabitch!' he exclaimed.

*

Joe burst through the door of his wife's delivery room and stopped dead in his tracks.

Topaz was sitting propped up in bed, two minute bundles cradled one against each breast, her face transformed with such a look of love that he thought he'd never seen her so beautiful.

She lifted her head as he entered the room. 'We've got a son and a daughter,' she said.

'I love you, Topaz,' said Joe, looking at his family, his eyes filling with tears.

Outside in the corridor, Rowena Gordon found a payphone and rang Josh Oberman on his mobile.

'Josh? Are you at some kind of party?' she asked, hearing wild shrieks in the background.

'Gordon? Is that you?' her chairman demanded. 'Where the fuck have you been all day? Everyone's been trying to get hold of you for ever! I'm at Maughan Macaskill with the whole goddamn team!'

'What? Have we announced a bid?'

'Yes, we announced a bid! We've also given them an ultimatum, forced them to accept, exchanged signatures and *BOUGHT THE COMPANY*!' Oberman half screamed. 'And you *missed* it!'

She glanced back down towards the delivery room, where Jacob and Rowena Goldstein were being held by their father for the first time.

'No,' she said. 'No, I didn't.'

Epilogue

Rowena and Topaz became close friends.

Matthew Gowers resigned from the chairmanship of American Magazines four months later and named Topaz Rossi his successor, making her one of the most powerful women in journalism. Topaz and Joe continued to adore their children, fight about everything and be madly in love.

The engagement between John Metcalf and Rowena Gordon was cancelled.

Barbara Lincoln divorced Jake Barber, then remarried him. The second time around they were very happy.

Atomic Mass's third album, *Questions*, sold sixteen million copies worldwide.

Joshua Oberman was rushed to hospital in New York a few days after the takeover of Mansion Industries with a heart attack, which he survived. He had been defying doctors' orders to retire for several months, refusing to leave Musica when it was under threat. This time he quit, insisting on signing all his stock over to Rowena Gordon.

'Don't be stupid, Oberman. This is worth millions,' Rowena said, protesting.

'I've got millions. Do what I tell you,' the old man snapped.

'So give it to your family.'

'I am,' Oberman said gruffly.

He came round to Rowena's apartment every Monday for dinner, and rang her every Friday to tell her how she was screwing up.

Rowena Gordon became the first woman in history to be Chief Executive of a major record label. She stopped seeing Michael Krebs.

'I want marriage and a family,' she said. 'I want us to be with each other the way Joe and Topaz are.'

'You know how I feel about that,' Krebs said. 'I care about you, but I just can't do it.'

Rowena nodded. 'I know,' she said. She reached out and stroked his cheek, softly. 'I know. And I'm grateful to you for everything. We'll always be friends.'

'What is this? Goodbye again?' Michael asked, his eyes narrowing. 'You can't be serious. What the hell's changed?'

She shrugged, her eyes bright with tears. 'I saw Joe and Topaz,' she said. 'I'm sorry, Michael. I wish I could separate everything, but I can't. I wish I didn't love you, but I do.'

'I love Debbie,' Krebs said angrily.

'So be with her,' Rowena said. 'I don't want this life any more.'

Rowena saw Michael often, both socially and over Atomic Mass. She amazed both him and herself by sticking to it this time.

People live without love.

She loved her job, she saw a lot of her friends, and she was happy enough.

It was three years later that Michael Krebs turned up at her door.

'Notice anything different?' he asked.

Rowena looked him over. 'Since last Tuesday? I don't think so. New running shoes?'

Krebs held up both his hands.

For a second, she nearly didn't register.

'Where's your wedding ring?' Rowena asked, feeling her heart stop beating.

'I asked Debbie for a divorce,' Krebs said.

'Why?' asked Rowena, numbly.

'Because I'm in love with you,' Michael said. 'Because I haven't been able to get you out of my head. And because Josh Oberman rang me last week and told me that I'd always loved you and that I was the only person who couldn't see it. He said one day you would just leave, and I'd never see you again, and I thought about it, and it would break my heart.'

'It would?' Rowena repeated, feeling almost faint with joy.

'Yes, it would,' Krebs said dryly, producing a diamond ring. 'So what are you doing for the rest of your life?'

They called their first son Joshua.

Now you can buy any of these other **Headline Review** titles from your bookshop or *direct from the publisher*.

FREE P&P AND UK DELIVERY
(Overseas and Ireland £3.50 per book)

Monday's Child	Louise Bagshawe	£7.99
Tuesday's Child	Louise Bagshawe	£7.99
Sparkles	Louise Bagshawe	£6.99
The Godmother	Carrie Adams	£6.99
Making Your Mind Up	Jill Mansell	£6.99
Not That Kind of Girl	Catherine Alliott	£6.99
Sheer Abandon	Penny Vincenzi	£6.99
The Lost Art of Keeping Secrets	Eva Rice	£6.99
Fame Fatale	Wendy Holden	£7.99
Welcome to the Real World	Carole Matthews	£6.99
My Fabulous Divorce	Clare Dowling	£6.99

TO ORDER SIMPLY CALL THIS NUMBER

01235 400 414

or visit our website: www.madaboutbooks.com

Prices and availability subject to change without notice.